The Latchkey Kids

By Vivian Munnoch

Copyright 2016 L.V. Gaudet
All rights reserved

ISBN 978-1-989714-00-3
Library and Archives Canada
First edition published October 2019
Printed by IngramSpark

Cover photo by
Mehdi-Thomas BOUTDARINE
on Unsplash

Discover other titles
by Vivian Munnoch:

<u>The Latchkey Kids Series:</u>
The Latchkey Kids

The Latchkey Kids 2:
The Disappearance of
Willie Gordon

<u>The Wishing Stone Series:</u>
Madelaine & Mocha

For
Robyn and Sidney Gaudet.

Contents

1   Meet the Latchkey Kids

"I am freezing to death, it's so cold. Seriously, I am going to be a frozen dead body stuck to these stupid steps and they will have to pry me off with a crowbar and thaw me out just to bury me."

Madison is standing outside the locked door to her house. Around her, the world is covered in snow and ice. It is very cold despite the bright sun, possibly the coldest day of the year. She is fumbling in her parka pockets for the key, shivering with the cold. Her mitts make it hard to feel for the small piece of metal.

Madison is a slight thing, average height for the girls in her class, but skinny enough that they sometimes tease her about it. It's friendly teasing, not meant to be mean.

"Oh come on key, where are you?" Her breath hangs like a cloud in the air, each breath adding a new cloud of vapor.

"I had my key to lock the door this morning." She tries the door again, just in case it is somehow unlocked. Again, the door is still locked.

Feeling a surge of fear and hopelessness, Madison fumbles through her pockets again. "I can't find it."

She has the urge to dump her backpack out all over the steps, but that would be embarrassing. "Seriously, nobody does that except crazy people," she thinks.

Madison looks around, hoping no one sees her. At the same time, she hopes someone does, that they come and help her.

Taking off her mitts, she tucks them between her knees, the cold biting immediately at her fingers. Her hands hurt from the sharp bite of the cold without the protection of her mitts, a mix of burning pain and numbness. Her fingers won't cooperate. She fumbles in all her pockets, one after another and digs through her backpack again, breaking down and pulling stuff out and dropping it on the steps.

"My key is gone!" Tears burn at her eyes, but she is determined she won't cry. Someone might see.

"What am I going do?" Madison moans. "None of the neighbors are home and I have no way to get in." She looks at the house hopelessly. "I wish there was a way I can break in."

"If my parents would let me have a cell phone," she groans, "I could call them." She leans against the locked door, cold and scared and alone. The urge to cry is growing.

"Today is my first day going to school and coming home on my own and I completely blew it."

Madison has been looking forward to this day for three years as she watched the older kids come and go with a freedom not granted to mere children. She is finally a 'tween' between being a kid and a teenager, who has to come and go to school on her own, spending hours without adult supervision until her parents come home because both her parents work. Her twelfth birthday was just last week.

"I was looking forward to today. Finally no more daycare. No more being treated like a little kid. And I blew it." She was so excited all week, eagerly waiting for this day to come. She felt so grown up but she was nervous too.

Her mother's words ring again in her head, the constant reminder replaying over and over in the most annoying way. "Don't forget to lock the door when you go. Don't forget your lunch. And do not lose that key or you will not be able to get back in!"

She had repeated that so many times that it made her crazy. Madison got mad at her mother, thinking she was treating her like a child. She is a tween, not a little kid. Next year she will be a teenager, thirteen.

Now her mother's words are mocking her.

"My two biggest fears, and I would never tell them to anyone, are missing the bus and losing my key. And I lost the key on my first day." She sags even lower against the door in despair.

"Just great, Mom is going to be so mad and Dad will say I'm too young to be trusted with responsibility. They'll probably send me to a babysitter."

Madison moans. That would be the end of her life. It would be like going back to daycare.

"The worst part is that it's so cold out and I'm locked out of the house and Mom and Dad won't be home for a couple of hours. I'll freeze to death before they get home."

Madison thinks hard. "What can I do? I have to show them I can handle a little emergency like this or I'm sunk. If I leave they won't know where to find me and I can't just wait here and freeze to death."

She looks up and down the street as if the answer might be there. It isn't.

"Maybe I should go back to school. Maybe someone will be there to let me in to warm up and use the phone."

Madison's hands and feet are hurting worse with every minute from the cold. She shoves her stuff back into her backpack quickly, the touch of the nylon pack and zipper painful on her freezing hands. She puts her mitts back on, and starts the long walk to school.

"Lucky I know a shortcut." She tries blowing on her hands through her mitts, trying to warm them.

"I'm not supposed to go that way and usually I wouldn't do it because of Old Man Hooper's mean dog Caesar that chases and tries to bite everyone. That dog is as mean as Old Man Hooper himself," she thinks, "but it will make the walk a whole lot shorter."

"I just hope Caesar is inside," she mutters as she heads off down the sidewalk, the snow crunching under her boots.

Andrew just got home from school and is already so bored that he can't stand it.

He is in the living room playing half-heartedly on his Xbox game, the volume turned too loud, but there is no one there to tell him to turn it down. With only one game to play, he got bored with it pretty fast.

"I wish I had more games. The games are a lot of money and it's taking me forever to save up enough allowance to buy another one."

He snorts at the thought. "I guess I'd earn the money a lot faster if I did my chores, but chores are lame and boring."

He looks at the clock. Nobody will be home for a few hours.

"Man, that is just forever," he grumbles.

At twelve, Andrew has been a latchkey kid since last year and has never really gotten completely used to being home alone. He's fine except for one thing that makes him nervous; sometimes he hears strange noises in the house. It usually happens when the house is very quiet. When everyone else is sleeping or he's home alone. Because of this, Andrew doesn't like being home alone. It makes him nervous, but he won't admit that to anyone.

Andrew thinks he's the only person with this problem and that it's lame and for little kids.

Sometimes, he imagines the noises are giant rats in the basement, waiting for the right time to come squirming up the stairs to chew their noses off and devour their eyes in their sleep. Sometimes he imagines it's someone breaking into the house.

When he told his parents last year about his fear, they said it was ridiculous and laughed. He didn't talk about his fear again after that; not to anyone. He doesn't want anyone else laughing at him too.

Andrew is only going through the motions of playing his game, running his game player through a maze of bad guys, jumping and shooting without really paying attention. He doesn't miss a beat. He has this game down and figures he could play it blindfolded.

He freezes, eyes widening and hands locked on the Xbox controller while his helpless character is repeatedly beaten to a pulp and killed by the bad guy in the game, over and over, phasing back into the game with a new life only to be killed again each time. It's a repetition of music, weapon blasts, and his character's death scream playing on repeat.

"What was that?" he thinks. "That was a thump, definitely a thump from somewhere in the house."

He heard it despite the loud noise of the game. His stomach knots with anxiety and he keeps still, listening. The thump comes again, quiet, and then something that sounds like a wet slither. Andrew's knees feel instantly weak.

"It's coming from the basement," he thinks.

"It's nothing," he whispers quietly, trying to convince himself.

"Mom and dad would say I imagined it," he thinks. "They would say it's only my imagination, that there's nothing there. Or they would say it's just the sound of the house settling, whatever that means."

"More like settling its sour stomach after eating someone," he whispers.

Andrew keeps listening, a frozen statue, waiting for more noises. The television blaring the Xbox game in front of him is making him self-conscious now. If there is anyone, or thing, in the house, the noise will attract it.

He looks at the television anxiously, wanting to move and turn the sound off. "But what if the sudden silence alerts it or him or whatever that I'm here?" he thinks.

"Better leave it on," he whispers. He is growing more nervous with each heartbeat. The urge to get out of there is too strong to ignore. "Whatever made that sound can have the house to itself. I'm out of here."

Heart beating fast and too scared to move, Andrew yells at himself in his head, keeping his lips closed tight because he is afraid whatever it is will hear him breathe. "MOVE, COME ON AND JUST MOVE! STAND UP!"

Andrew finally makes himself move. He puts the game controller down as quietly as possible and creeps to the front door, grabbing his jacket on the way from where he had carelessly tossed it on a chair. He winces at the quiet hissing noise his jacket makes from the fabric rustling as he slips it on. Jamming his feet quickly into his boots, he grabs his hat and mitts, almost forgets his key, and slips out of the house. He closes the door quietly behind him, turning the key in the lock as quietly as he can to lock the door.

"If there's anything here, that'll slow it down," he thinks.

He runs down the driveway, turns, and races down the road, the cold snow crunching loudly beneath his boots and his breath pluming in a cloud that hangs in the air behind him for a span of heartbeats before vanishing. His heart is beating fast and he has to force himself to not look back to see if anything is chasing him. The feeling that something is won't go away, even though he knows it isn't likely.

Kylie gets off the school bus with a group of other kids. She pauses just long enough for a quick look around, then scurries to catch up and walk close to the bigger kids so it looks like they are together. Her breath is pluming out behind her on the cold air with each breath.

They aren't together and they ignore her. They used to give her odd looks, but after a while they gave up and just pretend she isn't there. She has done this since she started taking the bus when she was ten.

Kylie hears the sound of a car approaching from behind and moves so the other kids are between her and the approaching car, hoping the driver doesn't see her. She fights the urge to turn around and look.

"Don't look, don't look," she says silently in her head, "don't jinx it by looking. With everyone bundled up so much with hats and scarves, he might not even know it's me if it's him."

The car passes by, slowing a little as it passes the kids walking on the side of the road, and keeps going. She lets herself stop holding her breath, relieved. "It's not him," she thinks.

Her thoughts turn to her predicament.

"I don't have to pretend to be with the older kids anymore. It doesn't matter now that I'm twelve. Twelve is old enough to babysit even. But I still keep up with the older kids because I don't like walking home alone. It's not safe."

She breaks off from the pack of kids, turning up the sidewalk of her house. At the door, she fumbles for her key, finally having to take off her mitten to find it. The cold instantly bites her bare hand painfully. "Like it has a million tiny teeth," she thinks.

She gets inside and quickly closes and locks the door behind her. Dropping her backpack and lunch bag, she strips off her outerwear. Her scarf is frosted with fuzzy hard frost from her breath. She turns on the TV and plops into a living room chair.

"I wish I didn't have to come home alone. Even my annoying little sister Becca might make me feel better, even though she's just a little kid." She sighs unhappily.

"That's our big lie. I've been coming home alone for two years, since I was ten. I had to lie about being alone before and after school until I turned twelve. I still have to lie about it to everyone, even to Becca. As far as anyone knows, I just started being on my own. It's a hard secret to keep. Mom says you aren't supposed to leave kids alone at home at only ten years old. Mom said we could be taken away from her if anyone found out."

She pauses, feeling lonely. "I have a lot of big lies in my life."

The weight of the secret has been a difficult burden for her. She has lived for the past few years in fear that someone would find out and she and Becca would be taken away from their mom. They might be put in a foster home or worse.

Kylie is sitting in the living room blankly staring at the images on the TV. At twelve, she's already an expert at being a latchkey kid.

"Ugh, I'm so bored." Kylie needs a distraction. She flips through the few channels they have on the TV, finding nothing she wants to watch, and sits sullenly staring at what she considers a lame show for babies. The cartoon characters giggle like idiots as they run pell-mell in brainless circles.

"I miss having more channels. Just having the bare basic channels sucks. Everybody else has the movie channels, HBO and stuff. I wish Mom didn't have to cancel all the extra channels when money got tight."

"I hate being poor," Kylie thinks unhappily.

She sighs again. "There's nothing to do. We don't even have a computer that can play games or anything. That old computer that was given to us for free doesn't have enough memory to do much of anything. Even the simple games are too much for it. Maybe I'll see what's up on the chats."

She starts to get up and decides against it, feeling the familiar pang of dread in her stomach. There are too many trolls online and she isn't in the mood for it today. She makes excuses, not wanting to feel like they control her life.

"Dumb free dial up internet hardly even works anyway. It takes ages to load a single page. Even the chat sites won't work if they're busy. Forget about trying to watch any videos on YouTube or anything. I am bored bored bored."

Kylie is restless and feeling antsy to get up and do something, maybe go somewhere.

"Maybe I'll go to the park. It's not far."

The idea brings on a rush of anxiety, but she decides it has to be better than just sitting here doing nothing. She tries to push away the anxious feeling. Being home alone doesn't feel safe either, but it's safer than going outside.

"It's only the park. There's nothing to be nervous about, you nervous nilly," she tells herself. That's her own made up word. Taken from the term 'nervous Nelly', a favorite saying of her Aunt Cora's, meaning to be nervous all the time, and mixed with silly.

She puts on her coat, boots, hat, scarf, and mitts and locks the door behind her. Kylie pauses nervously on the front step.

She's not supposed to leave the house when her mother isn't home. That rule doesn't apply anymore now that she's twelve. Her mother made the rule when she was ten, but now it's Kylie's own rule.

Checking both ways up the street before leaving the safety of her doorstep, the snow crunches under her boots as she walks to the park and her breath makes clouds in the air. For a moment, Kylie imagines she is a fire-breathing dragon who can kill anyone who tries to hurt her with a blast of fire from her throat. She puffs big clouds of fog into the air, watching them slowly rise up.

Kylie has the unnerving feeling someone is following her. She checks over her shoulder. Nobody is there but the feeling won't go away. She checks at least half a dozen more times by the time she reaches the park.

There is no one at the park when she gets there. She can feel the extreme cold through her coat and shivers.

"It's not a good feeling to be this cold. I wish I had a warmer coat. Maybe I should just go home. It's too cold out. But there's nothing there to do." She hugs herself for warmth.

"I'll stay just a little while," Kylie decides.

Kylie finds a partially built snow fort in a corner of the park. She starts adding snow to it, packing and adding it to a wall. She stops, rubbing her hands together, trying to warm them. It does nothing with the mitts on and it's too cold to take them off. She tries blowing on them. Her cheeks are burning with the cold too.

She cups her hands in front of her face, blowing warm air to warm both her cheeks and her hands.

She stops when she hears voices. She looks around quickly then ducks behind the wall, trying to hide.

"Who is it? I hope they didn't see me." She thinks quickly. "Maybe it's no one, some old people. Adults won't care and probably won't even notice me. But what if it's someone from school? Worse, what if it's someone I know?"

Kylie is embarrassed at the idea of being caught making snow forts.

"Twelve year old girls don't build snow forts," she thinks in a panic. But she's just not ready yet to let go of all the things she did for fun as a kid. As a tween, Kylie doesn't know how to have fun anymore. "I'm too old for playing and stuff like a kid and what I see teenagers do looks so boring. All they do is hang out and message each other or play on their phones or listen to music. I don't even have a phone."

Kylie waits, listening as the voices come closer. It's a group of girls. The one voice is unmistakable. She recognizes it immediately. With it, she knows the other voices too. She tenses and her heart sinks, her stomach tightening with dread.

"Please don't see me," she begs silently, crouching even lower.

The approaching girls have been bullying her for a while and it has been getting only worse with time.

"The mean team," Kylie thinks miserably, "Amber, Jessica, and Brooke."

Her heart races. It's pounding so hard in her chest that she's scared they might somehow hear it.

The voices stop and Kylie holds her breath, waiting. She can still hear the crunch of footsteps in the snow, coming closer, then that stops too. She listens for the footsteps to go further away. There is only silence.

"Is that the quiet whisper of a coat rustle?" Kylie wants to press herself down lower, to disappear like she never existed. She's afraid to move. They might hear her.

"What are they doing?" she thinks, feeling a surge of panic rising up in her. "Are they just standing there? Are they gone? Please be gone."

Kylie wants more than anything to peek but she doesn't dare.

"It's fine, they didn't even see you," she tells herself, trying to convince herself that nothing is going to happen. Maybe if she tries hard enough to convince herself, if she believes hard enough, it will be true.

It was already too late before she got to the park. They saw her walking towards the park and followed her, keeping their distance and ducking out of sight when she looked back. That's why she kept having the feeling she was being followed. Her instincts were right.

Their heads pop over the edge of her partially made fort, looking down at Kylie with nasty grins.

"Oh, my gawd, is she building a fort?" Amber squeals nastily.

Before Kylie knows what is happening, Amber's hands are pushing down on her, putting all her weight into it. Kylie struggles and cries out, feeling the other two girls' hands pushing down on her too.

The first thought in her mind is "I've been seen," along with the feeling of abject horror at having been seen making a snow fort like a little kid. She wants to dissolve into the snow, having never existed, at the embarrassment.

As quickly as the first thought comes, she realizes she is being attacked and fear surges through her, the embarrassment becoming even worse because it's them.

They force her down, giggling and mashing her face into the cold snow, pressing so hard the snow feels like it's biting into her face. It hurts a lot. Kylie can already feel the sharp pain of frostbite on her face from the snow.

The moment feels endless, Kylie struggling hopelessly, unable to overcome the weight and strength of the three girls, her prone position leaving her helpless to defend herself. They push down harder, Amber taking even more joy in mashing her face harder into the cold hard ground.

Kylie screams and flails, trying to break free, the burning pain in her face unbearable. By the time they let the pressure up, Kylie is sure her nose must be broken and bleeding all over the snow, staining it red.

She feels and hears them scrambling over the wall of the fort. They step on her feet and hands, not caring, pushing down with their weight on her back and holding her down while they climb over the low snow wall.

"Get her coat!" Amber cries in vicious delight. "Pull it off!"

They start pulling and tugging at her and Kylie hears the sound of her coat ripping as she fights to protect herself against them, trying to cover her head and roll into a ball.

"No, no, no, Mom is going to be so mad," Kylie thinks desperately over the ruined coat. Despite the pain they are inflicting on her, she's more worried over the coat than herself.

"Mom will be furious when she sees it. She'll tell me that she doesn't have the money to buy me a new coat." Insanely, Kylie can only think now of what she thinks her mother's reaction will be. It pushes away the fear of the girls hurting her.

She wants to cry out for them to stop, but knows it's useless. "It will only make the attack worse. These nasty girls enjoy watching me suffer."

Kylie tries to fight against the three girls but there are too many of them. She manages to roll onto her back, to try to kick at them, her arms blocking their blows. This only makes it worse because now her stomach is exposed. She realizes the danger and tries to roll back onto her stomach. They take turns hitting and kicking at her sides and back as she struggles and rolls.

A blow to her stomach forces all the air painfully out of her lungs and she can only gasp for air that won't come. Every attempt to suck in air feels like it's pushing more air out instead, like a fist is pushing her lungs up and squishing them from inside.

"How is that even possible?" Kylie thinks wildly. "I'm going to die." She feels sick and dizzy.

They take her hat and mitts, tossing them back and forth in victory. Amber yanks on her scarf, but the scarf is tied around her neck and it only tightens, strangling Kylie. She can't breathe.

They get her jacket undone and pull it off while Kylie tries prying at her scarf with desperate fingers, gasping for air, but it's too tight. They pull on her arms, pulling her hands away from her neck, pulling her coat off. Kylie frantically grabs at the scarf again the moment her hands are free.

One of them is still pulling on the scarf, trying to yank it off her, stretching it out and making it impossible for her to loosen it.

"I'm going to die for real," Kylie's mind whirls in a panic. "I'm going to suffocate to death while they torture me for nothing more than their own amusement!"

She is so cold that it hurts, but it's the lack of air that is the worst. Every breath she cannot take burns like fire in her throat and lungs. Her head feels like it's swelling larger and stuffed painfully tight with cotton.

Every attempt to suck in air feels still like it is only impossibly pushing air out of her empty lungs, like her stomach and lungs are still being pushed in and up inside her, the breath knocked out of her.

Sounds seem farther away, her ears closing up and blocking it all out. She wishes desperately she's somewhere else, that she never left the house.

Kylie feels a tug at one of her boots. Crying silently, unable to choke out a single sound past the tight scarf and empty lungs, she kicks out, trying to kick them. Her boot is pulled off, then the other. They're laughing cruelly. Oh, what great fun this is for them.

Kylie is crying harder now and can't stop. It makes her head feel like it's swelling more. "Do they even know I'm crying?" They seem oblivious. "It's lucky for me they don't notice, or maybe they just don't care. No, they can't know how hard I'm really crying. They would only attack me worse if they knew."

"Take the rest of her clothes," Jessica squeals nastily. Amber laughs at this, grinning at the idea.

"Let's shove snow down her shirt," Brooke says. Amber gives them the nod.

The girls roll their victim in the snow, shoving fistfuls of it under her shirt and down her pants. It's so cold against her bare skin that the snow burns like fire.

Finally bored with the game, the mean girls take off laughing.

"Let's go," Amber says, scooping up and taking Kylie's stuff with her. The other two follow, leaving Kylie laying in the snow, wet and cold, her clothes stuffed with snow, and with no coat or boots to get her home.

Kylie feels dizzy from lack of air and fumbles at the scarf with frozen fingers. The knitted wool is already starting to freeze hard, wet and caked with snow from the attack. It's turning to ice and she doesn't think she'll be able to loosen it.

She is terrified. "I'm going to die!" Kylie thinks frantically. Everything seems darker, further away. The sounds of the neighborhood muffled behind a cotton curtain. Even her body feels somehow further away.

At last, Kylie manages to loosen the scarf just a bit, managing to suck in the first shallow breaths of air since the scarf was pulled tight. The air barely comes. She is still winded from the blow to her stomach. The air is sharp and cold and hurts, but she gasps at it anyway, trying to suck in as much as she can. Her stomach still hurts from having the wind kicked out of her and she feels like she is going to vomit.

"Oh my gawd, what if I throw up? I can't even breathe? Will the puke even come out, or will I drown in it in my own mouth?" The thought makes her feel even more sick.

Sucking in those frantic shallow breaths of air, Kylie gets to her feet, shivering and dizzy and weak. She tries again unsuccessfully to loosen the scarf, then to knock as much snow out of her clothes as she can without taking them off. Her fingers are burning and numb from the cold. She fumbles clumsily at her clothes with little effect.

With only an ice-covered scarf and wet clothes that are already turning hard as they freeze to ice for warmth, she wraps the long trailing end of the stretched scarf around herself as best she can, wrapping her arms around herself too. The scarf is still knotted tightly around her neck, constricting her breath and making her wheeze for air.

"I'll have to thaw it out to get it undone," she thinks.

Kylie is so cold it hurts as if she is burning up on fire. She looks for the blood that must be soaked into the snow from when they jammed her face hard into the ground and is surprised there is none. Everywhere, she feels the bite of ice fire.

"Why does being so cold burn so much?" Her whole body is in sharp agony from the extreme cold.

She starts for home. Before she even gets out of the park her toes hurt so much that Kylie thinks they must be frozen solid and ready to shatter at the slightest bump. She walks with extra care, the slightest jarring sending sharp pain ringing through her feet and up her legs. By the time she reaches the corner her toes have become numb and the pain distant.

Kylie stops and looks down, making sure her toes are still there, afraid they really have snapped off. Her feet are nothing but blocks of sharp pain that can't feel anything else.

"I'm never going to make it home," she whimpers miserably. She forces herself to walk on.

Unbearable pain fills her feet before she gets more than a few houses from the park, getting worse with every step. They feel like clumsy blocks of white-hot agony. After a while, numbness seeps into her feet again. As much as it scares her, the numbness comes as a relief. She can't feel her feet anymore and she stumbles, having trouble walking with the bricks for feet that she can't feel. Even her hot tears are freezing on her face.

That short distance around the corner and up the street home is the longest walk she has ever had to make. She stumbles on.

Kylie feels so very tired. "I don't know how I can take that next step," she thinks piteously. The cold is taking over; her body temperature is dropping. She is getting sleepy and weak. Kylie is in the early stage of hypothermia, but her reaction is from the stress and not from freezing to death. That would take much longer than the few minutes that have passed, feeling endlessly impossibly long. She is giving up already.

"Maybe I should just lie down and let the cold take me. Maybe it won't hurt in the end to die like this." The pain of her whole body freezing pushes her on. She feels so exhausted and sick and weak that every step feels impossible.

"I -I-I'm not going to make it," Kylie chatters, her words barely whispering out her constricted throat, rough and weak. She feels more distressed than she ever has in her life.

"I wish I was just dead."

Anna gets off the school bus and waits for it to drive away before crossing the street. The driver isn't supposed to drive away until after the kids getting off have safely crossed the street, but he gave up in the first week of school on waiting for this one. She had stood there defiantly staring him down, not crossing until he gave up and drove away.

He watches her in his side mirror as he drives away. "Stubborn one, that one is," he thinks. "She's going to be nothing but trouble and more trouble when she gets older."

Anna saunters down the street until the bus is out of sight, then speeds up to walk brusquely, wrapping her arms around herself against the extreme cold, her breath puffing out in big clouds that hang in the air behind her.

"Why is it so bloody cold," she complains.

Anna arrives at home, fishes out her house key, and lets herself in, gratefully closing the door against the cold.

"Hi, I'm home."

She is greeted by silence. She didn't expect anyone to be there.

Dropping her backpack and kicking off her boots, she hangs up her coat and goes to the kitchen, looking for something to eat.

At thirteen, Anna is already well practiced at looking after herself.

Dylan shoulders his backpack and gets off the school bus, walking up the sidewalk. He scuffs his boots moodily against the pavement with every step as if lifting his feet is too much bother. He is thirteen, almost fourteen, and after more than a year as a latchkey kid, his parents now send him to a babysitter after school again.

"A babysitter," he thinks angrily, "just like a little kid!" It's the same sulky walk and moody thoughts he has every day on the way to the sitter's after school. And just like every other day, he glances around surreptitiously for anyone who might see. "Nobody better see me going to the stupid babysitter's."

Dylan resents having to go to a babysitter's house after school. It's embarrassing.

"Nobody my age has a babysitter."

He arrives at the sitter's house, Mrs. Foster. With a last look around to make sure nobody is around, a noncommittal shrug, and an I don't care slouch, he scuffs his boots up the sidewalk to the back door on the side of the house.

Dylan pauses at the door, pushing away the urge to knock. Mrs. Foster said to not bother knocking and to just walk in, but it still feels weird to just walk into someone else's house. He opens the door and goes in.

"Mrs. Foster, I'm here," he calls out, kicking his boots off and slouching out of his backpack and coat.

"I'm downstairs doing laundry," Mrs. Foster calls back. "Help yourself to a snack if you're hungry."

Another thing that feels weird to Dylan, helping yourself to a snack at someone else's house. Especially someone you don't feel like you know that well.

Dylan shrugs and cuts through the kitchen to sit in the living room, plopping himself on a chair glumly.

2   The Shortcut

Madison arrives at the forbidden shortcut and stops, staring at it uncertainly.

The tall wooden fence looms above her like an impossible fortress wall stretching down the road in both directions across the yards of multiple homes edging this street. The eight-foot fence has been here for as long as she can remember, blocking access from the sidewalk on this road to the alley on the other side.

She looks down its width in both directions, then up at its height.

Madison is having second thoughts about taking the shortcut. She always feels nervous using this shortcut. She has always been told not to go into other peoples' yards uninvited, and the shortcut means cutting through the yard on the other side of the fence.

"I don't get why I'm not allowed to go that way. Mom and Dad said it isn't safe and only made vague comments about buildings there. Maybe they are scared of Old Man Hooper and his dog. Who isn't scared of Old Man Hooper and Caesar?"

"Everyone knows about Old Man Hooper and Caesar," she thinks. "Mr. Hooper is flat out weird. He is as crazy as crazy comes and even meaner. He hates everyone. There are all kinds of rumors of Mr. Hooper locking people in his basement or killing them. And Caesar is the biggest, loudest, and meanest dog around. Caesar is kept chained up in the yard and it's a good thing too. He tries to attack anyone who walks past. Everyone knows Caesar eats any squirrel, rabbit, or neighborhood cat dumb enough to enter his yard too."

Madison leans closer to the fence. She peeks through the cracks between the fence boards, spying on the alley on the other side. There is no sign of life or movement. She looks up and down the sidewalk again.

The shortcut is blocked by the tall fence. "That's the trick part of the shortcut. The shortcut is to go through the fence. Only those who know its secret can use the shortcut and I know which one is the loose board."

She finds the little notch mark in a board and counts three boards over, swinging the board on its rusty nail. She squeezes through the hole in the fence. It's a tight squeeze with her bulky winter coat on and she gets stuck halfway through. She sucks in a breath, trying to suck everything in and make herself skinnier. She panics for just a moment.

"Come on, you can fit. You know you can."

You have to be skinny enough to fit to be able to use this shortcut. Not everyone in her class can do it. She feels the pressure of the fence against her, wishing she had a thinner coat, and squirms past it, popping out the other side. The board swings back into place behind her when she lets go of it.

Madison glances at the house nervously, hoping no one is home to see her, and quickly runs across the back yard to the alley bordering the other side of the yard. Stopping there, she pretends she is just walking down the alley and only just stopped. She looks up the alley towards her destination.

On the other side of the fence she squeezed through and just past this corner of an odd shaped backyard, the back alley runs behind the back yards of homes on two other streets running parallel to each other. Down the length of the alley are short driveways, half of them with old garages. Most of the garages look like they should be painted or replaced. Garbage cans clutter the end of most of the driveways, the homeowners taking their trash out to the cans instead of bringing the cans in. They are usually full whether or not the garbage trucks have come by recently.

Today there is a yellow-stained mattress leaning against one of the garages. It makes her stomach turn at the sight of its ripped and stained top side. A few houses past this, Madison sees an old couch missing two of its three cushions. It is an ugly plaid fabric that looks like it must have been from a hundred years ago.

"Maybe even a thousand," she thinks wryly. It is stained, holes worn in the back and arms, and the frazzled arms and sides look like a cat probably used it for a scratching post.

Four houses past the chair there is a short road branching off midway down the alley. The road is the distance of a single house and yard and spits you out on the next street on that side. The road has no name as far as she knows.

That road is her goal. Once she reaches it, she gets to the next street. One of the two houses bordering that little road without a name is Old Man Hooper's.

This is the other part of the shortcut that makes her nervous. The thought of passing Mr. Hooper's house makes her whole body cold with dread.

Madison stops a few houses away and studies Mr. Hooper's yard, looking for any sign Caesar might be outside. "Probably even the grass is too scared to be in that yard," Madison thinks.

At the moment, all the junk cluttering the yard is mostly uneven bumps in the snow, the larger stuff like a rusting metal kitchen chair skeleton missing its back and seat, stick up from the snow. Large paw prints have trampled the snow down in crazy crisscross patterns around the yard, especially along trails that must be Caesar's favorite path to take through the yard.

"I don't know how that dog manages to get through the yard without getting his chain tangled up in the junk." Madison sees no sign of the dog. She swallows and tries to push down her fear of the yard.

"It's just an empty yard and if he's out Caesar is chained. It doesn't even bother you," she tries telling herself.

Madison heads down the alley, slowing as she approaches the short access road and Mr. Hooper's house. She pauses and listens for Caesar, searching the yard for any sign of the black and brown dog. The dog is big. He looks like he probably has Rottweiler, Doberman, German Shepherd, and she suspects he probably has some Tyrannosaurus Rex in him too. And he is meaner than anything.

She does not see him and is filled with relief. "The dog must be in the house."

Nervously, she starts walking past Old Man Hooper's yard.

Kylie is not even halfway home before she's sure she will never make it.

"I hurt so bad everywhere from the cold and I can't decide if I even feel any pain in the numbness that has replaced my feet. I can't even feel my feet touching the ground anymore!"

The walk is pure torture in this extreme cold without her coat and boots. The road seems to stretch out longer and longer before her with every difficult step.

"Oh my gawd, is the road getting longer?" She gapes at the impossible distance ahead. "It feels like the house is getting further away instead of closer."

"I could just lie down here," Kylie thinks again, feeling the extreme exhaustion wearing her down, making her feel so weak. "If I stop, I'm done. I'll die here. Maybe that would be better."

The thought both terrifies and relieves her. "I can rest if I'm dead. I won't feel any more pain. I won't have to keep going."

Desolate and wanting to just give up and lie down, Kylie pushes herself on, not knowing where she will find the determination to keep going, making her mind focus only on being warm and inside the house. She focuses on each step, one step at a time.

Finally, she makes it home.

Kylie doesn't even realize she is home at first. She is forcing one foot before the other in blind determination, staring down at her feet as she stumbles along, unable to feel anything more than a distant sharp block of pain with each step, and looks up to get her bearings. She's expecting to yet again see an impossibly long way to go.

She is shocked to find herself standing on the sidewalk in front of her own house. She looks up the walkway to the front door and it looks a hundred times longer than it should.

"It's so far," she whimpers.

Kylie stumbles up the walkway, making it to the door. But her torment isn't over yet.

"I don't have a key to get in because they stole my coat with the key in the pocket." She feels again like giving up. She knows what to do, but isn't sure she can do it right now.

"That isn't such a big problem," Kylie says through teeth that are clenched tight from the extreme cold. Her words are a lie meant to push away her own doubts. She feels absolutely lost.

She looks around as if afraid someone might see her, and limps around to the back of the house, huddling down near a basement window.

"It's a good thing I figured this trick out before, or Mom would be coming home to find me frozen to death on the front steps."

Kylie is picturing herself lying on the front steps, curled up in a little ball for warmth and frozen hard as a statue. Her mother would come up the steps, wondering first why she is there, and then noticing that she has no coat or boots. She imagines the horror on her mother's face when she realizes her daughter is dead, frozen stiff as a Popsicle. "A kidsicle on her front step," she thinks.

Doubt almost stops her from even trying. "What if it doesn't work? It worked before, but it was summer then. This time it's winter. The window could be frozen shut. My fingers are so numb I might not be able to do it."

Kylie steels herself and pushes on the window in the middle where the two windowpanes slightly overlap, pushing on the inner pane overlapping to the inside of the house. They are the kind of windows that have two sliding pieces of glass in a window frame. She has to press hard enough to bend the one windowpane in enough so the latch does not catch while trying to slide it over with the pressure of her palms and fingers on the flat surface. There is nothing to grab and pull or push on to make sliding it easier.

She tries sliding the window, prying at it with frozen fingers that are so cold they are nubs of numbness and pain that feel nothing else.

"I can't do it," she thinks, panicked. She is so cold that her fingers barely work.

"No, come on," she groans. "You have to work."

Crying and biting her lip through the pain from the cold, Kylie frantically attacks the stubborn window, desperate to get into the house. For a moment, she is sure she's not going to make it and won't be able to get the window open. Kylie is about to give up when it finally moves just a tiny bit. It's such a slight movement that she isn't sure it really happened.

"It moved. Did it move? Of course it moved," she mutters through clenched teeth.

Encouraged by that tiny success, Kylie attacks the window with renewed energy, pushing and trying to slide it. It is so cold out that the window is frozen stuck in its frame, just as she was worried it would be.

Kylie manages to slide the window a little more. It stops just at the edge of the latch by the width of a hair now, the latch not catching. One wrong move and it could slip back and latch again. She holds her breath and tries again. The window moves the tiniest bit and then suddenly the icy grip of winter releases it and the glass jerks open just a little.

She almost cries out with the relief and the feel of that movement and the small opening it makes. It's just barely wide enough to get her fingers into. She shoves her fingers into the narrow opening; the touch of the icy metal feeling like a sharp knife is slicing up her fingers, and slowly works the window open.

Her whole body both numb and burning with cold, Kylie fumbles as she turns and crawls backwards in through the window. She tries to ease herself down, but her numb fingers can't hold and she falls with all her weight. Kylie cries out in pain, her feet exploding with agony as they hit the floor. She falls to her knees, twisting and trying to roll, her hands going out instinctively to break her fall and only managing to half fall on her side and hurt herself even more.

Now that she is finally safely inside the house, Kylie has the problem of the open window. She looks up at it. The freezing cold air coming in is turning to fog as it hits the warmer air inside.

"I can't just leave it open, but I don't think I have the strength to close it. I am so exhausted and cold and I hurt everywhere. I just want to lie down and quit. No, Kylie, you have to close it. It will freeze open and even Mom won't be able to close it then. She'll be really mad."

Digging deep inside herself for a reserve of strength she is sure will fail her; Kylie grabs a chair and drags it below the window. Luckily, her mother keeps an old kitchen chair down there to use as a step stool to reach the higher shelves.

Climbing up awkwardly with her blocks of ice for feet to stand the chair, Kylie struggles with the window, but it's stuck open, already freezing in place. With the window stuck open and the cold air chilling her, her fingers and toes on fire with pain from the cold walk and her whole body still a numb pain without end, Kylie feels completely defeated. She lets out a sob.

"I can't just leave the window open," she groans, "and I can't get it closed."

Kylie thinks about hitting the edge with a hammer to knock it loose, but knows she will probably just break the glass. Sobbing, she attacks the window, trying to force it closed, and finally manages to budge it with a protesting squeak from the window in its cold-shrunken frame. Shrill squeak by squeak, she fights with the window, nudging it closed a tiny bit at a time. She cringes each time, instinctively dreading her mother hearing the sound from somewhere in the house and finding out what happened, even though she knows her mother isn't home.

With the window finally closed, Kylie can go upstairs. Getting off the chair is just as awkward as getting up.

She moves cautiously through the dark basement towards the stairs. It is lit only by the weak light coming in the few small basement windows. The basement makes her feel nervous. It always has.

Every step is a distant stabbing pain in the frozen blocks that are her feet.

Kylie hears a noise, just barely, and even though she knows it's probably just her imagination, her heart races faster and her stomach knots. She has always imagined there are things in the basement, bad things. Her imagination is fueled by her ears playing tricks on her, hearing things from down here that no one else ever seems to hear.

Swallowing her fear, she forces herself to move forward. She thinks she catches movement in the corner of her eye and turns quickly to look, but there is nothing there.

"It's all in your imagination, dummy," she scolds herself. "Just get to the stairs."

When she reaches the stairs, she stops and looks up at the murky blackness above. The light switch is at the top of the stairs.

She swallows and races up them, half on her knees, the odd numbness with sharp slicing pain in her feet proving too much. She almost gives up halfway up the stairs. Her feet feel strange on the ends of her legs, dull numbness like they are asleep but with less feeling. The pain seems somehow to move through her feet to her legs above, like steel blades. The numb and painful frozen blocks that they were are now getting hot and tingling but still numb. The darkness of the stairwell swallows her.

She reaches the top and grabs at the doorknob of the closed door at the top, throwing herself against the door and almost crying out when her numb pain-filled fingers have trouble working the knob. The knob turns, releasing the door to swing open, and she spills out onto the kitchen floor.

She slams the door closed against the invisible monsters in the basement. She leans against the door, breathing heavily, imagining the unseen monsters somehow getting her through the door, and quickly scoots away with a nervous look at the door.

"You are being so stupid, scared of the dark. Are you a baby now?"

Kylie is still shaken by the attack in the park and distraught over the panic of not being able to get into the house. She is shivering and in pain from the cold walk home, and is heartsick over being stuck in this wretched position of being her.

Her whole body feels like it's warming too fast, getting hot. Every inch of her aches with the pain and numbness of being frozen. But now she feels like she is burning up with a fever too. Exhaustion takes over and she feels like soft rubber melting into the floor.

"I'm not just thawing out, I'm melting like ice."

"Why?" she sobs. "Why do I have to be me? Why can't I just be someone else; someone who doesn't get bullied or locked out of the house in winter with no coat and shoes? Why do I even have to be alive?"

The pain in her hands and feet is getting worse as they warm up. They feel like they are on fire. The pain is so bad now that Kylie is sure she is going to lose her hands and feet.

She tries again to pry the tight scarf around her neck loose, but it's still frozen hard with ice and her fingers are burning nubs of numb pain that won't cooperate.

"I'll have to wait for the ice to melt."

The scarf's continued stranglehold on her neck only makes her feel worse. She can breathe, but the air is restricted by the tight scarf. She imagines herself slipping off, unconscious and dying, strangled on her own scarf in the safety of her own home, her mother coming home to find her cold dead body on the floor with the scarf still knotted tightly around her neck.

"It would probably be good that I'm dead," she mumbles miserably.

Thinking again about her mother and sister finding her like that, Kylie struggles to her feet, wincing and whimpering, and limps to the bathroom. She rummages in the cabinet under the sink. She finds the hairdryer and plugs it in, turning it on and fumbling with it in her painful still-numb burning fingers. She runs it back and forth, blowing the heat of the hairdryer on the scarf until the ice melts.

Turning it off, she leaves it on the counter and tries again to loosen the scarf. The wet yarn doesn't want to loosen. Finally, it gives and she is able to loosen it enough to get her fingers under it and then to grip her hands around it. She pulls it off with relief, dropping it on the floor.

Tears streaming and limping awkwardly, Kylie goes to her bedroom. She struggles to get out of her wet clothes. She stops and looks down at herself. She turns, looking at herself in the mirror over her dresser. The bruises are already starting to show on her stomach, back, legs, and arms from the beating in the park.

She pulls on warm sweat pants and a sweatshirt and pulls the comforter off her bed and wraps herself in it. The edge of the blanket dragging on the floor, she goes to the living room and sits curled up in the big chair, shivering. She picks up the T.V. remote off the table beside the chair and turns the T.V. on.

"I wish I was dead," she moans miserably. "I wish I was never even born. That I could just melt into the floor and disappear. That I never even existed. I hate me and I hate this life."

Kylie starts flipping through the channels, finds a show she doesn't like but isn't as bad as the rest, and stops.

She turns her head towards the large living room windows. The curtains are only half closed. Outside at the curb in front of the house is a car. Her father's car. She sinks lower into the chair, desperately hoping he hasn't seen her. She feels sick suddenly.

"No," she whimpers fearfully, "not him, not now, not today."

She can't see anyone in the car and that makes it even worse. She hates her father.

"Please mom," she begs, "hurry home."

Madison is almost past the backyard of Mr. Hooper's house. She watches carefully before turning up that little road next to the side of the house and walks as quietly as she can.

She breathes in and out slowly, watchful for Old Man Hooper or his dog. The front of the house faces the other street, her destination. Just a few more steps and she is past the backyard and beside the house.

All is quiet. And then she hears the chilling jangle of the chain. Caesar!

She almost freezes with fear, her heart racing, and with a yelp makes herself run for her life.

Madison does not dare look back. She hears the snarl that she knows is Caesar, the jangling of his chain, his panting breath, and the sound of his feet thudding on the ground and churning up the snow as he charges across the yard after her.

Madison feels like little red riding hood about to be eaten by the wolf, and she is sure Caesar must have eaten a few grandmothers and kids in his nasty life. Her breath catches and she stumbles, almost falling.

He sounds so close!

She looks at the second window on the side of the house.

"If I can just get to the second window I'm safe. Caesar's chain doesn't go to the first window, but it's the second one that is the safe window. It puts enough distance between me and the dog that I can dare to look behind me. At least, that's what everyone says."

Madison is about to test that out.

She passes the corner of the house, the dog's feet pounding after her in the snow and the chuffing of his breath through bared teeth is practically on top of her.

Madison feels like her pounding heart is going to stop beating with her fear. She passes the first window; sure she can feel and smell the dog's hot nasty breath on her back.

Before she reaches the second window, Madison is startled by a strangled yelp and a scuffle behind her. She waits until she reaches the second window before she turns around to look, just in time to see Caesar getting to his feet and shaking the snow off. He had run himself right to the end of his chain and flipped himself over.

Feeling sick with fear and relief, Madison makes a face at him and hurries on her way.

Caesar watches her go with just a few loud barks to send her on her way.

With that out of the way, Madison can focus on where she is going now, and her need for help. "Please, please, let there be someone at the school to let me in," she begs.

Madison jogs for as long as she can, and then slows to a walk. A painful cramp is cutting through her side and her lungs feel burnt by the cold air. Her hands and feet are beginning to feel frozen inside her mitts and boots. She is frozen by the time she reaches the school.

Madison's heart sinks. There is not a single car in the parking lot. She goes to the front doors, pulling on them. They are locked. Cupping a mittened hand to block out the light, she presses her face and hand to the window on one of the front doors, looking in. Not a soul in sight.

"Oh no, there's no one here," she groans with a sinking feeling in her stomach. Just knowing she can't get out of the cold makes her feel colder.

Madison goes around the school looking in all the windows she can reach and trying all the doors. "Maybe one of the teachers is staying late. Maybe they are getting picked up."

The place is locked up tight and completely abandoned. The classroom lights are all off and she can see only a security light on in the hall.

There is no one there and Madison is freezing and alone and stuck outside with nowhere to go.

"What am I going to do now?" she whimpers.

Amber, Jessica, and Brooke are feeling pretty smug about the fun they had at Kylie's expense. They giggle and chatter about what they did to her as they walk away from the park, Amber rolling Kylie's hat, mitts, and boots in her coat. She fingers the tear in the coat caused in the struggle, waggling her fingers through it to peals of laughter from all three.

"We should have taken the rest of her clothes too," Amber sneers nastily, "and stayed to watch." She starts limping and groaning, holding herself in a mockery of how Kylie must have made her way home.

"Oh, I am so cold," she mock wails and then breaks into laughter.

"It would have been much funnier if we left her in only her underwear," Jessica agrees with a nasty laugh.

Brooke laughs too, her laugh and smile faltering a little. She had been caught up in the moment, enjoying tormenting Kylie just as much as the other two, but now she's not so sure.

She keeps her feelings guarded, not wanting the other two to know that she is having doubts about what they did. She feels the painful bite of the cold through her own mitts and boots and feels bad for making Kylie walk home with nothing to protect her from the severe cold. And stuffing snow down her pants and in her shirt, she cringes inside, imagining how much more painful that must have made the cold walk home.

"Maybe we shouldn't have done it on such a cold day," she thinks to herself. She glances at the other two, who are oblivious to her lack of enthusiasm. "I can't ever tell them about my doubts. They'll turn on me and start doing these mean things to me. You never show weakness to anyone who treats others like this, and Amber would definitely see my secret doubts as weakness."

As they walk back to their homes together Amber realizes they can't bring the clothes back with them. How would they explain them to their mothers? They would be in a lot of trouble, both for stealing and for leaving Kylie to walk home coat and bootless in this cold.

She smirks at the painful bite of the cold seeping through her own mitts and boots, making her fingers and toes burn and tingle with the cold. "Hah! Serves her right," she thinks nastily, though if you asked her she could not have told you what it served her right for. There is nothing Kylie has done to deserve the abuse other than just being there. Amber also would not be able to explain why she hates Kylie so much, she just does. She doesn't need a reason.

She pauses, turning to her friends. "We have to get rid of this junk." She raises Kylie's clothes for emphasis.

The other two nod. They know what she means. They will all have some explaining to do about the clothes if any of their mothers see them.

"Where?" Jessica asks.

"First place we see," Amber says.

They walk on up the street, watching for a good place to stash the clothes.

Amber stops with a cruel smile. "There!" She spotted a trashcan next to a garage.

The others follow her as she darts to it. The lid is frozen and she has to work at it, but it finally comes off and she shoves the clothes inside and puts the lid back with a satisfied smirk.

"We better hurry," Brooke says, eyeing the trashcan and feeling bad for throwing Kylie's clothes in the trash. "She'll never get them back now, that's for sure," she thinks.

She has more urgent things to worry about right now. They were only supposed to be out for a little while and all three have to get home soon before they get in trouble.

"We're going to be late," Brooke says.

The other two nod and they hurry off down the street.

Dylan is sitting morosely staring out the sitter's living room window when he sees three girls coming up the street, Amber, Jessica, and Brooke.

Dylan isn't all that interested in what they're doing, but they are girls and he has nothing else to do, so he watches them. Amber is carrying a bundle.

"This is so boring," he thinks. He's always bored at the babysitter's. "Mrs. Foster is nice enough, but she just doesn't have anything to do. No video games or anything. She doesn't have kids and has nothing in the house for them. All I can do is sit here waiting for one of my parents to pick me up. I wish they would hurry."

Dylan watches the girls stop while Amber jams the bundle into a trashcan next to the garage across the street. From their nervous looks around, he has no doubt they are hiding something.

Curious about what they are hiding, he waits for them to move on.

"I'm going outside," he calls out to Mrs. Foster. Shrugging on his coat and pulling on his boots, he goes out.

The chill air feels like it's biting his lungs when he inhales. He hurriedly zips up his coat, wishing he had grabbed a hat to cover his already stinging ears.

Dylan checks up and down the street to make sure no one is watching and darts across the street to the trashcan. No one is home at the house, but someone might drive by and see him digging in the trash. He looks again before lifting the lid to look in. Pulling the bundle out, Dylan looks it over then unwraps it to reveal a coat wrapped around boots and a hat and mitts.

He studies them. They look familiar. He realizes they belong to Kylie.

"What are they doing with Kylie's stuff?" His eyes narrow. "Those three are the nastiest girls in school and Kylie is Amber's favorite victim."

Dylan looks back at the babysitter's house, debating what he should do. "Kylie just lives on the next street. If I run the stuff over there, the babysitter might notice me gone and I'd be in trouble. Besides, who knows why those girls have the stuff?"

He's about to stuff the clothes back in the trash can but thinks better of it.

"They stole it from Kylie. There is no other reason they would have it." He thinks it over, feeling guilty for his automatic response to shove it back in the trash. His conscience wins.

With a last glance back at Mrs. Foster's house across the street, Dylan darts between the houses, cutting through the back yards to the next street.

Dylan doesn't want Kylie to see him. He approaches her house from behind, sneaking as he cuts through the next-door neighbor's backyard towards the front.

He is just about to break cover from the neighbor's yard and sneak up to the front door when he spots a car parked in front of the house. He looks up and down the street. It's mostly empty, so there is no reason for someone at another house to park in front of this one, and besides, the car is parked on the wrong side of the street. Street parking is on the other side.

"Her mom probably isn't home yet, so who would be at her house?"

Dylan studies Kylie's house and yard and spies a man skulking around the house, peeking in windows.

He ducks behind the bushes between the yards, hiding out of sight. He is still beside the house and he moves quietly and stealthily along the row of bushes, watching the guy from his hiding spot as he goes around to the back of the house. He watches the man try the back door. It's locked.

"Is he a burglar? Who is this guy?" Dylan watches the man turn over things in the yard, tipping a large snow-filled flowerpot on its side and breaking the top off it. His feels like his veins are turning to ice.

"He's looking for a key," he thinks. "He is a burglar."

Dylan's mind races, remembering his own house getting broken into, how much that scared all of them, and the terror his dog still suffers every time someone comes to the house. That was the worst part, not knowing what they did to the dog.

"I have to get out of here." He's about to dart away and run back to the safety of the babysitter's house, but he stops instead, spotting the frightened face of Kylie peeking out a window.

A cold chill fills Dylan. "She's home alone and some guy is trying to break in." He holds his breath, his mind reeling, trying to think what to do.

Dylan is frozen, unable to move or act, and can only watch helplessly while the burglar searches for a way in. His mind moves strangely, thinking, "He doesn't look like what you'd think a burglar would look like." He's picturing the stereo-typical burglar hunched over and dressed all in black with gloves and a mask. This guy is dressed like any other man, kind of dorky looking even.

Finally the man gives up, gets in the car parked in front of the house, and drives away.

The extreme cold is seeping through his clothes, but Dylan still can't make himself move. He is in shock and filled with a numbing dread. After what feels like forever, he manages to break his paralysis. Shivering with fear shock, he sneaks to the front door of the house, skulking low below the level of the windows so Kylie doesn't see him, and leaves the bundle of clothes on the front step before sneaking away.

As soon as he's far enough, Dylan sprints for the sitter's house, his heart pounding and his chest tight with anxiety.

"Should I tell someone?" he thinks as he runs, uncertain. "The guy is gone, but what if he comes back? What can they do anyway, since he's gone? Probably nothing." By the time he reaches the sitter's he has decided not to bother saying anything.

Andrew is wandering aimlessly. He doesn't want to go home yet and feels completely foolish about it. It will be a while before his parents get home and he doesn't want to be alone in the house right now. He can't put the thought of that noise he heard in the house out of his head.

"There's nowhere to go and no one to hang out with, except Dylan, and that isn't an option.

Dylan was my best friend for years and probably would have understood my fear of being alone in the house for hours. The focus is on the was. We don't hang out anymore, not since Dylan became withdrawn for a while and wouldn't talk to anyone. Not even to me."

Andrew feels a pang of regret and hurt at that.

"Dylan is back to going to a babysitter's instead of going home anyway, and he has no interest in being friends anymore."

When he first found out about the babysitter, he didn't believe it. He had to ask. Dylan reacted angrily and has avoided him ever since. He knew Dylan would be embarrassed and wouldn't want anyone to find out, so he kept the secret. Dylan is close enough to hang out after school if his sitter lets him, but Dylan doesn't seem to want to anymore. Andrew is fine with that.

"Dylan changed. He became a bully, picking on anyone smaller and weaker than himself. I don't like him much anymore. I don't think he'd bully me, but he's just a jerk now and I don't want anything to do with that."

Despite his thoughts, he has doubts. He is not so sure Dylan wouldn't beat up and bully him too. Dylan is bigger than most of the boys his age and so far everyone has been fair game, except him.

The cold is getting to him. His feet, hands, and face are freezing; his ears, too, despite his hat.

"I've got to figure out something now." Andrew stomps his feet, putting his hands over his ears, trying to warm up.

"I'll go to the store. It's not far. At least I can go inside and warm up."

He walks fast, alternating between a fast walk and a jog until he gets to the store. He's hanging around there for a while, staying outside and trying to find a sheltered spot where it might be less cold. He stays out as long as he can stand it, the cold biting his fingers and toes until they hurt. His ears feel like they are on fire and the cold air stings his nose painfully when he breathes in.

The cold is too much for him, driving him inside to find warmth. He looks at the inviting warmth through the window.

"They won't like me just hanging around and will kick me out, probably accusing me of shoplifting or something. People always seem to be suspicious for no good reason of kids on their own without parents. I have to do it. I'm going in."

He glances at the store clerk nervously as he enters the store and starts wandering up and down aisles, pretending he's looking for something.

34

3   The Parents Come Home

Kylie listens in fear to the doorknob being jostled. She knows it's her father trying to get in. She expects to hear the sound of breaking glass at any moment. She inches up cautiously to a window, staying low below the bottom edge, and carefully rises up just high enough to peak out. She needs to see, to know where he is. She is terrified he might see her.

He tries the front door first, and then moves around the house. He tries a side window.

Kylie skulks through the house, following him around. She almost steps into a bedroom doorway, catching the dark motion at the window barely in time and darting back, pressing herself against the wall. Her heart is pounding so hard in her chest it feels like it's going to come right through her rib cage and out through her chest.

His face is pressed against the window, looking in. He moves on to the back of the house.

Kylie sneaks into the bedroom and looks out, trying to see where he went. She moves on, following him to the back of the house, going into the kitchen now. She wants more than anything to look out and see what he is doing, but is terrified he will see her.

"Please don't let him know I'm home," she pleads silently. "He hasn't tried yelling through the door and pounding on it, so maybe he doesn't know. Maybe he thinks the house is empty." She crouches against the back door, below the window level, listening.

She can hear him out there, tipping things over, letting them fall, while he searches for a hidden key. She almost jumps and screams at the sudden shaking of the back door when he tries to open it, rattling the doorknob and shaking the door in its frame.

Kylie fights the tears, trembling, and holding her hands tight over her mouth to keep her whimpers from being heard on the other side of the door.

The rattling-shaking of the door stops. She can hear him muttering, but not what he is saying. He walks off, back around the house, trying another window.

Kylie scrambles away from the back door, staying low, peeking around a bedroom doorframe before scampering past the open doorway. She sees the dark shape of his form moving past and scampers into the room, ducking beneath the window.

She breathes deeply, holds her breath, and slowly rises up to peek cautiously out the window. She just catches her father moving out of sight, continuing on to the front.

Kylie scampers through the house to the front. She slips into the living room, staying down and against the wall, inching to the front window. She rises up against the wall beside the window where she is hidden by the partially open curtain, peaking through the small crack between the curtain and window frame.

She holds her breath, watching him walk away and get back in his car. He turns his head and looks back at the house, and just for a few heartbeats Kylie is positive he sees her, that he is staring at her. Then he starts his car and drives away.

She feels sick with fear and weak with relief. She sinks to the floor and sits there sobbing.

"I wish I was dead. I wish I was never even born, that I never even existed," she whimpers miserably.

After that, Kylie sits in a dark corner waiting for her mother to come home, scared her father will return and break into the house. It feels like time has stopped and will never move again while she endlessly waits.

"I'm going to have to explain to Mom how I lost my coat and boots," she moans. "I have another hat and mitts I can wear. They're old and worn out, and Mom fixed the mitts a few times, but that was my only coat and boots for winter. What am I going to wear tomorrow?"

Kylie is startled by a sound at the door. She freezes; her stomach knotting and her heart pounding hard in her chest and feeling like it skipped a beat. "Is he back?" She is terrified.

Relief floods Kylie when she hears the familiar jingle of the way her mother always jingles her keys just before she unlocks the door, followed immediately as the door opens by her mother's voice calling her and her younger sister's babbling mid-sentence about what she did today.

"Kylie, what are your coat and boots doing on the front step?" her mother calls out as she comes in the house.

Kylie is confused. "Coat? Boots?"

She gets to her feet and goes to see what her mother is talking about. She stops, staring in confusion at the clothes her mother is holding out to her. "I can't believe it," she thinks numbly, "there is no way any of those girls would have brought back my clothes. So how did they get there?"

"Well?" her mother insists impatiently. "Why are they on the front steps?"

"I don't know," Kylie says, staring in wide-eyed confusion at the bundle that is her coat wrapped around her boots and stuff. Tears pop to her eyes. She can't hold them back.

"How did they get there?" she thinks wildly. "Did he leave them? But, if Dad left them, that means he was following me. He followed me to the park, watched them beat me up and take my stuff, and he did nothing. Nothing to help. He left me walking home like that. No, even Dad wouldn't just watch and do nothing, would he? Would he leave me to maybe die walking home in this cold? No, I don't think he would. Then who? How?"

Seeing her distraught look and her red swollen eyes, her mother knows immediately that something is wrong.

"What's wrong?" she asks, concerned.

Kylie looks up at her mother, her face twisted with all the fear and sadness she has been feeling for the past few hours and it all pours out about being beaten up at the park, how her coat tore, and the three girls stealing her clothes and leaving her to walk home without them in the cold. She chokes on her tears and stumbles over the words when she starts telling her mom about her dad trying to get into the house.

Her mother listens, horrified. She is more upset about her ex-husband coming to the house than about the girls in the park, but she can deal with only one of the problems.

"We'll go to the girls' houses and talk to their parents," she says.

"No!" Kylie is stricken by the idea. "That will only make them bully me worse!"

"We can't just let them get away with this," her mother insists. "And, they left you without a coat or boots in this cold? Something has to be done about it!"

"Please mom, no," Kylie begs. "Don't you remember the last time? Their mothers believed them, not us. They wouldn't believe those girls were bullying. They were even worse to me for months after!"

Her mother looks at her, taking in the strain and fear no mother wants to see in her daughter's eyes, and realizes she's right. Saying anything will only make things worse for Kylie at school.

When she had confronted the girls' parents before they had sided with the girls, believing their story and saying Kylie made it all up and that she was the bully. The bullying did get worse after that. When she complained to the school, the principal pretended to sympathize and promised to talk to the girls and did nothing about it. But she could tell the principal believed the three girls stories that Kylie made it all up.

"I wish I could pull her out of that school and send her somewhere else," she thinks unhappily, "but how would she get to school? The other schools she could go to are full and wouldn't take her when I tried. We would have to move and I just don't have the money for that."

She sighs, feeling helpless to protect her daughter.

"Well, let's take a look at that coat," she finally says, closing the discussion about dealing with the bullies. She is relieved because she doesn't have to deal with a confrontation with the other girls' parents. But she still has the bigger problem, keeping them safe from her ex-husband.

One thought just doesn't fit, however. She cannot reconcile how the coat and boots ended up on the front steps.

"Kylie, if those girls took your coat and boots then how did they end up on the steps?"

"I don't know," Kylie says miserably. "I guess someone must have seen what happened."

"And they did nothing to help?"

"They brought my stuff back at least."

Kylie's mother frowns, not satisfied with that explanation. She unrolls the coat and together they look for the tears. It won't look very good, but it will have to be mended so Kylie can wear it to school tomorrow.

With no one at the school to let her in and no idea what else to do, Madison heads back home. She is getting colder, her fingers and toes are burning and painful from the cold now and she is getting very upset. She is also going to have to explain to her parents about locking herself out when they get home.

"Assuming I'm not frozen to death by then," Madison mutters miserably.

She retraces her steps, the walk feeling a lot longer this time, and stops when she reaches Mr. Hooper's house.

Caesar!

"I forgot about Caesar," she groans, "I have to go past him again."

The thought of having to go past the dog makes her whole body ache with dread, her muscles unwilling to go on even though she knows it's the only way. It will take too long to go the long way around and she is frozen.

"Come on Madison, you can do this. It's only a dog and he's on a chain that doesn't even reach past the edge of the yard. Yeah, only a big mean dog that'll probably tear you apart and eat you."

Madison loves dogs, but this one is scary, mean, and large.

She stares at the house and yard, willing the dog to not be outside or that Mr. Hooper comes out and controls that nasty dog.

"Mr. Hooper is as scary as the dog is. Maybe I am better off trying to sneak past the dog."

She jumps when the dog pops his head around the side of the house with one loud woof, staring at her from the backyard.

Madison swallows, trying to control her fear. The dog is only standing there watching her so far.

"His chain doesn't reach the road, so walking by should be safe, right?" It doesn't feel safe.

"Okay Madison, let's go," Madison urges herself on.

She takes a first cautious step.

The dog just watches.

She takes two more steps, almost reaching the point where she would be even with the curb in front of the house.

The dog moves, shifting position but not taking a step, and she imagines him coiling to spring at her.

"Just do it Madison," she mutters, "just go. Don't even look at him and just walk right past the house."

A few more steps and Madison is passing front yard, keeping to the far side of the little road, as far away from Old Man Hooper's house as she can without climbing over the fence on the other side. Every muscle is stiff and tense.

Caesar just stands there watching her very intently.

"Very hungrily," she thinks.

When Madison reaches not quite halfway past the back yard, the dog suddenly launches himself at her with a deep growl that becomes a barrage of loud angry barking, bounding after her with powerful strides.

Madison screams and whirls to face the lunging dog, putting her arms up to protect herself from the attack.

The back door of Mr. Hooper's house flies open with a bang and the old man comes barreling down the stairs on legs that are little more than sticks covered by loose pants. He is wearing a stained white undershirt with a hole in it and an unbuttoned plaid flannel shirt that is also stained and torn. Madison suspects the brown-red stains are the blood of his and Caesar's victims from cutting them up in his basement to bury them or feed them to Caesar. His wild eyes, unkempt hair, and grey patchy chin stubble make him look more frightening and wild, like a backwoods crazy man.

Fists clenched, he raises one and shakes it at her threateningly, the other gripping what Madison suspects is some kind of weapon to knock her senseless with so he can feed her to the dog.

"You quit teasing my dog!" he shouts at her. "Get outta my yard! Get outta here and leave my dog alone! You kids are always teasing my dog!"

Caesar reaches the end of his chain and Madison is relieved to see the chain holding strong. With the chain taught, still pulling and lunging at her, Caesar's jaws snap as if he is already chewing on her while he continues to bark ferociously.

"I'm not even in his yard," Madison thinks. With a scared whimper, she scurries off towards the back lane, putting Mr. Hooper's house and Caesar behind her as quickly as she can. The moment she reaches the corner where the little road meets the back lane, Madison breaks into a run.

Behind her, Caesar is still barking after her and she can hear the old man yelling and muttering.

Madison is still shaken by the confrontation when she reaches the fence with the loose board. She looks up at the fence, picturing for just a moment Caesar breaking his chain and coming after her, pinning her helplessly against the fence while he tears her apart, tearing first through her coat to get to her skin beneath. She sees its height as an impossible barrier, and then almost panics when she doesn't find the loose board right away.

"Okay Madison, calm down," she tries to sooth herself.

Fingers numb with the cold and her toes like numb blocks filled with a distant sharp pain that are there weighing her legs down but somehow detached, not a part of her, Madison tries again, looking for the notch in the board and counting the boards.

Her fingers will not work when she tries to move the board. Madison pulls her mitts off and blows hot air on her fingers, putting them in her mouth and sucking on them to try to warm them up. It only makes the pain in her frozen fingers worse. Putting her mitts back on, she tries again and this time moves the board.

Madison starts squeezing through the board when she hears the sounds of footsteps and heavy breathing behind her, and then the jingle of a dog's chain.

"That heavy breathing is definitely a dog panting," she thinks. "Caesar! He got loose!" Terror grips her and she squeezes frantically through the fence, almost falling through on the other side.

She turns as she lets the board fall back into place just in time to see a woman jogging up the alley with a big fluffy white dog.

Madison leans against the fence and lets out a nervous giggle. "It wasn't Caesar," she says in relief.

She walks the rest of the way home, each step seeming to take her farther away instead of closer. The pain in her frozen fingers and toes is getting worse. She tries walking faster, and it makes the pain in her feet worse but at least she should get home faster. Her nose is burning too now and she walks holding her mitts to her face, blocking the cold and warming her face with her own breath cupped beneath the mitts. She leaves only a crack to see through between her mitts.

"Will I ever get home?" she moans in despair.

When Madison finally gets home, she is so cold that her hands and feet hurt so much she is crying. She still can't get in, though, because she lost her key and locked herself out. Madison sits on the steps and just cries.

"Are you okay?"

She looks up, startled, to see the woman who lives next door.

"I locked myself out," Madison sobs.

"You look frozen!" the woman exclaims sympathetically. "Come inside my house to warm up and we'll watch for your parents to come home."

Madison gratefully goes with her.

Inside the neighbor's house, she is given a warm blanket and a cup of hot cocoa. Her fingers are too frozen at first to hold the cup. She sits there, rubbing her hands together, trying to warm them. When her fingers and toes start to warm up the pain is terrible. Frostbite had been setting in. She has to wait for the pain in her fingers to lessen before she dares try picking up the cup of hot cocoa. She sits there drinking it thankfully and watching a television show that is way too young for her that the neighbor put on to entertain her.

A few hours later, Madison's mother arrives home.

The neighbor notices the car in the driveway. "Someone is home at your house."

Madison looks up at her with fear in her eyes.

"I'm going to be in trouble for locking myself out," she thinks. "Worse, my parents are not going to trust me to be home alone now."

"Do you want me to go with you?" the neighbor asks sympathetically, seeing her fear.

"No, I can manage," Madison says unhappily. Her mind is working, thinking through what she will say to her parents. She gets up reluctantly.

"Thank you for letting me wait here, and for the hot cocoa," she says as she pulls on her coat and boots at the door. She waves goodbye as the woman closes the door behind her.

Madison trudges home reluctantly. "I'm going to be in so much trouble," she thinks again miserably. "They'll make me go to a babysitter now. I'm too old for babysitters." She opens the front door to find her mother frantically searching the house and calling her.

Hearing the sound of the front door and the thud of Madison's boot dropping on the floor, her mother rushes to the door.

"Where have you been?" Her voice is as anxious and harsh with worry as the expression on her face.

Madison shifts nervously, standing there with one boot on and one off, her coat open, and hat and mitts dropped carelessly on the floor with her backpack.

She looks down at the floor, not wanting to meet her mother's eyes.

"I lost my key," she mumbles quietly.

"What? Look up at me when you speak. What did you say?"

Madison huffs in frustration, not wanting to repeat herself. She looks up at her mother, her mother's worried look making her want to hide.

"I got locked out."

"How? Where is your key?" She advances on Madison. "Take your jacket off, give me your backpack. Where is your key, Madison?"

Madison lets her mother take the offending backpack. She takes off her other boot and jacket while her mother searches the backpack.

"I don't know. I got home and I couldn't find my key." Her voice is cracking and sounds small, making her sound years younger.

She stands there watching her mother pull stuff out of her backpack, shaking them out and finally dumping the rest of the contents on the floor in a mess.

"So where were you?"

"I was next door." Madison decides not to tell her that she walked all the way back to school and then home again before finally ending up next door.

The front door opens behind Madison and her father walks in.

"What's all this?" he asks, looking down at the mess scattered on the floor and at his wife rifling through Madison's backpack.

"Madison locked herself out. She lost her key." Madison's mother doesn't pause in her search of the backpack and its contents.

Her father takes his shoes and coat off, hanging up his coat, and gives Madison a disappointed look.

That look makes a red flush burn her cheeks. She would have preferred anger to his disappointment.

He shakes his head. "Did you check her backpack and coat?"

Her mother looks up at him with an annoyed look.

He picks up Madison's coat from the floor and searches the pockets, feeling along the bottom hem in case it somehow slipped through a hole in the pocket into the inner lining.

Madison just watches. There are no holes in her pockets.

"How did you lock yourself out?" her father asks while he searches the coat. "This was a pretty big responsibility we trusted you with. I guess you just aren't ready for it."

"There is no key," her mother exclaims, dropping the violated backpack on the floor. "I guess we were wrong. You just aren't responsible enough yet."

She turns and heads for the kitchen.

"Mom, I am. I'm twelve," Madison begs, following her. "What are you going to do?" She has a pretty good idea what her mother is going to do and she is mortified at the idea.

"Mom, no, please, I'm too old for babysitters."

Her mother picks up the phone and digs her little phone book out, turning on Madison. "What if the neighbor wasn't home? Where would you have gone? It's too cold out; you could have froze or had frostbite."

Madison blushes at the memory of her freezing walk and the pain of frostbite in her fingers and toes.

"I'm finding you a babysitter." Her mother starts flipping through the little phone book.

"Mom, please," Madison begs, fighting the tears she can't stop. Twelve is too old to go to daycare or a babysitter. Too old to cry. How can she show them she's old enough if she cries like a baby?

"You just aren't ready yet for the responsibility of getting yourself to school and home," her father says, entering the kitchen and pacing angrily.

The tension in the air between them all is heavy. Madison watches helplessly as her mother is determined to find a babysitter and her father continues pacing angrily and scolding her and complaining about the locked door. She doesn't even hear his words anymore, seeing only the teasing and taunting at school when the other kids learn she's going to a babysitter.

Madison looks at her father, usually her biggest ally when her mother is set on something and is being unreasonable. She has no ally there now. Madison isn't sure if he is angry with her, himself, or at the door that kept her from getting into the house.

Madison is mortified. "Babies go to babysitters," she thinks. "I'm old enough to be home alone. I'll show them!" Her heart sinks. "But how?"

With no mature options, she resorts to what has always worked in the past. Madison cries and begs them to give her another chance.

This goes on for some time, a battle for who has more stamina. Her mother keeps threatening to send her to a babysitter, her father pacing angrily and lecturing her, and Madison keeps crying and begging for another chance. Finally, her parents wear down first and relent. Madison is given another chance to show that she can handle the responsibility.

Andrew walks around the store, trying to be invisible. He can feel the store clerk watching him and, when he risks a quick look at the clerk, sees the man is watching him suspiciously. The clerk looks like he is ready to confront him and accuse him of stealing something, even though he hasn't done anything.

"I just want to keep warm without having to go back home and wait alone for Mom and Dad to come home," he thinks, feeling dumb just thinking about it. "What's there to be afraid of being home alone? There's nothing there."

Andrew is afraid someone might find out. "I'm too old for this kind of little kid scared of nothing stuff."

The clerk's suspicious stare is making him more nervous. He's starting to feel panicky; scared of being caught even though he isn't doing anything wrong.

He tries to pretend he's shopping, hoping the clerk will leave him alone. He looks around him and grabs something off the shelf without looking at anything but the price tags below the items on the shelf. It has to be something he has enough money to pay for, and he doesn't have very much. He has no idea what it is that he grabbed.

He's only buying it to show that he's not there to make trouble.

Andrew shuffles up to the counter, keeping his head down, and puts the object on the counter.

"Are you really going to buy that?" the clerk asks with a smirk. He still looks suspicions and is eying Andrew with a distrustful look, judging him either insane or a criminal, depending on his reaction to the question.

Andrew looks up at him with a nod, a flush creeping up his neck, and then looks down at the item in question. He stares at it in horror.

There, for all of the world to see, is a pink box. He feels like it is staring up at him in gleeful accusation, yelling to the store, "HE IS LYING!"

Andrew swallows, feeling suddenly sick with embarrassment, the red flush rising up his cheeks. He looks around quickly to see if anyone is looking.

The object pictured on the bright pink box looks similar to that bullet shaped lipstick candy, only longer and white.

Andrew doesn't know what it's used for, but the word Tampon glares up like an announcement and all he knows is that it's something very private that boys are not supposed to know about and has to do with women and teen girls and puberty.

The package says it's a mini pack just for the purse. He suffers a sudden flash of thought, envisioning having to explain to his mother why he bought it.

Andrew turns redder, his face burning with a flush of shame, and the clerk behind the counter laughs. His expression shows pain for the boy's predicament and relief that he isn't a shoplifter after all.

"Your mom sent you, didn't she?"

"Yes," Andrew mumbles, looking down and hoping no one sees him.

He pays for his unwanted purchase and makes a beeline for the exit, running halfway home before he slows down and starts looking for somewhere to ditch the little bag.

When Andrew gets home, the tampon box has been safely disposed of in a random trashcan along the way. He lets himself back in the house and goes back to playing video games.

He plays for the next hour, nervously listening for the noises from the basement that sent him fleeing from the house. The noises never repeat themselves, but that almost makes it worse because he can't make himself stop expecting them.

Finally, his parents come home and he can put this day behind him.

4   Some Mornings Are Never Good

The three bully girls are sitting in their usual spot at the back of the bus. That's where the bad kids sit, the ones who are tough and mean. They are the kids who the other kids shrink at the sight of and generally try to avoid out of fear and self-preservation or who just have a reputation for making other kids' lives miserable.

Their chatter stops and they turn to look out the window when the bus stops, watching to see who is getting on the bus. They know who gets on at this stop, and are watching in gleeful anticipation.

Getting on the bus, Kylie keeps her head down but can't help nervously looking around. She catches the shocked angry stare of Amber glaring daggers at her and knows it's because she got her stuff back. The embarrassment of what Amber and her friends did to her at the park burns her cheeks red, even though probably nobody even knows about it.

She is wrong. Before she even sits down, Kylie hears muffled snickers and whispered words about it. Some kids give her sidelong glances while they whisper behind their hands to their seatmates.

"Okay," Kylie thinks, "so Amber got online and told the whole school. Figures."

Amber's eyes narrow and her lips become a tight angry line. She glares hatefully at Kylie as she gets on the bus and takes a seat closer to the front of the bus.

"Of course she sits in the front," Amber thinks nastily. "The front seats are for meat, the kids who are weak and pathetic, targets for the kids in the back seats."

Amber is furious. She is not mad that Kylie got on the bus, at least no more than the usual anger every morning when she sees Kylie get on the bus. Amber's hatred is boiling at the sight of Kylie wearing the same coat and boots they took yesterday.

Amber turns to her two friends, glowering at them suspiciously, and mouthing the words, "How did she get her stuff back? Was it you?"

They both quickly shake their heads, looking worried and confused, denying having anything to do with it.

Amber fumes over it all the way to school, glaring at Kylie's back and ignoring her two friends' attempts to talk to her.

Kylie can feel Amber's hate-filled glare burning into her back all the way to school. She doesn't have to turn and look to know the other girl is staring at her.

Andrew is waiting at the bus stop with the usual couple of kids, huddling inside their coats and trying to keep warm. He huffs and watches his breath hang in a heavy cloud, motionless in the air.

He looks around at the other kids and up the street. There it is in the distance at last, the orange beast with its stinky exhaust, worn seats, and tired scuffed body.

They are all relieved to see the school bus coming around the corner. They line up and Andrew gets on the bus last, taking an empty seat. The seat cushion sinks with his weight and he settles in to stare out the window for the ride to school. Around him, the bus is filled with the usual roar of kids talking and laughing.

He glances quickly at the driver.

"If we get too loud, the driver will yell at us to be quiet. If anyone gets out of their seat or doesn't listen, he'll stop the bus to yell at us to be quiet. That usually happens once every week. It should be today or tomorrow," he thinks.

The driver just drives on and Andrew turns his attention back to staring out the window.

Madison is puttering around her room, not really doing anything. She looks at the clock and her eyes widen, her mouth dropping open to form a panicked "oh".

"I'm late!" Madison looks around in alarm, sizing up what she needs and where it is. She's not ready for the school bus yet. She flitters around the room grabbing clothes and pulling them on without looking at them, puts her hair in a hurried ponytail without brushing it, rushing through the house to the front door and struggles to get her jacket and boots on fast enough.

She grabs her backpack and remembers, "My lunch!" She drops the bag and bolts for the kitchen. "I'm going to miss the bus!"

Grabbing her lunch bag from the fridge and racing for the door again, she crushes it in her hurry to jam in into her backpack, groaning with the thought of what she might have done to the lunch inside.

Madison leaves, struggling with the key and moaning, "come on key." Finally, it locks and she bolts down the street.

She has to run all the way to the bus stop. Halfway there she is sure she can't run another step. Gasping, the cold air burning her lungs, she has a painful stitch stabbing her in the side, her backpack feels like it weighs a million pounds, and her legs are so achingly tired she is sure they can't move anymore.

Madison pushes herself on, forcing herself to keep going.

She is just nearing the bus stop and the bus is waiting ahead. She puts her head down, pushing herself to run harder. Her heart skips when she hears the hiss of the bus's brakes releasing as the driver starts slowly pulling away.

"No!" she cries, trying to push her exhausted legs to run harder.

Madison reaches the corner, bolting into the street without looking, dodges a car that blares its horn at her when she runs in front of it, and chases the bus while waving her arms and yelling for the driver to stop.

Luckily, the driver spots her in the rear view mirror and stops. The bus's door opens and Madison runs for it with a gasp of relief. She reaches the bus and climbs gratefully inside, using the handrails to pull herself up the steps because her legs feel like they are ready to give out.

The driver gives her an over the glasses stern look as she climbs the stairs, shaking his head in disapproval. He puts an arm out, stopping her before she can pass him.

"It's your responsibility to make it to the bus stop on time. It's not my responsibility to make sure you don't miss the bus," he lectures her right there in front of everyone. "Next time I won't stop."

He pulls his arm back, letting her pass with a disapproving shake of his head.

Face flushed with embarrassment and cold, Madison mumbles an apology and sheepishly stumbles back through the bus, finding an empty seat and gratefully sinking down into it. She wants to hide and pretend none of this happened.

"Maybe nobody was paying attention and noticed the driver giving me a lecture," she thinks. Glancing around at the smirks and snickers sent her way she knows she's lying to herself. The whole bus witnessed her shame.

Anna stretches and yawns lazily in bed before rolling over and looking at the clock. She stares at it, blinking sleepily. Her eyes widen.

"Oh my gawd! I missed the bus again!" she squeals. Normally, she wouldn't care, but she is already in trouble for being late for school twice this week.

Anna jumps out of bed and dresses in record time, pony-tailing her hair without brushing it. She grabs her toothbrush, quickly dabs toothpaste on it, and runs for the kitchen, barely brushing her teeth on the way. Dropping the toothbrush on the table, she swallows and grabs her backpack and lunch, racing out the door without locking it, pausing just long enough to pull her coat, boots, hat, and mitts on quickly. She pauses outside the house, looking around.

"Oh buggers, it's too far to walk to school in this cold, I have to find another way. Bike!"

She runs around the side of the house to the shed in the back yard, her feet sinking in the deep snow with every step, drops her stuff in the snow, and struggles to open it. Luckily, the doors slide sideways on tracks. There is no way she could open it with all the snow blocking the doors if they were the type that swung out on hinges. The snow collapses in a big chunk and falls into the dry shed as she leans in for better purchase and forces the door open wider. She tramps more in when she steps into the shed. Fighting with the tangle of bikes, she manages to get hers out and wrestles it out the door.

Retrieving her stuff, Anna drags the bike through the snow to the street in front of the house and jumps on it, riding hard for school until she is too exhausted to keep up the fast pace. Fighting her bike through the snow to the road exhausted her before she even started. She slows her pace for a while. Luckily, the streets are clear so it's not hard to pedal.

"Staying on the roads is the long way to school. I don't have time for that. I'm taking the shortcut."

She swerves off route, and hops off the bike, dragging it through deep snow as she cuts through a yard to get to the next street, mounting the bike again on the other side and taking off like a shot down the street. At one point, she hits an icy patch and almost wipes out, the bike wobbling dangerously before she regains control. At this speed, she would have hurt herself pretty good. She has to drag her bike through the deep snow of a few more yards, cutting across to the next street.

"If I'm lucky, I'll make it by the second bell and Mom and Dad won't get another phone call about me being late for school.

The bus pulls to a stop in front of the school and Kylie gets off the bus with the other kids. She weaves through the crowd of kids arriving for school, looking around at everyone.

"Who could have left my stuff on my doorstep?" she thinks. "Someone did it, someone who had to have known what happened in the park and what those girls did with my clothes after stealing them. There's no way it would have been any of those three bullies. They'd never have given my stuff back."

She stops herself from looking back. The three bully girls are on the bus behind her, waiting their turn to get off. The bus always unloads from front to back, giving the kids at the front a running chance to escape anyone sitting further back. She quickens her pace, wanting to be nowhere around there when they are released from the bus.

Kylie is confused and torn with emotions. "I'm grateful to whoever it was, but it's so embarrassing too. They must have seen what those girls did."

She clenches her jaw angrily. "Whoever it was saw what happened and didn't try to help." She hurries into the school, ducking away from everyone else to be alone, looking behind her often for her tormentors.

"If they saw, why didn't they try to stop them? How could they just watch those girls beat me up and take my stuff and do nothing? How could they just leave me walking home like that? To maybe freeze to death and die?

Maybe whoever it is was scared. I can't blame them for that. They might have been beaten up too. Then they would become targets of the mean girls' campaign of torture too. I guess I can't blame them for that. I have to forgive them. At least I got my coat and boots back."

What Kylie feels the most, though, is alone. Utterly, completely, absolutely, and undeniably wretchedly alone.

"No one is more alone than the person being bullied," she thinks miserably.

"I wish I didn't have to go to school. I feel like everyone is looking at me, laughing behind my back and making fun of me for the things those jerks do. I feel like everyone is against me. I have no friends. I have a few kids I kind of hang out with sometimes, but you aren't supposed to feel this alone if you have friends. Are you? And friends are supposed to stick up for you. Nobody dares go against the three worst bully girls in the school."

She sighs unhappily. "I wish I was never even born, that I would just die, that I never existed. I wish I didn't have to go through day after day of this cruel life, being tormented by those three nasty jerks. I wish I was dead."

An icy dread fills her. Amber must be furious. She had seen the cold hard hatred and anger directed at her when Amber saw her get on the bus with her stuff back.

She ducks around a corner.

"If I'm going to survive this day, I need to avoid those three at all costs. Maybe I should run away. Skip school and just take off.

Mom will be worried, but the mean team also won't be able to torture me anymore."

When the bus arrives at school, the kids pour off it in a less than orderly way while the bus driver sits back watching and hoping none do anything he'd have to step in and stop. Other buses are dropping kids off too, competing with parents' cars also trying to pull up to drop kids off.

Sitting at the back, Amber has no choice but to silently sit and wait her turn. She glares at Kylie getting off ahead of her and hurrying towards the school.

"They should let us off from the back first, not the front," she fumes. Kylie is out of sight by the time the kids at the back of the bus can get up and get off the bus. She gets up, impatiently elbowing past someone getting up at the same time and pushing her way ahead of her.

The moment they are on the ground, Amber pulls her two friends off towards the school and straight to the bathroom, her expression grim and her friends glancing at each other nervously. As soon as the bathroom door closes behind them, she whirls on them with a furious look, glaring from one to the other.

"Which one of you gave Kylie her stuff back?" she demands.

They stare at her with identical shocked looks. Jessica and Brooke saw Kylie get on the bus too and noticed Amber's fury, but neither had though much of anything about it.

They only realize now, as their friend faces them with an anger that makes the blood in both their veins turn cold with fear, that Kylie was wearing the coat they took.

Jessica and Brooke have both always been afraid of Amber despite their friendship. With a nasty girl like her, you just never know when she might turn on you too.

They shake their heads, exchanging nervous looks, denying it.

"No, I didn't!"

"I wouldn't! Never!"

Amber glares at them both suspiciously. "Well she got her stuff back somehow and nobody but us knew where it was," she hisses.

"Maybe someone saw us stuff it in that trash can," Jessica suggests.

"Maybe whoever lives there found it and recognized it," Brooke says. "Maybe they gave it to her."

Amber can't argue with the logic of their suggestions. Both are possible answers.

"Maybe," she admits reluctantly, still eyeing them both suspiciously. But, this is not over yet.

"They don't always agree with the things I want to do," she thinks, "especially Brooke. She is kind of wussy sometimes, trying to back out of doing stuff."

Amber turns and paces the bathroom, watching Brooke out of the corner of her eye suspiciously. "Did you give that little witch her stuff back?" She keeps the thought to herself. "When I find out who did it, I will make them pay, no matter who it is. It's time to drop it for now and move on to more important things."

Her silent pacing is making both girls nervous.

"We have to do something about it," Amber says conspiratorially, turning to look at them directly. "We are going to get even with Kylie for getting her stuff back."

The three start plotting their revenge.

"Why do we have to punish Kylie just for getting her own stuff back?" Brooke wonders. She doesn't dare say what she thinks.

In minutes, they are back in the hallway looking for their victim.

Dylan's morning is a rushed mess. From the moment he got out of bed, everything seems to be going wrong. He is woken up before his alarm by the sound of his parents' angry voices in another room.

"They're at it again," he groans, "fighting." He pulls the pillow over his head to try to drown them out and go back to sleep. The incessant buzzing of his alarm starts. He groans again. He has to get up.

His mind is foggy with sleep and he feels sluggish. He stayed up late playing video games in his room last night when his parents thought he was sleeping and is too tired now. He forces himself to get up and staggers to the bathroom. He's wearing a pair of shorts, he prefers them to pajamas. He gets too hot sleeping in anything else.

Finished in the bathroom, Dylan heads for the kitchen where his parents are still fighting. They clam up at his entrance, leaving a cold silence between them in the room.

He looks at Lucy huddled in her cage, shivering and looking absolutely miserable.

"You already put Lucy in the cage," he complains.

"We don't have time to be tripping over the dog," his mother snaps.

Lucy whimpers in response, staring at him with her head low and sad eyes.

Dylan's little sister comes in, seeming annoyingly unaffected by their parents fighting. She sits down to happily eat her toaster pastry breakfast.

Dylan opens the fridge and pulls the milk out, placing it on the table. He gets out a bowl, spoon, and cereal, placing them next to the milk and pours cereal in the bowl. He pours milk over the cereal and starts to eat.

That first mouthful tastes foul, making him gag and choke on it, spitting it back out into the bowl.

"Dylan! That's disgusting!" His mother's voice is still shrill and angry from fighting with his dad.

"It tastes gross!" He leans in and sniffs at the cereal with a disgusted look, inspecting it. Now he sees the lumps in the curdled milk. "The milk is spoiled."

"What do you mean it's spoiled?" His mother rushes over impatiently as he picks up the milk carton to inspect it. Sure enough, it is a week past the expiry date.

"It's expired," he tells her.

"There's no way it's expired, I just bought it." She snatches the carton away to inspect it herself. She sniffs it and makes a disgusted face, then checks the date. She almost swears, catching herself.

"Find something else to eat." She takes the carton to the sink and pours it out, running water to wash the sour milk down. She returns for his bowl while he pulls out bread and makes toast.

Dylan is watching his mother carefully pour the milk out of the bowl, using the spoon as a dam against the cereal and trying not to pour the cereal into the sink. He smells burning toast.

He leaps up and reaches the toaster just as smoke begins to rise. Popping the toast out, he handles the hot bread gingerly, dropping it unhappily on a plate.

"Scrape it off," his mother snaps, her temper still short. "You don't have time to re-toast."

Dylan grabs a butter knife and unhappily starts scraping the burn off the toast into the sink, doing a poor job of rinsing the crumbs out, which only makes his mother more annoyed. He can see the angry set of her lips pursing tighter when she re-rinses his crumbs from the sink.

"We are all going to be late now," she complains. She rushes out of the kitchen to finish getting ready for work, thankfully leaving him to eat in peace.

Dylan is almost finished his toast when his dad comes rushing in and starts pouring coffee into two travel mugs. He can tell by his stiffness that he's still angry too. Whatever they are fighting about, they aren't letting it go.

"You're still eating? Hurry up. You are going to be late." His father's angry tone makes Dylan feel like he's in trouble.

"I'm done," Dylan mutters, dumping his unfinished toast in the garbage and putting the plate in the dishwasher. He leaves the room stiffly, his parents' anger rubbing off on him. He goes back to his room to get dressed and comb his hair. He can still hear them talking angrily at each other through his closed door.

Last night Dylan talked his parents into dropping him off at school today instead of going to the babysitter and taking the bus from there and is now regretting it.

"Sitting in the car with them fighting like this is going to make the drive miserable," Dylan mutters.

"Dylan!" His father is yelling, "let's go!"

"Coming!" He yells back, loud enough to be heard through the closed door. He starts grabbing his books and jamming them into his backpack, his ears burning now with the anger in his dad's voice. He dreads stepping out of that bedroom and facing their anger. It doesn't matter that they are angry at each other, not him, anger is anger and it makes him feel like crud.

Someone starts knocking loudly on his door. It isn't his dad. It would be a pounding, not a knock, if it was.

"Dylan, come on," his mother's shrill voice is getting angrier from her anxiety over running late. "You're making us all late! Let's go!"

The red flush on his ears spreading, Dylan grabs his backpack and yanks the door open, stalking angrily out of his room. He is at the door trying to get his coat and boots on when his mother is on him, impatiently shoving his lunch at his already full hands.

He snatches the lunch and drops it on the floor to pull his boots on.

She gives him an annoyed look that says, "Seriously?" and turns her attention to his little sister, shooing her out the door with her backpack and lunch.

Lucy's panicked cries follow them out the door.

They rush out to the car where his dad is waiting with even less patience. The drive is as unpleasant as Dylan expected, the car filled with an awkward angry silence, no one talking to anyone else. He is not having a good day and is frustrated and angry.

When the car pulls up in front of the school, Dylan gets out, waving goodbye with a grunt and a scowl, and heads into the school, pushing his way ruthlessly through anyone who doesn't move out of his way fast enough.

"I don't know why they have to be mad at me just because they're mad at each other," he thinks.

Inside, he stops and looks around the hallway. He feels a strong urge to punch something, a locker, anything, to destroy something. He is filled with frustration and anger to the point he feels ready to explode. Seeing a scrawny boy in a plaid shirt only irritates him. Dylan heads for him.

"I'm going to show this jerk what's what," he thinks, not connecting the thought to his built up frustration and anger over his horrible morning.

The three bully girls are waiting for Kylie. She got off the bus first, and they had their little meeting in the bathroom, but they still have a few minutes before the first bell rings. The halls are packed with kids. They see her coming through the crowd and pick their spot, waiting for her to reach them to attack.

Jessica and Brooke watch Kylie's slow approach, wishing she would hurry up so they can get their stuff for their first class. Being late for homeroom is the worst because that's when you are marked absent or late for the day.

"Come on, hurry up," Jessica mutters. "You better not make me late."

Brooke glances at her and goes back to watching their prey. "It's Amber who's making us late," she thinks, secretly hoping Kylie turns and goes another way so they can get to their lockers. Kylie just keeps on coming. "Don't you know anything? Why are you still coming?" Brooke thinks.

Kylie is almost on them. Jessica turns her attention to Amber, watching for her signal to attack, but Amber is not paying attention to their approaching victim.

She follows their leader's eyes to see what she is looking at.

Amber watches Dylan walk quickly towards a scrawny boy in a plaid shirt. She cringes inwardly at having to be in the same school as such a dork as the scrawny boy. Everything about Dylan says anger, his aggressive walk, the angry way he holds himself, his fists clenched at his side, and the reckless look in his eyes.

She thrills as she watches Dylan put his arm out straight, slamming the smaller boy's locker closed with a loud bang just as he is opening it, and then slams the boy into the lockers with a shoulder check in one practiced fluid motion, towering over him and saying something. She can't hear what he is saying. It doesn't matter.

Jessica nudges Brooke, pointing at Amber and then to Dylan. Brooke looks, shaking her head and shrugging to say, "What can we do?"

Amber is too busy mooning over Dylan and doesn't even see Kylie passing them until it's too late. Jessica watches her pass with disgust. Brooke is relieved. Now maybe they can go to their lockers.

Annoyed, Jessica nudges Amber, whispering harshly, "I thought we were going to get her?"

Amber turns to her in confusion, having completely forgotten for a moment why they are there.

Jessica points at their victim who is already vanishing in the crowd of kids.

Amber's eyes narrow as she stares after Kylie just before she vanishes in the crowd. "I missed my chance!" she thinks.

"We'll have to get her later," she hisses and leads the other two off to get their stuff for homeroom.

Kylie sees the three girls waiting for her up ahead and cringes. There is nothing to be done about it; she has to go past them. She steels herself for the inevitable, walking on stiffly.

As she's approaching with a sick feeling in her stomach, watching the evil trio while trying to look like she doesn't see them, she sees Amber's attention turn to Dylan and stay there.

"Am I wrong? Maybe they aren't waiting for me. Please don't be waiting for me; please don't be waiting for me," she thinks. She can see Jessica and Brooke whispering and looking at her as she gets closer to them.

Kylie makes a point of not looking at them, watching them through the corners of her eyes. "There's no point in jinxing it if they aren't waiting for me by letting them catch me looking at them."

Amber's interest in Dylan also draws Kylie's attention to him. He's focused on a smaller boy and is going in for the kill. She knows that look he has as he stalks the smaller boy in the plaid shirt. Kylie knows immediately what he intends without knowing exactly what he plans to do. His exact plan doesn't matter; it's all pretty much the same.

"Dylan is as bad of a bully as Amber and her friends are." Kylie feels sad for the smaller boy, who doesn't even see it coming. For a moment she is tempted to call out and warn him.

"If I warn him, I'll definitely get the evil trio's attention and I don't want that." Feeling helpless to do anything, Kylie can only watch as she walks on.

Kylie cringes when Dylan slams the other boy's locker door on him with a loud bang that startles him and everyone else around. She feels a little sick watching him slam the boy into the lockers hard with a shoulder block. "That had to hurt." The smaller boy cowers and bravely tries to play it down, a sickly look of pain and fear on his face.

Kylie looks away, her face tight and stomach sick. She can't watch anymore. She keeps going, desperately hoping Amber doesn't notice her. Amber is too busy staring at Dylan with a love-struck look that makes Kylie even more nauseous. Jessica and Brooke stare at her with shocked looks as she walks by, whispering and nudging each other and their leader.

Kylie slips past the bully girls without incident. Relief floods her, turning her knees weak.

"I was sure by the angry glares I got from Amber on the bus and as I was approaching them in the hall that they were up to something; and it wouldn't be anything good," Kylie thinks.

A tight pain in her chest reminds her to breathe and she exhales quickly, realizing for the first time that she was holding her breath.

Still not satisfied, Dylan takes his bad mood out on a couple more boys, both smaller and weaker than himself, before rushing to get his stuff from his locker and racing off to his homeroom.

Kylie is seated at her desk and looks up to watch Dylan rush into the homeroom classroom, roughly pushing his way past a couple kids going through the doorway before him.

She turns away with a disgusted look. "Who else did the big jerk bully before he got here?" she thinks.

Dylan gets into the room and quickly looks around. There she is, Kylie. His heart beats faster and his hands feel clammy, his stomach tightening into a knot.

"She is so pretty today," he thinks. "She is so... looking at me with complete disgust and revulsion."

She looks away and he knows it's because she can't stand to even look at him. He stiffens. That look of disgust is like a knife in his chest.

"She hates me," he thinks miserably. "She thinks I'm disgusting and gross."

That look directed at him from her hurts him inside, worse than his parents' anger and fighting. Dylan has a crush on Kylie. It's his secret. He slinks down the row of desks and slides into his seat, staring gloomily ahead. The pain hardens, turning to anger that is directed at no one and everyone. He feels the overwhelming urge again to punch something.

Kids are still filing into the room and taking their seats. He sticks his foot out and trips the next boy to pass his desk, laughing cruelly at the boy sprawling on the floor, his books scattering.

Half a dozen other kids snicker at their classmate's embarrassment. Others look embarrassed for him or angry at Dylan's cruelty.

Kylie makes a point of not turning and looking. "Jerk. Why do some kids have to be so mean?" she wonders sadly.

5   Bully's Revenge

Through her own cleverness and determination to survive the day, Kylie manages to avoid her tormentors. It was pretty close a few times. She even rushed up to strike up a conversation with a teacher walking in the direction of her class to avoid them.

By the end of the day, she is feeling almost victorious. "I just have to make it to the bus and run home, and then I'm safe for today."

"Nice coat," Amber sneers at Kylie with a mocking smirk as she and her two friends walk by her while she's standing in front of her locker putting her repaired coat on to go home.

Kylie blushes, her stomach souring instantly and a rush of fear rushes through her. The stitching is obvious and ugly where the rip was repaired. Jessica and Brooke giggle at the insult. To Kylie's relief they go past her without stopping. The bus will be coming soon and kids are hurrying to get their stuff ready to get on the bus for the ride home.

Her face burning with embarrassment at Amber's comment about her coat, Kylie grabs her books, locks her locker, and heads down the hall.

When Amber and the others reach the corner down the hall, they quickly dodge around the corner out of sight. They wait there for Kylie, watching as she walks past them without seeing them.

"She's not headed to the exit, so she must have somewhere to go before the bus comes," Amber whispers. "We have to be fast in case she comes back to her locker."

Stifling their giggles, the three girls race back down the hall to Kylie's locker. They stop and look around. A girl is walking towards them. They wait impatiently for her to walk by, waiting for her to reach the other end of the hall. They pull out juice boxes, jam the straws into them, and quickly stick the other end of the straws through the open vent slits in the top of the door, squeezing and spraying the juice into the locker.

"Hurry!" Amber urges. She still has other plans for Kylie before the bus comes. They don't have much time.

Madison has nothing left that she needs to do and has those minutes before the bus comes to just hang around and wait. She is heading for the door where the bus stops to line up to wait for the bus.

She sees Kylie putting her coat on at her locker down the hall ahead of her. Amber and her two nasty friends say something to Kylie as they go by but they don't stop, disappearing around the corner. Kylie grabs her stuff and hurries down the hall past that corner and keeps on going down the hall and turns at another corner.

Madison is still walking towards that end of the hall when the three meanest girls in the school step out from around the corner and start heading straight towards her. She is immediately nervous; worried they'll do something to her, although she has so far been lucky enough to avoid their attention. The three girls stop and are looking right at her, making her even more nervous.

"They're going to do something to me, I just know it," Madison whimpers silently. She almost turns around and goes back the other way. "They're going to make me miss the bus."

"If I can walk past Caesar I can walk past them," she tells herself. She steels herself and continues on towards them, ready for the worst.

Madison is relieved when she walks past the three girls without them doing or saying anything.

After she passes them and makes it all the way to the end of the hall, she turns around and looks back to see them messing around with one of the lockers. The three of them have juice boxes. Giggling, they punch the straws through the holes, shove the other ends through the vent slits in the locker door, and start squeezing the boxes, spraying the juice inside the locker. Madison turns to the door and pushes it open to escape outside.

"At least it's not me."

Amber and her friends catch up with Kylie just as she is opening the door to come out of the girls' washroom.

Jessica and Brooke move quickly to each side of Kylie, grabbing her arms.

Kylie is startled. She looks from one to the other in surprise and resignation.

"I knew this was coming," she thinks unhappily. She had known all day and spent the whole day feeling sick with dread of it.

Amber steps in front of her, blocking her path, sneering at her with a nasty superior look.

Kylie struggles but can't break free. Jessica and Brooke drag her back into the washroom, making her drop her books in the hall outside the door in the struggle.

"Let me go!" Kylie complains.

Amber follows them in, looking pleased with herself.

In the privacy of the bathroom, Amber looks Kylie up and down, smirking nastily.

"Nice coat." It's both an insult and a threat. "Now, how do you think she got it back?" This last is directed to her friends.

"She must have followed us and pulled it out of the trash," Brooke says, still hoping Amber will stop suspecting either of them of giving it back.

"Are you a garbage picker?" Amber says nastily. "I'm not surprised. You probably get all your pathetic clothes from the garbage."

Kylie stares at her defiantly. "I wish I was anywhere else but here," she thinks. "I wish I was anyone else but me." She wants to cry but is not going to let these girls see her do it.

While the other two hold her, Amber steps forward. She takes Kylie's scarf off her with the slow deliberateness of someone who is thoroughly enjoying herself.

"I know I saw this in the trash." Amber eyes the toilet stalls behind Kylie. "Or maybe it was in the toilet. Toilet, trash, it's all gross. Just. Like. You."

She ties one end of the scarf tightly on one of Kylie's arms.

"Get her on the floor," she orders.

Jessica and Brooke start wrestling Kylie to the floor. She puts up a fight, trying to stay on her feet, lashing out with her feet and trying to kick them. Amber joins them and the three of them force Kylie down to the floor on her back.

"Get her in the stall!" Amber says, stepping back because they can't all fit in the stall. They start dragging her head first towards the toilet stalls.

Kylie tries to fight back harder. "They're going to shove my head in the toilet," she thinks wildly. She's not strong enough to beat the two of them. With her head and shoulders in the stall, they have to sit on her to hold her down, keeping her down with their hands and weight.

"Let me go!" She keeps screaming it until she gives up. They won't let her go and no help is coming.

While they hold her down, looking to their leader to find out what to do next, Amber runs the scarf around front foot of the stall wall between the two stalls. She steps over Kylie and Kylie is sure she is planning to step right on her. Kylie is surprised when the bully only steps over her.

Amber runs the scarf through the stall they dragged her partially into and back out around the foot on the other side. She steps over Kylie again to leave the stall. Kylie kicks out savagely, trying to knock her down, and misses.

"You even kick like garbage," Amber says. "No, you kick worse than that. You kick like poo. You are poo. You should be in the toilet. But since you won't fit, we'll just have to bring the toilet to you."

While the other two continue to sit on Kylie, holding her down, Amber stretches the scarf as hard as she can to make sure it can't stretch anymore and ties the other end of the scarf around Kylie's other arm, making sure it's good and tight.

Kylie struggles but is trapped, tied down by the arms. The scarf is stretched so tight that she can't pull herself up even a little. It's tied painfully tight on her wrists and the pull on her arms feels like they are being pulled out of their sockets.

They finally let go and stand over Kylie looking down at her, inspecting their handiwork with pride.

"Let me go," Kylie cries again, trying to pull herself free and get up. Giving up, she just lays there glaring at them, angry and afraid.

Smirking, Amber pulls something out of her coat pocket, some kind of plastic bottle that she had barely been able to force into her large pocket. She eyes the toilet in the open stall behind Kylie. Stepping over their helpless victim, she starts yanking toilet paper out of the holder as fast as she can and tossing it in the toilet.

Amber's grin grows. She scoops up Kylie's mitts and hat, and tosses them into the toilets.

"Do the others, plug them up," she tells her two followers, "hurry. We don't want to miss the bus."

With a shrug and giving each other a nervous look, they obey. The girls are reluctant because they don't want to get in trouble if they get caught.

Brooke yanks out handfuls of paper towels, knowing they'll work better, handing them to Amber and Jessica.

"Good idea," Amber nods, taking the towels. They fill the bowls with paper towels and toilet paper.

With the toilets clogged with too much paper, they follow Amber's lead and flush them over and over again, making the toilets overflow. With the hissing of the running toilets, the water rises in all three, breaching the top of the toilet bowls to flow over and down the outside. Water begins pooling and spreading across the floor. Now Kylie is trapped on her back on the floor, arms tied, with toilet water flooding the floor around her and soaking her clothes and hair.

Amber stands over Kylie with a nasty smirk, holding the bottle out for her to see and wags it mischievously. It's a plastic jar of bright yellow paint stolen from the art room.

"No, please don't" Kylie begs.

Smiling cruelly, Amber opens the bottle of paint and slowly pours it out on Kylie, pouring it all over her head and clothes.

Jessica giggles, grinning with pleasure, and Brooke pushes down her bad feelings about this, forcing a smile on her face.

Kylie tries to struggle, to break free, to at least dodge the paint, but it's useless. She can't move.

Amber tosses the empty container on the floor.

"Looks like you peed yourself," she sneers.

Yellow paint drips from Kylie's hair and clothes into the water pooling around her.

With a beckoning wave to the others from Amber, the three girls leave, their laughter echoing down the hall as they race for the bus, scooping up their backpacks from the floor where they left them on the way.

The bus is already pulling away when they burst out the doors. Seeing the retreating bus, their faces fill with panic and they run harder, yelling and waving for the bus to stop.

Seeing them in the side mirror, the driver sighs and stops the bus, waiting for them to catch up. He opens the doors with an unhappy grunt and gives them his over the glasses unimpressed stare.

"You almost missed the bus. You'd better be faster next time."

Amber gets on the bus, rushing down the aisle to a back seat, grinning and giggling. Jessica follows with a curt, "We will." Brooke looks down apologetically, frowns, and mumbles, "Sorry," before following them to fall into her seat.

Brooke looks out the bus window unhappily, looking back towards the school. Oblivious, her two friends giggle and grin next to her.

Anna isn't thrilled about having to ride her bike back home in the snow and cold. With no reason to rush since she can't take the bus, Anna is taking her time. She is walking down the hall and notices books scattered on the floor down the hall. The bathroom door opens and three girls come out of the bathroom laughing. Two of them step over the books, the third steps on them, giving a few of them a kick. They rush off, running for the school bus. They are Amber, Jessica, and Brooke.

"That explains the books," Anna mutters. She watches them go curiously and keeps walking. She reaches the washroom door and hears crying. She stops and listens. It's coming from the bathroom.

"No surprise, with the three that just left laughing. No doubt they were just in there tormenting someone."

Anna pushes the bathroom door, opening it cautiously, and is horrified by what she sees. For a moment all she can do is stand mutely in the doorway staring in shock at the helpless girl lying trapped on the floor in a pool of water. She recognizes her as someone she has seen around school, but doesn't really know.

Kylie is tied to the stall feet on her back in a pool of water, water still running over the sides of the plugged toilet bowls, yellow paint dripping off her head and clothes to mix with the water. Her face and eyes are red from crying.

Kylie looks up at her with horror at being seen in such an embarrassing position and relief at being found. When the bullies left, she was terrified that no one will find her until school starts in the morning.

Anna snaps out of it and rushes forward, kneeling down by Kylie and struggling to untie the tightly knotted and now wet scarf.

"What did they do to you?" she squeals with a shocked gasp.

She tries to be careful not to get her own clothes wet with the water pooled on the floor. She gets one side untied and helps Kylie get up, worrying over her ruined coat. She doesn't know this is the second time these girls have ruined the coat.

"Your coat, it's ruined! I guess your mom's going to have to get you a new coat," Anna says.

Kylie shakes her head miserably. "She won't. She can't afford it."

Kylie goes to the paper towel dispenser and starts trying to pull out towels. She is such an emotional mess that she can barely manage to yank paper towels out of the dispenser. Her hands are shaking too hard and she fumbles at the towels.

"Here, let me help," Anna says, pulling out a bunch of towels. She tries to help Kylie clean herself up. She rubs the coat with paper towels and they get wet too fast, crumbling and sticking to the coat. She grabs more and tries blotting at the paint and water dripping from the coat and Kylie's hair. Some of the paint comes off, but the coat is still paint-stained and ruined. The paint is starting to stiffen and Kylie is soaking wet.

"This isn't working. Take the coat off." Anna helps Kylie take the coat off and tries rinsing some of the paint off the already soaking wet coat and wringing it out over a sink. Water pours out from the wringing. She hangs the coat off a sink and grabs another handful of paper towels.

"You missed the bus," Anna says as she tries to rub paint out of Kylie's hair.

"So did you." Kylie's voice is still shaky with tears.

"Nah, I missed it this morning. I rode my bike and have to ride it back home. How are you going to get home? You're soaked!"

Kylie breaks down, sobbing harder. "She's right," she thinks. She looks at Anna miserably.

"I still have to get home and I'm soaked through. I have no choice; I have to try calling Mom to come get me. She's going to have to leave work early, and that won't be good. Her boss isn't very understanding and gives her a really hard time any time something happens where she has to miss work.

It's going to take her a while to get here too. They'll have locked the school doors by then and I'll have to wait outside in the cold and I'll freeze. I can't walk home like this either, it's too cold. I'd probably freeze even worse. I wouldn't be able to try to find shelter from the wind; but I wouldn't be making Mom leave work early."

Anna feels bad for Kylie. They aren't friends or anything. She sees her around the hallways and on the bus and stuff, and they have classes together, but she has never even talked to her before. "Nobody should have to be in the spot she is in," she thinks.

"Can your mom come and get you before they lock the doors?" Anna asks.

"No," Kylie sobs, "she'd never get here by then."

Anna thinks about the problem for a moment and gets an idea.

"Come home with me. I think my dad might have something that can get the paint out. At least we can wash and dry your stuff so you can get the rest of the way home without freezing."

Kylie looks at her skeptically, rubbing the tears off her cheeks and blowing her nose with a paper towel.

"I-I am soaked. I'll freeze," she says miserably.

"Well, you can't stay here either," Anna says. "Come on, we'll double on my bike and it will be faster than if you walk."

Kylie sniffles. She really doesn't want to. She is embarrassed and miserable and just wants to be left alone. "I wish I was dead," she thinks.

"Come on," Anna urges again. "It's ok. Nobody will be home. They never get home until really late."

"Okay, thanks," Kylie reluctantly agrees. She feels really weird about it, going to this girl's house; a girl she's never even talked to before.

Anna helps her pick up her books in the hallway and they head for her bike. It takes a little awkward maneuvering to get Kylie up on the handlebars, her hands quickly freezing and not making it easier. She has never doubled on a bike before. Soon they are on their way, moving quickly on the cleared road and struggling together to drag the bike through the deep snow when they cut through yards to make the trip shorter. Anna's tracks from the morning make the way a little easier going back home.

One of the last to get on the bus, Dylan walks down the aisle and slinks down into one of the few empty spots, this one midway to the back and next to Andrew, grunting the universal greeting. "Hey."

"Hey," Andrew grunts back and that is the end of their conversation.

Dylan looks around the bus, noticing Kylie isn't on the bus, and wonders about it.

The bus starts pulling away and he hears some girls shouting for it to stop. The bus slows and stops, the aggravated driver waiting for them to reach the bus before opening the door.

The three mean girls get on the bus, unapologetically pushing their way down the aisle to their favorite spot at the back. Panting and giggling, they make a kid move so they can take the seat. Others who were there before them give them distasteful looks as they get on and take their seats.

Dylan looks out the window. There is no sign of Kylie.

Amber and her friends' constant snickering and whispering behind their hands at the back of the bus as the bus pulls away again grates on him.

"They're up to something," he thinks, glancing back at them. They are still excited and winded from their run for the bus.

Kylie expected the trip to Anna's house to be worse with wet clothes than her walk home the other day was without the coat and boots, but surprisingly it isn't. Even wet, the coat keeps her warmer than she was without it at all, although she is definitely getting very chilled by the cold wet clothes and coat.

When they reach Anna's house, Anna abandons the bike at the edge of the front yard and rushes them both into the house.

"Hurry, take that coat off, you must be freezing," Anna says, closing the door behind them. She leads Kylie to the kitchen, helping her peel off the wet coat. It's heavy with water and stiff with ice and hard to get off. It hits the floor with a clunk.

Kylie is shivering so hard her hands are hardly working.

Anna rushes off and comes back with a couple large fluffy towels. She wraps them around Kylie, rubbing her arms and back, trying to warm her.

"Wait here." Anna runs down to the basement.

Kylie sits there feeling awkward and weird in Anna's house, a virtual stranger from school. She is chilled and feels sick. She listens to the sounds of stuff clattering and being shifted around downstairs.

Anna comes up holding up her prize proudly for Kylie to see.

"What's that?"

"Turpentine." Anna shrugs, looking down at the metal can and old rag in her hand. "It might work." She sounds unsure.

Kylie blinks at her, not sure what to say. Finally, she nods.

Anna soaks the rag with the stinky liquid. With a pause, a deep breath, and a mental, "this is it, last chance to stop," she starts rubbing Kylie's hair with it, trying to get the paint out.

"I hope this works."

Kylie sits there letting Anna scrub her head. Anna frowns. They are both enveloped in the stink of turpentine.

"That stuff really stinks."

Kylie's head starts to itch as Anna works, her scrubbing making Kylie's scalp sensitive.

Then it starts to hurt. "Oh, hey, that's starting to burn."

Kylie tries to bear it, but it's just getting worse as Anna keeps scrubbing.

"Ow, that's really starting to hurt now," Kylie says, her voice full of stress from the pain.

Anna stops and studies her scalp. It did remove some of the paint, but her scalp is an angry red now.

Kylie looks up at her, blinking her eyes to try to keep the tears away. "It's really starting to burn."

Anna looks down and sees the tears in her eyes.

"Oh no, I'm sorry," she says. "Hurry, let's get you in the shower!"

Kylie nods. She is shivering so bad her teeth are chattering.

Anna suddenly realizes. "You are chilled!" she says. "And your clothes are still all wet and full of paint. We have to get you out of them.

Come, have a hot shower to warm up and get that turpentine out of your hair. Pass your clothes to me and I'll toss them all in the wash. Hopefully some of the paint comes out."

While she rushes her to the bathroom, Kylie can't stop whimpering and moaning from the growing pain in her scalp. Every second it burns fiercer because of the rubbing making her scalp raw. It hurts almost as much as pouring alcohol hand sanitizer on a cut.

Leaving Kylie standing awkwardly at the bathroom doorway, Anna rushes off and comes back with a big fluffy housecoat. Without giving her a chance to say no, Anna pushes the housecoat on her and pushes Kylie into the bathroom. She closes the door, making it final.

Kylie looks around the bathroom, feeling absolutely retched. "I can't do this. I can't shower in a stranger's house." She stands there for a long time, wishing this would all go away.

"Why does this have to be happening to me?" she moans.

"Hey, are you okay?" Anna calls through the door. "What's taking so long?"

Kylie swallows and reluctantly strips down in the bathroom and passes her wet stuff through the door. It feels really weird showering in someone else's house, especially someone she doesn't really know. She feels so self-conscious that she has the urge to scream. She keeps half expecting someone to barge in on her.

When Kylie steps under the spray of hot water, it feels so good that it makes her feel the need to cry all over again, and she does. She stands there under the water, scrubbing at the paint and turpentine in her hair, sobbing.

When she finishes, she dries off and wraps herself in the warm housecoat. "It feels so good to be warm again." Then she just stands there uncertainly, feeling really weird about it and not wanting to come out of the bathroom.

"Are you okay in there?" Anna calls through the door.

"Um, yeah," Kylie calls back hesitantly. She opens the door and comes out.

"I made hot cocoa to warm you up on the inside," Anna says brightly.

Kylie follows her back to the kitchen where she sees that Anna had been working on scrubbing her coat with turpentine.

They both work on the coat with just as little success. All it does is leave an oily stain behind. Turpentine is meant for oil based paints and this is latex paint, but neither girl understands there is a difference.

Finally, Anna shrugs, giving up.

"This isn't working. Maybe we should just throw the jacket in the wash," she suggests. The water, which froze to ice on the way, had kept the paint from completely drying. With the fabric wet, the paint turned rubbery, not hard.

Anna tosses the paint-smeared jacket and clothes in the washing machine with soap and stain remover, adding extra soap just to be sure.

They hang out for a while, awkwardly talking about nothing and anything, waiting for the wash and then the dryer, Kylie's boots clunking loudly in the machine echoing throughout the house.

The paint doesn't come out completely, but Kylie's clothes do look much better despite the oily looking stains left behind by the turpentine. The paint is mostly just in the seams and stitching now. Finally done, it's time for Kylie to go home.

"Is your mom going to be home before you?" Anna asks.

"I don't know. I'm going to be cutting it pretty close. Thanks for... you know." Kylie looks down at her feet awkwardly.

"Yeah," Anna says. "Guess I might see you at school tomorrow."

"Okay." Kylie leaves, heading for home. She walks quickly, breaking into a run now and then until she is too tired and has to walk again. She gets home only minutes before her mother and sister.

She takes off her coat, looking around and trying to decide what to do with it. Her coat and clothes still stink of turpentine despite being run through the wash. She shoves it in the closet, hoping her mother doesn't notice.

She quickly sets out her books open at the kitchen table and sits down, pretending she's doing homework. "I have homework to do anyway."

When her mother walks in with her sister, she pauses in the front hall, sniffing the air.

"What's that smell? Is that the garbage?"

She goes to the kitchen, pulling the bag out of the garbage and sniffing it as she ties it up to put it in the can outside. She returns, walking around sniffing, trying to figure out where the smell is coming from. She stops and looks at Kylie with an odd look.

"What is in your hair?"

"What? Nothing," Kylie starts, but her mother is already on her, picking at her head. She wants to bat her hands away, but sullenly sits there and puts up with it.

"Is this paint?" Her mother tries to catch her eyes, but Kylie just looks down. "Look at me, Kylie. How did you get paint in your hair?"

"Um, there was an accident in art class."

"Look at me," her mother orders again. "You're lying. What really happened?"

Kylie sags, finally looking up to meet her eyes. Her mother sees the pain and despair in her eyes and it makes her worry.

"What happened?" she asks more gently.

"It was those girls again."

Her mother purses her lips. She wants to call the school and the girls' parents to rage and demand justice, but she knows it's no use. They've been on this merry-go-round too many times. Her anger deflates and is replaced with hopelessness. She is unable to protect her daughter.

"Let's see what we can you about your hair."

Relieved her mother isn't asking for details, Kylie decides to break it to her about the coat. "They got my coat again."

"Show me."

Kylie gets up and fetches the coat, showing her mother the oil-stained coat with paint still in the seams. She points out the same on her clothes.

"We tried to clean it up."

Her mother sighs heavily. "Ok, let's see what we can do to fix this too."

6   Surviving the Winter

A few months have passed since the bathroom incident and school life has moved on. Amber has been trying all winter to get up the nerve to talk to Dylan. She has had a big crush on him since grade three but he doesn't even seem to know she exists.

Every morning she watches for him on the bus, and again every afternoon when the bus takes them home again. Her pulse races and a flush burns her cheeks as she watches him get on the bus. She daydreams about him sitting beside her, giving her that dreamy slightly crooked bad boy smile of his as he slouches into the seat, but he never does.

She pauses when she sees him in the hallway, wishing he would stop next to her, smile at her, or talk to her. He always just goes past her as if she's not there.

Today is no different. Amber is sitting at the back of the bus with her friends. She isn't paying attention to their conversation, lost in her own thoughts.

"Do you know who you know who asked to the spring dance?" Jessica gives her friends a conspiratorial look, rolling her eyes towards a boy in their class sitting with a couple of other boys. He is the most awkward looking boy in their class.

"He didn't," Brooke gasps, snickering.

They both cover their mouths with their hands to express their delighted shock. The most awkward looking boy in the class has a major crush on the prettiest girl in the class. There is absolutely no way she would not say no. She wouldn't just say no; it would be a soul crushing defeat. She would stomp his feelings into the dirt and laugh at him.

They revel in the knowledge he had been humiliated, probably publicly, and put in his awkward geekish place.

The bus jerks to a stop and the doors open. Amber's head pops up and she stares at the door. This is his stop.

Dylan gets on the bus and she can't stop herself from staring at him. Jessica and Brooke keep on talking, but she barely hears anything they say.

She imagines Dylan pushing his way to the back of the bus, making some kid move out of his seat to sit next to her, and giving her that slow crooked bad boy smile of his as he sits close to her. He would put his arm over the back of the seat, the closest you dare go to putting your arm around someone on the bus. That would let everyone know that she is his girl.

He doesn't make it to the back of the bus.

Her heart sinks as it always does when he picks another seat. This time he takes an empty seat halfway to the front, bordering the geeks and the meats. That would be coolness suicide for anyone else.

"He just doesn't care what anyone thinks," she sighs to herself. She keeps staring at him as the bus continues on, making more stops to pick up kids on the way to school.

One of her friends nudges her and Amber turns on her with a dirty look. Jessica points ahead, motioning. "Go sit with him," she whispers.

Amber shakes her head, horrified. "I can't possibly!" she thinks. "But, oh, I really want to."

The school is going to have a spring dance before school lets out for spring break and, if she has any hope of him asking her to dance with him, she will have make sure he knows she exists before then.

"He's not going to ask you to the dance if you don't talk to him," Jessica whispers in her ear.

Amber gives her an annoyed look, turning her attention to watch Dylan wistfully. She snaps herself out of it, quickly glancing around to make sure nobody saw.

Her eyes settle on someone else. Kylie. They narrow and a rush of hatred fills her. There is so much of it that she's sure it must be pouring out of her to affect everyone around her. "Good," she thinks, "they should all hate that little witch!"

Amber is still miffed that she has had little chance to get revenge against Kylie after she got them in trouble.

"We got in a lot of trouble over the bathroom incident when that sissy Kylie's mother came to the school demanding we get punished," she thinks. "The stupid principal was more upset about damage to school property from flooding the toilets than us tying up and tormenting Kylie.

We were even blamed for the juice sprayed all over inside Kylie's locker. Nobody had any proof we did it. We made sure no one was around to see. The school even made our parents pay to replace the ruined schoolbooks in her locker. We were grounded and almost kicked out of school."

She clenches her teeth, seething with anger just thinking about it.

"This is MY school and if I had to go to a new one I'd have to start all over making my reputation. Dylan wouldn't be there either. Kylie is so lucky the principal decided to give us a two-week suspension instead. I was in enough trouble just for that."

Jessica glances at Amber, seeing the clenched jaw and hateful glare. She follows her eyes and picks out the target easily. Kylie.

"No surprise," she thinks. "She's the one who wanted to plug the toilets and spray juice in the locker. But, it's never her fault when we get caught. It's always someone else's fault." She smiles inwardly with cruelty at the thought of Amber actually having to admit anything at all was her fault.

"She's still on about blaming Kylie, but it's her fault we got in trouble, not Kylie's. It's not Kylie's fault Amber hates her. Okay, maybe it is. But it wasn't Kylie who made us tie her up in the bathroom and flood the toilets. And it wasn't her who made us spray juice in her locker. That was Amber."

She risks a sulky look at Amber. Brooke is still talking next to her but she's not paying attention to what she's saying. She's almost afraid to even think it. She certainly would never say it out loud. Amber would be furious if she knew what she really thinks. Nobody is supposed to go against anything she says or thinks or does.

"I'm kind of glad we got caught," Jessica thinks. "Amber has been lying low and hasn't been able to get Kylie again because of that weird Anna hanging out with her. She hasn't had us do anything, not really, in a while. Just some online stuff and that doesn't really count. Maybe she's finally settling down and we can stop doing all these mean things all the time."

She huffs involuntarily. "It's exhausting," she thinks.

Amber just keeps glaring at Kylie sitting ahead of her on the bus, oblivious to Jessica's disloyal thoughts. If hatred had a smell, hers would smell like old moldy rotting egg salad that had been left sitting in the hot sun.

"Ever since the bathroom incident, I haven't seen Kylie without that other girl, Anna," Amber fumes to herself. "The two have been inseparable. I don't dare go after Kylie with Anna around. That girl is weird and tough." The truth of it is that she's a little scared of Anna.

Anna is one of those kids who just doesn't seem to care about anything. She comes to school late, wears whatever she wants, and doesn't bother to do her homework if she doesn't feel like it. She sits wherever she wants on the bus, if she even makes the bus, and doesn't follow any of the rules.

She gets letters and phone calls home, detentions, and any other punishments the school thinks of, and none of them ever seem to affect her. They just never go anywhere and the teachers and principal forget about them. When she has to eat lunch in the detention room, she goes with an attitude that suggests she's only doing it because it suits her to eat there. She gets away with anything because nothing they can punish her with seems to affect her. When anyone else's parents would be called to the school for a meeting, hers never do.

She never hung out with anyone at school either, not until she started hanging out with Kylie. She has always been a loner, on the fringes, and seemed entirely too comfortable staying there. The teachers gave up on Anna and just let her do her own thing. Anyone with that kind of power has to be pretty tough. Even with Jessica and Brooke to back her up, Amber does not want to mess with Anna.

"We had to resort to getting even with Kylie only online for the last few months. We post nasty stuff about her and spread rumors. I posted all about what we did to Kylie in the bathroom. I left out a few things of course; that we tied her down and purposely plugged the toilets. I said that it was Kylie who plugged them up and then slipped and fell in the toilet water. I bragged about pouring the yellow paint on her because she smelled like pee. This should have made me feel better, but this time it didn't. Kylie just keeps ignoring my attempts to get at her online like she doesn't even notice.

It doesn't make sense. I hear the whispers around school. Everyone is saying what I say online. I've seen the looks people give Kylie, how they avoid her and laugh at her behind their hands. How can she not notice all that? How can it not affect her?"

She fumes. She should feel the power over Kylie, the ability to control her life, to ruin it as she pleases. Instead, she feels like nothing she does matters. It's infuriating, frustrating. It makes her feel useless. She does not like the feeling.

She leans in closer to whisper to her friends. "We have to come up with some plan to get those two apart," she hisses. "Break up their friendship, even just get them apart long enough to get Kylie."

Jessica giggles and nods, a shadow of nervousness flashing across her eyes while Amber stares at Kylie with a nasty gloating look. Brooke looks a little uncertain.

Madison is getting better at being home alone. She hasn't locked herself out again and only almost missed the bus a few times, never actually missing it.

"I'm getting into a pretty good groove," she thinks, expertly running through her school day morning routine. She has the routine down and is feeling confident handling herself in the mornings.

"I'm so happy Mom and Dad decided to give me another chance instead of making me go to a babysitter. Babysitters are for babies, thus the name 'baby' sitter."

Madison looks at the clock. She is still good for time. She moves on to jamming her books into her backpack and putting it at the door with her house key and feeling good about how good she is at being home alone.

She stops, her head snapping up at a sound. She listens. She hears it again.

"It's just a car door next door," she decides.

"I wish it was this easy after school." A shadow creeps over her good mood. Madison is still a little nervous at home alone, and she feels it more after school.

"In the morning, I don't have time to think about it," she reminds herself. "I'm thinking only about getting ready for school. After school, there is no rush; just waiting for Mom and Dad to come home. That's when the time drags on. Sometimes, I'm not sure the clock even moves."

She pushes the thought away even as it creeps into her mind. The house makes strange noises, especially when you are alone. She hears creaking and popping sounds that her parents told her is just the house settling or the roof making noises from the weight of snow on top of it.

But that doesn't explain the other noises. She hears them at any time of day or night, mostly when the house is very quiet because she's alone or the only one awake at night.

"Stop thinking about it," Madison scolds herself. "You're just going to give yourself the heebie-jeebies."

The thought of the noises, and the voices, keeps edging into her mind despite her efforts to push them out. Sometimes she thinks she hears voices in the house. She tells herself they can't be coming from inside, but they sound like they are.

The voices are the worst. They're the kind of low voices that are so quiet that you almost think you are imagining them, but they won't go away.

A faint sound teases the edge of Madison's hearing. She holds her breath and listens. It almost sounds like low murmuring, like a radio playing quietly somewhere far away and she can just make out the announcer's voice, but not what he's saying. It's so quiet that she's not even sure it's a voice or that she hears it at all.

She moves around the house silently, listening and trying to find out where it is coming from. But as she follows the faint sound of voices they seem to come from somewhere else.

"Great," she thinks, "now you're making yourself hear things."

She hears a voice, louder. She still can't quite make out what was said, but there's no doubt it came from outside this time. It's followed by the thud of a car door.

"It's the neighbors, dummy." Madison almost laughs at her own ridiculous fears. She pulls her focus back to getting ready for school and checks the time.

"Time to go." Madison puts her winter stuff on, grabs her backpack, and heads out the door. She locks the door, pausing to look at the lock for a moment before turning away and heading down the street to the bus stop. She thinks about that first day when she lost her key and has an urge to double check that she still has it. She gives in, reassuring herself the key is there, safe and sound.

She reaches the bus stop in time to see the bus coming around the corner up the street. She waits, standing back while the bus stops in front of her, its air brakes making those awful popping and farting sounds, and finally gets on, taking a seat. She stares out the window as the bus pulls away.

"The problem is that I'm lonely and bored," she thinks. "Waiting for Mom and Dad to come home would be much easier if I could have a friend over. Mom and Dad won't let me have anyone over or go anywhere but home after school, not until they get home, and by then it's suppertime and after that it's too late. I could go to their house, they could come over, or we could sometimes just talk on the phone.

I'll never admit it to anyone, but that's the one good thing about daycare that I miss, having other people around."

The hours waiting alone for her parents to come home always feel like forever.

Kylie pulls her hood up, yanking her jacket tighter around her and trying to hide inside it when the school bus arrives. It doesn't do any good. There is no hiding from who she is. She gets on the bus, blushing and glancing around the bus quickly as she mounts the stairs, taking stock of who is looking at her and how many of them are laughing at her.

"Why can't I just disappear?" she thinks miserably. Every set of eyes she feels on her burns with the shame of what she is sure their owner is thinking.

She stumbles; tripping over a foot that she's pretty sure was stuck out on purpose, and makes it past the first few rows of seats. She takes the empty seat next to Anna.

Ever since the bathroom incident, Kylie and Anna have been best friends, although Kylie still can't understand why Anna wants to be her friend. Anna insists on sticking by Kylie's side whenever possible in school. "Safety in numbers," Anna would say.

"You haven't been online have you?" Anna whispers in her ear, giving Kylie a look warning her that she had better not have been.

"No hi, just have I been online?" Kylie whispers back with a pout, but doesn't really mean it.

"I'm serious. Those three won't bother you with me around. They're just a bunch of weak cowards and are scared of me because they know I'll stand up to them. But that won't stop them from attacking you online."

Anna has expressed her dislike of cowards many times.

Kylie's blush deepens. She did go online and regrets it. She also knows she's a coward herself; all the more reason to wonder why Anna hangs out with her.

"I'm glad she's my friend," Kylie thinks, "but at the same time I sometimes wish she isn't.

Ever since the bathroom incident the despicable trio haven't had a chance to get me again because of Anna staying close to me at school. And when I'm not at school I don't dare leave the house.

It seems like such a bother for Anna, always having to be with me. I'm sure she'd rather be somewhere else doing something else. Besides, I'm used to being alone. Now I'm never alone at school.

Those nasty girls have resorted to using the chat groups and apps that everyone is on to wage their campaign of psychological torture against me."

Kylie feels the flush of shame turn her face hot just thinking about it. They said such nasty things online that Kylie is embarrassed to come to school.

"I wish I could just disappear, fall into a big bottomless hole and keep falling forever," Kylie thinks. "Sometimes, I wish I was dead."

Anna nudges her with her elbow, bringing her attention back to her. She's still waiting for an answer.

Kylie looks down in her lap when she answers. "No."

"You looked down. That's a dead giveaway you're lying." Anna makes a disgusted face. "The stuff they post is just ugly lies. It's garbage. You don't need to look at that. If you look at it too much you start believing it."

Kylie still doesn't meet her look. "The whole school probably knows what they're saying."

"They probably do. Anyone who believes their lies is stupid; stupid and not worth worrying about. You have to stay out of those chat rooms and apps and off any of the sites. Don't give them the chance to hurt you. You have to promise me you'll stay away from those sites."

Kylie nods. It's not a verbal promise, but Anna accepts it.

"I still hear the rumors being spread about me at school. I see the looks everyone gives me and I hear them laughing at me when they think I don't hear," Kylie says quietly, still looking down at her lap.

"We'll have to see what we can do about that." Anna grits her teeth.

Kylie glances at her. It's a determined look Kylie has already come to know, and to know it probably means trouble for someone.

"I hope it doesn't just make things worse, whatever she's planning to do," Kylie thinks.

"The evil trio aren't the only ones I need to worry about," she thinks.

"We're friends now and they won't dare to bother you as long as we're together," Anna says, as if she heard her thoughts. But Kylie is only safe at school with Anna at her side.

Anna looks at her friend. She had been online herself last night and saw what Amber and her friends posted about Kylie. Kylie isn't their only online target either, but it's the ugly things they said about Kylie that made her angry. She was so angry that she woke up this morning still feeling mad. She turns to look out the window.

Kylie feels the usual unpleasant tingle in her back as they sit and the bus rolls on towards school. It's that feeling you get when you know someone is staring a hole through your back. She itches to turn around. Kylie can feel Amber's hate-filled glare burning into her back. She doesn't turn to look, but she is sure Dylan is staring at her too and it adds to the awkward discomfort.

"Don't turn and look," Anna whispers, picking up on her tense posture. "Don't give them the satisfaction."

Kylie swallows the lump in her throat, nodding almost imperceptibly. "I think he's staring at me too."

Anna risks a quick look back. She shrugs.

"What does he want?" Kylie whispers.

"Who?" Anna whispers back, pretending she doesn't know. She's just toying with her friend.

"Dylan," Kylie hisses. "He's staring at me again."

"He likes you," Anna shrugs, smiling.

"Eww." Kylie makes a disgusted face. "Does not! He's a big bully. He's probably thinking about mean things to do to me. Or, he's laughing at me for the things Amber says about me."

Her face flushes with embarrassment over the horrible things she saw online last night. It's still a raw open wound of pain inside her, making her feel absolutely wretched. "I feel like every single kid in the whole school must hate me," she thinks, "except for Anna, and I can't understand why she wants to be my friend."

"Just ignore it," Anna reminds her. "Nasty girls like them only have power to hurt you if you let them."

Kylie looks at Anna, needing to change the subject. "Why do you always get on at different stops? I mean, who does that?"

"I do," Anna says, winking. "I like to be mysterious." She looks down quickly.

"A sure sign she's hiding something," Kylie thinks.

They sit in silence for the rest of the bus ride.

Andrew's alarm clock beeps in a rude high pitched incessant beeping, jerking him out of sleep. He groans and rolls over, pulling the pillow over his head to block it out. There is no blocking out that incessant beeping. Finally, he pulls the pillow off his head and reaches his arm out, slapping blindly for the clock and its snooze button until he finally lucks into hitting it, silencing the alarm.

He lays there for a few moments, wishing he is still sleeping but unable to go back to sleep with the knowledge the alarm will beep again in seven minutes. Andrew makes himself sit up, swinging his feet to dangle them over the edge of the bed, yawning and scratching under one arm. He reaches and turns the alarm off, then stands and staggers sleepily forward.

On school days, Andrew gets up after everyone else is gone. The only thing different about the weekend is that everyone else doesn't always leave the house and he sleeps until noon, if he can. He lies in bed and pretends to if he can't.

It doesn't take him long to get ready for school. Andrew pulls off his pajamas and puts on jeans and a shirt. Then he remembers his mother's constant reminders about putting on clean underwear.

He hears her voice nagging him in his head. "What if something happened? What if you were in an accident?" she would say. "You would have to go to the hospital and they would see you don't have clean underwear!"

"Ah yes," he thinks, "the age-old threat of the doctor seeing your dirty gitch. I'm pretty sure my grandparents said the same thing to Mom, and their parents to them, for all the generations back to the start of mankind."

"If they can see that my gitch is dirty, then I probably messed them because of the accident," he mutters.

Andrew imagines himself staring down a speeding car in fear as it is about to run him over, he leaps out of the way just in time. But he is not safe because he jumped into a yard of ferocious dogs. Their teeth are big and their faces mean. They snarl and bark and foam at the mouth. Mad dogs. He fights them off bravely only to end up in a pit of poisonous snakes.

After wrangling the snakes, he escapes and manages to get safely home.

But then he hears a noise come from the basement, and whatever made the noise down there comes up the stairs with a wet slithering sound.

Andrew is sweating at the thought of something lurking down in the basement and imagines his body being brought to the hospital. He is still alive, at least his body is, but his mind is gone. It was stolen by whatever was in the basement and he messed his pants at the very last minute before it leapt for him. His last conscious thought before it sucks his mind out is that they are going to see his dirty gitch.

"Look Marge, we've got a dirty one here," the doctor says, pointing and laughing. "The boy did not put on clean underwear this morning."

The doctor parades around the hospital with the soiled underwear held in front of him with tongs, holding his nose and chanting. "Dirty underwear, dirty underwear, the boy did not put on clean gitch!" And the whole hospital follows him around, a parade for the dirty underwear, showing them off. They go marching off down the street and everyone who sees joins the parade.

He shudders, unable to play this game further.

Andrew laughs at how stupid it all is, but it's an uneasy laugh. Thinking about some monster in the basement getting him spoiled the game. It left him on edge and nervous.

"Hah, I'm not stripping again to change them," Andrew says with fake casualness. He goes to the kitchen to have some toast before school.

As he is pressing down the button on the toaster, Andrew hears a clunk and a dull sound that sounds like something rolling. He freezes, listening. He is alone in the house.

He realizes why his game turned to thinking about a monster in the basement.

His heart beating fast in his chest and a cold sweat breaking out over his whole body, Andrew feels like he is frozen in place and unable to move.

He forces his legs to move forward towards the closed basement door. He stops at the door, listening carefully and thinks he hears a quiet slithering noise on the other side of the door. He holds his breath.

"It's your imagination, dummy," he thinks. "It's just the sound from your stupid game."

He hears a crash in the basement.

Swallowing, Andrew runs to his bedroom and grabs his baseball bat from the closet, racing back to the closed basement door and listens.

"I should go down and check it out." Suddenly Andrew wishes he had put on clean underwear. "What if there is something down there? The doctors will see that I didn't change my underwear!" he thinks.

Andrew knows the thought is ridiculous. His underwear doesn't look dirty. Nobody would even know the difference.

Andrew wrinkles his nose, sniffing. He smells something burning. The toast!

He rushes to the toaster and pops it, smoke curling up from the appliance. The toast is charred black.

"Oh man!" he groans and plucks out the burnt toast. He almost drops it, shaking his hand and sucking his finger when he burns it. He looks at the ruined toast in disgust.

Andrew gives a nervous look at the basement door.

"Whatever is down there can stay there." Tossing the toast in the garbage, he grabs his lunch and heads for the front door. He puts on his coat, boots, hat and mitts, grabs his backpack and leaves the house.

It's too early for the bus, but it beats having whatever is in the basement get him.

"There's nothing there you big dummy," he reminds himself as he locks the door behind him.

He quickly pushes away the thought that spring is coming and soon after that it will be summer break. He'll be home alone all day long then.

Dylan is hurriedly getting ready for school. Their dog, Lucy, is glued to him, cowering and shivering and tripping him up. She always knows when everyone is leaving. Dylan isn't getting a ride today, and has to take the bus.

"The best part of taking the bus," he thinks, "is I don't have to listen to them fighting or yelling at me for taking too long," referring, of course, to his parents. He doesn't let himself even think about the other best part; that Kylie is on the bus.

It wasn't that long ago that he had to go to the babysitter before school too and catch the bus from there. He doesn't dwell on why he only goes to the babysitter after school now.

Ready to go, Dylan goes around the house, Lucy following at his heels, checking every window and both doors. He sets traps in every room, except the basement.

They are the kind of traps that will not catch anything, just little things that will tell him if someone had been in the house. A thread draped across an opening that would be gone if someone walked through; that sort of thing. He goes around again, double and triple checking them. He'll check his traps when he gets home from the sitter.

He puts a very unhappy dog in her kennel, trying to give her dog cookies out of guilt, which she refuses to take. That only makes him feel guiltier. Getting his stuff together and coat on, he returns to check Lucy too many times. She is trembling and whimpering in her cage, knowing she's going to be left alone all day. They never put her in a cage before. Now they have to or she will poop all over the house, as if she's punishing them because she's mad or terrified at being left alone all day.

Dylan heads out the door for the bus. Lucy starts crying and yelping inside the house, making him feel miserable for her and full of guilt for leaving her.

He arrives at the bus stop and watches for the bus to come.

"Maybe today I'll be able to sit near her." Sometimes he tries to sit behind Kylie where he can see her. Other times he sits ahead of her, but is always still very aware of where she is behind him. He chickens out the moment the bus pulls up.

His eyes automatically scan the bus as he gets on, taking in the familiar faces. Dylan picks a seat close to the front of the bus, where only The Meat sit. The safe zone. Close enough to the driver that nobody dares bug you on the bus. He feels like meat today.

Dylan had gotten off okay this morning. He even almost felt good about getting himself off on his own instead of being dropped at the neighbor's house until time for the bus. But now he just can't get rid of that anxious feeling.

"I missed something," Dylan thinks, "maybe forgot to lock something. Someone could break in the house while we're gone. It's going to be my fault."

He tries to focus his thoughts on something else and ends up thinking about Kylie. He can't deny it; he thinks she's cute. He likes her and has for a while.

Thinking about Kylie brings his attention to the three girls who always sit at the back of the bus where The Toughs sit; Amber and her friends, Jessica and Brooke.

He can feel Amber staring at him.

"She always stares," he thinks, feeling icked out by the goo-goo eyes she gives him, and is pretty sure she likes him. The thought makes him want to shudder with revulsion. "I don't like anything about that girl. She's kind of chunky, cakes on the makeup, and has the most annoying laugh that makes me think of a donkey when I hear it. Her face isn't all that attractive either with that nasty grin she always has.

Mostly, I can't stand her because she's just a jerk. She's rude and selfish and thinks everything revolves around her. There's nothing nice about Amber at all.

Those three have been picking on Kylie all year. When I see Kylie walking down the hall every day looking like she's trying to be invisible and wants to hide, I feel bad for her. When I saw her in tears, looking cute even with the blotchy redness from crying on her face that usually makes girls ugly, and her face twisted into a look of pain, I wanted to run to her side and protect her.

When I see those girls being cruel to Kylie, I get so mad that I want to punch them. I can't, of course. Boys aren't supposed to ever hit a girl. Any boy who does is just showing how weak and pathetic he is if he has to hit a girl."

He doesn't see the hypocrisy of his thoughts, how his own bullying behavior is a reflection of their cruelty. He sees these girls as horrible people and their cruel treatment of others as wrong, but he's no different from them. Dylan is just as much a bully as they are, but he doesn't see himself as one.

The only difference between Dylan and those girls is that he acts without thought, going after weaker kids when the urge strikes him, lashing out in frustration. Amber and her friends plan their attacks, getting as much joy out of planning the cruelty as they do acting it out.

Kylie is sitting with Anna again. He noticed that immediately when he got on the bus.

"I'm happy to see Kylie finally made a friend, even if her new friend seems kind of weird. She's the last person I would have expected her to become friends with. Anna is a loner who doesn't seem to care about anything and is always getting in trouble.

I just hope she doesn't get Kylie in trouble or take advantage of her. She's so quiet and shy. But those other girls have backed off bullying Kylie since she started hanging around that other girl and that's good."

Even better was when he saw Kylie actually smile and laugh for the first time the other day. It made him feel all warm inside, though he would never tell anyone that.

Dylan glances back at Kylie. She stares ahead, making a point of not looking at him. He frowns. "She won't even look at me. She purposely looks away to avoid looking at me. I wish I could just talk to her, even just to say hi, but I'm too nervous every time I'm around her. Besides, she hates me.

Maybe she won't hate me anymore if I tell her I'm the one who left her coat and stuff on her step." From the torn and stained condition of her coat now, he is sure it has to be the only one she has.

"Why don't her parents get her a new coat? Can't afford it maybe? It's a good thing I saw those girls and got her stuff from the trash can."

The bus is stopping in front of the school. Dylan makes himself a silent promise.

"Before school finishes for the summer, I am going to talk to Kylie, maybe even tell her I'm the one who got her stuff back."

Kylie is troubled and can't get the things that are bothering her out of her mind. There are too many of them. She spends her day distracted and barely managing to pay attention in class. In between classes, when she walks with Anna to their next class, she's barely there at all.

Kylie and Anna are separated in the last class before lunch, put into different groups working in separate rooms. Kylie's group is sent to the library.

Kylie grabs her stuff and heads for the door with her group, taking one quick look back. "Lucky me," she thinks, "I wasn't put in the same group as the mean team."

Kylie struggles to concentrate, annoying some of her group with her lack of participation in the group project. After a while they ignore her, leaving her to her own thoughts. By lunchtime, Kylie can't take it anymore. The need to talk to someone is overwhelming.

"This is driving me crazy," she thinks. "I need to talk to someone. I need to tell someone. I don't think I can take it anymore." She feels it like the sharp edge of a knife inside her, pressing against her ribcage.

Despite her anxiousness, Kylie is one of the last to leave the library when the noon hour bell rings. She picks up her stuff with a sick feeling of dread. Her stomach cramps with the pain that has plagued her all day.

"They will probably be waiting for me," she thinks, "the mean team, the trio of terror."

"It's now or never," Kylie tells herself. "You can't hide in the library all lunch." She reconsiders, "Or maybe, can I?"

She steels herself. "Just go. Do it. You definitely can't get away with hiding here all day."

Feeling suddenly ill and uncertain, she forces herself to move out that library door. She navigates the halls quickly, dodging kids and feeling a rush of panic that she'll run into them. She ducks into the cafeteria, looking around for Anna, and is disappointed to not see her. Her heart sinks with dread. The mean team are there.

Amber looks up to see Kylie alone and smiles a wicked smile.

"Hey." Anna comes up from behind, startling Kylie and making her jump.

"Jumpy," Anna teases.

They find seats at an empty table in a corner, giving them space and almost privacy from the cafeteria full of kids. The loud volume of all the talking makes any conversation almost guaranteed not to be overheard unless you talk loudly.

"Does it ever bother you being home alone after school?" Kylie asks.

Anna shrugs. "Not so much. I'm used to being alone." It does bother her, much more than she would ever admit to anyone, but for different reasons than Kylie is about to reveal.

"I'm scared when I'm home alone," Kylie says, looking down at her lunch with very little appetite.

"Still? But you've been doing it since you were ten. You should be over that by now."

"I know," Kylie, says self-consciously. She thinks about how much to reveal, settling on the lesser of her problems. It feels trivial, and maybe if Anna agrees it's dumb, she'll have one less thing stressing her out. "It's the basement."

"You're scared of the basement? What, do you think that there are monsters down there or something?" Anna teases. "Do you have to check under your bed for monsters before you go to bed too?"

Kylie rolls her eyes, giving her an annoyed look.

"I can't help it," she thinks. "I'm nervous of the basement. Anna must have some silly fear too. Doesn't almost everyone? Sure, I have an active imagination, at least that's what Mom always says. But, I just can't help that nagging doubt that clenches my stomach with fear even though I know there can't be anything down in the basement to be scared of. I know it's dumb and I have no idea where this fear and the doubt in the pit of my stomach come from."

She swallows her pride and goes on.

"Sometimes I think I hear things that sound like it's coming from the basement," Kylie confesses self-consciously. "Quiet little noises that no one else ever seems to hear. Then my mind starts playing tricks and I imagine there are things hiding down there; waiting for who knows what. Bad things. I know I'm just being stupid, and I keep telling myself that, but it just won't go away.

I feel like something is down there, listening to me. Like it can sense me and is staring up at me through the floor, like it can feel my fear through the floor."

"Wow, you are one seriously messed up girl." Anna says.

"Isn't there anything that scares you?" Kylie asks. "I mean dumb things that you know shouldn't."

Anna thinks about it before answering. "Sure. Everybody has some dumb thing they're scared of, don't they?"

"So what's yours?"

"Dark holes," Anna says, "the kind that could be caves with a wild animal, snakes, or giant spiders hiding inside."

She is maybe a little afraid of dark holes if she really thinks about it. But that isn't the thing that really scares her. It's only something to throw out there because she doesn't want to admit to what she's really scared of.

"What I'm really scared of is being alone and not wanted," Anna thinks, "of being abandoned. My parents mostly ignore me, when they aren't mad at me and giving me heck for something, if they're even around. But I'm not going to tell you that.

And much worse than that, I hate Cole and sometimes I wish he would just die. And knowing that I am such a horrible person to think that way about my own little brother scares me more than anything else. I'm not going to tell you that either. That's my ugly dark secret and I can't tell anyone."

"Dark holes," Kylie repeats, nodding. It sounds reasonable. "So you understand, then, about the basement. It's kind of dark down there, and creepy."

"Not ours. Our basement isn't just cement. It's all finished like a living room."

"That would help," Kylie says, thinking that nobody could be scared of just another living room.

Kylie is itching to say what's really on her mind, and she almost blurts it out, but she backs off. She's not ready yet to tell Anna just how bad her problems are. All the problems in her life are making her feel like a wreck. She feels stretched too thin, at the end of her frayed nerves.

She's not sleeping so good either. All her problems seem to close in on her at night when she lays in bed trying to fall asleep. They whirl around in her head and she just can't get rid of them. She imagines all kinds of bad things then. When she does finally fall asleep, she has nightmares. All the time. Sleeping is bad.

Anna picks up on the tension. She knows Kylie isn't telling her something.

"You didn't answer on the bus. You haven't been going online on any of the chats, have you?" Anna watches Kylie, studying her reaction to see if she's lying. She knows Kylie will deny it, whether she's guilty or not.

Kylie shakes her head, a guilty flush creeping up her cheeks.

The three bullies have been tormenting her mercilessly online. Anna made her promise to stop looking online so she wouldn't have to see it. Mostly Kylie doesn't, but sometimes she just can't help it and has to see what nasty things they are posting about her. When she looks, she is so upset that it makes her stomach hurt for days after.

Anna eyes her suspiciously.

"You have been online." She shakes her head with disappointment.

Kylie's blush rises higher on her cheeks and she gives her a guilty shrug.

"I couldn't help it. They've left me alone here, but that's only because you are with me most of the time at school."

"They won't dare touch you with me around." Anna has a reckless gleam in her eyes.

"You can't be there all the time. It's only a matter of time before they catch me alone." Kylie's eyes are hollow and wide, haunted with the fear that won't go away. It's just one more fear to drag her down.

"Ever since they did," she swallows, "you know, in the bathroom, it feels like I'm just forever waiting for them to get me again and this one is going to be a doozy."

Her cheeks flush redder with the memory. Her mother had dragged both her and her little sister to the school and she stood there in mortified embarrassment while her mother yelled at the principal for everyone to hear. She has never seen her mother so angry. It made her a little proud too, because she has never seen her mother stand up to anyone like that before either. Usually her mother avoids confrontations, especially when it comes to their dad.

"That one was a doozy," Anna says. Her expression turns grim. Well, you just stay off those chats. You don't need that poison in your life. Whatever they have to say, you don't have to look at it." She turns her attention to her sandwich, signaling the discussion is closed.

Kylie looks down at hers, not feeling like eating, and mechanically taking a bite and chewing. She doesn't taste it.

She glances at her friend now and then as they eat their lunch in silence, wishing she could tell her what is going on.

With her own problems weighing on her, feeling like she's drowning under a huge weight of stress, Kylie has no idea that Anna is dealing with her own problems too.

Sitting next to her, woodenly eating her own sandwich, Anna also wants to tell her friend what she is going through, to be able to get it off her chest. But she is so used to keeping it all to herself, of acting as if none of it bothers her, that she just doesn't know how to stop.

"I hate school," Kylie says, interrupting Anna's thoughts. "How about you?"

Anna shrugs. "Who likes school? I don't really see the point in it. It's boring and I'd rather be at home watching T.V. and playing games." This is a lie, but it doesn't matter.

Kylie laughs. "I knew it. You always miss the bus and come late."

"I'm doing better," Anna smirks. "I'm coming to school every day now."

Anna sleeps in most mornings, often misses the bus, and sometimes didn't bother going to school at all. Her parents are always on her case about it and she is really sick of hearing about it.

Anna looks at her friend, Kylie. She hasn't been missing school since they started hanging out. "If I skipped, Kylie would be at the mercy of those jerks," she thinks. Her parents have laid off nagging her about school too. "Probably just because the school stopped bugging them," Anna thinks grumpily.

The sudden freedom from her parents getting on her case and yelling and threatening her also left her with more time to think about her other problem.

She doesn't really know why, but she just kind of blurts it out, surprising herself by the words coming out of her own mouth.

"My brother is sick," Anna says.

Kylie looks at her. "He's got the flu?"

"I wish," Anna mutters.

Kylie is curious now. "Who would wish the flu on anyone?"

"I would," Anna says, turning and staring ahead at nothing now, fiddling with her shoelace and picking at the cracked plastic tip that is still left on one side. She idly wonders what those plastic things are called.

"The flu would be better," Anna says. "He's very sick. He is sick with so many things that he is sick on top of being sick. He is so sick that even his medications are making him sicker."

She sits silently for a long moment before continuing. Kylie just waits, expecting she will go on.

"It's like they're killing him trying to make him better. Everything just makes it worse."

"Sorry," Kylie says quietly.

"Yeah," Anna says.

The bell rings, interrupting them. It's time for their mandatory twenty minutes of fresh air and sunlight. Outdoor time.

Anna gets up with a sigh. "Let's go."

Kylie scoops up her stuff and follows her out of the cafeteria. "This is so archaic, making us go outside like grade schoolers in middle school."

Dylan passes the table they sat at and notices a small folded piece of paper. He looks around quickly, doesn't see them coming back for it, and stops long enough to snatch it.

"I don't know which of them left this, but they might want it."

Curiosity pulls at him. He unfolds it and reads it as he walks to his locker. He stops dead in his tracks and looks at the two girls stopped at Kylie's locker ahead of him.

"I know your secret, but which one of you is it?"

He quickly folds the piece of paper and shoves it into his pocket, going to his own locker instead.

7   Spring Brings Hearts Aflutter

March came in quiet and calm and left in a fury with a late season blizzard that left a mess of cars stranded all over highways and city streets and brought the entire area to its knees for two days. "In like a lamb, out like a lion" was a phrase that was repeated so often that everyone was sick of hearing about it.

As usual, Groundhog Day also came with its typical ridiculousness. Groundhogs of all kinds were dragged out, from actual animals to jokers in lame costumes that even made their school mascot look less ridiculous; and even pathetic looking sock puppets and stuffed toy groundhogs. They all had crazy names that made the whole thing even more a joke. The news shows and papers ate it all up as if it was the biggest event of the year. It was anyone's guess whether any of the rodents, fake or real, actually saw a shadow or if they just reacted to the glaring media lights, storm of camera flashes, and too loud crowds.

One groundhog, an actual animal name Monteberry Montebue, even charged and attacked a news lady, trying to crawl up her legs. It was clear to anyone watching that the "attack" was nothing more than a frightened animal trying to find safety. They replayed that one over and over all over the T.V. and YouTube videos got millions of hits with the woman shrieking and trying to climb on top of her cameraman who just stood there laughing and cracking jokes while trying to continue filming it.

In the end the groundhogs were all over the place in their predictions, leaving people to rely on the weatherman instead. So much for Mother Nature whispering in the old groundhog's ear to let him know what she is planning.

With spring and the melting snow came a lot of things. Talk of the threat of new wars and fears of terrorists and more shootings in schools and other public places filled the news.

But a lot of this seems distant and far away to the kids at school, happening somewhere else.

The big thing close to home that is real to the kids is what happens between Kylie and Anna.

Kylie is so stressed out that she just wants to scream and break things. She feels like this stress has been grinding at her forever like someone poking you over and over and over. The last few weeks have been the worst.

Kylie and her sister are sitting in the living room watching T.V. Becca was dropped off at home by her babysitter today. Their mom is late coming home.

Kylie turns at the sound of the familiar jingle of keys at the door, waiting expectantly. The door opens and her mother comes in, barely waving at them as she disappears down the hallway, going straight to her bedroom without a word, and locks the door.

The two girls look at each other.

"Why does Mom look like that?" Becca asks. The look on her mother's face scares her.

"She went to court today," Kylie whispers. Her sister nods understanding.

Worried, they follow their mother down the hall, stopping and listening outside her bedroom door. Becca knocks tentatively and tries the knob.

"It's locked. Mommy never locks the door."

"I guess she needs some privacy."

Kylie and her sister stare at the door, scared and confused.

Kylie leads her sister back to the living room, motioning her to go back to watching her T.V. show.

"We need to give Mom some time. You keep watching your show and I'll make supper."

Instead of going to the kitchen, Kylie sneaks quietly to stand listening outside her mother's closed door. She can hear what she thinks is muffled sobbing and is sure her mother is crying into her pillow to hide the sounds so they would not hear.

"This isn't good," she thinks, "Moms are not supposed to cry. If they can't be the strong one then who's going to be?"

She turns to head to the kitchen and sees her sister standing at the end of the hall watching with a worried look.

Becca starts towards her and she moves to head her off.

"I want to see Mommy," Becca says.

"Shh, come."

"No, I want Mommy."

"We need to leave her alone for a little while. She'll be okay. She just needs a little time alone."

"She's crying, isn't she?"

Kylie nods.

Becca nods back, her look too knowing. "She's been doing that a lot."

Kylie blinks at her surprised. "Why do you think that?"

"She always locks herself in her room when she cries."

Kylie can't deny that. Their mother did that for years before she kicked their dad out. She's surprised at her sister's perceptiveness. She never thought Becca noticed.

"Come on; let's play a game until she's ready to come out." Kylie tries to keep her sister busy and away from their mother's room.

"I'm hungry," Becca complains after they've been playing a little while, looking up at Kylie unhappily.

Kylie looks at the time. It's way past supper and they haven't eaten yet. "Me too. Come on, I'll make you something. What do you want?"

"Peanut butter and jam."

"OK."

Kylie makes them both peanut butter and jam sandwiches. Becca eats hers hungrily. Kylie only picks at hers. She doesn't feel like eating.

She plays more games with her sister and gets her in her pajamas and her teeth and hair brushed for bed. The whole time she keeps looking towards her mom's room, worried. She feels hollow and scared inside. Her mother has never done this before. She's locked herself in her room to cry, but only for a little while. She's never locked herself away for the whole evening, and it scares her to death.

"It's time for bed," Kylie says, looking at the clock. It's past time for her sister to be in bed.

"I can't sleep without Mommy."

"She'll be in to say goodnight. I'll knock on her door."

Becca nods unhappily, letting Kylie tuck her in. "Can you read me a story?"

Kylie doesn't want to, but the absolute sadness in Becca's eyes breaks her heart. She gets a book, one of her sister's favorite Biscuit the dog books, and starts reading, trying to make her voice sound happy. It's impossible when she feels so miserable and worried.

After that book, she ends up reading two more. Kylie is on the third book when she finally hears the soft click of her mother's bedroom door opening.

When her mom appears in the doorway, both girls look up and Kylie's throat catches.

"She looks horrible," she thinks. "Mom looks so frail and thin, like she's sick. She's been crying for sure, and looks like she just lost the most important thing in her life. This is going to bad, really bad." She's terrified. She has never seen her mother look this bad.

To the girls' mother it feels like she has just lost the most important thing in her life; the two most important things actually. She looks at her daughters, feeling haunted. Haunted and hunted and wrung out.

"How do I tell them?" she wonders. "How do I tell them that I lost in court? Worse, it was the same judge who gave my ex-husband visits before. The judge was angry that I stopped sending the girls. He threatened to find me in contempt of court if I don't send the girls for the visits with their dad. I might even go to jail."

Nobody has to tell her what that means. With no one else to look after the girls, they would be sent to live with their dad for as long as she is locked up.

When she was leaving court her ex-husband made a point of catching up to her. She was hurrying, watching for him, hoping to get away before he leaves the courthouse. He grabbed her arm from behind, jolting her to a sudden stop. He held her arm painfully tight and pulled her close to whisper in her ear.

"This is only the beginning," he whispered. His voice was cruel and his eyes gleamed hard, his smile nasty. "I am going to take custody of the girls away from you and have you declared an unfit mother who should not be allowed to even visit the girls. You will never see them again." He released her arm roughly and swaggered away, smiling smugly.

She could only stare after him mutely, rubbing her arm where a bruise was already starting, fighting the tears that burned at her eyes and trying to make herself breathe. She is going to lose her girls.

She reflexively moves her hand to rub the bruise and stops. The motion pulls Kylie's eyes to her arm.

Kylie stares at the bruise on her mother's arm. She can tell it was fingers. She has seen bruises like that before.

"Girls, I have to tell you something," their mother says. Kylie can see that whatever it is, it's breaking her mother's heart.

Their mother sits down with them on Becca's bed. She fidgets with her fingers like Kylie often does herself when she's nervous and then looks the girls each in the eyes, her expression grave.

"The judge says you have to visit your dad," she says softly. She tries to keep her voice from cracking and the despair from showing.

"Maybe if I make light of it the girls won't be so upset," she thinks.

Kylie looks at her little sister. Her eyes are big, widened and filling with tears. She looks shaken and pale.

With a strangled sound and a horrified look, the little girl jumps up and runs from the room. She is crying hysterically by the time she reaches the doorway and she races out of sight, going to hide somewhere.

Kylie swallows the knot that seems to be suddenly choking her throat. She feels like someone just yanked a mat out from under her feet, throwing her off balance hard, and she just keeps on falling and falling. She feels dizzy, cold, and confused.

It's only long moments later that Kylie realizes she is laying down and her mother is staring down at her with a worried look, talking to her. She had fainted. The world seems to be spinning and she feels like she's wrapped in a blanket of ice, her skin cold and clammy.

Kylie feels sick. The world is swimming and it all feels so wrong. Nausea is spinning in her stomach, a sickening carnival ride that won't stop.

"Can you sit up now?" her mother asks worriedly.

Kylie nods mutely and tries to sit up with her mother's help. She's still weak and dizzy. She realizes she's shivering.

"I have to go find your sister," her mother says and Kylie nods.

After what feels like an eternity, Kylie's mother returns.

"I can't get your sister to come out."

"Mom looks lost," Kylie thinks.

Kylie nods. Still dizzy, she follows her mother.

Becca had wedged herself into a crawl space beneath the basement stairs that had been boarded up years ago, but the board is now loose.

Kylie looks into the hole. It's dark and Becca is scared of the dark. Her face hangs in the darkness of the hole like a sad little moon with large sad eyes.

"Becca, please come out," Kylie begs. "You can't stay in there."

It takes a few hours of coaxing for Kylie and her mother to convince Becca to come out. When she finally does come out they both hug her tight, trying to sooth the sobbing little girl.

"I don't want to see him," Becca sobs. "I hate him."

"I know," their mother sooths, "but this time I don't have a choice." She looks at Kylie over Becca's head, her eyes begging for understanding.

"The judge was very angry with me for not making you go."

"It was the same judge, wasn't it?" Kylie says.

Kylie's mother is surprised by the level of maturity she sees in her at that moment. She nods, swallowing and trying to keep her voice steady.

"I'm going to fight it, but I might not win."

"Can't we just not go while you fight it?" Becca asks, her voice small.

"No. You have to go," their mother says gently.

"That's not fair," Kylie says angrily. "Why is the judge punishing us?"

"It's not punishment."

"It feels like it," Becca says.

"Can't we just not go like before?" Kylie asks.

Their mother sighs heavily. "The judge says you have to see your dad. If I don't make you go he's going to put me in jail and make you live with him." She keeps this to herself.

"I'll be in a lot of trouble if I don't make you go," she says. "And please don't say things like you hate him when you're there. Don't do anything to make him angry."

Becca just cries harder, clinging to them both. Kylie nods solemnly.

"Kylie," her mom says, getting her attention again. "I have to get another job to pay for court."

Kylie stares at her mother in disbelief. "But that would mean you'd be working three jobs! When would you ever have time to look after us? When will you even sleep?"

She sees then just how hollow and drawn her mother looks. The dark circles under exhausted eyes, the worry lines in her face, her pale face. No, her face is not pale; it's kind of grey, sick looking. Her mom looks awful. She looks like she did before she kicked him out.

This is her big problem. Bigger even than Amber and her two nasty sidekicks. And having no one to talk about it to makes Kylie feel like she is swimming in a pool of slimy stinky swamp water with no control over where she goes or what happens to her.

Kylie blinks her eyes, woken by her alarm. They feel grainy and dry, sore. Her whole body feels grainy and dry, achy like she has the flu.

She sits up, feeling woozy with exhaustion. She did not sleep that night after her mother broke the news.

Food would not stay down, coming up soon after she ate. Kylie has lived on nothing but a little dry toast and water all weekend

She is so stressed and upset she can't deal with it. She did not sleep the next night either. All weekend, Kylie moved in a thickening fog of distress, barely sleeping and feeling sick all the time. When she did fall asleep, she had terrible nightmares.

When the weekend ended, her nightmare did not. The visit is coming.

Each morning she gets up, managing to dress and go to school, muddling through the day, locked within herself. Anna tries to talk to her and she only answers in nods and head shakes, leaving Anna to stare at her in worry.

This has gone on for two weeks now. She kept it all bottled up inside, telling no one, and all her fears and anxiety just keep building up inside her.

This morning looks like it will be no different. Kylie gets dressed and brushes her hair, completely devoid of life, moving like a mindless zombie.

She goes to the kitchen. She stops, looking at the breakfast on the table in surprise then at her mother.

"Something is wrong" she thinks. "Mom should already be gone, not home making breakfast."

She sits down woodenly, her stomach sour, and stares down at the food she can't stomach eating. She looks up at her mother standing across the kitchen gripping a coffee cup like it is somehow going to save her.

"What happened?" Kylie asks.

Her mother swallows, trying to control her voice before speaking. She blinks a few times and tries to look at Kylie steadily, and fails.

"The first visit with your father is set."

Kylie's world swoops and her stomach heaves. She throws up.

Anna could tell something is wrong with her friend, Kylie, for the last few weeks and that it has been getting worse with each passing day. She is worried. She has made attempts to get Kylie to talk about it, but she has been mostly preoccupied with her own problems and didn't try very hard.

"I thought we were supposed to be friends," Anna mutters as she brushes her hair in front of the mirror. She yanks the brush through a tangle, ruthlessly tearing out hair. "Friends talk to each other. They tell each other their problems."

She stops, looking at her reflection guiltily. "I guess I've been doing the same thing."

Anna is under her own load of stress and has been for months with her parents spending more and more time out of the house. When they are home, they talk in hushed whispers in another room and walk around with haunted eyes.

She puts the brush down and goes to the kitchen. She stops in the kitchen doorway in surprise.

"Mom, Dad, you're home."

The sight of them sends her stomach sinking in a tailspin of doom. She is already feeling out of sorts and very much alone. It has just gotten a whole lot worse. The look on their faces says it all. Resignation, pity, loss.

"Anna, we have some bad news," her mother starts, choking on her words and unable to continue.

Pushing down the lump of pain constricting his throat, her father manages to finish.

"Your brother has taken a turn for the worse. It doesn't look good. We-we just thought you should know."

Instead of the shock, betrayal, and pain they expected, Anna's face twists into a mask of anger. She fights it, but it's too late. The pain in their eyes reflects that.

Her father looks away and her mother leaves the room, grief stricken.

"We have to get back to the hospital," he says.

Anna would have felt remorse if she were not so angry. She stares after them long after she hears the door close and the car start.

"He has taken a turn for the worse. What does that even mean? I haven't seen them in two days, and they just come in and drop that on me with no explanation and just leave."

Her eyes burn with angry tears. Anna is pretty sure it means her brother has gotten a lot sicker. She suspected he was dying before, but her parents would not tell her that.

"It's like I don't even have parents, like I just don't exist to them." Anna's voice and face are bitter. "Ever since Cole got sick months ago and they took him to the hospital. They spend all their time there.

I haven't seen Cole in months. They never let me go to the hospital with them. It's like he doesn't even exist and they just made him up so they don't have to be with me. They are always there.

I thought they were finally going to spend some time with me this weekend. They promised. Then they rushed off to the hospital to be with Cole when the hospital called. They called the house a few times over the weekend to tell me if Cole is getting better or not and that was it."

Hot tears are running down her cheeks.

"I wanted to tell Kylie what's happening, but it's like she doesn't even care. She's not talking to me at all and I don't know why. Kylie doesn't want to hear about my problems. She doesn't care."

"I don't care either."

At least that is what she told herself. Anna just wants her parents and she is flat out feeling angry at the world.

She tries to compose herself. She has to leave for school soon.

The day everything between Kylie and Anna comes to a head Anna is filled to bursting, angry and resentful towards her brother and her parents. She hates him so much and wishes he would just die, and hates herself for feeling that way.

Kylie doesn't look up when the school bus stops and Anna gets on. She still doesn't look when Anna takes another seat. There were no empty seats together when Kylie got on.

Kylie and Anna both sit on the school bus in brooding silence, Kylie in her seat and Anna a few seats away. The tension coming off each girl can be felt like a physical force surrounding them.

They barely speak to each other as they get off the bus, walking towards the school side by side, each girl's bad mood feeding into the other's mood.

They both can feel the other's anger and wonder if the other girl is mad at her. They walk together stiffly into the school. Not knowing makes them both feel more on edge.

The kids all move singly and in groups into the school, no longer cooped up together on the bus. They feel the tension in the air leave with the distance between them and the two girls and are relieved without knowing why they are relieved.

"What are you doing later?" Anna asks Kylie.

"I don't know," Kylie says, her voice more harsh than she intends.

Her tone of voice annoys Anna. Anna feels like her friend is blaming her, but has no idea what for.

"Well, you should know what you're doing," Anna says more snappish than she means to. She covers it badly, by being rude and defensive instead of with an apology. "You have to be doing something! Do you even know if you are going to class or eating lunch?"

Kylie gives her an annoyed look. "That was just mean," she thinks. "I don't know what got into her and I'm having none of it."

"Well maybe it's just none of your business and that's why I don't know!" Kylie says angrily.

The comment would have hurt Anna's feelings if she wasn't feeling so angry. She is in no mood to put up with anything and when her friend Kylie is snappy, she gets snippy right back.

"Well maybe you should keep your stinky business to yourself! I don't want to know!"

That is the breaking point. Kylie whirls on her and blows up at Anna, yelling at her with a fury that makes the other girl step back.

"Why are you even on me all the time? Can't you find any real friends?" She regrets it the moment the words are out of her mouth. That did not come out the way it sounded in her head. She meant that she doesn't know why Anna wants to be her friend when no one else does.

Angry, Anna steps forward again, lashing back with her own nasty words.

"I felt sorry for you, jerk! Now I know why you don't have any friends!"

Before either girl knows what's happening they are screaming at each other in the middle of the hall with everyone around stopping and staring.

It's the grandmother of all fights. Bigger even than the big friend fight of 2003 that is still talked about in hushed whispers, even though it's a new generation of kids in the school now.

The fight finally ends just when everyone is sure it will become physical.

Kylie and Anna both turn and stomp off in opposite directions, declaring their friendship and each other stupid and over forever.

The sudden quiet that is left behind them makes the hallway feel empty. Some kids snickering, some embarrassed for the two girls, the students all move on to continue with whatever they were doing before the fight.

Anna is so furious as she storms off that she feels like she is about to explode. She just can't hold it in and has to take that violent anger out on something.

Anna goes outside and looks around, shaking with anger. She spots a stick on the ground and picks it up, gripping it tight and testing its weight. It's not very thick or long. She wishes it is bigger.

Anna turns to the offending tree next to where she found the stick and starts beating it furiously with the stick. Chunks of bark break off the tree and go flying, the stick snaps and cracks, the tip breaking off repeatedly, flying away with the ruined tree bark.

Her face twists from fury to a grimace of pain, turning red, as the tears begin to flow.

The poor tree is damaged from Anna's temper tantrum of epic proportions, the stick breaking smaller and smaller as she continues to strike the tree harder with each blow.

Finally, a teacher notices and hurries from the building with a stern look. Unfortunately, it's old Mrs. Crampshaw, who has no sense of humor and even less sympathy. She is yelling at Anna before she even reaches her, her finger wagging angrily.

Anna stops and looks guiltily at the tree, dropping the stick.

Mrs. Crampshaw hauls her off inside to the principal's office where she deposits Anna on a chair and shouts at the principal with her story of what she caught the girl doing before storming off.

Anna sits there miserably in "the bad chair" outside the principal's office waiting while he talks on the phone. She is sure he is trying to phone her parents.

"Hah! He won't get them. They aren't even home," she mutters under her breath. "They're never home."

She looks down and realizes there are a few drops of red paint or something on the floor at her feet. She looks at it curiously and sees a drip hit the floor.

"Where'd that come from?" Anna wonders.

She notices the gash in her hand from the stick at the same moment the school secretary comes racing over from her desk making a big scene over the injury, having just spotted it too.

Spring break is coming and everyone in school is already talking about the end of the school year, that long anticipated moment when the doors close for the summer and the kids don't have to spend all day long learning anymore.

The halls are full of speculation and gossip about what the spring dance will be like.

Jessica and Brooke are talking about what the theme of the dance might be when the fight between Kylie and Anna breaks out.

Brooke whirls around wide-eyed and stares at the two girls screaming at each other. She's a little frightened by the sudden ferocity of the fight.

"I feel a little bad for them, especially Kylie," Brooke thinks. "Amber will be so all over this when she finds out. Sometimes I really hate Amber, but being friends with her is safer than not being friends with her."

Jessica turns to watch the fight with a cruel smile, delighted. "Oh, this is so awesome," she whispers to Brooke.

She watches the fight eagerly, almost giggling when the two friends storm off, their friendship over. She grabs at Brooke, pulling her along.

"Come on, we have to find Amber!"

Brooke's heart sinks when the fight ends and the two girls go their separate ways, declaring their friendship over forever. She follows Brooke dutifully, feeling resigned to it.

"This is not good," Brooke thinks. She's not happy about the fight for her own reasons. "I enjoyed the break from Amber's constant drive to "get" Kylie. Her constant push and anger over this pointless vendetta is so stressful."

Brooke also feels somewhat bad over the mean things they do. Not while they are doing them so much. She gets wrapped up in it and has fun or is more worried over her own fear of Amber than how wrong their behavior is. But afterwards she feels bad.

"The end of that friendship makes Kylie an open target again and Amber will be after her harder than ever."

They find Amber quickly and Jessica eagerly shares the news.

A slow cruel smile spreads across Amber's face as she listens. Her biggest regret is that she was not there to see the fight herself.

"Open season on Kylie has just started," Amber says.

"I am so bored sitting at home alone after school every day," Madison thinks, looking out the bus window as it drives her towards home. With the nicer weather, being cooped up is driving her even more crazy. "Mom and Dad are going to be late getting home tonight. I'm going to have even longer to sit there bored."

She stares out the window vacantly for a while, wishing she has something to do. Then the idea hits her. "I'm going to go visit my secret fort before I go home."

Madison found a new place to hang out. She calls it her fort. There is only one problem with her fort; to get there she has to take the shortcut through the loose board in the fence and down the alley where she is not allowed to go.

It also means going past Old Man Hooper's house and Caesar.

The bus pulls up to Madison's stop, letting her off. She glances back at the bus once, taking her time walking more slowly than usual towards home. She goes towards home so the driver doesn't stop and ask where she's going.

After the bus pulls away and continues down the street to drop off the next kid, she turns and races back the other way to take the shortcut to her fort.

Madison manages to get past Hooper's house without trouble. "Caesar must be inside," she thinks with relief. She doesn't say it out loud in case she jinxes' it and the dog comes charging out at her.

When she arrives at the lot with the abandoned building, she races around its side to the back where her secret fort is. She glances up at the boarded up old brick building, half expecting someone to come out and yell at her for being there. No one does, of course; there would never be anybody there.

Her spot is an old dilapidated shed in the back corner of the lot. The door is half hanging off, the one window cracked and boarded up, and the walls themselves are crumbling and rotting boards with gaps and holes. The ceiling droops a little and has a big hole in one corner, as if a giant puppy came along and chewed the corner off. The yard is partially fenced in and the paved part of the lot is filled with a tracery of cracks. Some look like someone dropped something very large and heavy that pushed the cement down as it cracked it. The old painted parking lines are mostly worn away. Weeds grow up everywhere through the cracks in the concrete and the abandoned lot is sometimes used as a dumping ground for large trash items the garbage truck won't take and someone is too cheap to pay to have hauled away. There is always something new dumped there. Today there is an old armchair sitting in the middle of the cracked pavement parking lot.

Madison pauses to look at the chair.

"I wonder where the stuff disappears to. You would think it would just sit here forever."

When she discovered this place, there was an old broken dresser with all the drawers missing. The next time she came that was gone and there was an old mattress with a big hole and its guts falling out. She took a close look at that. The springs inside were like the mattress's skeleton bones. When a rat poked its face out at her with a squeak, she had squealed back and ran away.

Now the mattress is gone and the chair is here. For a moment, Madison imagines strange creatures coming in the night to take the stuff. It would take a bunch of them to carry them away because they are small like the little monkeys at the zoo. Only these creatures are bald and twisted and ugly, not cute with large human eyes. The creatures have human eyes too, but they are scary human eyes.

"Who leaves the stuff here and where do they take it?"

Madison imagines the homeless people she saw once when she went downtown with her mother. In her imagination, they take the stuff from the back lane she passes through between home and Mr. Hooper's house, dragging it here very early in the morning before anyone wakes up. They look around in fear and run away quickly, leaving the treasures for the creatures, payment for the strange little creatures to leave them alone. The junk sits here all day and, when the next night comes, the ugly twisted little creatures come crawling out in the dark to take their gifts.

"Or maybe they aren't little twisted creatures at all. Maybe they're the homeless people and they live in there."

Except instead of homeless people, her mind conjures up images of strange children who live and hide in the shadows.

Madison turns and looks at the abandoned building.

"That must be where they take it," she whispers as if afraid they might hear her. She imagines them struggling with the heavy objects and somehow squishing them through the small cracks and holes with their evil magic to drag them down to the basement where they hide during the day.

Madison shudders and pushes the thoughts away. She can't push away the fear her own imagination makes her feel though.

"Stop it Madison," she mutters at herself. "You're just being silly." She continues on, nervously inspecting the shed before going in.

She tries to push down the unwanted thought in the back of her mind that those child-like creatures could be hiding in the shed too.

This shed is her secret place. Madison is sure she would be in even more trouble for coming here than for going down the forbidden back lane. She hasn't even told any of her friends about it.

Andrew gets off the bus at his stop and starts walking home. Halfway up the street, he turns a corner and sees Madison ahead. She's running and looking around as if she's worried about being seen.

"What's she up to? She's not going home." He pauses to watch, pulled by curiosity. He shrugs.

"Heck, it's not like I have anything else to do," he mutters. His parents won't be home for at least a few hours.

He follows, keeping a good distance behind and trying to stay out of sight. He hides behind a tree while she walks up a sidewalk bordered by a tall fence.

When he thinks it's safe, Andrew peeks out from his hiding space. The sidewalk is empty. He looks around quickly

"Where'd she go?" He jogs up to where he last saw Madison on the sidewalk next to the tall fence, stopping there and looking around.

He looks at the fence and smiles. "She can't just disappear. That leaves one option, she went through the fence."

Andrew finds the loose board, swinging it aside and squeezing through. He reaches the alley on the other side just in time to see Madison turn to pass Mr. Hooper's yard. She turns up the next street.

He hesitates. "Caesar didn't freak out. He must not be out." Fear churns his stomach and stiffens his muscles.

"Everyone is scared of that stupid dog. If she can do it, I can do it."

Steeling himself for the inevitable attack, Andrew sucks in his breath and holds it as if it will somehow help, sprinting up the back lane.

He's almost choking on his held air by the time he's approaching the yard. His lungs are going to explode. He can't hold his breath any longer.

Andrew pushes himself harder, flying past the house and skidding in the street in front of it, his face turning red. Three houses past, he gives out, his breath exploding out and sucking in hard deep breaths of sweet air.

Andrew ducks behind a car parked on the street, doubling over and wavering dizzily, gasping and panting. He has to cover his mouth with both hands to stifle an attack of coughs.

When he's ready to move, Andrew races up the street to catch up with Madison. He spots her ahead and drops to a walk, still keeping his distance to follow her discretely.

Madison turns and cuts across the front yard of an old abandoned building. She runs around to the back of the old boarded up brick building. Andrew stops in front of the building, staring up at it. Andrew is in awe of the place.

"This place is so perfect!"

He pulls his attention away from it and sneaks along the side of the building. He stops at the back corner and peeks around, watching Madison as she stops in the middle of the back lot to look at a chair.

"What the heck is a chair from a living room doing here?"

He watches her vanish into an old dilapidated shed by the fence in a back corner of the lot. Hoping she doesn't look back and see him, it's open ground from here to the shed, Andrew takes a chance and steps out.

Distracted by his curiosity, Andrew forgets himself and starts wandering around the brick building, inspecting it and wondering what it is. All the windows are boarded up. Some of the boards are broken or missing to show the smashed out windows behind them.

"Probably kids throwing rocks at them," he thinks while looking around absently for a good rock to throw.

The back of the building is not a straight wall. A section juts out in a big box shape. At the back and tucked in a corner there is a part of the building that seems more like a shed added on to the outside of the building. The shed roof is lower than the rest. He has seen little storage add-ons like this next to the door on some track housing.

Looking around the other corner of the building, he takes a few steps up that side. There is nothing of much interest here, just wall and weeds. There is something in the weeds near the wall, an empty space and a partial view of something brown.

"Is that a door lying on the ground?" He shrugs. It doesn't matter. Door or a board, it's probably just more junk. Although, who knows what might be living under it.

He returns to the back of the building.

Andrew starts poking around and finds a basement window with half the boards missing. The glass is broken and jagged, what is left of it is grimy with years of dirt. He hunches down, kneeling and looking around. He has completely forgotten about Madison.

He peers into the darkness below, thinking how cool it would be to go in there and check out the place.

Andrew practically jumps out of his skin in fright, startled by a girl's voice right over his shoulder.

"I wouldn't go in there," Madison says. She's leaning over his shoulder looking into the dark interior of the building's basement with him.

Dylan was not there for the big fight in the hallway. He turns to watch Anna storm by looking like she's ready to tear a strip off the next person she sees.

"What's up with her?" he wonders.

By the time Dylan reaches his science class, he's heard the gossip about the big fight in the hallway between Kylie and Anna. Kylie isn't in the classroom.

"She's always here before me," he thinks.

The last stragglers are filing in when Kylie comes slinking into science class looking embarrassed and like she wants to just crawl under the floor and hide. Dylan hears the comments and snickering nearby and knows immediately it has to do with her.

His buddy in the next seat makes a rude remark and Dylan jabs him hard with his elbow.

The other boy turns to him with a look, muttering. "What was that for?"

"Just don't," Dylan warns him. His friend gives him a knowing look and turns his attention to someone else.

Dylan watches Kylie take her seat, huddling into herself as if she could actually make herself disappear that way. She looks lost, a kind of emptiness in her eyes. The look he sees reflected there fills him with his own empty void.

"I know that look," he thinks. He had seen it in his own mirror after his house was broken into.

His thoughts turn back to that awful day. The damage to Dylan's house was pretty bad. The moment he walked in the door alone, home from school, to find the mess still haunts his dreams.

He came in the front door completely unaware something was wrong. They had kicked in the back door. If he would have come in the back he would have immediately seen that the door was not closed and the doorframe torn apart where the lock bolt ripped through the wood frame. The boot print on the door was too obvious to miss.

Unaware anything was wrong, Dylan had kicked off his boots and dropped his jacket and backpack carelessly on the floor by the front door even though he knew he was supposed to hang up his jacket, line his boots up in the bottom of the closet, and put his backpack in his room.

He thought he smelled something odd. "Smells like poop in here," he complained. Stepping forward to the living room doorway, his jaw nearly dropped to the floor at what he saw. He stood there staring in confusion, mouth open and slack.

Everything in the living room was tossed all over the place. The tables were smashed, the chairs tipped, and their fabric and cushions looked like they had been ripped apart with a big knife. The television lay face down in a pool of its own shattered screen. Books and magazines from the bookcase were shredded and tossed all over, ornaments smashed everywhere, and his mother's favorite figurine of a woman was embedded in the wall. The walls were smeared with something brown, the paint gouged, and holes knocked in them. He immediately suspected what was smeared on the walls.

Instinct had told him to back away, get out, run and get out of there because someone could still be in the house. He didn't.

Dylan felt sick. He was more scared than he had ever been in his life and was sure his face must be as white as a sheet. He felt clammy, his teeth started chattering, and his knees went weak.

He went further into the house. Dylan could not stop himself. His mind was numb and he could hardly even think. He stopped at the kitchen doorway, taking the scene in.

In the kitchen every single glass plate, bowl, and glass was smashed. The room was littered with glass shards, looking like an explosion had gone off. The smell was stronger here. It smelled like something burning. The air was hazy with smoke still.

He sniffed the air and looked around.

The orange light on the stove glared at him and he looked at the knobs. Dark smoke trailed up from the stovetop element where the oven vent is. The oven was on, turned up to broil.

Dylan did not want to do it but felt he had to. He went to the stove, turned it off, and opened the door. Smoke billowed out, blinding him and making his eyes burn. The smoke made him choke when he breathed it in.

"Why didn't the smoke alarm go off?"

Dylan looked up and saw that the alarm had been ripped out of the ceiling and smashed.

He turned his attention back to the oven, looking inside now that most of the smoke was gone. Whatever was inside was unidentifiable and still smoked.

"Lucy!" Dylan cried in sudden panic. But no, whatever was in there was too small to be Lucy. He had to convince himself of that, even though the doubt tore at his chest.

He turned in a daze, looking around.

The microwave door seemed somewhat rippled at the top. He went to it, tried to swallow the hard lump in his throat down, and opened it. The inside was blackened and a charred lump lay inside.

Whoever did this had tried to burn the house down. He was sure of it. Andrew stared at the lump in the microwave. He was not sure, but he thought whatever was in there might have included a Barbie doll, cutlery, and a popcorn bag.

Luckily, the fire had burned itself out by chance, the microwave zapping and popping and melting some wiring so that it died before the stuff inside could catch fire good. They had made the mistake of wrapping the stuff in his mother's new potholders. The package the potholders came in had boasted that they would never catch fire.

"I guess they were sort of right." Dylan said and moved on.

He left the kitchen and went down the hallway. The bedrooms were tossed too. He went from room to room, his heart beating fast, his chest a hollow knot, and his stomach sick.

"Where's Lucy? Where's the dog?"

He searched the whole house and the yard without finding any sign of her. When his parents came home they found Dylan huddled in a corner of the destroyed living room, hugging the dog's blanket and crying.

It took them two days of searching before they finally found Lucy hiding in the tight space behind the walls in the basement. She had chewed through the wall behind the dryer to get in there.

They tried everything to coax Lucy out but she would not come out. She just stayed hunched and shivering, whining so quietly they could barely hear her and refusing even to look at them.

Faced with having the animal die and rot behind the wall, his dad ended up pulling out the washer and dryer and tearing a hole in the wall to get her out. She backed away, squeezing further down the wall out of reach, shaking and crying. Finally, they had to make another hole further along the wall with the dog between and people at each end systematically tearing the wall out until they got to the dog.

Lucy's screaming was terrible when they pulled her out. She peed and pooped on the floor in terror, her eyes rolling until nothing but the white showed. She fought and tried desperately to get away; trembling so hard that nobody thought it was possible for a dog to shiver that hard.

They took her to the vet where they had to sedate her to sleep so the vet could look her over. Lucy had bruises, some of them pretty bad, and some bone fractures, but they would heal.

Unfortunately, her body healed but her mind did not.

It was anyone's guess what had been done to the animal to put her in such a terrified state. They only knew that she had been badly beaten. It was months before anyone in his own family could get near the dog without her freaking out. The vet said to take it slowly. Ignore her, but talk to her and say her name. Let her come to you when she is ready.

Dylan did not think she would ever be ready. Nobody can touch her still, but at least she doesn't tremble and cry anymore every time one of them walks in the room. She will go outside to pee and comes back in and goes straight to her kennel. The kennel has become her safe place, except when they all leave her alone. Lucy is terrified of being left alone. They cover the top and sides so she would feel like she is hiding.

Any time someone who is not part of the family comes to the house, Lucy would hear or smell them. She would start crying and frantically digging and tearing at the cage to escape and run away, trembling in terror. People stopped coming to the house, embarrassed or annoyed by the dog's reaction to them.

Dylan still can't get rid of the empty feeling of fear, wondering what they did to his dog. He is terrified whoever broke into the house will come back.

What if he's home alone when they do?

It's that same look of fear that he saw in his own eyes reflected back to him in the mirror that day after their house was broken into that he sees now in Kylie's eyes.

8   Amber Gets Her Way

Jessica is sitting in her room thinking about Amber and writing her thoughts in her diary. She can't help the blush of jealousy she feels, or the resentment.

"Amber the untouchable," she complains, "Amber who always has to have her way, like anything could ever go any other way.

Amber could not possibly have things going any better for her than they are right now. With Anna not hanging out with Kylie anymore, she can go after Kylie as much as she wants and she is making up for that time when her victim was mostly untouchable.

Amber is merciless and relentless, obsessed with getting her revenge on Kylie. She stalks Kylie everywhere in school and out. When she can't go after Kylie in person, she's on the phone or the internet spreading her nasty gossip and lies, making the ugly rumors about Kylie grow.

Ugh, it's getting sickening having to always follow Amber around listening to her obsess about Kylie."

Amber and her friends assault Kylie at every chance, pushing or knocking her down, knocking her books out of her hands, and hitting or tripping her. One morning Amber even ran up to Kylie as she walked along the edge of the road and shoved her into the path of a car. The driver barely managed to swerve around the girl suddenly stumbling in her path.

Jessica makes a face to show how unimpressed she is.

"Amber's vendetta against Kylie has become the only thing she can think or talk about, that's how bad her obsession has become. When she can't talk about or act on her need to hurt Kylie, she becomes so grouchy that nobody can stand to be around her."

Jessica pouts, letting out a little sniffle.

"I enjoyed going along with Amber's games for a while. But I'm getting sick of her obsession with Kylie. I miss talking about other stuff and doing other things.

I can't take it anymore. I have to tell Amber that this is going too far. I wish I could talk to someone about it, but I don't dare. If Amber ever finds out I even had a single thought against her, well I don't want to find out what she might do about it. I'm just so sick of always having to get Kylie."

She finishes writing and hides her diary away and then turns her attention to the computer. Jessica logs into their favorite site and sees that Amber is already online.

"Just great," she complains.

She barely got online when messages start popping up from Amber. She scans the messages without really bothering to read them. There's no point; it's all just the same stuff about Kylie.

Jessica sighs. "Can't you just take one day off?"

Jessica sends a few half-hearted responses, knowing Amber will be mad if she doesn't join in. Unfortunately, they only fuel Amber's fire. The other girl goes on a tangent about Kylie, most of it making no sense.

"Why does she even hate Kylie so much?" Jessica asks herself. She has no idea. She just plays along with Amber because she enjoys feeling powerful and in control going after someone weaker, and it was fun. It's not fun anymore. She's also afraid of becoming a target if she doesn't go along.

Feeling protected by the distance and faceless feeling of anonymity from chatting online, Jessica taps out a comment. She feels exhilarated and reckless as she types it, and regrets it the moment she clicks on the send button.

MG2: TAKE A BREAK GF. UR OBSESSION WITH KYLIE IS GONE OVER TO CRAZY. THIS IS LONG GONE OLD AND BORING.

Jessica's eyes widen as the messages begin to pour down the screen. She winces and her face reddens at what is popping up on her screen.

Amber's online rant over Kylie was sane compared to the nastiness coming from her now.

Jessica is shocked by Amber's reaction to her comment and how severely she suddenly turned on her with a stream of nasty threats and accusations. She swallows a hard lump in her throat, beginning to sweat and feel sick.

"What have I done?" Jessica whispers.

"Ok, get a grip on yourself girl. You have to fix this."

She starts typing; trying to convince Amber that she didn't mean it, it was a joke. Jessica tries to convince her that her message meant something different from what she had really intended. She meant it was crazy good, not loony. She tries to tell her old and boring meant the months they didn't do anything. She types that she wants to get Kylie just as bad and can't wait to get her again.

At the same time, Brooke is at home thinking her own thoughts about Amber's obsession with revenge against Kylie.

"The new intensity of Amber's attacks on Kylie is crazy. Amber is crazy. She's crazy in a dangerous way."

Brooke is sickened by this new level of cruelty and by Amber's obsession. Seeing this new level of crazy has made her more afraid of Amber.

"I just want all this to stop. I don't want to hang around with Amber anymore. I don't want to do these awful things all the time. I mean, look at me," she stares into the mirror on her dresser, lifting up a clump of hair and letting it flop back down, "I'm pretty sure I'm going bald from stress."

She is miserable and feels horrible about the pure nastiness of this ongoing vendetta against Kylie.

"Kylie doesn't deserve this," she mutters. "She never did anything to Amber. So why does she hate her so much?"

But as much as Brooke wants to separate herself from her two friends and this crazy obsessed chasing after Kylie all the time, she can't. She is terrified of Amber.

She doesn't dare disobey.

Madison and Andrew have started hanging out together regularly at her secret fort.

"I didn't want anyone to know about the fort, especially a boy," Madison thinks, "but I have to admit I'm actually having fun with Andrew. I'm less nervous about being here too with someone else around."

She looks at Andrew. They are there now at the fort, just hanging out in the lot of the abandoned building. They explored the lot for the hundredth time, walked the cracks like tightropes, and swung sticks at invisible enemies.

"I know I'm getting too old for playing fort games, but I'm not a teenager yet either."

Like the other kids her age, Madison is in that awkward age when you are too old for the kid stuff, but still kind of a kid. She isn't old enough for boys and dating, although she has to admit she has kind of been noticing boys lately. Of course, even if she is old enough, Andrew would not be the sort of boy she would be interested in. Well, that's what she tells herself anyway.

Madison is examining a gross looking ripped up mattress that appeared in the lot today. She shudders and doesn't want to get too close, remembering the ugly rat face that poked out of a similar mattress left here before. It stared at her with its beady eyes. That look gave her chills and she imagined the rat wanting to eat her eyes.

Andrew is off by the old brick building, examining its walls again.

She looks across the lot at him and watches him for a moment.

"I don't know what he's looking for, but it probably won't be anything good." she mutters. "Boys!"

She shakes her head and tisks.

Anna is walking home from school feeling angry and unhappy. She missed the bus again this morning and was late for school. Then she missed the bus going home because her homeroom teacher kept her back to drag her to the principal's office so they could both lecture her on being at school on time.

"They yell at me for missing the bus and then make me miss the bus. Isn't that jut bloody ironic? Well, maybe I won't even go to school at all tomorrow, how's that? Maybe I'll just pack a bag and leave, go somewhere far away where I won't be such a disappointment to everyone. They'll all be glad to be rid of me anyway."

Anna's parents are just as absent as they have been for the past months. Between her dad working three jobs now to pay all the hospital bills and her mom spending all her time at the hospital with her brother, Anna is alone more than ever.

"Worse," she thinks unhappily, "when they are around, they're always so grumpy and are always mad at me."

She notices too how they seem somehow hollow inside and dark eyed with dark circles under their eyes from lack of sleep. It scares her.

"I feel like my parents are slipping away somehow," Anna thinks miserably. "Fading away to leave their bodies empty husks like that empty body of a grasshopper I saw once." It looked like a grasshopper until she realized there was nothing inside the body.

"I know they are both under a lot of stress. The bills are piling up and unpaid, we hardly have anything to eat in the house anymore, and we are all living under the dark shadow of my brother's illness.

I feel guilty, but I can't help feeling angry and resentful towards him for doing this to us, to me especially. I know it's not his fault he's sick and I shouldn't feel this way. He's the one dying. I just do.

I'm such a horrible person.

Sometimes I even wish I'm the one dying in the hospital just so I could get some of the attention, so Mom and Dad would love me as much as they do him."

Without her friendship with Kylie and the need to protect her from the bully girls, Anna has nothing to care about anymore. She has lapsed back into her old habits of sleeping in late, missing the bus, and skipping school.

Finally, she reaches her street.

"I'm so late, but nobody will even know. They won't even be home, they never are."

Anna walks into the house, surprised to find the door unlocked. She pauses cautiously, and listens. She shrugs. "I must have forgot to lock it."

She gets only a few steps in and freezes, turning to stare in shock into the living room. Her parents are sitting there looking very unhappy, both of them. Her dad should be at work at one of his jobs and her mother should be at the hospital sitting next to her brother's bed holding his hand.

A tidal wave of emotions pours through Anna. She's happy that her parents are home, then in a few heartbeats the realization hits and she's gripped with fear that her brother has died. Why else would they be home? Why else would they look so unhappy?

Before she can identify the grief tearing at her heart, she feels relief that it's finally over. Their world no longer revolves around suffering over her dying brother, and then guilt for wishing it.

She feels sorry for the pain and suffering her parents must be feeling over his death, happy to finally have her parents back, hopeful that they will love her now like they did him, and guilt for feeling relief.

Resentment at her brother for stealing them with his sickness tugs at her. Then grief washes over her at the loss of her brother and hatred for herself for her own selfishness.

That is washed away by desperate hope that he is okay and that maybe he came home and that is why they are here. The hope breaks as soon as she feels it. She knows he will never come home. It's terminal, despite her parents' refusal to accept that. That is what the doctor said, that he will never leave the hospital alive.

Anna wants to laugh and cry and scream all at once.

She looks at her parents and realizes the tears in her mother's eyes are not grief. They are desperation and anger and frustration. Her father's haggard face is not pale and grey from loss. It is exhaustion and defeat. His mouth and eyes are angry, not lost.

All the emotions flood out of Anna to be replaced with the empty numbness she has become used to feeling. Nothing but grey soppy emotionless nothing. The sudden loss of all those emotions raging inside her leaves her deflated like a used party balloon that is too tired to pop when someone sticks it with a pin, slowly and silently leaking its air out instead.

She crosses her arms defensively and stands there waiting for it, staring at her parents. She has a pretty good idea what is coming. It doesn't matter for what. They never talk to her without her being in trouble for something.

With a heavy sigh, her father gets up and steps forward, waving a piece of paper that he has clutched in his hand at her. His fingers are gripping it too tight, crumpling it.

"We got another letter!" he says angrily.

Her mother wipes a frustrated tear away, staring at her hard.

Anna stiffens, instantly on the defense.

"We've been getting letters and phone calls all year. We had to leave your brother alone to go to meetings at your school. We have gone past that now. They are contacting the truancy officer," her father continues. "Do you know what that means? It means they are going to investigate us for neglect! They are going to come in here and ask a lot of questions and treat us all like criminals! Like bad parents! All because you just can't bother going to school! We are at our wits end with you! How can we get it through to you that you have to go to school?"

Anna wants to yell back at him. The words scream out angrily in her head. "Maybe you are bad parents! You should not forget that you have two kids just because one is sick! Maybe it would be better for everyone if the truancy officer or family services just came and took me away since you don't have time for me and don't want me around anyway!"

She says nothing. Anna just stands there listening to her parents yell at her. Her parents continue yelling and lecturing at her, threatening all kinds of dire consequences both in and outside of their control. She lets their anger wash over her, tuning them out and not hearing the words anymore. She's heard the same lecture many times over.

"Yeah yeah," she says silently in her head. "I have to smarten up, straighten out, and stop messing around. I have to go to school. No more skipping, missing classes or being late.

You are taking away my allowance and grounding me. No TV, computer, or leaving the house except for school. But, how does an absent parent punish a child when they are never home to enforce the punishment? Grounding me doesn't mean anything when you are never here to make sure I obey."

"Do you understand?"

"Huh?" Anna almost says, looking up at her parents, shocked out of her internal dialogue with herself.

They are both standing there staring down at her angrily. Her mom's arms are crossed over her chest like an impenetrable shield, and she wonders for a second what her mother is defending against. Her father's hands are at his sides, tense like he is one word away from clenching them into hard fists.

For just a second fear courses through her and she thinks, "He's not going to spank me, is he?"

"I understand," she mumbles, trying to think fast and unable to remember what they just said.

"What? Say it so we know that you understand. You understand what?"

"Uh oh," Anna thinks. "What did they say? Ok, you got this. Just say something that sounds good. You are in trouble for missing school." She swallows to clear the lump from her throat.

"I won't miss the bus and be late anymore. I won't miss school."

"I'll try harder-," she pushes that though down. Try is always the wrong word to use. It makes it sound like she is not serious about doing what they want.

"I'll do better at school and help out more at home," Anna finishes.

She can tell by the slight nod of her mother's head and the lessening of the tight muscles in her dad's posture that she said the right things.

"Go to your room. You are there for the rest of the night." Her dad's hard voice has a hint of defeat. Her mother's grim expression has a new layer of fear as she watches Anna.

Anna turns and walks away obediently, going to her room and closing the door.

"Guess I'm not having supper tonight," she complains, sitting on her bed unhappily and looking around her new prison. She can already feel the hunger of an empty stomach gnawing at her.

"At least they're home for a change, even if I don't get to see them or anything because I'm stuck in here alone."

She looks at the computer, but thinks better of it. "If they come in to check and catch me on it when I'm grounded I'll have to stand through another lecture."

With nothing else to do, she swings her legs up and lies on her back on her bed, hands crossed over her stomach.

The sound of murmuring voices comes to her once she is quiet and still.

She can hear them talking even through the closed door and across the house. The house is too quiet, so sound carries through the heat grates and ducts. She listens, but can't hear what they're saying. She just knows it is about her and the desperate and frustrated tone tells her it's nothing good.

"I don't want to know what they're saying about me anyway," she pouts.

Anna sits up, staring at nothing and feeling miserable and alone.

"Even with them both home for once, I am still alone. I feel even more alone than I do when they're not here."

She looks at the door. It is not locked, but it might as well be. She looks at the window, thinking about crawling out, that they probably would not even notice. Not until the school calls to say she missed school again, anyway.

"They don't even care about me," she moans. "They would probably be happier if I was taken away. Then they wouldn't have to get letters and phone calls. They could just worry about Cole.

I wish I had someone to talk to."

She thinks about the months that she spent hanging around with Kylie after finding her tied down in a pool of toilet water in the bathroom.

"I finally didn't feel so alone. I was so busy worrying about Kylie and protecting her from those bullies that I didn't spend so much time thinking about Mom and Dad and Cole and being alone."

She misses her friendship with Kylie and still feels hurt over their fight.

"I wish I could take back the things I said to Kylie," she says unhappily. "I didn't really mean them. I was just mad, and not even mad at her. It's no use. Kylie will never forgive me. Why would she? If my own parents don't like me, why should anyone else? My friendship with Kylie is dead forever."

Andrew has been hanging around with Madison after school at the old abandoned building and the shed fort behind it regularly since that first day. They are there again today, having braved the route past Old Man Hooper's house and that nasty dog Caesar.

He won't admit that he is just as scared passing that house as Madison is. Boys are supposed to be tougher and braver. He is not sure which scares him more, Caesar or Old Man Hooper.

"A girl wouldn't have been my first choice for someone to hang around with," he thinks, watching her across the field, "but it sure beats sitting at home alone waiting for Mom and Dad to come home. I don't hear the noises from the basement when I'm not home to hear it."

Andrew is wandering aimlessly around the abandoned lot while Madison investigates a nasty looking old mattress, the latest piece of furniture to be dumped here.

"This lot seems to be a place for people to leave their junk that's too big for the garbage truck to take," he thinks. "The strangest thing is that it always vanishes within a day or two and then something else is left here. Who would take the stuff? Is there some weird garbage trade going on? Is someone leaving their junk to be picked up by someone else who would then leave theirs for someone else?"

He imagines people coming in beat up old pickup trucks or old cars pulling old utility trailers. They drive in behind the abandoned building and get out to check out what treasure was left this time, looking it over with interest and discussing its merits. If they decide they want it, they struggle to lift out whatever piece of junk furniture they have in the truck or trailer, depositing it next to the other before struggling to get their new treasure loaded. They drive away feeling very satisfied, taking it home to furnish their house.

"Must be pretty bad houses," he mutters, picturing shacks that are barely hammered together, probably windowless with a sheet for a door and an old wood stove for heat and cooking. They wouldn't even have electricity.

The basement would be one of those basements dug out from outside the house with the double doors that lay on the ground against the back wall of the house. It's the creepy kind of basement that feels more like a bomb shelter than a basement.

He pictures a boy like him struggling to open one of those heavy wooden doors, pulling it up and over on its hinges. The door bangs down on the ground when he drops it, leaving the dark rectangle of open blackness below. He moves around and struggles to open the other door, widening the hole in the ground.

Steep stairs that are more ladder than stairs vanish down into the blackness below.

The boy looks down into the darkness, trying to dare himself to go down. He hears a noise. Something is down there. The boy jumps to the other side of one of the doors, lifting it up to push the door over its apex and letting it fall closed with a loud bang. He hurries to close the other door too then scrambles for a branch to shove through the door handles, locking whatever is down there in.

Bored and a little unnerved with that game, Andrew turns his attention to the old brick building. The darkness of the building is an invitation that is pulling at him. He has no idea what the building was. You can see where there used to be a sign on the front, but it's long gone, probably fallen off.

"The whole building looks decayed and rotting. But brick is strong, so it can't be in that bad of a shape."

Madison has lost interest in the mattress. She looks at Andrew across the field, studying the big brick building. She knows he is itching to go in there. She leaves the old mattress and walks over to Andrew.

"Don't go in there," she warns him. She can see he's not really listening. Andrew is too interested in that old building. She shakes her head at him.

"It is not a good idea to go in there. There is nothing in there. It is just old and nasty and dangerous."

Madison takes him by the arm, pulling him away. Andrew reluctantly lets her pull him away but he can't help but look back.

Curiosity may have killed the cat, but it is eating away at him. He wants to know what it's like inside. He is sure it would be really cool going into an old abandoned building.

He looks back again as Madison drags him away towards the shack at the back of the lot. His breath catches and he blinks to clear his eyes.

"My eyes are playing tricks on me," he thinks. "For a second I thought I saw something move inside one of the broken basement windows, but it was gone so fast I must be imagining it."

"Come on, we'll explore over here," Madison says, still leading him towards the shed. They are pretending to be explorers discovering a new land.

Andrew can't shake the image out of his head. He goes along with Madison's game. They stomp around poking sticks at the ground. His mind keeps going back to that window. It makes him even more interested and he convinces himself it must be a cat.

"If a cat will go in there then there can't be anything to worry about," he thinks.

"I'm pretty sure I saw something in the window," Andrew says, finally telling Madison what he is thinking. He is sure she will tell him that he is just being dumb and refuse to have anything to do with it. He continues anyway. As brave as Andrew thinks he is and as much as he wants to go inside and explore that abandoned building, he would rather not do it alone.

"I'm pretty sure it was a cat," he says. "We should go check it out. Maybe it's stuck and needs help to get out."

Madison gives him a look that says she doesn't believe him. "Cats can jump and climb. If it got in then it can get out."

Andrew frowns, not willing to be put off so easily. "Come on, it won't hurt to look. We won't even go inside."

"I don't think it's a good idea."

"Chicken?"

She turns to look at his impish smile. He is daring her. "I can't let a boy win," she thinks. She gives in.

"Fine, we'll go look. But we'll only explore the outside of the building."

"Just the outside," he says. "We won't go in or anything, just look in through the windows."

Andrew is itching to get into that little storage shed built off the back of the building.

"That shed on the back could be a good second fort. I'll bet there's cool stuff in there. There has to be. I could test the door. There's another door near there too that looks weak. If we can get it open, we can get a look inside the building. Just to see of course; not to actually go in or anything."

Madison frowns doubtfully. "Maybe we should leave the doors alone."

"We aren't going in or anything, just looking."

Madison agrees despite having a bad feeling about this. "Fine, we'll check out the doors, but not go in," she says firmly.

Andrew nods eagerly.

"I don't feel safe anywhere anymore," Kylie whispers to herself unhappily, sitting on her bed alone with the door closed. Her eyes have dark circles from not sleeping and she looks like a hollow-eyed waif who is only half in this world.

"Not that I felt safer before. It's more than that now. I don't just not feel safe, I feel threatened. I feel like I'm always under attack, even when I'm tucked safely in my own bed with the doors locked and Mom in the next room.

Amber and her friends are absolutely everywhere now. They're constantly threatening and hurting me. It's worse than it has ever been. I have to watch for them on the way to the bus in the morning, all day at school, and going home from the bus every day.

They've never been after me this bad before."

Kylie is absolutely sick over it.

"The rumors the evil trio are spreading about me are worse than ever too. Everyone at school is giving me weird or mean looks and whispering about me. The whole school knows about the rumors and are talking about them. It doesn't matter that they are all lies. Nobody cares because it's more fun to believe nasty rumors they know aren't true."

She sighs miserably, her posture deflating with the air blowing out like a sagging balloon.

"I wish I never have to go to school again. I wish I was just dead, never even born. I hate myself for being so stupid."

Of course, she knows she isn't actually stupid, and she hasn't done anything really dumb, but she feels like she must be.

"I'm stupid and useless and dumb, or they wouldn't constantly be mean to me and everyone else wouldn't believe their lies about me."

If the constant stress of those three bullies always waiting for her everywhere wasn't bad enough, Kylie is also sure she has seen her father following her in a car a bunch of times.

Between the physical, mental, and emotional pain from those awful girls, and the fear that every car she sees is her dad, Kylie is beside herself with stress. She is absolutely desolate about it all.

"I just wish I was dead." Unhappily, she gets up and leaves her room, walking more like a zombie than a living girl, depression dragging her down into a black pit. She goes to the living room and drops into a chair.

Today her fears come true.

Kylie is sitting in the living room when she notices a car pull up and stop in front of the house. She gets up and goes to the window, peaking outside.

Her heart catches in her chest and her whole body tenses, her mouth going suddenly dry.

It's the very same car she thought she had seen following her; that she thought she had seen her dad in. "No, it can't be!"

Kylie starts to panic. Then she remembers. "Today is our first visit with Dad. The visits are starting again." Kylie feels sick and weak. Suddenly she can't think.

A car horn blares angrily outside.

Kylie hears her mother and sister coming from Becca's room, their voices soft murmurs as they talk quietly. She only makes out a few words. Her mother is trying to comfort her little sister, telling her everything will be okay.

"No, it isn't going to be okay," Kylie thinks.

She turns when they come into the living room. Her little sister looks pale and shaky like she does sometimes after having a bad nightmare. Her mom looks strained and tense. The deepened lines at the corners of her mouth and eyes show just how anxious she is.

"Mom is trying to be strong and not cry," Kylie thinks.

"It's time to go," her mother says with a little tremor to her voice.

"If she can be strong then so can I," Kylie tells herself silently. She nods and steps forward, taking her sister's hand.

She looks up at her mom. "It is going to be okay," she says.

Her mother looks at her, seeing the attempt to be brave, and has to swallow. Her breath hitches in her chest as she fights the tears, giving her girls a weak smile. The fear still shows through the smile.

"Come on," Kylie says, leading her sister to the door. They put on their jackets and shoes and go outside.

Their father is just leaning on the horn again as they step outside, letting loose another rude impatient blast. He looks annoyed.

With a last strained hug at the door, their mother hugging them a little too tight, she whispers in their ears as she releases them from her embrace, "Everything is going to be ok." But Kylie still doesn't believe her.

The girls reluctantly go down the steps and cross the yard to the car waiting at the curb while their mother retreats inside.

Their father waves at them as they approach the car, trying to smile.

Kylie reaches for the back door handle, hesitating. She doesn't want to touch the car.

Their father waves at them impatiently to get in and she grasps the handle and pulls the door open.

Scared, the girls slide into the back seat. The thud of the car door closing feels more like the door to a prison cell. Kylie looks out the window, feeling trapped and isolated.

Their father turns in the front seat to look back at them, smiling. His smile is off. It doesn't reach his eyes. His eyes are hard and angry.

"Not like they would be if he's happy to see us," Kylie thinks.

"Well now there's my girls!" he says too loudly, "Finally, I get to see my girls!"

The girls' mother watches through the crack between the closed living room curtains as the car drives away, tears streaming down her face.

He takes them out for ice cream, making a big show of it in the ice cream parlor. The girls follow him in, heads down and unsmiling, trying to be invisible.

"What kind of ice cream do you want?" he booms, looking around at the few other customers before leaning in over the ice cream cooler filled with tubs of colorful ice creams. "Only the best ice cream for my girls."

He waves them over and they mutely approach the display, not really looking. Becca caves, drawn by the enchantment of an ice cream treat. She starts eying the ice cream, her lips curling up in a small smile and her eyes devouring the selection.

"Which flavor do you want Becca?" he asks.

She points at a bright orange ice cream that tastes like creamsicles. Oblivious to her pointing, he announces, "I know, you want Tiger Tiger." He looks at the clerk, who is looking at the child doubtfully. "One Tiger Tiger."

Becca's lip comes out a bit and she looks at the clerk for help.

"What is it?" their father asks, impatience already showing.

"I don't like Tiger Tiger," she says in a small timid voice.

His eyes flash. "Since when? It's your favorite. She'll take Tiger Tiger. You think I don't know my kid's favorite ice cream?"

"She never liked Tiger Tiger," Kylie thinks, keeping her thoughts to herself. "It tastes like black licorice and she hates black licorice."

"Kylie, what kind do you want?" He turns to her.

Kylie shrugs. "I don't know. Vanilla, I guess."

"Oh come on, you can have anything. Sorbet. How about Sorbet? She'll have Sorbet. I'll have Rocky Road."

Becca watches while the lady behind the counter scoops out the black and orange ice cream, taking the cone when it's handed to her and looking at it with disgust. She is crestfallen as she watches the orange ice cream she wanted be scooped into a cone and handed to Kylie.

Kylie takes the ice cream unhappily. "He doesn't even know that I don't like Sorbet," she thinks. "He doesn't know what either of us like."

With the ice creams handed out and paid for, their dad leads them out. With his attention elsewhere, Kylie nudges Becca, offering her the orange ice cream.

"Trade," she mouths the word.

Becca glances uneasily at their dad, worried he will get mad.

Kylie pushes the cone towards her again and she looks at it wistfully.

"You don't like it either," Becca says, meaning the black and orange ice cream.

"That's okay."

They trade and Becca happily eats her Sorbet ice cream. Kylie tries not to make faces while she eats the licorice ice cream.

Their dad finishes his ice cream quickly and looks at them impatiently. Kylie has made little progress on her ice cream, and her sister is only half finished.

"Hurry up, let's go." He gives them enough time for one more lick before he snatches their ice creams away and tosses them in a nearby garbage. "You're done. You're taking too long."

Becca almost cries, but manages to hold it back. He doesn't like it when they cry. Kylie is grateful she doesn't have to finish the awful licorice treat.

"Next stop, the mall," their dad announces, taking them back to the car.

"Your mom kept you from me for so long," he complains as they are driving. "I missed out on so much time with my girls. Today we are going to make up for that. We are going to the mall and you can get whatever you want."

Kylie rolls her eyes, not believing him. Her sister gives a little uncertain smile.

At the mall, he walks fast and proud, talking too loudly about how he's shopping for his girls. He drags them through the mall, making a big show of taking them shopping. They go from store to store, loudly showing off how generous he is without actually buying anything. He keeps looking around proudly as if to make sure everyone sees and hears what a wonderful father he is. The whole production feels phony and makes Kylie embarrassed and sick.

"The man he tries to pretend to be in front of all these strangers isn't who he really is," Kylie thinks. "Are these people really buying this? He's so phony."

Being younger and desperately wanting to have a normal happy family, Becca's guard slowly drops and she buys into their dad's pretend happy family. She even starts enjoying herself and looking at things she likes.

They enter a store filled with toys and games, and Becca's eyes fall immediately on a doll. The doll's arms and legs are chubby like a baby. Large yellow curls of soft hair cover her head and hang down past her waist. Her cheeks are round and lightly colored with a pink blush, her pouty lips pinker, and her large bright blue eyes are bordered by long dark eyelashes. The dress is a fancy number that looks like she should be at a garden party with princes and princesses.

Becca's eyes grow larger and her face breaks into a big smile. "I found it Daddy, I found what I want." She rushes over to the doll, almost afraid to touch it.

He gives her an annoyed look, walking past the doll towards the other end of the aisle and boasting again about how he's buying gifts for his kids as if he didn't hear her. The girls know they are expected to follow.

"I haven't seen my girls in so long. Their mother is getting revenge on me by keeping them from me. I'm going to buy them anything they want. I'll buy them the whole store!"

"Daddy, can I get the doll? I really really want it. Please? Please please please. It's the only think I want and you won't have to get me anything else. Please Daddy?" Becca looks up at him hopefully.

The facade slips and the real man shows. His mouth and eyes turn ugly with anger, his body stiffens, and he turns to her, speaking with a low threatening voice.

"Shut up. I'm not buying that."

"But Daddy, you said you would buy us whatever we want." Becca's enthusiasm slips a little. But as the very young are prone to, she holds onto hope. "Please Daddy, please. You promised."

"No. Stop it." He starts trying to move them on.

Kylie tries to signal her sister to drop it.

Undeterred, Becca tries again.

"It's the only thing I want. You won't have to get me anything else. Even if you get Kylie ten things, I only want this." She's looking up at him hopefully, a whine in her voice by the end.

Their dad turns away, a string of foul language erupting from his mouth in an angry torrent. He turns on Becca, swearing at her.

The store clerk gives them an annoyed look at the foul words that come from his mouth as he swears at the little girl. The clerk's look changes to alarm when she sees the man grab the little girl roughly by the arm, his fingers digging in painfully as he squeezes too hard, and gives the child a sharp little shake.

"Not another sound!"

Becca stares up at him, her eyes filling with tears, afraid.

He shoves her off, looking around quickly to make sure no one saw, catching the clerk's concerned look and looking away.

"She didn't see if he pretends she didn't," Kylie thinks. "It always works that way. It's easier for adults to ignore it than to say something; to tell him not to treat kids that way."

He gives Becca a hate-filled glare and puts a smile back on his face before he turns around again. He scans the area for an audience and starts talking loudly about how generous he is when it comes to his girls, walking out of the store and expecting them to follow.

"This is my day with my girls after their mom kept them from me. It's a big day, finally getting to see them again. Anything for my girls. What do you want? Let's go look in another store. I'd give my girls absolutely anything they want. Whatever you want, girls, it's yours."

He seems oblivious to the hurt and scared look on Becca's face. She stares at the lost doll, turns and watches him walk away.

Kylie tries to comfort her sister without him seeing. If he sees, he will get angrier. Becca just stares after him mutely, her newly found excitement over her dad gone, her bottom lip sticking out and pouty and tears burning at her eyes.

"Do not cry," Kylie whispers the warning quietly into her sister's ear. "It will only make him worse." She leads her out of the store, dutifully following him.

He leads them around, store to store, the two girls following submissively while he keeps announcing what a great caring and generous father he is. Their mopey behavior isn't lost on him, and he finally stops and whirls on them, startling them.

They cringe and freeze in their steps, trying to be smaller when he stops and turns on them, leaning down threateningly over them.

"What's the matter with you two?" he hisses. "I take you out for a treat; this is for you, not me. Do you think I want to spend the day wandering the mall? This is all for you. And you two just sulk and mope. If that's how you want it, then we're going home. Let's go."

A glimmer of hope sprouts in Kylie and Becca. He's going to take them home.

He turns away again, the girls half jogging to keep up with his angry pace, leading them out to the car.

Their hope dies when they realize the moment he pulls up in front of an apartment block; they are not going home yet.

He takes them back to his apartment where, on entering, his mood switches gears again. Smiling, he spreads his arms, sweeping them out to direct their attention to the apartment.

"What do you think? Huh? How do you like it? It even has a second bedroom. Go on, look around."

The girls step forward hesitantly, uneasily looking around the strange apartment.

"You've never been in my new apartment. Come on. Make yourselves at home. Are you thirsty? Do you want something to drink?"

He hurries to the kitchen area, the kitchen and living room making up one room, and gets them sodas.

"Mom doesn't let us-," Becca starts, her voice small.

Kylie flashes her a warning look, but it's too late. The words are already coming out of her mouth.

Their dad is turning from the fridge as Becca speaks. He bangs the soda cans down on the counter so hard they are sure to fizzle up and spray out when opened.

"I don't care what your mother doesn't let you do. She's not here, is she?"

He puts a forced smile on his face. "I'm so happy you're here. This is going to be a great visit. Wait! I have presents for you."

He rushes off to one of the bedrooms, leaving the two baffled girls staring after him. They exchange uneasy looks.

"Whatever it is, pretend you like it," Kylie whispers.

He comes back with the presents, giving them to the girls eagerly. The girls open them without the joy that usually come with unexpected gifts.

Kylie takes the gift bag he hands her, nervously peeking inside. She feels like she is walking a thin wire over a bed of broken light bulb glass and one wrong step will make her fall into those very sharp shards of glass that will cut her to pieces. The stress is absolutely exhausting.

She pulls out a shirt with great relief. It's not even ugly and it looks like it will fit. She holds her breath when he hands a gift bag to her sister.

Becca doesn't smile when she digs through the tissue paper inside for the gift.

"Please don't make a bad face, please don't make a bad face," Kylie prays silently. Again, relief brings her anxiety down a notch as her sister pulls out a doll that isn't too bad.

They continue this through the rest of the presents, three for each girl. Surprisingly, the gifts don't totally suck. They are all cheap, but decent.

"Thank you," Kylie says, trying to sound like she means it. She nudges her sister.

"Thank you," Becca says, her voice still low and sad, still upset over how he treated her earlier.

The girls sit meekly waiting for instructions, unsure what to do and feeling awkward.

"What should we do now?" their dad asks. "I know; a game." He gets up and pulls out a game. It's an old game that he must have borrowed for today.

He sets it up and they start muddling through playing. None of them know how to play it and there are no instructions in the box.

He keeps a big smile on his face, talking loudly, and making a big production about the visit. He doesn't fool the girls though.

They can see the anger barely controlled beneath his pretending to be happy to see them.

The girls act stiff and uncertain and it only makes him angrier, so they try to act more normal and that makes him angrier too.

Finally, with both girls intentionally letting him win, the game comes to an end.

"Time for supper," he announces. They sit in uncomfortable silence, mostly looking at the floor, while he cooks supper. When it's finished, he sets plates on the table, calling them, "Come and eat."

They come to the table obediently and sit looking down at their plates. It looks completely unappetizing to both girls. Their dad never had been able to cook.

Kylie picks up her fork and pokes at the food on her plate. Her sister doesn't move. Their dad clenches his jaw, holding himself back from snapping at them to eat. Kylie pokes something on her plate and brings it to her mouth, her sister watching her to see if she survives. She chews and swallows, working hard to keep her face blank. It tastes awful.

Encouraged by Kylie's lack of falling out of her chair dead, Becca takes a tentative first bite. She doesn't have the same control as her sister and her face twists into a grimace at the foul taste.

"What's wrong?" Their dad's expression is hard, his eyes and mouth angry.

"N-nothing," Becca manages, forcing herself to chew and swallow.

They continue through supper, having trouble eating, but they do their best to swallow it and keep it down without a complaint.

When Becca almost vomits up her supper, Kylie gives her a terrified look and her sister bravely swallows against her stomach trying to gag and spit up the food. They both feel sick as much from the stress as they do from the horrible food.

Seeing Becca gag, their father slams his hand on the table with a loud bang.

"What's wrong with it?" He glares at each of them defiantly.

Becca cringes when his arm lashes out towards her. He snatches Becca's plate away, inspecting it and glaring at her over the plate.

"N-n-nothing," she manages to squeak out.

"Then eat it!" He smacks the plate down in front of her so hard he nearly breaks it, making her jump and almost cry out.

They manage to get through the rest of dinner without more than his angry glares while he wolfs down his meal and gets up and starts angrily washing dishes. He keeps looking at them, insulted by their slow eating.

After supper he turns on the television and plops himself in a chair, angrily sulking.

With nowhere else to go, the girls can only sit there on the couch in silence. They are strung out on a thin wire of anxiety. The tension is terrible.

As the evening continues, both girls feel his anger growing. Kylie keeps looking at the clock, trying to be discrete, watching the time tick by painfully slowly towards the time he's supposed to return them home.

At the end of the visit, things turn ugly. Their father turns on them suddenly, jumping from his chair to tower over them, his posture threatening and his eyes full of hatred.

"Why are you two acting so weird?" he demands. "Your mother has been putting junk in your heads about me hasn't she?"

Kylie flinches even though she tries not to and Becca inches closer to her for safety.

"Your mother turned you against me, didn't she?" he yells, followed by a string of foul words that makes both girls' faces turn red. They are frozen in fear, staring at him.

Kylie wants to tell him to stop, but she knows that would be a dumb thing to do. It will only make him madder.

Their father's rant goes on and on. He is working himself up, getting himself angrier, and it's a terrible and frightening thing to see.

Kylie almost jumps at a touch. She turns; her heart feeling like someone is holding it tight in their fist. It's Becca moving closer, half hiding behind her and clinging to her. She looks down at her frightened face, the big teary eyes, and puts a comforting arm around her.

"I won't let him hurt you," Kylie whispers, afraid their father might hear.

Suddenly he is on top of them, looming over them and glaring down.

Kylie's breath catches in her chest. "He heard," she thinks desperately.

"Your mother will be sorry," he hisses. "She'll pay. I'll kill her before I let her get away with this."

"Get away with what?" Kylie's mind reels with confusion. She has no idea what he's talking about. What did her mother do? Then she remembers. His rant started with him saying her mother turned them against him.

"But you did it, not her," she thinks. You're the one who has always been so angry and mean to us." She keeps silent, not daring to say a word.

"I'm going to take you away from her forever," he says, staring directly into Kylie's eyes with a cruel smile as if to make sure she understands. Or, perhaps he is looking for a certain reaction. Fear? Despair? She doesn't know. Whatever it is, if they react wrong it will make him furious.

"One of these visits I won't take you back home. You'll live with me forever and she'll never see you again." He is gloating over the pain he knows this will cause their mother.

"This is horrible!" Kylie thinks. "He doesn't even like us! If he did, he would be nicer to us. He wouldn't treat us like he hates us. We don't want to live with him! And never see mom again?" Her thoughts turn to Becca hiding behind her.

Kylie mentally wishes her sister to keep quiet, to not react, but it's too late.

Becca is crying with a look of horror. The tears are flowing freely, her face is scrunched up and turning red and she is openly and loudly bawling.

Their father turns his head to stare at Becca behind her. His mouth tightens and his eyes harden even more.

Kylie's nerves are jangling and screaming "DANGER!"

She flinches but is powerless to move or act, frozen with shock and fear, when he suddenly reaches out and grabs Becca by the arm.

He pulls her towards him too roughly, banging her into Kylie as he yanks Becca from behind her, pulling her off the chair. His grip is painfully tight and he shakes the little girl angrily, scaring and hurting her more.

"WHY ARE YOU CRYING?" he screams in her face.

Kylie's heart breaks for her sister as the little girl trembles before his rage. Kylie manages to break her paralysis and tries to help.

"Sh-she just m-misses you," Kylie sputters, having trouble making her tongue work in her fear, getting up to stand before the chair.

He lets go of the younger girl and turns his attention to Kylie. She steps forward, putting herself between her father and her sister. It was the right thing to say. He's still angry, but he walks away instead of continuing his attack on Becca.

The remaining minutes left in the visit feels like it drags on for days. Their father continues to be a volcano of anger bubbling beneath the surface and ready to explode at any moment.

"Let's go," he suddenly barks. "It's time to drop you off with your mother."

The girls look at him in shock, trying to hide the relief that floods them. Becca moves to collect her presents.

"That stays here." He glares at her, snatching the doll out of her hands. "I don't trust your mother. She'll probably throw it out. Anything I give you stays here, where it's safe."

Unhappy she can't keep her gifts, Becca would have pouted if she wasn't afraid it would make him angry. She follows her father and sister out.

By the time he drops the girls off at home, they are both upset, out of sorts, and feeling traumatized. They spent the endless minutes of the car ride home in fear that he will keep his threat about not letting them ever go home again.

Neither girl really believes he will let them go until after they quickly exit the car in front of their house and run for the door, expecting him to chase them and catch them and drag them back to the car.

It's not until the door is closed and locked behind them that the girls can breathe a sigh of relief.

Their mother had been anxiously watching at the window all day and only managed to stop crying a short time before her daughters came home.

She meets them at the door, quickly closing and locking it against the hateful man in the car. She grabs her daughters and holds them close, the three of them clinging desperately to each other and crying in their relief.

They each listen for the sound of the car driving away, afraid he will not leave and feeling alone in that fear they each keep to themselves.

"Okay girls," their mother says at last, "it's been a long and tiring day. Let's get you ready for bed."

It's early for Kylie to go to bed, but she's exhausted from the hours of stress and fear and doesn't complain. Becca is too upset to sleep and ends up going to bed with their mother.

Kylie lays in the growing darkness of her room, staring at the shadows the last weak fading daylight casts across the wall through the window.

"I wish I had someone to talk to," she whispers to the darkness. She thinks about Anna.

"I miss our friendship and still feel hurt over our fight. I said some mean things that I didn't mean. I wish I could take back what I said."

She swallows, but the lump in her throat won't go away. She fights the tears.

"We are going to have to go back and see Dad again. I hate him. I don't ever want to see him again. Why? Why is the judge making us see him? Why does the judge hate us so much?

I wish I was dead. Then I'd never have to see him again. I wish I was never even born, that I never existed."

It will be a long night with little sleep for the troubled girl.

Dylan is in the hallway at school when he spots Kylie moving down the hall. She seems to be all hunched into herself like she is trying to be invisible.

"She looks more upset today than usual, all haunted and broken inside," he thinks. "I wonder if something happened. I bet it has something to do with the nasty rumors Amber and her friends are spreading about her. They are all lies. Everyone knows it. But it doesn't stop them from repeating them and having fun with them."

A few heads turn to follow Kylie as she makes her way through the kids in the hall, keeping her head down, arms hugging her books tight to her chest, and doing her best to pretend she doesn't notice. She avoids looking at anyone and ignores the looks and comments directed at her.

"Don't look, don't hear. Don't look, don't hear," she keeps repeating the mantra in her head, trying to block out the snickers and comments she hears as she goes by.

Dylan's anger flares. He tenses, his weight shifting into a fighting stance, his eyes narrowing. "I want to grab every one of them and shake them until they stop and just leave her alone," he thinks.

Kylie passes him and blanches. She still has to look up enough to see where she is going so she doesn't walk into anyone and she sees his angry stare directed at her as she approaches.

"Don't hurt me," she pleads silently, forcing herself to not openly look at him, "please just leave me alone."

"She still can't even stand to look at me," Dylan thinks, feeling the stab of pain at the imagined rejection.

He watches Kylie go and sees Amber before either of the girls see each other. His jaw clenches and his whole body tenses as he watches the inevitable about to happen.

"Those three have been going after Kylie worse than ever before. They left her alone while she was hanging around with that other girl. I was happy Kylie finally found a friend, and one that protected her. But now they aren't friends anymore and Amber and her friends are after her all the time. I don't like it, but I don't know what to do about it. I wish I could do something."

Amber pauses when she spots Kylie. Her expression changes to cruel delight and she starts pushing through the crowd towards Kylie, moving in for the kill.

Dylan decides to try intervening by distracting Amber. It's a sudden decision that he acts on before he has a chance to think about it. He is stepping forward thinking, "What are you doing?

Do you even have any idea how to stop her? No, you don't. Just stop Amber. That's it? The other two just do whatever Amber says. They can't think for themselves. She's the one I have to stop."

Amber feels the rush of thrill as she heads for Kylie. She has no idea what she is going to do, but she is determined to do something. Suddenly her path is blocked by a body as Dylan steps in front of her.

Amber barely pauses, moving to go around the body only to have it move with her, still blocking her path. Her lips tighten into an angry line and she looks up, ready to tear into whoever is in her way.

Amber blinks in surprise to see Dylan standing before her and her heart skips a beat. Her breath catches in her chest. She looks past him quickly to her victim, but is so thrilled that he is actually looking at her like he might talk to her that she can't move.

"Hey," Dylan says in the universal greeting of their school, looking down at her.

Amber barely manages to squeak out a "hey" in return and silently scolds herself for being so dumb.

Kylie sees Amber appear from behind a couple of kids, headed straight for her with that hateful glint in her eye that she knows all too well, and blanches.

"Why won't she just leave me alone?" she moans inwardly, wishing she could just shrink and disappear.

She quickly assesses possible escape routes and knows it is useless.

"I'm dead meat," she thinks. She braces herself for it, whatever the attack might be. Amber could shove her hard, trip her, slam her books out of her hands, anything.

Dylan steps between them and Kylie watches Amber's eyes flash with irritation as she tries to dodge around him, only to have him move with her. She sees the anger.

"What happens when the worst she bully in school goes after the worst he bully?" But the anger quickly turns to confusion and an awe that makes Kylie's stomach feel sick.

"My tormentor and the jerk," Kylie thinks. They're standing in the hall staring at each other and she shrinks at the sight of the two worst bullies in school together, talking.

"They're probably conspiring against me. I have to get out of here!" She slinks away feeling absolutely wretched and hollow inside.

Dylan has no idea what to say to the girl standing before him. He is still in shock that he said hello to her. He has never had to talk to her before and would have preferred to keep it that way.

"Ugh," he thinks, "I don't like Amber. What do I even say?" He has hardly talked to any girls before. It turns out it won't be a problem.

After a brief awkward moment staring at each other, Dylan flees, walking away quickly like nothing happened.

Amber stares after him in confusion and excitement.

"I don't know what to do to keep Amber and her friends from constantly going after Kylie," Dylan thinks, feeling his face flush with the shame of fleeing from a girl. "I can't hit them and threaten them because they're girls. I'll have to run interference somehow whenever I see Amber ready to pounce and go after Kylie."

The same clumsy moment repeats itself over the next few days with Amber trying to go after Kylie only to find Dylan standing in her way looking at her, tongue-tied and unable to talk.

After the first couple of very awkward times that he stopped Amber to try to talk to her, she broke the silence. Once Amber started talking, she just would not stop. He never had to talk. Unfortunately for Dylan, Amber thinks the sudden attention means he likes her back.

Seeing the two together often all of a sudden, Kylie only becomes more convinced the two are going to gang up to get her.

"The two worst bullies in the school working together against me," she moans, watching them with a sick feeling.

"Between worrying about whatever they're plotting and having to see Dad, my life is more miserable than it has ever been. I just wish I was dead."

She is so stressed out worrying over Dylan and Amber and what they might be planning to do to her that she doesn't even notice that Amber's attacks have mostly stopped again. Of course, Amber's two hench-girls didn't stop. They still shove her, trip her, knock her books out of her hands, and anything else they can do whenever they see her.

Amber is so thrilled. Dylan moves off from one of their brief hallway encounters and she turns and rushes to her friends waiting a little way down the hall. Jessica looks a little miffed. Brooke's expression reveals the hope in her heart, that this will mean an end to Amber's obsession with Kylie.

"He likes me!" Amber beams at her friends. "I'm sure he's going to ask me to the spring dance."

"Dylan is going to be my boyfriend!" Amber squeals.

Still in earshot hiding around a corner, Kylie hears this. It sickens her. She leans against the wall to steady herself, feeling it wash through her.

"This is even worse than them just ganging up on me. They aren't just two bullies now, they are boyfriend and girlfriend bullies."

She stumbles off down the hall, feeling hollow and wrung out.

9 The Spring Dance

It is the day of the spring dance, and with it spring break is only days away. After that, summer break will come fast with all the extra work being put into preparing for the last projects and exams for the final report card marks. The dance is only a few days away.

Most of the girls in school have been excited and in a tizzy over the spring dance for weeks. None of them are really allowed to date yet, but that doesn't stop them from dreaming about it and talking about it.

Then there are the officially unofficially dating couples. Those who everyone knows are 'dating', although they may not even talk to each other for days or even weeks. Everyone is wondering who will take who, unofficially of course, to the dance and which boys will ask which girls to dance.

Amber was getting more anxious and excited the closer it gets to the day of the spring dance. Today she is bursting with it.

"I was so sure Dylan was going to ask me to go with him. So why hasn't he? The dance is tonight and he hasn't asked me yet." She stares dreamily at Dylan across the way, him oblivious to her watching him.

"Well I'm going to the dance anyway!" Amber says with an exaggerated pout. "Just because he hasn't asked me yet, doesn't mean he won't ask me to dance." She sighs, smiling. "He probably thinks I should just know he's taking me, since he is going to be my boyfriend."

Her eyes light up. "Maybe he'll ask me at the dance to be his girlfriend."

Jessica and Brooke are jealous and getting really sick of hearing her go on about Dylan. They don't think anyone would ask them even to dance one dance.

Jessica tries not to roll her eyes in annoyance. They just smile and nod and agree with her. Neither wants to tell Amber what they are thinking.

"I wish she would just shut up and stop talking about him," Jessica groans inwardly. "If he didn't ask her yet then he probably won't."

"Ugh, Dylan Dylan Dylan," Brooke moans inwardly, "enough already. He seems to be more tolerating Amber hanging off his every word than acting like a boy who wants to impress her. But then, boys like Dylan don't have to make an effort to impress a girl. They only have to acknowledge her and that's enough."

Amber just keeps talking on and on about herself and Dylan, completely oblivious to the eye rolling boredom of her friends.

"There is just one thing I haven't figured out yet," Amber continues. "How am I going to see Dylan after school closes for summer?"

All around school heads are filled with visions of everyone dancing and having a great time just like in the movie dances. The decorations will be great, the music better, some kids will get into trouble, and they will all leave feeling like new people. Others are imagining the awkward moments with dread, planning to avoid the dance.

"Dance smanse! I don't care about the spring dance and I'm getting sick of hearing about it. I wasn't even going to go until some of my friends convinced me to." Madison is looking through her closet, trying to decide what to wear.

"I'm looking forward to spring break. Two weeks of no school. No homework. No daycare. Just home and doing whatever I want."

She pauses, looking at herself in the mirror. "Oh yeah, I forgot. I was so excited, this is going to be my first spring break out of daycare. All summer long too, I'll be home alone all day."

The idea is a little scary. What if someone is at the door? Her parents warned her against answering the door to strangers when they aren't home. "What if someone breaks in while I'm home alone?"

She thinks about the basement with a sinking feeling of dread, and the strange noises she sometimes hears. She is pretty sure it's coming from down there. Worse, she thinks about the absolute unfailing total and complete boredom. All summer long she is going to have nothing to do. She starts changing her clothes, getting ready for the dance.

"I need to make a plan. I am not going to just sit at home alone all day every day if I can help it. At least I have the secret fort and Andrew to hang around with. But I don't think that will be enough. I need to find some more kids in the area to hang around with. Some of my friends are going away for part of the summer with their family or are staying with relatives. Andrew is the only one who will be around all the time."

"Madison, are you ready to go?" her mom calls.

Madison scrambles to finish getting ready, calling out, "I'm ready."

She sits on the edge of her seat for the drive to school, both excited and dreading this. It's her first dance. She never bothered going to the others, feeling too self-conscious to go.

"Have fun," her mother says as she gets out of the car. Madison looks back at her mom and waves, then turns and jogs to the school door. She stops at the door, taking a deep breath, and pulls it open. Other kids are arriving. Some were already there and are talking excitedly, grouping up in their cliques before they go inside. She can hear music coming from the gym, where the dance is being held.

Madison walks into the dance, stopping to take in the decorations. It's not nearly as dark as she expected. The gym is decorated with a few balloons and steamers and a big banner painted with spring flowers. Some of the chairs used for concerts and other big events in the gym are set up for people to sit on. A row of tables has bowls of punch and some potato chips. The gym teacher, Mr. Barns, is sitting at a table playing music on the gym P.A. system. It sounds just as bad as it does for everything else they use that old machine for.

"There are not very many kids here. Not like in the movies, where the whole school shows up and the gym is packed."

Madison looks around at the kids awkwardly standing around until she spots one of her friends. She rushes over to her, feeling better not being alone.

Anna wasn't planning on going to the dance, but her dad is working and her mom is at the hospital as usual. She is home alone and is bored and lonely.

"Dances are stupid." She thinks about the other kids who will be there having fun. She will be by herself alone in a crowd, probably sitting in a corner somewhere. Nobody even knows she's there because they don't care. "Dances are totally lame."

She pushes down the sadness and loneliness that fills her. She is just so tired of feeling lonely and unhappy all the time.

"The other kids always seem to be happy. On TV they are stupidly happy in their perfect little worlds." She pushes the thought away. It will only bring her down.

She looks at the clock impatiently, then at the dead television set, and shrugs.

"Whatever," she grumbles. "I might as well go. It's not like I have anything else to do. At least I can maybe laugh at everyone there."

She hopes nobody will notice that she doesn't have a parent dropping her off and picking her up. That could be a problem when she tries to leave to go home.

"They probably won't even notice," she mutters. "They never notice whether I take the bus or not anyway."

Anna makes a brief half-hearted attempt at fixing herself up. She's not a girlie girl, so there's no wasting time fussing over her hair and stuff. Just a quick wash of her face, brush through her hair, and making sure there is no obvious dirt on her clothes, and she is good to go.

She checks the clock. "Good. I won't be one of the first ones there. Those kids will look dumb hanging around the gym by themselves. I also won't be so late that everyone will notice me coming in.

I should get there right when mobs of parents are dropping kids off," she nods.

Anna hops on her bike and rides to school.

Andrew is getting ready for the spring dance. He puts his hands under the running water in the bathroom sink, slicking back his hair with his wet hands. He shuts the water off and quickly runs the comb through his hair. If he doesn't, his mother would just send him back to comb his hair anyway.

He's not going because he wants to go to the dance. He thinks the whole dance thing is pretty lame. He's going because he has a plan.

"After Mom drops me off I just have to go in long enough to make sure I'm seen," he thinks. "Then I'm out of there.

I've been itching to check out the attached shed and back door on that old abandoned building. Madison chickened out when I tried to pry it open and wouldn't let me. This is my chance.

I'm sneaking off on my own tonight to go there and inspect the doors to see if I can get inside to check that place out."

He goes to the kitchen to find his mom. "I'm ready," he announces.

She looks him up and down, giving him a little frown. "Is that what you're wearing?"

He looks down at himself. He's wearing the same jeans he wore to school, the hems at the bottoms of the legs worn rough, a few broken strings of fabric hanging loose, and a small hole in one knee. The shirt is the same he wore all day too, complete with a spaghetti stain from supper.

"What?"

She sighs. "Go change your shirt at least. It has a stain on it."

Andrew grins. "That way everybody knows what I had for supper."

"Go change."

He shrugs and slouches out of the room to change his shirt; coming back a minute later with a new shirt and his hair messed from the quick change.

"Shouldn't you dress better than that?" his mother says, clearly not impressed. "It's a dance. You should dress up just a little."

"Nah," Andrew shakes his head. "Then I'll look like a wuss. All the guys will be dressed like this. Nobody dresses up for these things."

She looks at him skeptically, thinking that a boy going to a dance should at least wear nicer pants than blue jeans with ratty bottoms and a hole. She lets it go. It's just a junior dance. The kids aren't even old enough for dating yet.

"Your hair," she says.

"I combed it. You made me change," he complains, flattening it down with the palms of his hands.

"All right then. Let's get going. I'll pick you up out front of the school when it's over."

"Ok Mom," he nods with a grin.

She catches the eagerness and wonders. "Andrew isn't the going to a dance kind of boy," she thinks. "I half suspect he is up to something, but can't think what." She grabs her purse and keys and they get in the car.

"Who are you meeting there?" she asks.

"The guys." It's the expected noncommittal answer.

Dylan walks into the dance trying to look casual and looks around. He doesn't see Kylie and feels an instant pang of disappointment.

"Maybe I should just leave, go back home," he thinks. "Should I wait and see if she shows up or leave?" He can't decide.

"I don't know why I even bothered coming. School dances are for nerds, jerks, sucks, and girls." The decision to go was last minute. The other guys all said they weren't going either and horsed around making fun of anyone who was. Dylan won't admit it to anyone, but he was hoping to see Kylie there even though he doesn't have the guts to talk to her or anything.

He spots a couple of the guys across the gym, trying to look casual and obviously feeling as awkward and out of place as he is. They duck when they spot him, not wanting to be seen.

"Huh, cowards," Dylan mumbles.

Dylan is just about to turn when he is suddenly surrounded by girls. His first reaction is surprise and thinking he's just in their way. He tries to step aside, but they cluster around him, blocking him from going. He feels a rush of anxiety. He looks around at the faces and his heart sinks.

Amber is hanging onto his arm and staring up at him with a dreamy smile. Jessica and Brooke are at least keeping their hands off him but they are staring up at him expectantly too.

"Uh, hi," he says awkwardly. If he had any idea that Amber thinks she is going to be his date he would not have come.

"I'm not going to this stupid dance," Kylie complains, sitting on her bed pouting. "I don't even know why Mom is making me go. I don't want to go. What for? So the whole school can look and point fingers and laugh at me? So Amber and Dylan and the mean team can come after me and bully me? So I can get beat up?

With everything going on in my life right now, going to a stupid dance is the last thing I want to do."

She gets up unhappily, looking at her sallow face in the mirror, seeing the bags under her eyes, her hollow cheeks.

"Oh yay," her voice is sarcastic. "I get to go look stupid standing by myself in a corner, the only one with no friends." She is wallowing in pain and misery from every side; because of the bullying, losing her only friend, Anna, and now having to see her dad again.

Kylie also can't stop worrying constantly about what her dad might do. She is scared he will follow through on his threats to steal her and her sister from their mom.

Her mother knocks on the bedroom door, opening it and walking in. She gives Kylie a hopeful smile that she doesn't feel. She wants her to go to the dance, hoping it will get some of the worry off her chest, even only for a couple of hours.

"Ready?"

"Mom, I don't want to go," Kylie whines, looking at her hopelessly.

"Come on," her mother insists, "it will do you some good. You'll have fun, I promise."

"No I won't," Kylie mutters stubbornly. "Amber and her friends will be there and I don't have any friends at all."

"None at all?" Her mother asks, not believing it. "What about your new friend, Anna?"

"She isn't my friend anymore," Kylie says moodily. "With all the stuff Amber says about me, the whole school hates me, even Anna."

Her mother looks at her thoughtfully. She knows girls always exaggerate these things. They always say they have no friends at all, but then you see them running off with a whole gaggle of friends.

The haunted look in Kylie's eyes pulls at her and she almost changes her mind.

"No," she decides, "Kylie is going. It will do her some good to get out with her friends."

"Get dressed, you're going," she says.

Kylie stalks off angrily to her dresser, yanking clothes out roughly.

"I do not want to go to that stupid dance!" she complains.

"You have five minutes." Her mother leaves her to get dressed.

Kylie angrily yanks her clothes off and the new ones on. She savagely rips the brush through her hair and shoves it into a ponytail. She looks at herself in the mirror.

"I hate you Kylie. I hate you and I hate everything about you. I wish you were dead."

She turns to leave the room, thinking sadly, "I wish I could just disappear, that I never existed. I wish I was dead."

When her mother stops the car in front of the school, Kylie looks around nervously for the bullies.

"It's not going to be that bad. You'll have fun," her mother says.

"No, I won't," Kylie thinks. She gets out, waves goodbye, and goes into the school, trying to be invisible. She peeks out to see her mother's car still sitting there.

"She's making sure I stay," she sighs miserably. The car drives off, making her thought a lie. She looks around at the other kids and towards the gym where the music is coming from.

"I already feel out of place at school. I just don't fit in anywhere with anyone. Going to the dance will be pure torture. I belong at the dance even less than I do at school."

The dance started more than half an hour ago and kids are still showing up. The gym isn't filling up like everyone's expectations and they didn't turn the lights low enough for the flashing colored lights to look like much of anything.

There will be no slow dances in the dark.

The girls all sigh in disappointment and relief as they look around at the boys clustered across the gym from them.

As with every dance, the boys are mostly standing around awkwardly on one side of the gym trying not to look at the girls. They know the girls are staring at them and expecting them to ask them to dance but are too scared to do it.

The girls are standing on the other side of the gym giving the boys nervous glances and anxiously wondering who will ask them to dance and if anyone will. They secretly hope they don't. Even the ones that have unofficial "dates" for the dance are standing awkwardly on their side of the gym looking across the invisible barrier that none dare to cross.

Kylie walks in slowly, hoping no one will see her, and tries to keep to the wall. She looks around unhappily. Everyone is either too busy to give her any looks or comments, or they haven't noticed her.

"Good," she thinks. "Hopefully I can just lay low and nobody will see me and I can get out of here when it's over in one piece."

She sees Anna standing in a corner with a moping look. Kylie turns away. "I am not going to go over and talk to her. Anna would probably just say something mean and walk away anyway."

She spots Amber and her friends with Dylan. "Oh great, this just gets better," she mutters. She looks around. "I need to find somewhere to hide until this awful dance is over. If that bunch see me, I'm dead."

She sighs unhappily. "I just want to leave."

Amber is hanging off Dylan despite his best attempts to avoid her hanging off him. No matter which way he turns, he just can't seem to get her off him. He tries to pry her off without being obvious, but it doesn't work.

"I've got to slip off to the bathroom to get away from them and think," Dylan decides. "Hopefully they won't follow me in there. I have to plan my escape. Leave this dance. Kylie isn't here anyway and I'm not spending the next hour and a half listening to Amber nattering and having her hanging off me. She is so annoying!"

He is getting ready to make his move.

Amber spies Kylie and a wicked grin spreads across her face. She tugs on Dylan's arm eagerly and grabs at her friends to pull them closer to listen.

"There she is!" Amber hisses excitedly.

"I can't believe she actually came," Brooke complains. Secretly she wished Kylie wouldn't come. Now instead of having fun, they will have to spend the whole time following Amber around while she obsesses over getting Kylie.

Jessica nods and smiles. "This is going to be fun!" she says. She is really thinking that it would be more fun if one of Dylan's friends would ask her to dance. But since that probably won't happen, this might be the next best thing.

"Come on," Amber urges, "let's go get her!"

She releases her grip on Dylan and starts stalking her prey, the other two girls trailing along. She looks behind her eagerly for them and realizes with a disappointed jolt of surprise that Dylan is not with them. He is standing where they had been moments before, just watching them.

"Don't bother with him," Jessica says. "We don't need him for this."

Amber frowns. She hoped he would come too, that he would be right there into this with her. She shrugs. Maybe he didn't know.

"Yeah, I guess he can't come because she is a girl and he's a boy. Boy's aren't supposed to hit girls and stuff," she decides. "This is girl stuff."

Dylan watches the girls suddenly dart off after Kylie. His first reaction is to feel stunned. There's no reason really to feel that way. They are doing what they always do. Somehow, though, he thought the dance would be off limits to the normal school stuff. He thought they would leave Kylie alone, that an uncalled truce would be in effect.

Suddenly the girls are back in front of him again.

"Where did she go?" Amber asks, annoyed. "Did you see where she went?"

"There she is!" Jessica pipes up, pointing.

"Let's go!" Amber is about to trot off.

"Wait!" Dylan cuts in, grabbing Amber's arm to stop them.

She looks up at him expectantly, thinking, "This is it. He's got a better plan or he wants to come with us."

Dylan is annoyed and his expression shows it.

"Why don't you just leave her alone?" he scowls at them, keeping his voice quiet to not attract the attention of the people around.

Amber is shocked. She stares up at him in stunned fury. "What? Why?" she splutters. Her eyes narrow like they could stab him with tiny daggers and she spins on her heel and storms off.

Jessica shakes her head in surprise. Not knowing what else to do, she takes off after Amber.

Brooke blinks in confusion and follows her friends, leaving Dylan alone at last.

He watches them go in relief, but it quickly turns to a cold lump of dread sitting in his stomach. The look of fury Amber gave him is enough to make anyone tremble in fear. He isn't worried about what she might do to him, he can look after himself.

"I think I just made things a lot worse for Kylie," he whispers. He looks around the gym for her but does not see her. He can't find Amber and her friends now either. There is a big lump in his chest suddenly and his arms and legs feel like they are made with lead. They are so heavy that he doesn't think they can move.

"I'm going to have to try to keep an eye on Kylie, even if it means stalking her over summer," Dylan said, feeling cold as if his leaden legs and arms are sending a chill through him. "Amber is coming after her and it is going to be worse than ever."

Brooke hesitates as she follows her friends, pausing to look back thoughtfully at Dylan. She suddenly realizes something.

"The way he was looking at Kylie, how he stopped her when Amber wanted to go after her, and telling her to leave Kylie alone." Her mind is spinning. "I think Dylan likes Kylie," she gasps. "He's not into Amber at all. She just convinced herself he is.

I don't know what I'll do with this information, but I might be able to use it some time." She hurries off to catch up with the other two girls.

Anna sees Amber and her friends start going after Kylie, Kylie duck behind some kids, then they stop and look around when they lose her. They rush back to Dylan.

"Obviously to get his help," Anna thinks. She watches them as they search around, spotting Kylie again, and go after her again. Dylan stops Amber. She is too far to hear what they're saying, but Amber and her friends walk right past her when they storm off angrily.

Anna hears part of Amber's angry outburst as she goes by with her nasty friends obediently following.

"I can't believe he told me to leave her alone," Amber complains. "Why is he even protecting her? Ugh, I HATE her!" She lets out an angry growl. "I'm going to get her worse than I ever have for this."

Anna looks back to where she last saw Kylie and she's gone.

"Amber is on the hunt for Kylie and whatever she is going to do will be pretty nasty," Anna mutters. "I have to find her and warn her." She rushes off through the crowd to find Kylie.

After long minutes of searching, Anna spots Kylie trying to hide in a corner by a door that is blocked open. There is an open space between her and the door where she will be in full view of the nasty trio and she is eying it up for a chance to make a break for it and escape out the door.

Anna rushes over to her. "Kylie, we have to get you out of here!"

Kylie looks at her suspiciously. "What do you want?"

"Amber is here," Anna says, trying to pull her along.

Kylie resists. "So? She's always everywhere."

"But she's extra mad about something and she is coming after you," Anna says urgently. "I've never seen her this mad about anything. Everything she has done to you before will be nothing to what she is going to do now if she gets to you."

Kylie looks around anxiously. "Why? What did I do?"

"I don't know. "Does it matter? Is there anything you have ever done? She just hates you. She doesn't need a reason. She never does."

"No, you're right." Kylie says sadly.

"Come on," Anna urges.

Kylie holds back still. This is her ex friend. "Why would she try to help me?" she wonders. A pang of fear runs through her. "What if it's a trick? What if Anna is on their side now? What if she is about to take me someplace where they can all gang up on me and there will be no teachers or parent chaperones to see and stop them?"

She looks at Anna, saying nothing, and then glances at the open door and what might be freedom or a trap.

"Come on," Anna says again. She stops pulling and looks at Kylie.

"Ok, so I said some mean stuff I didn't mean. I was upset about other stuff at home and took it out on you. I'm sorry. I wish I could take it all back, but I can't. It's too late. You have no reason to trust me, and after all the stuff they have done and things everyone else says I don't blame you for not trusting anyone. But you have to trust me.

I'm all you have."

Tears spring to Kylie's eyes and seeing them makes tears spring to Anna's eyes too.

"I-I'm sorry too." Kylie's voice cracks with emotion. "I didn't mean what I said either. I was just upset about… stuff."

"Ok, so let's go." Anna hugs her and pulls on her arm again, dragging her off. "Let's get you out of here before they do something." They break into a jog, ducking and dodging though the crowd.

Dylan is watching Kylie when Anna suddenly springs at her. He watches the heated conversation, though he can't hear what they are saying, and feels an urge to step in. When they suddenly hug and take off together, he is glad he didn't.

"Anna and Kylie made up being friends. That's good," he thinks. "She won't be alone as much for Amber to go after her."

Amber spots Anna and watches her. She sees her pounce on Kylie, and a sly smile spreads across her lips. "There you are."

She watches the exchange between Kylie and Anna, becoming angry when it turns from animosity to hugging.

"I'll have to put off getting my revenge on Kylie. But not for long."

Something is bothering Amber. She is even angrier with Kylie now because Dylan actually told her to leave her alone.

Why does he even care?" she growls. Then she spots him, standing there thinking no one is looking. "He is staring at her, at Kylie."

"Why? Why is he staring at her like that?" Jealously rears its ugly head as Amber starts to suspect she might have a rival for the boy she wants.

"He is going to be MY boyfriend," Amber growls quietly. "I'm going to hurt Kylie and hurt her so bad that she never comes back. I might even kill her for real. I am not going to let her of all people take my boyfriend."

Andrew sneaks out of the gym and down the hall, looking behind him to make sure no one is coming to catch him leaving. With a sigh of relief that nobody is following him, Andrew slips out of the school, keeping low and close to the shadows. He darts off from one shadow to the next between pools of vapor light and finally runs off across the lot.

He runs down the street and the next, cutting through yards and taking shortcuts. He has to slow down to rest a few times.

Finally, he is there. The old abandoned building. He stops on the sidewalk in front of it and looks around nervously.

"This place sure is extra creepy at night," he says quietly. "It's creepy enough in the daylight, but even creepier now."

It is not quite dark out yet, but the light in the sky is beginning to fade to dusk. The shadows are growing deeper and the sun seems a weak mimic of its daytime self. It will be dark soon.

Andrew scurries around the building to the back, keeping close to the wall. The shadows in the next property and by the old shed at the back seem like they are moving in the darkening dusk.

"They can't possibly be moving," he whispers to himself, trying to sound convincing. "It's just a trick of the light on my eyes. An optical illusion. It has to be."

He makes his way to the little shed attached to the building and inspects its outside walls and door again. The brick is a little crumbly and looks dirty, just like the rest of the building. The wood door is rotting. He presses on the door in a few spots. It feels a bit spongy and soft.

He presses harder and then slams his weight against it a few times. It takes surprisingly little to break the door open. The rotting wood gives fairly easily around the lock, the doorframe breaking apart. Andrew almost falls inside when the door suddenly gives with a moist cracking sound.

Andrew brushes himself off and looks around so see if anyone heard, then he goes cautiously inside.

There isn't much here; an old rusting lawn mower, a couple of shovels, and a rake. One of the shovels is laying on the ground. He looks up at a row of hooks on the wall. One is missing.

"Probably rotted off," he decides.

There is an old coil of garden hose piled carelessly in a corner and nothing else but a lot of old spider webs and a couple of motionless big fat hairy spiders that he suspects are either sleeping or dead.

Andrew backs out with a grimace of dislike, staring at one of the large spiders distrustfully.

He looks around. Still, no one is around. He walks around the other side of the building. They haven't really bothered inspecting that side before because it puts them in view of the houses on that side and anyone going by on the street.

There is a tangle of overgrown bushes, tall grass, and weeds next to the building near the back corner. Andrew has a vague sense they are hiding something.

He takes a step towards them and stops when he sees a car approaching up the street. He retreats to the back of the building where he is out of sight.

He starts poking around, examining the mostly boarded up windows, covered with two by four boards nailed across them with gaps between the boards. The glass behind the boards is so dirty, it is nearly impossible to see through.

He freezes. Just for a moment, he thought he saw movement inside the basement through a broken window.

"Nah," Andrew mutters. "There is nothing in there. An old cat or something maybe, but that's it."

He goes to the back door. He had wanted to try this door before but Madison would not let him. He tries the knob and it is locked. Gripping the knob, he rattles the door in the frame. It rattles louder than he expected. It is loose in its frame. He inspects the edges.

"The hinges are probably rotting right out of the wooden doorframe. The frame looks even more rotten on the outside than the door does."

"I think I can get it open without too much trouble!" Andrew whispers eagerly.

He hears a noise. It is a slithering kind of noise, like he imagines he sometimes hears coming from his basement. He stops, listening. His blood turns cold and his face pales. Suddenly scared, he turns and runs away.

Madison sees Andrew look around and slip out of the gym. "He is acting suspiciously," she thinks.

She hurries to the gym door and spots him scurrying off down the hall. She follows him, keeping at a distance. When he stops and looks back, she quickly ducks down behind a large garbage pail. She holds her breath and waits and then dares a peak just in time to see him slip out a door, leaving the school.

"Oh, you are going to be in so much trouble Andrew," she mutters under her breath. "I know exactly where you are going, and you are not supposed to leave school during the dance except with your parents."

Madison jogs over to the door, looks out the window, up the hall to make sure no one is watching, and slips out too, following him. She follows him all the way to the old abandoned building.

"I knew that's where you are going!" she says, ducking behind the fence of the property next to the abandoned building to watch

Andrew. When he moves around the back, she jogs out to follow, keeping close to the building. She stops at the back corner.

Madison watches from the shadows, peaking around the corner of the building. She watches Andrew break open the old rotting door to the attached shed. It didn't look that hard. She holds her breath, worried, until he finally comes back out.

Andrew goes around the other side of the building and darts back a moment later. She sees the movement of an approaching car up the road between a few houses.

Back behind the building, Andrew looks around, pauses, and starts trying the back door.

Madison's heart thumps in her chest and her lungs feel tight as she watches Andrew play with the knob, turning it, and then pushing and pulling at the door, testing it.

"Oh no you don't!" Madison gasps quietly. "Don't you dare go in there." She is about to step out of hiding and call out to him to get out of there when he suddenly freezes.

Andrew turns and looks around him quickly, and then he stares at the open hole of the broken basement window. He looks scared as he listens and studies the window. He turns and runs as if some invisible monster is chasing him.

Madison ducks and he does not see her, but she gets a good look at his face as he races by. The look on his face is one of terror.

She watches his retreating back, and then moves quickly to the window, looking in. She sees nothing but darkness.

"What he is so scared of?" She hears a slithering sound that chills the blood in her veins.

"I am not waiting around to find out," she mutters and runs back towards the school. "Mom will be picking me up soon."

She tries to convince herself that is the only reason she is running. "Besides, there will be a lot of people there. Whatever is at the abandoned building will not come around all those people," she thinks, reluctantly admitting to her fear.

Madison's heart is thumping hard in her chest as much from nerves as from the run by the time she gets to the school. Panting to catch her breath and holding a painful stitch in her side, Madison slips back in the same door she snuck out of. She looks around for a clock. It is only minutes before the parents are to start arriving to pick kids up.

"I was gone longer than I thought," she pants. She heads back to the gym and steps inside, looking around for Andrew, but does not see him anywhere.

"Where is he?" she pants, still trying to catch her breath. "Didn't he come back here?"

10   The Dance is Over

The dance is ending and Dylan is reluctantly still hanging around and trying hard to avoid Amber and her friends.

"I just want to be left alone to watch Kylie, if I can find her. I haven't seen her since she slipped out of the gym with Anna. Those pests just won't leave me alone."

He is hanging around in a corner, keeping a group of boys between him and Amber and her friends, when he notices a girl looking lost and worried, searching the crowd at the dance.

Dylan recognizes her. He has to think for a moment before he remembers her name. Madison.

"I've seen her and Andrew hanging around after school, walking by on the street," he thinks. "I saw Andrew at the dance earlier and saw him sneak out. Obviously, he was up to something and the dance was just a trick to get out of the house without telling his parents where he was going.

Or he was ducking out to avoid a girl. She is probably looking for him. Andrew probably gave her the slip too." He chuckles inwardly a little at that, thinking of how annoying Amber and her friends hanging off him is.

Dylan is curious. Andrew doesn't hang around this girl in school. It's only an after school thing. It's not something he would need to hide from either.

"Maybe I should see what's up," he decides with a shrug and walks over to her.

"What's wrong?" Dylan asks, stopping in front of her. She is turned looking the other way and didn't see him coming.

Madison turns and looks up at him, startled by the question. "Um, I," she stammers uncertainly. "I'm looking for someone."

Her face flushes with a blush, sure the bully is going to do something mean to her. She glances around for help or an escape route, seeing neither.

"Andrew," Dylan says with a knowing nod. "He skipped out."

Madison shakes her head. "I know. I followed him. But when he ran off I thought he would come back here and he didn't."

The worried look in her eyes bothers Dylan. Something is wrong. He looks out the door and sees Dylan's mom looking for him in the groups of kids milling around as they slowly make their way to their parents' cars.

"He didn't come back?"

Madison shakes her head, looking up at him. Her eyes are big and round and suddenly Dylan thinks he can see what his ex friend would like about this girl. He knows Andrew would never admit it if he did have a crush on any girl.

"Where did you follow him to?"

"Our secret fort." She looks down, blushing at the admission. With this taller boy staring down at her, forts suddenly seem for babies. She makes herself look back up and meet his eyes.

"I think something happened to him."

The spring dance was a week ago and Andrew has not been back to school since the dance. Dylan and Madison are both worried about him. Every morning they find each other when they get to school to find out if the other has heard anything.

It's second period, math, and Dylan is sitting at his desk doodling on his paper instead of listening to the teacher's mindlessly bland voice droning on at the front of the class. He does not notice the teacher stop talking or when the door opens and the principal waves the teacher over. He does not notice the teacher slip out of the room, closing the door behind him.

It is the slow increase in volume around him that gets Dylan's attention. He looks up to see the teacher missing and everyone looking around curiously and talking.

The door opens and he looks. The teacher walks in, ushering Andrew in with him. Andrew enters reluctantly, keeping his head down, and quietly dodges desks and feet to slip into his chair. He does not look up, does not look back at any of the kids staring and whispering.

The teacher calls their attention back to him and resumes his lecture.

Dylan watches Andrew sit there. Andrew slowly pulls out his math book and paper and pencil, setting them on his desk with deliberate slow motions, as quietly as possible. He watches Andrew out of the corner of his eye all class and through the next. He is more quiet than usual and seems kind of pale, like he has been sick.

When class breaks for them to change books at their lockers, Dylan approaches him in the hall.

"You ok?" he asks.

"Why?" Andrew asks defensively.

"Hey," Dylan puts his hands up, taking his ex friend's defensiveness wrong. "I'm not going to do anything to you or anything. We're friends still, aren't we?"

His look is uncertain. He is not sure if Andrew will say yes or no.

Andrew relaxes a bit. "Yeah, I guess. I'm ok. I was just sick."

"I heard you've been hanging around some abandoned building."

Andrew's eyes flash with suspicion. "Yeah, a bit." His voice is defensive.

"Sounds cool."

The bell rings for class and they both head off down the hall. The bell. That wonderful device that cuts through an awkward moment with its shrill ring and instantly frees you to escape.

Madison is relieved to see Andrew back at school even if he does look kind of grey and seems off. She does not approach him at school. Instead, she rushes off to their secret fort after school to wait for him. It is the day before the last day of school before spring break.

She is sitting inside their fort at the far back of the abandoned lot. She gets up and goes to the door, looking across the lot to the abandoned brick building. The place unnerves her. She can't stop thinking about that strange slithering sound she heard the night of the dance and the fear she saw on Andrew's face when he fled.

Madison looks past the building, hoping to see Andrew. She starts wandering around outside her fort, not going near the old brick building, staying close to the old shed at the back of the lot.

She hangs around there for as long as she dares before scuffing her feet and heading for home, unable to shake off that feeling of dread.

"He is not going to come," she decides and leaves. She takes a wide path up the side of the building, keeping her distance from it.

Madison is preoccupied and not really paying attention as she walks home. She goes up the street, cutting down the next, towards the alley.

It is almost a fatal mistake.

The sudden surge of hairy flesh, hot breath, and loud barking right in her face scares Madison so bad that she jumps back instinctively and falls to the ground.

Straining at the end of his chain just inches from her, Caesar barks fiercely. He is so close she can smell and feel his nasty dog breath.

Madison gasps, but can't inhale any air. It feels like the breath has been knocked out of her. "Move!" she cries inside her head. She is frozen with fear, unable to cry out or move.

The door to the house flies open and Mr. Hooper comes hobbling out as bad tempered as ever.

"Get out of here! Leave my dog alone!" he yells, followed by threats that her shock turns into wordless babble. It is enough to break her paralysis.

Madison scuttles back and gets to her feet quickly, running. Her heart is pounding so hard in her chest that she is afraid it will break.

"So this must be what a heart attack feels like," she thinks desperately, sure she is having one. "I'm going to die of a heart attack here in the back lane and nobody will even know where to find me. Old Caesar will probably get loose and eat me, or rats will."

Madison can't breathe, but she pushes on for as long as she can. She has to stop, gasping, to lean in relief on the other side of the loose fence board where she is safe. The air burns in her throat and lungs as she takes great mouthfuls of air, trying to catch her breath.

Ever since the dance Amber keeps trying to get Kylie but she is hanging around that other girl again, Anna. Amber is not happy about it. She is determined to make Kylie pay for what happened. Dylan actually told her to leave that witch alone.

"I can only think of two reasons," Amber thinks as she watches Kylie and Anna in the hall at school. "Either he likes her or he thinks I should spend more time with him instead."

That second brightens her mood a little bit. "That has to be it," she decides. But it does not make her feel any less hatred towards Kylie, or want to get her any less.

Amber turns and walks away to find Dylan. Dylan can't avoid her despite his best efforts and Amber is intent on jealously guarding her man from Kylie, "Just in case," she tells herself, "although I can't see any boy wanting that." Her reference is to Kylie.

It is only in this last week of school before spring break that Amber realizes she has no plan for how she is going to see Dylan over the break.

"I tried all week to get him to make promises about how we'll see each other, but he just mumbles and shrugs. Ugh, boys.

There has to be a way. Tomorrow is the last day of school. I know; I have to find out where he lives, where he goes, everything he does. Wherever he goes, I will go too. Well, when I'm not busy trying to get that Kylie, that is."

Madison is sitting in her bedroom. She is supposed to be cleaning it before her parents get home, but she just can't get motivated to do it. Music plays softly on her radio alarm clock. If she turns it up much louder, it starts to crackle with static. She likes this station best, but it has a weaker signal than the rest.

"We were going to hang out at the fort over break. Now I don't know if that's going to even happen."

She keeps thinking about Andrew. She still can't shake that feeling from the night of the dance. The spookiness of being at the abandoned building in the quiet of evening and hearing that strange sound after seeing the look of absolute terror on Andrew's face has given her the heebie jeebies.

"With spring break coming, I'll be home all day. I'm kind of looking forward to it, but kind of not too. I'm feeling pretty confident being home alone before and after school now, but staying home alone all day is going to be so boring."

Thoughts of spending all day home alone kind of scare her, but she tries not to think about that.

"I could go back to the fort myself." That feeling of dread comes over her again. She hasn't been able to convince herself to go back to the fort after the night of the dance, except that one time she waited for Andrew and he never showed up.

"It's just the fear of going past Old Man Hooper's house and Caesar," she tries to tell herself. But she knows it is more than that. She is scared to go to the fort alone after school.

She can't erase the memory of Andrew's fear.

"I can handle that old dog," she tells herself bravely. "He just startled me."

Madison hears a single knock. She stops, looking around.

"I don't think that was the door. It sounded like it came from above, from inside the wall."

She leaves her room, checking both front and back doors just in case. There is no one there.

She is heading back to her bedroom when she hears a low groaning somewhere above, like the sound wood might make under strain. She stops, looking up. The house is silent now except for the dull rhythmic thock thock thock of the clock on the living room bookcase and the low music coming from her room. She listens. It doesn't repeat.

"Was that in the roof?" Madison tries to push away the uneasy feeling gripping her. "It's just the house settling. That's what Mom and Dad always say."

She's about to start walking again when she hears a thud from below.

"Did something fall downstairs?"

She goes to the basement stairs, opening the door and peering down into the dark basement. "I should check it out. If it's something spilled it will be worse to clean it up later."

She reaches for the light switch and imagines she sees movement in the darkness below, that she hears quiet scuffling like something is scampering. It is so quiet she can't be sure she heard anything at all.

"Now you are imagining things. You are just seeing and hearing them because Andrew told you he hears strange noises when he is alone at home or when everyone is sleeping. He was just being silly and now you are the one who is being silly. Just go down and check it out, there is nothing to be scared of."

She thinks she hears another muffled sound from somewhere upstairs. "It's your radio in your room."

Madison looks at the darkness below again and hesitantly reaches out, flipping the light switch. She steps down the first step, then the second. An unsettling image comes to her of some unseen thing waiting down there for her. She chickens out.

"It's probably nothing." She pushes the thought in her head away; not wanting to voice it, afraid someone might somehow know if she does. "If there is anything spilled down there I'll just pretend I never heard anything. Mom can clean it up."

She retreats to the safety of the main floor, leaving the basement light on and closing the basement door. Madison walks just a little bit faster than usual back to her room.

She turns up the music a little louder, feeling a little security in the noise, and sits on her bed. "I guess I have to get cleaning before Mom and Dad get home."

Being busy should push away any unwanted thoughts, but she keeps thinking she hears little noises in the background. Madison turns down the radio to listen.

"The house seems to be making a lot of noises all of a sudden." The anxious feeling won't go away.

When she told her parents before about the noises that made her nervous, they said it was just the house settling. "Houses always made sounds like that when the seasons change," they said.

But more than once Madison could have sworn she heard something in the basement. Quiet footsteps or the rustle of something moving. The scrape of something being pushed or the clatter or thump of something falling. Her parents never found anything out of place when she did manage to convince them to look. She knows they won't believe her now either.

"It's only in my imagination. You, girlfriend, have a case of the nervous mouse because of whatever scared Andrew at that old abandoned building. You are being completely dumb. And that was probably just a cat or something. That's it; you are going to get rid of this fear once and for all. You have to go back to that old building and prove to yourself that there is nothing there. If you can do that, then the noises of the house settling won't scare you anymore either.

But first, I need to talk to Andrew and ask him if he has gone back to the fort and the abandoned building since the dance. I also need to ask if he is planning to go there during spring break. It should be safe in the daytime to hang out at the fort if we don't go near the building."

Kylie is sitting at her desk daydreaming and not paying attention to the teacher droning on at the front of the classroom. She has been thinking a lot about the things that have happened in the past weeks, how she went from no friends to one friend; from being bullied every day to almost getting to feel like a normal kid.

"The kind of kid who doesn't have to be scared to come to school and who isn't bullied," she thinks. She thinks about their big fight where she and Anna broke up being friends.

"It's such a big relief to have Anna as my friend again," she thinks. That's one less thing to feel pain in her heart over. "It's going to make the spring and summer breaks better too. The whole summer spent cooped up at home all alone with nobody to talk to all day long just seems unbearable. I don't dare go anywhere alone. Between those bully girls and my dad stalking me, it's just not safe to be out alone."

Another thought makes her frown. "It's not safe home alone either. I hear noises sometimes. Sometimes it sounds like someone is trying to get in the house. When I look later there is sometimes something out of place. A flowerpot tipped over, things moved.

I know it's Dad trying to find a hidden key or checking the doors to see if one was left unlocked. But we are too smart for that. We never hide a key outside and we always keep the doors locked even when we are all home."

The idea of her dad breaking into the house while she is home alone makes Kylie's blood turn to ice, sending a shiver of fear through her. She doesn't know what he would do if it ever happened. She doesn't want to know.

"Sometimes I hear noises in the basement too. I think we have rats down there or something, as if worrying about Dad getting in wasn't enough. I've never found any rat poop, but sometimes I find something that was moved."

Her thoughts turn to last weekend when her mom and sister were out grocery shopping and she was alone. She was startled by a wet crash that sounded like it came from the basement. While she was still registering what it was, there was a dull clunk and rumble and a loud thud.

She went down to investigate. She found the source of the crash, a glass jar knocked off a shelf where her mom keeps food that won't fit in the kitchen cupboard. The canned beets and their purple red juice were splattered on the floor in the remains of the broken jar like purple red blood and organs. She searched around some more. The clunk and low rumble followed by a loud thud was a large can of tomatoes that had apparently tipped and rolled along the shelf all on its own, falling to the floor and denting the can when it hit. She could see the trail it left in the dust on the shelf.

"It had to be rats or something. Gross! I tried to get mom to call an exterminator, but she wouldn't. She said it would cost too much. She bought some big ugly rat traps instead."

Kylie shudders at the thought of going down there and finding a dead rat in one of the traps. "That's even grosser than knowing they are down there trying to raid the canned food."

She turns her attention back to the teacher talking at the front of the class, only partially listening, and then looks at the clock on the wall. The bell will ring soon and she will have to try to get through the halls without being assaulted by Amber and her friends. She watches the clock's second hand tick slowly around with dread.

"At least I'll have Anna to hang with for spring and summer breaks," she thinks.

Sitting at her own desk, Anna watches the clock too, waiting impatiently for the day to end. She is still grounded. "What a joke," she thinks, "grounded with nobody around to ground me."

She sighs, trying to cover the sound.

"Spring break is about to start and it's going to be the loneliest spring break ever. Summer will be even worse. Cole is still hanging in there and my parents are still never home.

I never would have thought I would say it, but I have to. I'm going to miss school. Without school and all the classrooms full of kids and teachers, I have no one.

No one except Kylie. I have her to hang out with at least. I've never been very good at making friends.

I don't know what I'm going to do this summer, but I have a feeling it's going to be a very different kind of summer. I just can't decide if that will be good or bad."

Andrew looks down at the papers in front of him on the desk. With it being spring break and report cards, the teachers are either playing catch up for the next term or giving them useless busy work. He scratches mindlessly at the paper with his pencil. No one will actually be looking at it anyway.

His thoughts turn to the abandoned building with their fort in the back corner of its lot. He hasn't gone back to the abandoned building since the night of the dance. He had been so shaken and pale when his mother found him wandering towards home that night that she immediately thought he had come down sick. She whisked him off to bed and worried over him, giving him no peace.

"I guess it was good Mom wouldn't leave me alone," Andrew thinks, "I didn't really want to be alone, not even with Mom and Dad just in the next room."

All week after the dance he was tormented by the sound and creepiness of the abandoned building at night. He had bad dreams about it that left him bleary eyed and dark circles under his eyes from not sleeping.

Convinced he was sick, his mom let him stay home from school that week.

"Staying home all week wasn't such a good thing. Mom stayed home with me the first day, but then she had to go back to work. I was left home alone. Staying home didn't feel safe. I could hear the noises. Nobody believes me, but I hear things that I'm sure are coming from the basement. I've always heard them.

Spring break is going to be unbearable if I have to stay home alone. I asked Mom and Dad about it and they gave me the okay to go out during the day to hang out with friends, but with limits. I have to be home by four every afternoon and I have to always let them know where I'm going to be that day and who I'll be with. If they say "no" then I have to stay home.

I have to find someone to hang out with. There's Madison, but she's a girl. I can't spend the whole break hanging out with a girl. Some of the guys are going away for spring break. Others are going to day and week long camps."

There is only kid he can think of who will not be going anywhere. Dylan.

"We were friends before; before Dylan's house was broken into and he started acting all weird, and before he started bullying everyone. I'm not sure about this. Will Dylan even want to hang out and be friends again? How do I know he won't just bully me too? There is no one else who will be around, just Dylan and Madison.

I'm going to have to try making friends again with Dylan."

Dylan is sitting in his desk staring down sullenly. He has no idea what he is going to do for spring break. His mom broke the news to him that morning that he will not be at the babysitter anymore.

"That's good and it sucks," he thinks. "Good because only little kids need babysitters and I'm too old. It's embarrassing. It sucks because I'm going to be at home alone all day."

An involuntary surge of fear rushes through him, making him frown angrily. He still has nightmares about people breaking into the house even though that happened months ago.

He pushes the thought away, but it comes anyway. "What if I'm home alone and someone breaks in? What will they do to me?" The idea of being home alone scares him. Dylan is not going to admit it to anyone though.

What he did not realize until suddenly feeling lonely at the idea of a couple weeks home alone, is that he has been too wrapped up in being a loner on the outside of everything. He was just going through the motions everyday of going to school.

"I don't have any friends anymore. I'm an outsider looking into everyone else's lives. It's lonely but it's where I belong. I don't fit in anywhere or with anyone. I'm better off alone. I'm just fine this way, happy," he lies to himself.

He looks up, looking at Kylie sitting closer to the front of the classroom. "She always seems so sad. That's how I feel." Dylan doesn't really know why he feels that way.

He looks at the clock. It's almost time. School will be done for spring break. He isn't worried about seeing Kylie. She only lives on the next street over. He's sure he'll see her hanging around somewhere. Dylan is not planning to spend the next few weeks just hanging out at home alone all day.

The final bell of the last day of school rings with dull finality.

Eager to escape the boring life of school, the kids are soon pouring out of the doors in an excited babble. When the last school bus drives away, the last parent picks up the last kid, and the stragglers make their way towards home, a stillness settles on the school.

A lone paper flutters in the breeze, blowing across the front pavement, rattling and flapping in the wind when it catches on a bush by the curb.

The janitor moves silently through the school, slowly sweeping the floors for the last time, oblivious to the silence as jazz music blares into his ears through the ear buds plugged into them.

School is over for spring break.

11   Hanging Out in the Neighborhood

The first days of break are filled with an exhilaration that soon languishes into boredom.

Madison is sitting staring at the television and not really watching it. The show is a repeat and one she's never really liked.

"Ugh, I am so bored. I had so many things I wanted to do over spring break that I didn't even know where to start. It feels like I've done it all before noon on the first day. I have nothing to do now."

She feels the now familiar itch to go to her secret fort, along with the rush of fear.

"I haven't had a chance to talk to Andrew. Maybe Andrew will be at the fort. Then I won't have to hang out there alone. I don't even know why I feel scared of that old place. It's kind of spooky looking, but it's perfectly safe in the daytime."

She still can't shake that uneasy feeling the place gives her.

Kylie spent her first days of spring break sitting at home alone. Her sister is at a babysitter all day for the break. Her mom doesn't think Kylie is old enough yet to look after her sister that long.

Kylie suspects it's more fear of what might happen if their dad showed up.

"I'm glad I don't have to be stuck with my little sister, but I also kind of wish I was. Then I wouldn't be all alone."

The silence of the house weighs down on her.

"Maybe I should go to the park. No, I can't. I'd be risking running into Amber and her friends. No way!" She shakes her head.

Kylie decides to go online and almost immediately regrets it.

She turns on the old computer, waiting forever for it to boot up. She waits even longer to get onto the chat site on their obsolete dial up internet.

Going into a chat room that is popular at school, she starts scrolling and immediately sees that Amber and her friends are on their usual nasty crusade to defame and humiliate her.

"Don't read them, just skim down."

Kylie skims down the posts, but can't help herself, reading some of the foul comments that leave her feeling hollow inside. She leaves the chat to try another chat site. She finds the same thing there. The evil trio had already been on this site too.

"No point bothering to read them. I already know what they say."

She scrolls down anyway, skimming through comments, reading some and bypassing others. The comments made against her only get worse. She feels them like a physical pain in her chest and feels like her soul was just crushed.

Feeling suddenly sick, Kylie turns off the computer and lies down on her bed. Tears soon come.

"I wish I was somewhere else, anywhere else. I just can't understand why Amber and her friends have to be so cruel. I never did anything to them, so why do they hate me so much?"

She rubs the tears away angrily, but they just keep coming. She rolls over, half burying her face in the pillow.

"Maybe something will happen to me," she murmurs into her pillow. "Something so bad that I'll either be dead and never have to be bullied again, or they will all feel so sorry for me that even Amber won't be mean to me anymore. Then they will be sorry they were so mean."

She punches the pillow, sobbing harder. "I hate them! I am so stupid! I am so stupid that everybody hates me! I wish I was never even born! I wish I was dead!"

Amber is having fun online. Every keystroke is power at her fingertips. She loves this.

"With a few words, I can make or break anyone."

She goes into one chat room, scouts the posts, and picks a victim. Chattymay1. She doesn't know the victim and it doesn't matter to her. It's just some random person out there, faceless and unreal.

Amber reads through Chattymay1's posts, deciding from both the name and language that Chattymay1 has to be a girl. It doesn't take long to get into a verbal battle. She grins wickedly, the light from the monitor glowing off her face.

"Easy pickings."

Thrilling in the nasty outpouring coming from her fingertips, she presses on; upping the nastiness and watching her victim squirm and react with hurt and anger. Her victim's posts are becoming more desperate and crazy. After a frenzy of nonsense posts, her victim vanishes from the chat. Amber looks at the time and laughs.

"That was fast. I think I broke a record. It only took me twenty minutes to break her and not a lot of effort. Hah! She's off crying somewhere," she gloats.

Other posters are starting to attack Amber for her unprovoked nastiness against Chattymay1, so she leaves that chat room in search of more play.

Amber moves onto some of her favorite chat sites where she knows she will find Jessica and they gang up to take down other innocent victims. They move from chat room to chat room inflicting emotional damage. In the ones she knows Kylie visits, they leave nasty chat bombs for her to find.

Unknown to Amber, Chattymay1 is as that very moment sitting in her room with the razor blade from her dad's shaving razor on the desk next to her computer keyboard. She took it the other day when she was at a really low point.

"Nobody can hurt me if I'm dead," Chattymay1 says sadly, staring at the bare razor. She feels so lonely.

"Nobody would even care if anything happened to me. Nobody would come to my funeral. I have no friends. Even the kids who pretend to be my friends are probably laughing behind my back."

With tears streaming down her face and wondering why a total stranger attacked her, why everyone seems to always be so cruel and hurt her and bully her, she looks at the sharp piece of metal.

Her real name is Kerry. She picks up the razor blade, fingering the sharp edge. A bead of blood sprouts. She sliced her finger.

Kerry looks at the wet red bead and the thin almost invisible line of the cut.

Her arms are crisscrossed with scars and healing scabs from where she had cut herself previously in the only way she can find to purge herself of her emotional pain.

"It would slice so easy. I could just do it right now. A few simple slices and then they would all feel sorry for me. Nobody would bully me again."

Jessica is going along with the game online with Amber. She gets a rush out of making up stuff about people she doesn't know, although it's more fun when it's someone she does know. Jessica almost slipped a few times though.

"Oh my gawd, I almost posted nasty stuff about Amber!" She stares at the screen, her eyes wide, and a wicked grin on her face. "All I'd have to do is make another profile and log on with it, and BOOM. I can say anything to Amber I want and she won't know it's me.

It is so tempting. Amber is my friend but I don't actually like her or anything. I only hang out with her because I no one else will be my friend."

The thought brings up the too familiar loneliness.

"Besides, if I'm not friends with Amber, I would be a target for her. There were only two people in Amber's world, those who go along with her and her victims."

Brooke is bored. She turns on her laptop, going online to the chat rooms and trolls for a while, reading everyone else's posts without commenting.

"Nobody likes a troll," she thinks, "someone who just sits back reading posts and watching without posting to let anyone know they are there. Then BAM! You hit them where it hurts with a well-placed nasty comment."

She finds a tempting target and is about to strike, typing a nasty comment and reaching for the enter key, when she sees Amber's login name show up.

MG1. It's their own joke. The mean girls, MG1, MG2, and MG3. As their leader, Amber naturally declared herself number one. When they all attack the victim online together, sometimes they don't pick up that the furious onslaught of nasty comments are coming from three, not one.

Brooke sits there, finger poised over the key, watching to see what happens. Amber starts attacking someone posting as Chattymay1.

Brooke pulls her hand back, scrolling down and watching the exchange. Seeing the viciousness of the attack sours her stomach. She frowns, watching until Chattymay1 leaves the chat. She turns off the computer.

"Maybe I can find something else to do."

She thinks for a while. "I'll see what Mom is doing. Maybe she'll take me shopping or something."

Brooke goes searching for her mother. "Hey Mom, what are you doing?"

The answer is pretty obvious from the stacks of folded laundry and half-empty laundry basket. Her mother looks at her. "Folding laundry."

Brooke shrugs. "Whatever. Mom, can I go to the mall?"

"Who are you going with?"

"No one."

"I don't think I want you going alone yet, maybe when you're a year older."

Brooke pouts. "But I'm so bored."

"You could help me fold laundry."

She makes a disgusted face. "Please Mom."

Her mother looks at the piles of laundry and sighs. Brooke is in luck. Her mother is bored with the laundry. There are so many things to get done, but she just can't get into housework today.

"All right, but we're both going."

"She must be bored too," Brooke thinks. "I don't know how Mom can stand just sitting at home all day every day."

She has to wait while her mom spruces herself up. After laundry and floors, her mom is looking somewhat rough. She sits impatiently waiting, wishing she would hurry up.

"I wish she'd hurry, but I'm glad Mom decided to change her clothes. I would have been embarrassed to be seen with her looking like that."

Anna is sitting in her bedroom moodily. "Ugh, this is so lame, just sitting around here doing nothing."

She gets up, paces, and stops. "I'm going out."

She goes to the park and hangs around there for a little while, but nobody is there. It gets boring fast. Anna decides to go exploring the neighborhood, something she has done so many times she already knows the area very well. She wanders out of the park, turning one way and going some distance, then starts to turn again and changes her mind.

"I always go this way. I'm taking a different route."

She changes direction and walks on for a while, then stops, realizing where she is.

"This will take me past that crabby old Mr. Hooper's house and his mean dog Caesar. No way. I'm taking a longer route."

She detours, going the long way around to avoid Hooper's house. She ends up detouring again to avoid another house where a large dog is laying quietly watching her as it suns itself.

She ends up having to pass another dog, smaller than the other one, behind a fence. It watches her approach the yard, tongue lolling and tail wagging, then breaks into loud barking that makes her cringe. She tenses as she passes by, walking on the other side of the street. She speeds up to get past the dog quickly.

Anna is scared of dogs and avoids any house with a big or noisy dog. Any time she comes face to face with a dog she freezes in fear and can't move. It doesn't matter if the dog is not barking or if it's trying to eat you and rip you apart.

"At least it isn't Caesar. He's the worst. He is big and only on a chain with no fence. What if he got off the chain? What if Old Man Hooper forgot to chain him? I'd rather go through a pit filled with poisonous snakes and spiders than meet up with a loose Caesar. That dog is mean! And the old man is pretty scary too, like a snarly old dog."

Anna looks around to get her bearings, and keeps walking, absently roaming further than she normally does in this direction. There isn't much here. This is where the uglier old worn down looking houses are, while the better houses are a few streets over.

She feels embarrassed thinking that. Kylie lives on one of these streets in one of these ugly old houses. There are some old stores and stuff, a little garage for fixing cars, and some other buildings she doesn't really know what they do in.

Anna walks past the front of a large boarded up brick building, looking at it with indifferent curiosity.

You can see where there was once a sign on the building, but the sign is gone. The place looks like it was abandoned a long time ago. The lot is not looked after. The grass is too long and probably was butchered when the city worker guy came by to cut the grass on the medians and boulevards.

As she walks past, Anna notices a ratty old chair sitting in the back yard behind the building. It's the kind of padded armchair found in most living rooms and often bought to match the couch. Beyond it at the back corner of the lot is an old rotting shed.

"Who would want to sit there," she mumbles. "I bet the chair is full of bugs and mice and stuff."

Andrew is playing video games with the volume too loud. His character races through the town chasing down bad guys and shooting them. He has a snack on the floor next to him, a glass of chocolate milk and a stack of cookies. It's not the kind of snack he would be allowed, but there is no one home to say no.

He reaches over and grabs a cookie, munching on it as he fights single-handed with the remote in the other hand.

Andrew doesn't hear the first noise. It's a distant background sound against the crashing, blasting, and music of the game.

When the sound repeats, the noise registers on his subconscious. His ears pick it up but it doesn't register in his mind. Andrew pauses briefly without realizing it, anxiety tensing his muscles, but keeps playing.

He can't ignore it the third time. He stops and listens, unsure whether or not he heard something. The blaring game drowns out anything that might be there.

"Probably just hearing things," he mutters, sure it's his imagination. But an uneasy feeling deep down inside tells him he is wrong. He tries to ignore it, but the feeling doesn't go away.

After a moment of playing, his ears tuned to the house, Andrew breaks down and turns down the sound with the T.V. remote. He listens, putting down his half eaten cookie.

He thinks he hears a faint sound. It sounds like scratching.

Nervous, Andrew puts both remotes down and gets up, listening carefully as he takes a few steps towards the living room doorway. He is pretty sure it came from the basement.

"Glad the basement door is closed," he thinks. Andrew moves cautiously, going to the basement door and listening through the door.

"Is it just my imagination?" he whispers doubtfully.

He hears another noise and turns his head. "Did it come from the kitchen?"

He starts turning in the direction he thought the noise came from when he hears a distinct sound from the basement door. A scraping, like something brushed against the door.

Andrew starts sweating but feels suddenly chilled. His face is a blank mask of fear. Swallowing hard, Andrew has to force himself to move.

He walks slowly to the living room, trying not to make a sound. He grabs his keys, wincing with the slight jangle they make. He grips them in his fist to keep them quiet, and heads to the door, speeding up as he moves despite his efforts to stay calm and move slowly.

Andrew doesn't notice when he steps on the partially eaten cookie, breaking it into small pieces and crumbs and mashing it into the carpet.

Leaving the T.V. on with the game still playing, Andrew opens the door, slips outside, and closes it with exaggerated care. Cringing when the keys make a noise as he locks the door, he practically flies down the steps, bolting up the street.

He does not stop running until he is halfway up the street and completely winded.

"Where do I go?" He stops, looking around as if he might see the answer in front of him. "The fort? The abandoned building? No." He decides against it. He's not ready to go back there yet, not alone.

"Guess I'll just walk around."

With no destination in mind, wandering aimlessly, Andrew eventually finds himself by the old creek. The creek has always been off limits since he was first allowed to play outside unsupervised.

"I'm twelve," he grumbles, "the rule can't still apply."

He spots a figure in the distance tossing something into the water. "Probably little rocks."

Andrew shades his eyes and squints, trying to see who it is. He starts walking towards him. As he gets closer, he recognizes him. It's Dylan.

Dylan is hanging around down by the old creek. He had collected a bunch of small stones and pebbles and is standing there tossing them at the water one at a time, aiming for different things; a rock beneath the surface, a swirl of water, a weed, anything that catches his eye. It's not wide enough to try skipping stones. When he sees an insect, he tries to hit it with the stone. He always misses.

He doesn't notice the approaching boy until Andrew is close enough to talk to him without yelling.

"Hey," Andrew says.

"Hey." Dylan does not stop his throw.

"What'cha doing?"

"Tossing rocks."

They stand there for a while, Andrew watching Dylan toss rocks.

"Wanna do something?" Andrew finally asks.

"Okay, what?"

"I've got a secret fort. We could go there. It's behind some old abandoned building."

"Sounds cool."

Dylan stops picking up rocks and the two boys wander off following the creek for a ways before walking away from it. They cut across a few yards and up a back alley running behind homes.

They come to Old Man Hooper's house and are about to walk past it.

Seeing their approach, Caesar immediately runs to the end of his chain, ears alert and barking at the boys.

Dylan pauses and stares at the dog barking ferociously at the end of his chain.

"Hey, watch this," he says. Dylan looks around and then picks up a couple of rocks, hefting them to test their weight. They are not large, but they are big enough.

"I have a bad feeling about this," Andrew thinks.

Dylan waves one of the rocks in the air. The dog's ears perk up and his eyes follow the rock without slowing in his spittle-flinging barking. The dog's posture is aggressive and he is doing little hops with his front feet at the end of his chain as he barks.

Dylan nods and pulls his arm back and swings, sending the rock flying towards the dog.

Caesar dodges the missile and lunges, snapping at the flying rock, his teeth clacking as he just misses it when it flies past just beyond his chain's reach.

Dylan immediately lets the second rock fly and it hits the dog.

Caesar yelps and jumps sideways, dancing away from the pain and snapping at the unseen attacker. He is smart enough to realize almost immediately that it is one of the two boys who hurt him. He stops and stands there for a moment, staring them down, his fierce bark intensified.

With a powerful thrust of his hind legs, he lunges after the boys, intent on them, charging. The dog hits the end of his chain with a strangled yelp and is jolted backwards with the sudden stop of his collar held by the chain, flipping him over. He hits the ground with a muffled whuff and gets up looking a little dazed. He lunges at them again at the end of his chain, snapping and barking crazily.

The door to the house bangs open and Mr. Hooper comes hobbling out, arms in the air and fists waving. One fist holds a broom that he waves and brandishes like a weapon.

"Get out of here you little jerks!" he screams. "Leave my dog alone!"

He is coming after the boys, yelling and waving the broom like he will beat them with it. Caesar lunges and barks even harder, taking his cue from his master's agitation.

Dylan grabs Andrew's arm and tugs. "Come on, let's go!"

They run off down the street and don't stop until they are around the corner and out of sight.

Dylan breaks out into laughter.

Andrew looks at him, scowling. He doesn't think it's very funny. "Why'd you do that?" he asks, disgusted with what Dylan did.

"What? It's just some dumb old dog," Dylan laughs.

"Like your dumb old dog?"

That hit a chord in Dylan and he stops laughing, suddenly feeling shame for what he did. He thinks about the unknown cruelty and pain whoever broke into his house did tormenting his dog. She is still messed up by it, terrified of being left alone and of anyone coming to the house. His face reddens and feels hot with the heat of shame rising up his cheeks.

Dylan looks guiltily at Andrew. "Let's go find that fort of yours."

12   Investigating the Old Building

When Andrew and Dylan arrive at the old abandoned building, Dylan stops before it, looking up in awe. He had no idea this place even existed. His face spreads into a huge grin.

"This place is awesome! How long do you think this place was boarded up for?" He walks around the front of the building studying the old age-stained bricks and broken boarded up windows. Andrew follows, nervous of being here.

"I don't know. The fort is in the back. Lots of privacy. Nobody can really see back there unless they try."

Andrew leads the way around back and across the lot towards the old rotting shed that is their fort.

Dylan stops to inspect a stained old padded armchair sitting abandoned in the middle of the back lot. It is today's abandoned piece of furniture.

"That's the fort," Andrew says, pointing to the sagging shed.

Dylan looks up and his eyes gleam with joy at the sight of it. "Cool." He heads for the fort, Andrew following.

Dylan eagerly inspects the shed, testing the rotting wood and finding a stick to poke up at the sagging ceiling and the crumbling edges of the holes in it.

They hang around for a while at the fort and then Dylan wants to explore more.

"Let's check this place out," Dylan says.

Andrew smiles indulgently and follows. He did the same exploration when he found the abandoned property.

They wander around the yard, poking around the bottom of trees, checking out a lump of broken concrete that looks as if it could have fallen from the sky, and anything else that catches their attention.

"Hey, why are you always being such a jerk to people?" Andrew asks, feeling nervous about risking angering his ex friend.

Dylan shrugs. "I don't know. I'm just kind of mad all the time I guess."

"That's not a very good reason."

"No, probably not."

It doesn't take long for that moldy old chair to draw Dylan back to it.

"Hey, let's check this out," Dylan says. They inspect the chair again. Dylan almost sits in it but Andrew stops him.

"I don't think I'd want to sit in that." Andrew makes a disgusted grimace.

That makes it all the more fun. Dylan grins mischievously and starts horsing around as if he is now determined to sit in it. Andrew pushes him away and it turns into a wrestling match. They take turns trying to sit in the chair, fighting each other for who gets to sit in it and acting like they both don't want anyone touching it even as they both pretend they are uncontrollably drawn to sitting in it.

Tiring of the game, they stop and Dylan leans against the chair. He looks down at it with a grin and pushes, tilting it.

"I wouldn't," Andrew says, shaking his head and taking a step back.

Dylan grins and tips it over, jumping back as he lets it fall.

They watch it expectantly as the chair falls and hits the ground with a dust-raising thud. Both boys half expected a rat or something to jump out but nothing squealed or scurried from the chair except a big fat hairy spider that fell off from the impact when the chair hit the ground.

They shrug at each other. That was anticlimactic.

"Let's go check out the building." Dylan starts off across the yard, not waiting for Andrew.

Andrew looks at it, a shadow of unease crossing his eyes. He follows uncertainly.

Dylan starts poking around the boarded up brick building. Andrew watches him throw rocks at already broken windows where the boards had fallen off. They wander around the outside inspecting ground floor and basement windows and the locked doors. Dylan tries the door that Andrew thought he might have been able to open but could not budge.

"Maybe we shouldn't be trying to get in." Andrew tries to look casual.

"Nah, it's not like anyone is going to come around and catch us." Dylan pushes on the door again, putting his shoulder and weight into it. When it doesn't open, he moves on to a basement window that has a couple of missing boards, allowing possible access.

"Hey, come check this out." He waves Andrew over.

Andrew reluctantly joins him, both stooping down to look in.

Madison walks around the corner of the building to find Andrew and Dylan stooped down peeking in the basement window. She was heading for the fort, but changes course when she sees them.

As she approaches them, Dylan starts pulling on the remaining boards, trying to rip them off. The boys are unaware she is there.

Madison frowns and speeds up, walking purposely towards them. "I am going to give them heck and tell them to stay out of there," she thinks.

Madison is coming up right behind them, opening her mouth to speak, but just as she reaches them the board gives and Dylan tumbles backwards to land on his butt, knocking Andrew down too, laughing. Andrew can't help but grin at that, losing the serious look on his face.

"Andrew just what do you think you are doing?" Madison demands, hands on hips and looking a little too much like a mother scolding a naughty boy.

The boys look up at her and laugh even harder.

Madison's lips tighten into an angry line and she glares at them before she breaks down and starts laughing too.

"You looked ridiculous when that board gave and you both fell on your butts with a surprised look while still holding the board."

Andrew and Dylan get up and the three of them huddle around the window. Andrew is feeling braver now with two people to back him up.

They can see more now with another board out of the way. The glass is broken and a large portion of it is missing. The jagged edges are as grimy as the rest of the glass still there and a crack splits it into two halves. They look curiously into the darkness below.

"That was pretty tough to get off," Andrew says.

"Yeah, I thought it would be easier. The wood looks pretty rotten," Dylan says.

Dylan looks around, eying up the other windows. "Let's try some of the others."

Madison looks doubtful.

"It's okay," Dylan says. "It's not like we're going to go in or anything." He gives Andrew a conspiratorial wink when she turns to look at the other windows.

Against her better judgement, Madison joins them as they poke and prod at windows. They keep to the back and sides to avoid being seen. The other window boards are in the same shape as that first one and they return back to that first window.

"This looks like our best bet. It has the most boards missing," Dylan says, studying the last boards.

Andrew nods, studying the window. "I hope the last couple boards are not as hard."

Madison watches them suspiciously. She has a bad feeling she knows what they are up to.

"Let's do it," Dylan grins. "It's the best way in to check out what's in there."

Madison backs away. "You said you were not going to go inside," she accuses them.

The boys shrug at her with sheepish grins.

"Aren't you dying to see what's inside?" Andrew asks.

"I don't think you should go inside. It's dangerous and we are not supposed to be here at all," Madison says.

"Nah," Dylan waves her off. "What can happen? Nobody will find out if we don't tell."

"We'll be careful," Andrew says. His own doubt is creeping back with a sense of unease.

They struggle with the boards and, pulling together, get the last couple of boards off. They study the window again. There are sharp pieces of glass poking out here and there from the frame. In the bottom there is a brownish stain that they each privately suspect could be old blood.

They can get in now, but Andrew is suddenly unsure about it. The slithering sound he heard the night of the dance pops into his head. He can hear it in his imagination like it is happening again right at that moment.

Andrew thought the sound had come from the basement, but was filled with doubt later out of fear it was really outside where it could have gotten him. If it was outside, then it's long gone. But if it was in the basement, it could be still down there right now, waiting for them.

He had thought he saw motion in the darkness inside the windows a few times too. He had convinced himself it was a cat or something. But cats don't make a slithering sound.

Andrew feels an icy shock of fear climb up his spine. He doesn't want to go inside anymore.

"I think maybe Madison is right," he says. "We shouldn't go in."

Madison nods. "I don't think we should."

Dylan gives them both a look that says "chicken".

"Aw, come on. Really, what could happen?" He stares at them expectantly.

Andrew and Madison exchange uncertain looks. Neither of them wants to look afraid, despite their better judgement.

When they don't answer, Dylan takes it as agreement.

"We should try that back door again," Dylan says. "Maybe you are right about the window. We'd probably get cut and have to get a tetanus shot." He rubs his arm imagining how much that would hurt. He had heard they use an extra long needle and that it is very painful.

He goes over to the door, Andrew and Madison trailing reluctantly behind, and inspects it again. He looks around, wondering if there is something around that would help.

"Let's check this shed," he says.

They search the attached shed for tools they might use on the door. There isn't much in there of use and nothing that looks like it would help open the door.

"Maybe we can make a battering ram," Dylan says.

Madison remembers seeing an old rake abandoned in the grass next to the shed they made into their fort. It is almost completely buried under years of grass growing and dying and growing again.

"There's an old rake by the shed. It's hard to see. The ground has almost eaten it beneath the grass. It's lying right against the wall on the other side," Madison says. She regrets it the moment the words are out of her mouth. "Don't encourage them," she silently reprimands herself.

"I think I know where it is," Andrew says and runs off to get the rake. He has to pull hard against the years of dead grass grown over the rake. The ground does not seem to want to let the rake go and, for a moment, the thought occurs to Andrew that the ground is trying to protect them. It doesn't want them to go inside the abandoned brick building.

With a dull tearing sound, the grass gives way and Andrew pulls the rake free. Its underside is wet and discolored, slimy in spots where slugs had made a home beneath it. He races back with the rake.

The two boys study the door, trying to figure out the best way to use the rake to break it open.

They try a few different things that don't work.

Madison stands back watching and finally sighs as she steps forward and takes the rake from them.

"Like this." She shows them how they can use the rake as a lever against the door. "Now you just have to shove the teeth in the crack and pull it this way."

It is hard to do but they jamb the tips of the rake's teeth into the crack between the door and doorframe, managing only because the wood is rotting and soft. All three of them push together on the rake handle, using it as a lever.

The door creaks and groans and just when they are sure it is about to pop open the long rake pole cracks and snaps, breaking. They all fall.

The damage is done though. The teeth dug in and ripped up the edge of the door and the back of the rake head pressing against it splintered the doorframe.

They inspect the door again and, with a lot of tugging, they get it open, the bolt tearing through the softened rotten wood frame. Besides being locked, the door and frame had swelled, nearly fusing them together. If it were not for that, they may have been able to push the door open despite its lock. Over the years with the ground shifting the lock was no longer lined up.

Andrew, Dylan, and Madison stand staring at the yawning opening of the doorway into the darkness inside the building. They feel shock. None of them really thought they would get it open. Now they have to make a real decision. Talking about going in when they didn't think they could was one thing. Actually doing it is entirely different.

Dylan glances at Andrew, then at Madison. He can't look chicken in font of them, no matter how scared he feels right now. He turns back to the darkness beyond the doorway.

"This is it." He takes a deep breath, readying himself to step through the doorway.

"Wait," Madison says urgently. The two boys look at her. "What if it's not safe? What if the floor gives and you fall to the basement? What if the ceiling caves in? What if there's something in there?"

"What if there's some kind of weird monster that slithers," Andrew thinks.

"The only thing that might be in there is mice and maybe rats," Dylan says, regretting his choice of "rats", his own words making even himself less certain about going in. He looks at Andrew for support and reassurance.

Andrew stares into the darkness uncertainly. "Maybe Madison is right."

"Well? What do you want to do?" Dylan stares at him expectantly. "You can't decide, can you?"

Andrew shakes his head, meeting his look and wishing Dylan would just drop it and they can go do something else. He doesn't want to look like a wimp, but is afraid to go in.

"It's okay to chicken out if you are scared," Madison says, unintentionally sealing the deal.

Dylan looks at her quickly, bristling from her words. "I'm done with being a chicken whipped wimp," he thinks, fully feeling the unpleasant memory of the terror he had felt being home alone after his house was broken into. It makes him angry. Angry at the people who broke in, for the damage they did to the house, for stealing their stuff, for making him feel so stupid and useless and weak, afraid and helpless. For hurting Lucy.

His eyes burn suddenly at the thought of Lucy. The familiar pain of what they did to her flushes through him.

"I'm going in," he says roughly before his voice can crack with the tears he suddenly can't stop. He steps forward quickly before they can see the tears, not looking back, stepping into the darkness.

He takes a few steps in and is immediately blinded by the darkness. He has to stop to let his eyes adjust. It's not total blackness inside. The cloying dust makes his throat catch with a tickle and his eyes burn.

"At least I can blame it on the dust," he thinks, trying to swallow and not cough.

Outside, safe in the daylight, Madison and Andrew exchange looks. Andrew frowns.

"We can't let him go in alone."

"This is a bad idea," Madison shakes her head.

They step through the doorway together into the darkness, blinded and stopping to blink and let their eyes adjust. Madison can't stifle the cough from the heavy dust.

They look around for Dylan, not seeing him immediately.

It is dark and creepy with deep shadows everywhere. Enough light comes in through the cracks between the boards on the windows and more where boards are missing altogether so that they can see, although not well.

Andrew thinks about the slithering sound he heard before and the ground that was not willing to give up the rake. "Seems like two good warnings not to go in," he thinks.

"Where are you?" he whispers loudly.

"Here," Dylan whispers back, waving at them. They spot him among the looming darker shadows inside and join him, Madison walking very close to Andrew.

When they reach him, Dylan moves on. They go deeper into the building, unconsciously clinging close together nervously, exploring the building.

"What do you think they used this place for?"

"I don't know. Some kind of factory maybe?"

Anna is walking past the old abandoned brick building again, going back towards home. She hears voices and other noises and pauses to listen. She is sure they are coming from behind the old boarded up brick building.

Curious, Anna walks around the building to investigate.

Anna comes around the corner of the building just as Andrew and Madison vanish into the darkened interior. When she reaches the back there is no one to be seen.

At the back of the building, Anna walks along the back wall and finds the open door. She stops and listens, hearing the voices coming from inside.

She goes to the doorway and looks in. "Who would go in there?" She shrugs and steps through the doorway, going in to investigate.

Anna stops inside, the dust tickling her throat and blinded by the darkness. She almost sneezes, pinching her nose in time to stifle it.

Shapes loom in a shadowy world of grey and darkness as her eyes adjust. She looks around, thinking she saw movement. She goes in the direction of the motion.

Dylan leads the way, Madison and Andrew following him as they nervously explore the abandoned building.

Something touches Madison in the darkness and she screams, jumping back.

Andrew whirls, feels a tug on his shirt, and jumps, startled and squawking out a surprised cry.

Dylan stops and turns to them, arms coming up on the defensive, looking for whatever attacked them.

Andrew laughs nervously. "I must have caught my shirt on something."

"I felt something grab me." Madison looks at them, her expression afraid and her voice wavering.

Dylan tries to look tough and brave, looking around on the defensive. He laughs, pointing. "You both got scared by that handle sticking out of that machine."

Something grabs him from behind and he jumps and yelps, spinning around and stepping back towards the other two.

Anna jumps out of her hiding spot with a loud growl, arms raised and fingers hooked into claws.

All three of them jump and let out sounds between startled gasps and frightened squeals. Their hearts race madly with the fear gripping them.

Anna can't hold it in any longer. She snorts with the effort of stopping the laughter and the laughs come roaring out. She doubles over with laughter, stepping towards them.

"You should have seen your faces," she chokes out between laughs. Despite her own prank on them, Anna can't help but feel a little startled too at their frightened reactions.

They stand there looking at each other awkwardly. She laughs nervously and then Dylan does too. Andrew is still too numb with fear to laugh and Madison wonders if her heart will ever stop pounding so hard and feeling so tight in her chest.

"What are you doing in here?" Anna whispers. There really is no need to whisper; it just feels like the right thing to do in this creepy place.

"Just messing around, checking the place out," Dylan says, eying her warily and wondering if she will tell on them.

Anna looks around. "Sure is creepy in here."

Andrew and Madison nod.

"What is over there?" Anna asks, pointing. She starts off in that direction. The others follow and soon the four of them are investigating every inch they can of the main floor.

The floorboards creak and groan beneath their weight, sometimes whining out a warning against the softness of the rotting wood floor. When they hit a spot that feels spongy, they carefully test the floor around them, each pressing their weight down cautiously with one foot, until they find a more solid path to walk on.

"Someone bigger than us could go right through this floor," Anna gasps.

The others agree and only moments later they discover a hole in the floor that looks like that very thing may have happened. They look down to the blackness below.

"I wonder if there might be the bones of someone who fell through the floor down there," Dylan says, voicing what they are all thinking.

"How many latchkey kids are buried under that floor," Anna moans, trying to make her voice sinister.

"Latchkey kids?" Madison asks. "What's that?"

"You know, us," Anna says. "Don't tell me you never heard of it. It's a term from the 1940's for kids like us who spend a lot of time home alone because our parents work and there is no one home to look after us."

"That's dumb," Andrew sneers. "You made that up."

"I did not," Anna says, a little insulted.

"I think it sounds kind of cool," Madison says. "Like a club. The Latchkey Kids. That's us."

Dylan and Andrew both snort at that and Anna makes a face.

"Let's keep looking," Dylan says.

They continue on with the exploration.

The main floor is mostly empty, most of the stuff inside having been hauled away and sold off a long time ago. There is only the old rusted machinery in the large main room. They have no idea what it could possibly have been used for.

They are studying the machinery when Andrew speaks up. It is an act of his active imagination, blurting out what he is thinking without intending to.

"I think there's something in the basement."

The others look at him.

"More stuff like this?" Dylan asks.

Andrew shakes his head, feeing dumb and wishing he didn't say anything.

He is drawn on by the expectant looks of the two girls; that sweet wide-eyed stare of anticipation waiting for the thrill of a scary story in the darkness as the wind howls outside and tree branches tap against the wall like skeletal hands. It does not matter that they don't hear any of that, this place is spooky enough already.

"I heard noises when I was here before and trying to look in the windows. And I saw something moving inside the window we pulled the boards off of. I figured it was just a cat. But I came here during the school dance and heard something else."

He looks around at the others, still feeling dumb. Hopefully they think I'm just telling ghost stories, he thinks. He does not want to say what he heard but feels he has to.

"I heard a slithering sound, like a giant snake or lizard dragging its belly on the ground. Cats don't slither."

The others just stare at him, speechless.

Dylan grins, deciding it's a joke.

"Let's check it out," he says. Now he is even more excited to explore the basement.

There is something about basements that always seems just a little creepy. Maybe it is because being below ground makes basements seem a little like a cave, or it could be because sunlight just doesn't get down there the same way it fills the floors above ground.

Maybe it is long forgotten memories passed down in the same genes that make you instinctively afraid of some things, genetic memories from the Neanderthals who preceded us. Or it is an instinct, your nerves warning you against something your body senses that lies deep beneath the ground.

All four kids feel the taught wire of anxious nerves at the thought of going down into the basement.

Despite his eagerness to check it out, Dylan feels a sudden rush of fear over going down there.

Andrew is itching to find out what is down there in the same way the horror movie coward cannot help but look in the shed. He is afraid. The thought of going down there brings back that slithering sound loud and clear in his imagination. He almost thinks he hears it for real now.

"At least I won't be going down alone," Andrew thinks.

Madison shakes her head with a frown. "It's a bad idea. We should just leave."

Anna looks at each of them. She has never really had anything to do with any of them before, but she still does not want to look like she is weak and scared. Trying to act braver than she feels, Anna stands firm and tries to keep the tremble out of her voice.

"We should do it." Her determined smile does not cover the fear in her eyes.

Dylan is thinking about how to get out of doing this when he notices how much darker it seems. "It's getting darker in here," he says, suddenly realizing how much the light has changed.

He is the bad boy, the tough bully who gets in trouble and is supposed to be scared of nothing. He can't let them know that he is scared to go down there. Maybe tomorrow he will feel braver.

"It is getting late," Dylan says. "We should all get home before any of us get in trouble. We will meet here again tomorrow. Bring flashlights, we are going down."

None of them wants to show their own fear of going down into the basement. They all agree. At least they are putting it off. Tomorrow is another day and just because they agreed to do it; does not mean it will happen.

They file out of the building. The light in the sky is getting old, the sun hanging to the West. Some of them are probably already out past the time they had to be home.

They split up, each heading for home and lost in their own thoughts.

Dylan's thoughts turn to Kylie as he walks home. He will be going past Kylie's house. "Maybe I'll see her," he thinks.

13   It's Not Dad's Visit

Kylie is at home alone. Her mom is at work and her sister at a babysitter. She moves around the house restlessly, looking out the window again and moving around restlessly. She picks up a book, tries to read it, but can't get her mind to focus on the words and puts it down again. She turns the T.V. on, skims the channels, and turns it off again with a deep unhappy sigh.

She looks at the window again. She doesn't need to look out to know what is out there. It is so nice out and she feels cooped up inside.

"I'm going outside."

After milling around the yard for a while bored, Kylie decides to go for a walk. She locks the house and starts walking. She has no destination in mind. It just feels good to be out in the sun and warm air, but at the same time, she can't shake the uneasy feeling that has been bugging her all day.

"It's probably just stress from having to see my dad. I wish I never have to see him again. He's a horrible person who is always mean. I wish he would just die so we would never have to see him again.

Now that me and my sister have to have visits with him again, my life is worse even than those nasty bully girls make it. Every visit with him has been a nightmare. He is always so angry and mean. It takes nothing to set him off and we feel like we are walking on eggshells we don't dare break or else. He yells at us, towering over us. It's scary. Sometimes he hurts us; hits us, or shakes or grabs us hard.

Becca is like a little ghost when we go for the visits. She is there, but it's like she's not even in there. Sometimes I don't see her in her eyes and it scares me. She's like a silent spirit only partially in this world. Sometimes it's her being too scared to answer him that sets him off. When that happens and he turns his anger on her, I have to protect her. She's just a little kid. I try to distract him or turn his anger on me instead."

She scuffs her foot on the pavement, sighing unhappily again, walking without paying attention to where she is going.

"He keeps threatening to take us away from Mom too. He made the same threats all the time before, when we used to go for visits before Mom stopped making us go. He threatened to hurt Mom then too.

I even told him once that I hate him and would run away if he took us from Mom because I would never live with him. I told him I would take my sister with me. He hit me hard when I said that, knocking me to the floor. Mom cried later when she saw the bruise on my cheek.

That's when Mom refused to let us go for any more visits. Dad freaked out when he showed up to pick us up. Me and Becca were so scared he was going to hurt Mom. We watched out the window. It was the most scared I've ever been."

Kylie often has nightmares that her dad is following her. She sees his car at school, parked across the street. He is sitting there looking angry as always, and just staring at the school bus. Sometimes in her dream, Kylie knows it is summer break and does not know why she's even at school.

Often there are no other kids there at school or on the bus in her dream. She gets on the bus alone and it drives away while she takes a seat on the empty bus. She looks out the bus window and sees his car following it.

When she gets off the bus, he is somehow already there, waiting and watching in his car. She runs home scared, imagining him racing up in his car and either running her over to leave her bleeding and broken in the road or snatching her off the street and dragging her into the car kicking and screaming, never to see her mother and sister again, to be kept prisoner by the father she hates and fears.

"He would happily kill all three of us. He hates us all that much.

Sometimes Dad shows up when we aren't even supposed to have a visit. He just sits in his car outside the house or school watching. I feel like he is staring right through the walls right into my soul even though he can't see me. It really creeps me out. Especially when I'm home alone and Mom won't be home for hours."

She imagines him coming in and killing her, then waiting for her mom and sister to walk in and killing them too, standing over their bodies and gloating with an evil grin.

Kylie feels sick now after thinking about her dad. She feels the tight knot that makes her stomach hurt.

"Think about something else," Kylie mutters. She tries to push her thoughts away but can't find any happier things to think about instead. There doesn't seem to be anything happy at all about her life.

Her thoughts turn to Amber and the mean team. On top of the stress and fear over her father, Kylie is still being bullied by the girls who bullied her mercilessly all year at school.

"It's spring break and I don't have to see them at all for two weeks, but I still can't escape them. Why can't they just leave me alone? They are always saying mean lies about me online. And if they catch me on any of the chat sites, they attack me with nasty comments. I can't even leave the house. I'm not safe going anywhere in the neighborhood. If I run into them they will beat me up."

The thought reminds her how risky what she is doing is. Kylie looks around quickly for her stalkers, both the mean team and her dad. A sick feeling of dread washes through her. She defiantly pushes it down to the bottom of her stomach, refusing to give in to the urge to run home and hide behind locked doors.

"Ok, happy thoughts, happy thoughts," Kylie chastises herself. She tries to think of something else. It's not much better. Her thoughts turn to Dylan, one of the last people in the world she would want to think about.

"Dylan has been acting so creepy in the last weeks of school. He is always looking at me. Yuck." The thought crosses Kylie's mind that there might be another reason for his behavior.

"Could he like me?" She dismisses the idea just as quickly. "No, that's ridiculous. He was probably just thinking of ways to bully me. Since he started hanging around with Amber he is probably spying on me for her."

The idea that he could like her still sits heavy in her stomach even though she immediately dismissed it as a dumb thought.

"I don't like Dylan. He is always bullying other kids. He is mean, just like my dad!"

Kylie is not really paying attention to her surroundings with all these thoughts going through her head.

She sees a car out of the corner of her eye.

"Is it following me?" Kylie turns to look fearfully and panic grips her. "Dad!" She wants to run but is frozen with fear. The car gets closer, driving slowly, and finally passes her.

Kylie feels weak with relief. "It wasn't him. It was some woman in a car that only kind of looks like his car."

Then she spots the real danger ahead, Amber and Jessica. Kylie's heart sinks and starts beating faster, making her feel suddenly dizzy. She feels nauseous.

"Please, let them not see me." She dodges sideways and runs off between houses, looking behind her fearfully to see if they spotted her. "Are they following me?"

"I have to get home. I'll be safer there behind locked doors."

She cuts across back yards; careful to avoid anywhere the girls might see her. The next house is hers. Safe. The back door lock always sticks and she runs around the house to the front door out of habit. It is not until Kylie is coming up the side of the yard and gets close to the front that she spots the car.

She stops.

"No, it can't be." It's her dad's car. There is no doubt this time. Kylie looks around.

"I have to get safely into the house and lock the door. Where is he? I don't see him in the car."

Creeping up along the side of the house to get a better look at the car, she peeks and still does not see him in the car. "Where is he?"

Kylie holds her breath and goes back the way she came, keeping against the side of the house to get to the back door. She is unlocking the door, the lock stubbornly sticking, when she hears her father's voice immediately behind her.

"Hello Kylie."

Kylie turns around and stands there looking up at him with what she is sure is a stupid expression.

He is waiting for a response, but in her fear, she has no idea what he said. She just stares up at him numbly.

"Let's go," he says, reaching for her, "we're going for a drive."

Kylie backs away and his mouth hardens and his eyes are angry.

"I said let's go," he says sternly.

Kylie shakes her head no. "It's not time for the visit," she murmurs almost too quiet to be heard.

"I said to come!" He lunges at her, grabbing, and Kylie dodges him but he catches her arm. He grips it painfully tight as he drags her to the front of the house.

Dylan is walking up the street and he sees people ahead. It looks like they are fighting, like a man and a girl. The man is dragging the girl to the car and she is fighting. They are in front of Kylie's house.

"It's probably just some girl being difficult with her dad." But the fear that has haunted him ever since his house was broken into rushes at him, almost overwhelming him.

"That's Kylie's house," he mutters, "and she's home alone." He has a sinking feeling in his stomach and his legs turn weak.

Without thinking, he starts jogging then running, forcing his muscles to move when they would rather melt into a puddle on the ground.

Kylie is struggling to break free from her father's grip but he is too strong. He shakes her roughly and slaps her face, dragging her to the car.

"You are coming with me! Your mom is never going to see you again!"

Kylie screams for help and Dylan runs harder.

Her father pulls the car door open and is shoving her inside the back seat.

Kylie screams and twists, trying to escape. Then she is in the car and the door slams on her, hitting her painfully as she struggles to crawl out. Panicked, Kylie reaches for the door latch and pulls.

It's locked! She lunges across the seat and tries the other side while her dad walks around to the driver's door.

"He put on the child locks," she thinks wildly. "The back doors can't be opened from the inside!" Kylie attacks the window button but it won't work. She is trapped! She bangs on the window, crying and screaming.

She tries lunging over the seat to escape out the front door. The driver's door opens and her Dad is getting in. He reaches back and hits her in the face with the back of his hand hard enough to daze her, shoving her back roughly.

"Stop it!" he yells. "Stop it or I'll beat the living daylights out of you!"

The car pulls away from the curb just as Dylan reaches it. He stares after it. Kylie's frantic terrified look is blazed into his brain.

"She is being kidnapped by a stranger!" he gasps. Before he knows what he is doing, Dylan runs and lunges at the car, grabbing the rear door handle.

Seeing the kid lunging at the car, Kylie's dad hits the door lock button on the driver's door, just as the boy grabs the door handle and pulls.

Dylan is already pulling on the handle as the locks click. He yanks the door open. "Come on!" he cries breathlessly to a very stunned Kylie.

She is frozen for a fraction of a second that feels like forever, just staring at her impossible rescuer.

Dylan reaches in and grabs her.

The car swerves across the road as her dad tries to reach around to the back seat and loses control of the car.

Dylan is struggling to keep up with the slowly moving car. He pulls Kylie, dragging her across the seat and yanks her out of the car.

They both stumble in the road. He is trying to hold her up and get her on her feet and Kylie is trying to get her feet under her. She falls, skinning a knee, and Dylan pulls her to her feet.

"Let's go!" he cries urgently, hanging on to her and pulling her. They start running.

They race to the back of the house and across the neighbor's backyard, running for their lives.

Kylie's dad is out of the car chasing them, yelling at them.

Knowing the area better, the kids manage to evade him and escape. They don't stop running until they are both winded and suffering from painful stitches in their sides.

They cut across yards to go a few streets over and crawl through the loose fence board, Dylan getting stuck and almost too big to fit. Apparently, most of the neighborhood kids know about the secret board gateway to the alley on the other side of the fence.

They jog up the back lane, gasping and holding their sides, towards Mr. Hooper's house and Caesar.

"Where are we going?" Kylie pants breathlessly, still holding her side as pain cuts through her ribs.

Bruises from her father's attack and her escape are already beginning to show on her and the blood dripping down her leg from her knee is starting to clot and stop bleeding. The drips running down her legs are drying and turning crusty.

"I know a place we can hide," Dylan says, leading her on.

Caesar is lying in a corner of the yard, hidden behind some of the clutter. His eyes are closed and he appears to be sleeping. His ear twitches at the sound of the approaching kids. He raises his head to look around, sniffing at the air.

He picks up their scent. He puts his head down and ears back. It is the scent of the boy who throws rocks that bite. His senses heighten and cry out "danger!" He can hear them coming closer. His lips curl up, showing his teeth.

Caesar rises to his feet, looking intently in the direction the scent and sounds are coming from. This boy hurt him enough times for the dog to expect it. Fear tingles through him the moment the boy comes into view.

Dylan and Kylie reach Mr. Hooper's yard. They don't see the dog. They forgot all about him.

They hear the thudding of paws on the ground first, the heavy breath chugging in and out of the dog's mouth. They freeze instinctively, looking up in time to see the large dark dog charging them with powerful strides.

With nowhere to go to escape the boy who hurts him because he is restricted by the chain, the dog's fight or flight response is left with only one option. Fight. Caesar would rather run away and hide. Instead, he charges at the kids, lunging and barking loudly, showing his teeth to let the boy know he has them.

The silence explodes into fierce saliva spitting ferocious barking.

Both kids tense with the fear the dog is about to rip them apart. Kylie is frozen in place and Dylan manages to make the small move of stepping partially between her and the attacking dog.

Scared of the boy even though he is making a good show of being brave, Caesar keeps lunging and barking, ready to bite the boy to defend himself. The dog is trembling, but the kids are oblivious to all but those big teeth and his loud spittle-flying barking.

Kylie shrinks away from Caesar, but Dylan leads her past the angrily barking dog.

"It's okay, he's on a chain. He can't reach the road." Dylan looks at the dog as they go past; feeling sorry for the mean things he did to the animal.

"I wonder why he's so mean," Kylie whispers.

Dylan flushes with embarrassment, but does not offer his thoughts.

They just reach the front yard when Mr. Hooper opens the front door and comes hobbling out. He is hobbling even worse than Dylan remembers, like his legs or feet are giving him pain.

Mr. Hooper waves a fist and starts yelling but is caught in a fierce coughing fit that doubles him over.

The two kids quickly scurry past his house.

"That must be why the dog is so mean," Kylie says once they are out of the old man's earshot, "because Old Man Hooper is so mean."

"Let's go." Dylan looks around nervously, still worried about the strange man who tried to kidnap Kylie. He leads the way, finally stopping in front of the abandoned brick building he had explored earlier.

"This will be a good place to hide. No one will ever think of looking for us here."

Kylie eyes the building doubtfully. "This does not feel right," she thinks nervously.

"It's okay," Dylan says, seeing her unease. "It's safe. The place is abandoned. Me and some other kids were in there already checking it out."

Against her better judgement, Kylie lets the boy she hates lead her inside the dark building. She frowns as he leads her around to the back and in through the door Dylan and the others had broken in through.

14 Noises in the Basement

Andrew returns home from their exploration of the old abandoned building. He is just putting his key in the lock and turning it to open the door when he remembers why he left the house.

He had been sure there was something in the basement and it terrified him.

Suddenly nervous, Andrew pauses before opening the door. He opens it cautiously, listening, and peers around the partially open door into the house. He is ready to bolt.

There is no sign of anything. No sound except the dull humming of the refrigerator in the kitchen.

Andrew slips into the house and looks around for any signs of a four-legged rat-faced intruder.

The cookie is still mashed into the carpet and the glass of milk is laying on its side. The wet spot in the carpet is obvious, the moisture turning the carpet a darker color and turning the crushed cookie to mush. It is all soaked in.

"Great," he mumbles. "I have to clean it up before Mom and Dad get home or I'll be in trouble for having the food and drink in the living room."

The noises in the basement are forgotten.

Andrew gets a towel from the bathroom and scrubs the wet spot out of the carpet. He scrubs and scrubs, finally sitting back and staring at it.

"It's useless. No matter how much I scrub, I can't get the carpet completely dry. You can hardly see it now, but you can still tell where the carpet was wet." He shrugs. "Hopefully it dries enough by the time they get home so they don't notice it."

Andrew is startled by the sudden ringing of the phone that breaks the silence. His face turns red in a hot flush of embarrassment and he goes to the phone and answers it.

"Hello."

"Hey there." His stomach tightens at the sound of his mom's voice.

"It's like she knows I did something wrong," he thinks, expecting her to lecture him for the milk and cookies in the living room.

"Something came up. We are going to be late getting home. Your Auntie Stella is having another of her self-made dramas and we have to go over there. Will you be okay getting your own supper? I don't know how late we will be, but we probably won't be home until after you are sleeping. Be a good boy and clean up after yourself, brush your teeth and don't stay up too late."

"I'll be fine Mom." He tries to hold off the annoyed sigh at his mother's tone that suggests he's just a little kid.

His mother stares ahead at the road while her husband drives the car, feeling guilty for not going home to look after her son. "You can stay up late a little bit. An hour past bedtime and no more," she says.

"Ok mom, I'll be fine."

"Goodbye."

"Bye." Andrew hangs up the phone and realizes his heart is still racing and he still half expects her to be scolding him for having food and drink in the living room, for spilling it, and for taking a whole stack of cookies for a snack. His mom is big on healthy snacks and cookies are not a healthy snack.

Andrew goes back to the living room, looks down guiltily at the wet spot on the carpet, and turns on the television, watching mindless cartoons for a while. It's a small comfort, to watch shows he is too old for now.

He stiffens and looks at the video game machine.

"The game is turned off. I'm sure I left it on. Weird." Andrew shrugs, "Maybe it turns off on its own? Maybe it does that after a while when nobody plays it? I don't remember it doing that before, but Mom turns it off if I leave it on."

He looks back to the television set. "I left that on too. But it was off when I came back. It doesn't turn itself off. I must have turned them off. Or maybe the power went out?"

"I must be imagining things, probably from exploring that creepy old abandoned building." He feels a little on edge and decides to hide in the mindless jabber of the television and goes back to watching cartoons.

Andrew knows he's probably too old for cartoons, but sometimes losing yourself in a childhood activity feels like the safest place to be. A lopsided smile creases his face as he lets his mind go blank while staring at the colorful images playing on the screen.

A while later Andrew's stomach rumbles. He looks down at it and realizes he is hungry.

"Guess I have to find something to eat."

Andrew goes to the kitchen to scavenge for something for supper. Not finding anything he wants, Andrew settles on soda pop and a bag of potato chips. He plunks himself in front of the television with his supper, flips channels, and picks a scary movie.

He sits there mesmerized by the movie, munching on chips and drinking his soda as the darkness outside grows deeper with night. Without realizing it, Andrew's eyes get heavier as the movie progresses and the clock hands move around the clock face. His head sags and he dozes off.

The movie is still playing while soft snores come from the boy slouched on the couch. A woman on the movie screams in terror, running through the woods for her life without breaking into his sleep.

Andrew wakes feeling groggy and rubs his eyes. For a moment he is not sure where he is, then realizes he is on the couch in the living room. The movie is over and some lame old black and white western is playing. White guys painted and dressed to look like the old stereo type of North American natives are whooping and yelling, chasing a bunch of cowboys. Their horses and arms seem to be moving too fast and it just looks funny.

One man in a big white hat leading a group milling around on horses proclaims, "Let's go get those Indians." They take off, their horses and arms moving comically fast as they race to the rescue.

"Indians," Andrew thinks, "that's rude. It's not even what they are called." Nobody really told him what he is supposed to call them. He wonders why nobody ever told him what they like to be called. "What if I ever met one? I wouldn't know what to call him."

"By his name, dummy," he thinks and laughs at his own goofiness. Andrew looks around, wondering what woke him up.

"Probably nothing," he mutters. He can't shake the feeling that it was something.

He listens, thinking that maybe it was the sound of his parents coming home. He remembers the chips and soda and hurries to put them away before he gets in trouble for having them in the living room.

Andrew is in the kitchen putting them away when he hears a thud. He turns and listens. "Car door?"

He hears another noise. "Basement."

Andrew looks and the basement door is open. "Didn't I leave it closed?"

He stares at the open doorway and the blackness of the dark basement stairs. "Maybe Mom and Dad stopped by the house while I was out this afternoon. They probably turned off the T.V. and game too."

His own words ring false. They would not have left cookies mashed into the carpet or the milk spilled there.

Andrew goes to the basement door to close it. He does not like it being open. Light from the kitchen splashes down the stairs, fading into the darkness and doing little to light anything beyond the stairs.

Grabbing the door, he starts swinging it closed and pauses. He is sure he saw movement below. Just a flash of movement in the dark, unrecognizable.

"Are they home? Are they in the basement in the dark for some reason?"

He hears another sound down there.

"Mom? Dad?" he calls.

Nobody answers.

Andrew steps down the first step nervously. He bends down, trying to see, but he is still too high. He slowly descends a few more steps, stopping before he reaches the middle of the staircase, again bending to see. Somehow, it feels safer having a shorter distance to the top than the bottom.

He can see only the bit of floor near the bottom of the stairs. He continues down. At the bottom of the stairs, he looks around. Shadows loom where furniture would be if the lights were on.

He flips the light switch but the lights do not come on. "Maybe they are burnt out? Or the fuse popped?"

"Mom? Dad?" he calls again.

Again, no one answers.

Andrew hears something. Someone is moving in the storage area.

He moves slowly towards the other room, listening. His heart is racing in his chest.

Andrew enters the storage area. It is cluttered with stuff stacked on shelves and boxes stacked on boxes. A lot of junk that a family accumulates over the years and that makes its way to the basement in case they might ever need it again.

There is a blur of movement to the side and Andrew spins just in time to catch the quickest glimpse of something dark and crouched down low to the floor before it vanishes behind a stack of boxes the height of his waist.

Andrew turns as if sensing it just as another stack of boxes piled to the ceiling behind him starts teetering. Looking up at the falling boxes in horror, putting his arms up to protect himself, they tumble down on him.

Whatever is hiding in the basement darts past him, banging into his legs and knocking him down.

Andrew screams. "I'm being attacked by whatever lives in the basement!" he thinks wildly.

Bruised but not broken from the weight of the boxes, his fall inadvertently saving him from the worst of the avalanche of boxes, Andrew is a little dazed.

"How did I get under this pile of boxes?" He starts pushing one off and freezes. Now he remembers. He listens, his eyes darting around the dark storage room, willing them to see better in the dark.

He can hear them scurrying in the darkness, coming at him, whatever they are.

Andrew screams and flails around.

"I'm going to die! They are going to eat my eyes out and my guts and kill me!" he thinks in a wild panic.

Crawling from under the pile of boxes with a mewling whimper, he scuttles off to a corner behind where the fallen boxes had been stacked. He stops, breathing fast and looking around.

"Whatever it is, it had to push the boxes from this side," he thinks. "What if there are more of them? They could be hiding right here. I could have just taken cover where they are."

Andrew is filled with an icy panic.

The creatures are climbing over the boxes, but the jumbled pile is slowing them down.

In the darkness, with the boxes mostly blocking them from his view, Andrew cannot tell what they are. He is pretty sure they must be rats, very large and probably crazed rats. "Maybe they are some kind of escaped super rats with human intelligence. No, even smarter than people."

"That's ridiculous!" he tells himself in his head as he watches for them from the safety of his corner. But his corner is not safe. Nowhere in the basement is and they are going to get him and eat his eyes while he tries to fight them off. Andrew is sure of it.

Behind the bottom boxes still against the wall, Andrew sees a large hole in the wall.

"That must be how they get in!"

With the creatures between him and escape, coming at him, Andrew looks around desperately. There is nowhere to go. He looks in the hole. "I think it's a tunnel."

He looks back to the doorway with the dark movement of shapes between him and there. He looks back to the darker tunnel again. "It's the only way out."

Terrified, Andrew crawls into the tunnel to escape the attacking creatures. He only hopes he can crawl faster than they can scamper.

"Don't think about that. Just go as fast as you can."

With one last look at the dark shapes struggling over the fallen boxes, he grabs a large box, pulling it hard and wedging it into the opening. "Maybe that will slow them down."

Andrew starts crawling as fast as he can through the tunnel. He can hear them behind him, chewing and clawing through the box blocking the tunnel entrance. The tunnel goes downwards and suddenly opens up larger. He can stand up here.

He gets up and runs for his life through the tunnel.

15   Old Man Hooper – Caesar Runs Away

The cluttered junk in Mr. Hooper's yard sits oddly quiet. The dog's chain lies snaking across the ground, the bent open clip at the end empty.

The overpowering presence of the large dog is conspicuously missing.

Mr. Hooper hobbles up the street calling Caesar. He looks so frail and lost, worried about his dog.

He sees a woman pushing a stroller, looks at her hopefully, and hobbles towards her. She tries to hide her flinch at his approach, wishing he would not try to talk to her.

"Have you seen my dog?" He stops, staring at her. "He is big and black and brown. He kind of looks like he could have Rottweiler, Doberman, and German shepherd in him?" He waits for an answer.

Feeling stunned by his presence, Mr. Hooper, who is known to be a mean old coot, she blinks and tries to find something to say, finally managing a quick, "No, sorry, I haven't seen him." She scurries off quickly with her stroller, making her escape.

Mr. Hooper watches her go, his hopeful look falling to lost hope. He starts walking again, calling Caesar. A few hours of this and his loss is turning to doubt and suspicion. Caesar never broke off his chain before.

He keeps searching, stopping anyone he sees and questioning them about the animal, sure now that someone has done something to his dog. He knows they all hate him and his dog.

Two streets from Mr. Hooper's house, Amber is walking along the sidewalk. The house on the corner ahead has tall bushes running down both sides of the yard that block the view of the yard beside it and the sidewalk and street on its far side. She reaches the end of the street, turns the corner and stops dead in her tracks, a look of fear suddenly on her face.

A large dog is standing perfectly still only inches away, staring at her with his evil beady eyes. It is Caesar.

Amber swallows hard, terrified. "Everyone knows how mean Caesar is. I wish he would get hit by a car."

Caesar takes a step closer. They are face to face, only a few feet apart, and she can smell his awful dog breath.

"Oh my gawd, he's going to attack me and rip me apart," her mind reels. She can't make herself move. She wants to run. She does not want to move. "If I move, he will attack. If I don't move, he will attack. I'm dead."

Caesar's head swivels to stare at something that caught his attention. With a powerful thrust of his hindquarters, he bolts and runs away.

Pale and shaking, Amber runs in the opposite direction to avoid running into the dog again. She runs blindly, thinking only of putting as much distance as she can between her and that dog. Finally too winded to run any more, she stops and looks around, not sure where she is.

The street is unfamiliar. She is standing in front of an old boarded up brick building; the same one the other kids had investigated. She looks around to get her bearings.

"I came from that way, so if I go back that way and this way…" Amber nods. "I think I know which direction is home." She turns to look at the abandoned building. "That's a creepy looking old building. If I cut through that lot it will be a lot faster than going back the way I came."

With some trepidation, eyeing the abandoned warehouse suspiciously, she takes a wider path as she cuts across the yard to the back of the building, planning to keep going all the way through. It is a creepy old building and Amber does not want to spend any more time here than absolutely necessary.

She looks around quickly when she reaches the back corner of the building and can see the lot behind the building. She speeds up, cutting through the back lot. Amber sees an old rotting armchair dumped in the middle of the back lot, tipped on its side. There is something on the ground near it.

Amber pauses, watching it warily and unable to tell what it is. "Is it a cat or small dog?"

It moves around to the other side of the chair, moving out of sight.

Keeping her distance, Amber keeps the chair in sight, watching for whatever is there, taking a few steps forward. She has to walk past the chair.

"I'd rather know what it is," she complains. She catches another glimpse of it. Whatever it is, it is moving around the chair with her, keeping the chair between her and it.

"Is it some kid playing with me?" The idea makes her mad and she is tempted to storm over there and let whoever it is have it. She angles to walk partially around the chair, still keeping her distance, trying to get a look at who or what is there.

She gets a brief glimpse of it again before it scuttles around the chair, but not a good look. It is something dark, hairy, bigger than a cat, and hunched down. "Caesar? Did he follow me? What if it is him? There is no way I'm going near it."

Amber looks around, unsure what to do. "What if he chases me?"

She spots the open door at the back of the building. There is movement in the darkness just beyond the open doorway. She stares hard but cannot make out what it is. She quickly takes her attention back to the chair in fear that whatever is behind it is sneaking up on her and catches another quick glimpse of it before it dodges back behind the chair.

"Whatever is behind the chair there are more than one. There are two, maybe three. That's it, I am out of here!"

She hurries across the lot in a fast walk, reminding herself that her parents always say that running only makes an animal chase you. As soon as she puts the chair and building out of sight down the alley, she starts running.

Mr. Hooper sees Amber walking quickly towards him with an unsettled look. "What's that girl's name?" he thinks. "Bah, I don't care. These kids now days are always trouble!"

"Hey, girl!" he calls out to her as she gets closer.

"I do not talk to strangers," Amber says, not slowing down.

Mr. Hooper hobbles after her, having trouble keeping up with her fast walk.

"My dog, have you seen a dog loose? A big black dog."

"Everyone knows your dog Mr. Hooper. Old Caesar is the meanest dog around and one of these days he is going to hurt someone and get taken away," Amber sneers at him.

Hooper stiffens his jaw at this. "Rude disrespectful kid," he thinks angrily.

"Have you seen my dog?" he asks again. "You did, didn't you? What is your hurry? What did you do to Caesar?"

He is catching up and reaching out to grab the girl and make her stop.

She stops before he can and Mr. Hooper almost runs right into her. He stops unsteadily.

"I saw your dumb old dog," Amber says. "He chased me and tried to bite me. I am telling my dad and he is going to call the dog pound to come take him away."

"Where?" Mr. Hooper demands.

Amber shrugs, hoping the old man never finds his nasty old dog. "It would serve them both right," she thinks.

"He went in that abandoned building a couple streets over," Amber lies.

"I hope the floor falls out or a ceiling falls on you when you go searching in there for your stupid dog, you ugly old buzzard," she thinks nastily.

Mr. Hooper pales. "The old brick one?"

Amber nods smugly and the old man hurries off, muttering to himself.

"I told you not to go there; I told you never go there, not to the old brick building. It is a bad place. Bad bad bad." He is still muttering as he goes out of earshot.

"Crazy old coot," Amber smirks cruelly.

16   Entering the Lair

Alone and scared in the old abandoned warehouse, Dylan and Kylie wander the building, searching out the different rooms.

"I want to go home," Kylie says. "But what if he's there waiting? What if mom came home and he did something to her and my sister?"

"Do you think he would?" Dylan asks. "I mean, that guy is probably long gone. He wouldn't want to stick around for the police after trying to kidnap someone. He has a witness too, me."

Kylie looks down sadly. "That was my dad. He wants to hurt us. I don't think he cares about the police. Besides, he would just lie to them and they will believe him not me. They always did before, the judge, counsellors, everybody."

Dylan looks at her in surprise. "Harsh."

He thinks about it. He knows he should get home. His family will be worried. But he does not want to leave Kylie here alone, and he does not want to take her home either if she is not safe there.

"What if you come to my house?"

"Will your parents just send me home? If my dad is there will they let him take me?"

"Is he allowed to take you?" It seems like a dumb question to Dylan, but at the moment it feels right.

Kylie nods unhappily. "He has visiting rights."

"Then they will," Dylan says. He thinks again and nods, making a decision. "I am staying here with you. We will stay here until we know it's safe for you to go home."

"What if someone comes and searches this place?" Kylie says. "What if my dad comes and searches it?"

"We'll hide in the basement. Let's go find it."

Dylan and Kylie search the dark building for the stairs to the basement. They finally find it and go down into the deeper darkness below, moving carefully. There is just enough light coming in to make their way, everything darker shadows within dark shadows.

Something moves in the darkness. It watches them.

Madison arrives to find Anna already waiting at the fort behind the boarded up brick building. The armchair from the day before is gone and a small old kitchen table with only three legs sits crookedly on the ground where the chair was.

They lean against the old shed and wait for Dylan and Andrew but the boys do not show up.

"I guess they aren't coming," Madison says, shading her eyes from the bright sunlight as she gazes across the yard to the old building.

Anna looks at the building across the yard. "Maybe they are already here. They might already be inside."

Madison shrugs. "Maybe. I would not be surprised if they didn't wait for us and went inside."

"Let's go in." Anna pushes herself off the shed wall. Without waiting for an answer, she heads for the brick building. With an unhappy shrug, Madison follows.

The girls pause in front of the open doorway, eyeing the darker interior of the building nervously.

Not to be made to look weak, Anna takes a deep mental breath and holds it, stepping out of the sunlight into the dark building.

Madison stares after her with a feeling of foreboding, wanting to turn and run away, but also worried now that she can't see her. "I can't just leave her in there alone," she thinks. Scared, she tries to swallow her fear and follows. She takes only a few steps in, stopping next to Anna. They both take the place in as they wait for their eyes to adjust.

Sunlight splashes across their backs, creating shadows of them that stretch out across the floor ahead. Their shadows weaken and fade with the sunlight trying to shine through the dirty windowpanes and giving them enough light to see.

The dust dancing in the sunlight coming in where the boarded up windows allows gives the place kind of a hazy look inside. The shadows and thick layer of dust give it a graveyard creepy kind of feel.

Their footsteps from the day before are visible in the disturbed thick layer of dust on the floor.

"I bet they went down to the basement without waiting for us," Madison says.

"They better not be planning to try to scare us," Anna mutters. "Let's go find them. Maybe we can sneak up and scare them first."

Madison and Anna wander through the building searching for the basement stairs and the boys. They find stairs and look down them. It is darker down there but not total darkness. The light coming in through the basement windows leaves the basement dim and shadowy but it is enough to see shapes.

"Ok, let's go down," Anna says, trying to sound braver than she feels.

They descend the stairs, feeling more nervous as they go. They both have a bad feeling about this. In the dim basement, the girls call softly to the boys. They hear a noise somewhere down there.

"It must be the boys," Madison whispers, a nervous tremor shaking her voice.

They move off through the dim basement. There is an open area with hulking shadowy shapes and a hallway that must lead to more rooms. There is all kinds of junk down there and Madison recognizes it as the trash furniture she has seen dumped in the lot behind the building, the stuff that would show up one day and be gone the next.

"What's all this stuff doing down here?" Madison frowns, picking out individual pieces she recognizes.

"What is this stuff?" Anna studies the derelict furniture with interested disgust.

"It's junk that shows up out back. One day it's there, the next it's gone and something else is there instead."

Anna thinks about this. "There must be homeless people living down here." The suggestion does not make either girl feel any better about being down there.

They both have the uneasy feeling that something or someone is watching them but neither wants to tell the other. Staying close together, they move deeper into the basement looking for the boys.

In the shadows, something watches them. It follows, nails clicking quietly on the floor. If they were looking, they might have caught a glimpse of dark hair in the light as it moves deeper into the shadows behind the junk cluttering the basement. Beady eyes glow yellow orange in the light filtering in through the broken windows where it escapes in past the boards covering most of them.

17   The Beast in the Basement

Dylan and Kylie wake up in the dark feeling groggy, stiff, and lost. They are curled up in a corner, Dylan's arms wrapped protectively around Kylie.

It is damp and chilly and dusty and they both feel like they slept in an old dusty shoebox that has been left in a damp basement too long.

Realizing they are huddled together, Dylan mumbles in embarrassment and awkwardly takes his arms away, moving a little distance away.

Kylie tries not to look at him, just as embarrassed, glances at him quickly, and looks down. Her cheeks flush with a blush. She does not want to meet his eyes. She moves a little further away, retreating into herself.

"I can't believe I slept in his arms," Kylie thinks, feeling wretched. "Of all people, Dylan the biggest meanest bully jerk next to Amber. I feel soiled."

The dim light is hazy because there is so little of it. They can see, but dark shadows loom everywhere in the weak light. For a moment, they both feel panic, unsure where they are. But then they both remember the old brick building.

"This is just so weird," Kylie thinks. "Did we really fall asleep? Is it still night? No, I'm pretty sure it's morning. Last night I didn't know what I was more afraid of, being in this old abandoned building or being here alone with Dylan, one of the meanest bullies in school."

Her fear of her father was bigger than both of those and left her feeling trapped and unable to do anything but go along with what Dylan said.

"Is it daytime?" Kylie asks, her voice a small nervous tremor. She is sure it must be because it seemed like only minutes ago they were sitting in the dark. As darkness fell outside it had become too dark to see much of anything. If there had been no moon last night, they would have been completely blind.

"I think so." Dylan hangs his head.

"We are going to be in so much trouble," he thinks miserably.

They were waiting until they thought it was safe. Kylie's mom had to be home before they tried going back to her house. They also had decided it would be better to wait until it was dark so maybe her dad would not see them.

Dylan would have been in trouble for being late, but Kylie was sure her mom would understand. It was a risk Dylan was willing to take. That's if they had made their way home last night.

The last thing Dylan remembers is them sitting and talking in the darkness of the basement, starting at every sound, holding their breath and listening, sure their pounding hearts would give them away thudding so loudly in their chests, and relaxing only a little when nothing more happened.

"We fell asleep." Kylie feels like she is going to be sick. Her eyes are big and her face twisted with anxiety. "Our parents must be so worried!"

Dylan nods. "We better get going." He feels sick too with nerves and really does not want to go home and face his parents. "I might as well get it over with," he thinks.

"I bet they called the cops," he mutters unhappily.

Kylie nods, her eyes tearing. She feels wretched knowing how scared her mom and sister must have been all night. Then another thought comes.

"What if my dad came back? What if he did something to my mom and sister?"

Dylan gets to his feet and reaches down, taking her hand and helping her up. He answers as he pulls Kylie to her feet.

"I won't let you go home alone."

Kylie looks at him thankfully. "We won't let you go home alone either. My mom and me, we will explain to your parents. After we explain to Mom what happened, she will be willing to go explain it to your parents."

Dylan shrugs. "It won't make any difference," he thinks. "I'm going to be in the biggest trouble I've ever been in in my whole life no matter what." He looks around. The place is full of dark shadows and dim light.

"Which way is out?"

Kylie looks around. "I don't know."

Andrew runs, following the tunnel, his breath coming in ragged harsh pants making his throat feel sore like he'd been yelling his head off at a playoffs game. A sharp pain keeps ripping through his side, making him almost double over. It takes every ounce of willpower to keep going, a will that is spurred on by the certainty that he can hear them back there still chasing him.

He almost stumbles coming around a curve in the tunnel and skids to a stop, staring ahead in dismay. The tunnel has stopped, dead-ended. There is nowhere to go. He is trapped and he can still hear them coming.

He looks around in a panic and spots a grate in the floor. Inspecting it, he tries pulling on it. The grate shifts. It is heavy, but it is loose. Scared to death and with no place else to go, he pulls harder, almost losing his balance. The grate comes up with a sudden jerk as the built up rust and dirt gluing it down gives up its grip. He drags it aside and sets it down.

Andrew stares down into the hole, fear making him almost quit. He forces himself to move, crawling down into the hole. With a heavy sigh and sure he is about to die down here and never be found, Andrew reaches up and pulls the grate back in place. He has to crouch as he does so, too tall for the lower ceiling. The dull scraping sound is incredibly loud in his ears.

"I hope that stops them," he mumbles.

Beneath the grate is a narrow tunnel like the one behind his basement wall.

Andrew starts crawling through the tunnel as fast as he can. The sound of them scrabbling after him in the tunnel above chases him down the tunnel, echoing down the passageway. He can't tell how far behind him they are.

Madison and Anna are moving quietly through the basement. They freeze when they hear a faint dull scraping sound in the distance.

"What was that?" Madison whispers.

"Could that be the boys?" Anna whispers.

"Must be." Madison has a bad feeling inside that it is not them.

"I think it came from this way." Anna points, indicating the direction.

"I think maybe we should check that way." Madison points in another direction. She does not want to go in the direction the sound came from. "Maybe it is the boys," she thinks. "Probably it is. But what if it isn't? This place is way spooky."

Anna thinks about it. "Maybe you are right. If we go that way, we will run into them for sure. They probably know we are here and are just messing with us. They will be waiting to jump out at us and scare us. We should circle around and come up from behind."

"What was that sound?" Kylie asks, looking around nervously.

"I didn't hear anything," Dylan says.

"I think it was a scrape or something."

Dylan remembers his promise. He was supposed to meet Andrew and those two girls here.

"I bet it's Andrew. We were supposed to meet here to check out the basement." Dylan tries to look through the dim light, but it is useless. He can't see far. "If we find him we probably find the way out."

"Andrew!" he calls out.

They listen but nobody answers.

"Andrew!" he tries again.

When Andrew again does not answer, Dylan shrugs. "Let's keep looking. We got in, the way out has to still be there."

Mr. Hooper is sitting outside the old abandoned brick building, staring at the open back door. He has been sitting there for hours. He looks broken somehow.

He tried calling Caesar for a long time but the dog never came. Not even a bark.

He knows he has to go inside to look for Caesar. He can't. Finally, Mr. Hooper shakes his head.

"He isn't here," he mutters. "He would have come when I called if he is."

He is worried something has happened to the dog. That someone has stolen him, that he was hit by a car, or worse.

He gets up stiffly to his feet and hobbles off to keep searching for his dog.

"Caesar!" the old man calls, his voice cracking with emotion.

Light from above splashes down the basement stairs through the open basement door, weakening by the time it reaches the floor below. The light entering the open storage area door teases at suggesting shapes in the darkness. Jars and boxes stand sentry in the dark basement storage room. Boxes lay in a jumbled mess where the stack had fallen over.

Something moves behind the row of jars lining a shelf. It tips a jar over and it falls to the floor with a crash, splattering pickled peaches on the floor.

Nobody is home at Andrew's house to hear it.

It scurries off, startled by the sound, dropping to the floor with a dull plop and squeezing between a couple of boxes with a slithering sound.

Dark shapes move in the tunnel, following the smell of the boy. Their eyes reflect the almost non-existent light, making them glow dully.

He is fast, but so are they.

They let him move further ahead of them; let him think he has a chance to escape.

It makes the game more fun.

Anna hears a noise and stops. She grabs Madison, pointing and mouthing the words "the boys".

They creep closer in the dark basement of the abandoned brick building, watching for the boys so they can jump out and scare them before the boys scare them. They make their way past the dark shapes of rotting furniture; some of the treasures abandoned in the yard above and dragged down here by who knows whom.

Madison stops, ducking and pressing herself against a wall and motioning Anna to listen. Anna presses herself against the wall next to her, listening.

There is a faint rustling sound much too close. Their eyes are wide in the dark, trying to see what made the noise.

"Uh, I don't think that's the boys," Madison whispers. They both heard it, a hoarse squeak.

A large fat rat ambles out from beneath a chair and they both jump and scream. They turn and run the other way, running blindly through the dark basement with only the faint silhouettes of dark shapes to guide them.

Dylan and Kylie are moving through the dark basement of the abandoned brick building.

"This place is a bloody maze," Dylan complains, keeping his voice a low whisper. "It didn't take us this long to find our way down here, so why is it so hard to find the way out?"

"Maybe it's like one of those old magic mazes from fairy tales," Kylie whispers back, joking to try to hide how scared she feels. "You know, like a labyrinth. It keeps changing so you can never find the way out."

"Funny." Dylan's voice doesn't sound like he thinks it's funny. "Andrew has to be here somewhere. I'm sure that's what we heard. Maybe he has Madison with him too. They've been hanging out here."

Kylie gives him a funny look. She can't imagine Madison and Andrew, or anyone else for that matter, hanging around this place on purpose.

"It could be your friend, Anna, too. She showed up here earlier when we were here."

The idea of seeing Anna makes Kylie feel a little better, but not much.

A scream peals out from somewhere in the dark basement, echoing chillingly through the dark maze. They both freeze at the sound.

Dylan laughs nervously. "They are messing around, but at least we know which way to go now." He leads the way towards the scream.

Something large and dark moves almost silently behind a looming shape in the darkness of the basement.

It watches Dylan and Kylie go past.

Andrew freezes in the tunnel at the sound of the scream. His stomach sinks with a sickening feeling and then lurches in a threat of vomiting up his milk and cookies.

"They got somebody else!"

He is frozen, listening. He breaks out into an ice cold sweat. "The sound came from ahead of me, not behind."

He looks behind him. It is too dark to see anything. He can still hear them scurrying after him in the tunnel.

"I can't go back and I can't go forward," he moans.

Andrew does not know what to do.

"If whoever screamed is still alive, as least maybe we can fight them off together."

Pale and shaking with fear, Andrew continues ahead through the tunnel. His knees feel bruised and battered and his hands scraped raw.

A little further ahead he stops and stares hollowly at the path ahead. The tunnel dead-ends up ahead again.

He sits, letting out a defeated groan. "This is the end. I'm dead."

The only sounds in the tunnel now is the faint drip of water dripping somewhere far away, his hoarse unhappy breathing, and the distant rustling of whatever is chasing him.

"Wait, it's a little less dark up ahead. The tunnel must change. It's very little, but light is coming from somewhere."

He creeps forward, listening and trying to see in the darkness.

Andrew reaches the end of the tunnel with a groan, putting one dirty hand on the rough cool brick wall blocking his path.

"Now what?"

He looks up. The light is coming from above. Over his head there is a hole large enough to fit him just like the one behind him with the grate covering it. The grate is missing on this one.

He pokes his head up cautiously, expecting to be attacked. The empty tunnel above continues for just a short distance.

Andrew climbs up and looks around for a grate or anything that might slow down those things chasing him. There is nothing. He crawls to the end of the tunnel. There is a hole in the wall.

"I went in a circle and came back to the hole in my basement," he groans. His heart sinks. "I should be thankful to be home, but those things might still be there."

Andrew takes a deep breath and holds it. He lets the air escape in a slow soft hiss as he blows it out, trying to calm his fear.

"I have to get past them to reach the stairs and they will probably still beat me to the door at the top. Be fast. I have to be fast."

Bracing himself for the coming fight and flight, he crawls out of the tunnel and looks around.

"This is not my basement."

"Why are you always so mean to people?" Kylie asks. They are still moving through the dim basement trying to find the way out of the maze of halls, rooms, and cluttered junk piled everywhere.

Kylie wanted to ask Dylan that question earlier in the school year, but then she lost interest, telling herself she didn't care, that she didn't want to know the answer. She was too scared to ask it. She used to kind of like Dylan, before when she thought he was nice.

When he started being a mean bully, she felt awful at first. Kylie hated herself for liking him and felt like he had betrayed her. He was nice! She felt like his turning into a bully was done just to put her off. Like he somehow knew she liked him and was doing it just to make her not like him anymore. She vowed to herself that she will never like him again.

Kylie's question takes Dylan off guard.

Dylan does not know what to say to this. He still feels like he is in shock. The girl he has a crush on is actually talking to him. Not only that, but he came to her rescue. He saved her from being kidnapped by a strange man who turned out to be her father, guarded her through the night, and is now trying to get her home safe.

Waking up with her in his arms still feels like a strange dream that could never possibly be real. And the dream just keeps going with her staying close to him because she is scared in the basement of the abandoned building.

"Any minute I'll wake up to find myself alone in my bed, safe at home," he thinks. The idea makes him a little sad. As much as he wants to get out of there, he doesn't want this moment to end either.

Kylie looks at him, waiting for an answer.

"I-uh, I don't know." Dylan looks away, avoiding her eyes.

"There must be some reason. You used to be nice then you became mean. Why?"

Dylan shrugs, feeling awkward. He's scared she'll make fun of him or think less of him. Finally, he makes himself speak, telling himself to say something, anything.

"I just don't want anyone to know I am scared I guess." He is as stunned as she is at the words he blurted out.

"Scared of what?" Kylie eyes him skeptically.

"What does Dylan have to be scared of," she thinks. "He's bigger than a lot of the boys his age, and strong. Everyone else is scared of him."

Dylan hesitates. He doesn't want to talk about this, especially to her. Now that it's already out there, he decides honesty is best.

"My house got broken into. They really messed the place up and even worse, they really messed up my dog. She's never been the same. She is scared of everything and everybody ever since. She freaks out if anyone ever comes to the house and when we have to leave her alone."

"Oh," Kylie is speechless for a moment. She feels like she should say something. She finally comes up with something.

"I'm sorry. What did they do to the dog?"

"I don't know, but they really hurt her and scared her."

"That sounds pretty scary."

"Yeah, I guess." Dylan looks down, trying to compose himself. Just talking about it brings all the pain welling up inside. "I guess I've been kind of scared ever since. What if they came back? What if I'm home and they do to me what they did to Lucy? What if they do worse to her?"

"Lucy, is that your dog?"

Dylan nods.

"I'd be scared too, but I would not be mean about it," Kylie says quietly. She looks at him, trying to read his expression. It would be easier if he would look at her.

"So why are you mean?" she asks. "Why did you start being a bully?"

Dylan shrugs again. "I guess I just want everyone to think I'm not scared. It's embarrassing."

"That's a dumb reason to be cruel to people."

"Yeah, it is," Dylan admits. "I'm sorry."

A small nervous smile curls up the corners of Kylie's mouth.

"Let's try this way," Dylan says, trying to change the subject.

They start in that direction when Kylie sees something big looming in the corner of her eye. Whatever it is, it is moving fast.

She jumps forward with a yelp as it lunges for her.

Madison and Anna finally stop running from the rat and look at each other with lopsided grins, gasping and out of breath.

"Just an ugly old rat," Anna pants.

"Yeah," Kylie gasps. "But now which way do we go?"

They both look around and have no idea which way they just ran from.

"I think we're lost," Madison says.

"I think so too." Anna motions Madison to be quiet and listens.

"What are you listening for?" Madison whispers.

"The boys. If we hear anything that might be them then we know which way to go."

Madison pictures the dark rat with its ugly hairless tail. "We thought we heard them before, but it was an ugly rat."

"Shh, this time we will listen better and make sure."

The girls listen, holding their breath so they can hear the slightest noise.

They hear a frightened yelp. The sound cut off as quickly as it happened.

"What was that?" Madison asks nervously.

"I think it sounded like Kylie," Anna says.

"What would she be doing here?"

"I don't know."

The scrabbling slithering sound echoing down the tunnel is coming closer.

Andrew turns to the tunnel entrance. "They are catching up!"

He looks around for something to block the hole with and sees he is in a darkened space filled with all sorts of old junk. Some of it looks familiar.

"Is that the rotting and broken furniture that gets abandoned behind the old brick building?"

Suddenly he knows where he is.

"I'm in the basement of the old brick building!" he gasps, staring incredulously around him. "I didn't think I went this far. Is this where they come from? How they get to my basement? It must be. They must live here and come through the tunnel."

A chill courses through Andrew.

"Is mine the only basement they get in? How many more houses can they get into?"

He is startled by the sound of a frightened yelp. His head snaps around, peering into the darkness and listening. It was a girl but it did not sound like Madison, the only girl he would expect to find here.

"Is that...?" he listens, thinking, "Anna?"

Andrew moves quickly now. "I don't know how many of these things might be down here, probably lots if they live here, but I have to at least stop the ones in the tunnel from getting in."

He starts grabbing anything that looks like it might work to block the hole in the wall and dragging it over. If it is too heavy, he abandons it and tries something else.

"It's taking too long," he puffs through his exertion, dragging a heavy legless dresser, its bottom scraping loudly and the echoing sound seeming even louder. "I have to block that hole!"

Just as Andrew is pushing the dresser into place in front of the hole, he sees movement in the darkness inside the hole. "They're here!"

Andrew gets a view of something hairy like hairy rats. "I don't think these are rats."

Their beady eyes glow back at him as they rush for the hole just as he pushes the dresser into place. He leans against the dresser, pressing all his weight against it with his legs spread out behind him for more traction, trying to hold it there. The dresser pushes back.

"They are trying to force their way out! They are pushing against the dresser, all of them," Andrew grunts. He has no idea how many of them there are. The dresser pushes out a fraction and he manages to push it back.

"I can't hold it for long. If I heard Anna then the others must be here too." Andrew's shaky voice is almost a sob. "Madison at least must be with her. Dylan too I hope."

He looks around wide eyed at the dark, struggling against the creatures on the other side, fighting over the dresser.

"HELP!"

Dylan's first reaction to the unknown attacker lunging at Kylie in the darkness is to freeze. His stomach squeezes in a tight knot, his throat too, and he freezes. His mind is blank in those brief seconds of panic as he watches the dark shape latch onto Kylie. Everything seems to be moving at breakneck speed but time seems to not move at all.

Dylan comes around enough to yell at himself silently in his head. "Move! What are you doing just standing there like a big dummy?"

Finally, he manages to move. Dylan's instincts are to run. Instead, he leaps forward and tackles it. It is bigger than he is and turns out to be stronger too. Dylan wrestles with it and it loses its grip on Kylie.

Dylan looks up into a face that is twisted into a half-toothless snarl. Weather lines in the aged leathery skin are deepened with smudges of dirt and it stinks of decay.

Dylan almost screams, but manages to hold it in, instead sputtering at it, "Get off her! Let her go!" It tries lunging for Kylie again, swiping at her with a clawed hand while wrestling with him with the other.

It grunts and talks. "Get off me boy! I am trying to get you out of here!"

Dylan falters in shock at the words and realizes it is staring at him with human eyes. Most of its face is covered with long greasy hair and it is wearing dirt-smudged tattered clothes. Kylie also stops struggling in shock. Their attacker lets them go.

Dylan realizes this is no monster, it's a man!

Dylan backs away fearfully and Kylie rushes to his side. They eye the man warily.

He stands staring at them with red-rimmed eyes, breathing heavily from the exertion of fighting with the boy. He is a homeless vagrant. His hair and beard are wild, tangled and long, his clothes tattered and dirty layers over layers, and he has the stench of one who does not bathe.

"What are you kids doing in here?" the vagrant demands, his voice rough.

"N-nothing," Dylan says defensively. "What are you doing in here?"

"Getting you out while you still can," the vagrant spat.

"You live down here." It's a statement. Dylan has no doubt.

The vagrant shakes his head. "They live down here."

"Who are they?" Kylie asks fearfully. She is imagining a whole pack of smelly dirty homeless men.

"The creatures." The vagrant leans closer, his expression a warning.

"You mean rats, and maybe some stray feral cats." Dylan eyes him warily. "We aren't worried about rats or half-wild cats."

The vagrant shakes his head, his expression growing grimmer. "There may be the odd rat or cat that comes in here. Sometimes they are lured in here by the creatures. Those things are smart, like people. Those rats and cats are the dumb ones. The unlucky ones. They feed off them."

Kylie's eyes widen in shock and disgust.

The vagrant shrugs like it's no big matter. "What did you think they eat? They aren't eating the furniture."

"So these things, creatures, people, they bring all this junk down here?" Dylan asks.

The vagrant nods. "I bring it. I take the furniture and other stuff people don't want. They leave it out in the back alleys for the garbage trucks but they won't take it, not the big stuff. So it just sits there and rots or until some kid sets it on fire.

I drag it back here and leave it out there." He points in the assumed direction of the world outside this basement. "I leave it in the lot behind the building and they take it and drag it down here. The next day when I bring a new piece the other is gone."

He looks at the kids meaningfully and they stare back wide-eyed and scared.

"It keeps the monsters that live down here from coming out and getting me while I sleep," he whispers conspiratorially.

He narrows his eyes at the kids. "What are you doing in here? It's not safe to be down here. The monsters live here!"

He waves them to follow. "Come, you have to get out before they get you. We have to get out of here."

Dylan and Kylie both think he is crazy, but at least he knows the way out. They do not trust this dirty man, but they both feel they have no choice but to let him lead them out. They exchange glances and nod at each other. They follow the vagrant uncertainly, staying close together while he leads them out.

As he leads the way, not looking back to see if they're following, he mutters, "Have to come in to rescue a bunch of kids who do not know any better than to play in dangerous abandoned buildings. These kids these days have no better sense than that. It's amazing they survive to adulthood, I tell you."

"This building was abandoned for a reason you know," he complains, directing his conversation to the kids now instead of talking to himself, "years ago. I know because I used to work here. I saw the things that happened here. Something lives beneath the building in tunnels. It's been here since the plant opened, probably a lot longer.

There was an accident one day, a piece of equipment snapped and the force sent it right through the brick wall right down here in the basement. That's when we discovered the tunnel behind the wall.

Things started to happen after that; accidents and accidents that were no accident.

When they closed the plant, I was too messed up to work for a while. Then when they emptied out all the equipment, they started coming out. I guess they liked the clutter. It was like they disturbed their nest, although that has to be in the tunnels somewhere under the ground, outside the basement.

They are mostly just little like big rats, but they look after something bigger, like ugly nasty hairy ants looking after their queen. There is something else down here and it is much bigger than the little ones. And those little ones will drag you down to the basement and eat you. Or feed you to the bigger beast."

Madison and Anna hear a cry for help. They stop and look around.

"That sounds like Andrew," Kylie says, looking around nervously.

"He sounds scared." Anna turns her head, trying to determine where the cry came from.

They exchange fearful looks. "If he is scared, should we be scared too?"

Kylie is staring at the homeless man in shock. "This strange man's story is made up," she thinks. "It's crazy. He's crazy.

Creatures? I hope he isn't dangerous crazy. We need to get out of here before he hurts us."

Dylan shifts closer to Kylie, thinking, "This weird guy is crazy nuts. I've got to get us away from him and out of here. He can do anything to us down here and nobody will ever know."

Both their nerves are stretched tight with the overwhelming sense of dread, of being in grave danger. The tension is hanging in the air all around them.

The vagrant's eyes are hollow, drained of life, and filled with years of torment that they suspect are the product of his own deranged kind of crazy.

He leans in closer to whisper to them, causing them to take an involuntary step back. "I've seen it," he is about to whisper hoarsely.

"HELP!"

Kylie turns at the sound of the cry echoing to them from somewhere in the basement. She looks around, looking choked.

Dylan's head snaps up alertly, listening.

"HELP! SOMEBODY! I CAN'T HOLD THEM!" The cry comes again, dulled by the distance, a faint echo ringing after it.

Kylie and Dylan look around, startled.

"That's Andrew." Dylan looks at Kylie. "He's in trouble."

Kylie nods. "He sounds pretty scared."

The vagrant peers around into the darkness surrounding them as if looking for something.

"It is too late for the other boy. The creatures have him." He looks at Kylie and Dylan. They turn to stare at him in shock.

"We have to get out now or the beast will get us too, the big one," the vagrant says.

18   Caesar

Madison and Anna stare at each other in confusion and fear.

"Why did Andrew cry for help? He sounded terrified." Madison can't decide if they should run and escape.

"We have to get out of here." Anna looks at her fearfully.

"We have to help him," Madison decides. "We don't know what kind of trouble he's in."

Anna's heart sinks into her stomach. She is scared and only wants to get out of there.

"Did he say something about not being able to hold something?"

"Maybe he just got stuck," Madison suggests.

"Ok, let's go find him," Anna agrees reluctantly.

"Andrew! Where are you?" Madison calls out.

"Here! Help, they're getting in!" Andrew screams.

The girls look at each other.

"What?"

They run towards the sound of Andrew's voice

Dylan turns away from Kylie and the vagrant, staring off into the darkness, trying to figure out where the cries for help came from. He does not feel right just leaving his friend there. He looks back, catching Kylie's eye. She nods and he is sure she is thinking the same thing.

Andrew sounded scared. No, he sounded terrified. He is in real trouble.

Andrew is also smaller than Dylan and Dylan feels a surge of protectiveness over the smaller boy. Andrew hasn't come around much this past year, but he is the only one of Dylan's old friends from before the break-in who did not completely abandon him.

"We have to help him," Dylan says.

The vagrant growls at him. "Do not be a fool boy. There is nothing you can do for him. We have to get out of here while we still can!"

Kylie nods and the vagrant is visibly relieved. Maybe the girl can get the foolish boy to see sense.

"Come on, let's go," he urges.

"We have to help him," Kylie says.

The vagrant is surprised. He was sure the girl had more sense than the boy. He gapes at her wordlessly, reacting a moment too late.

Kylie moves so fast she is gone in an instant, running off into the dark shadowy maze that is the basement.

"Wait!" Dylan calls and runs after her.

The vagrant moves too slowly. He is left standing alone with one arm raised to snatch the girl, reaching just a moment too late to snarl her in his grimy fingers.

"No," he moans, shaking his head. His arm drops to his side and he visibly sags with defeat "Do not do it old man. You are too old for this. Just get yourself out, save your own skin."

He groans out a heavy sigh, his shoulders sagging further, and goes after them.

Dylan's heart is beating fast and a tightness grips his chest. He lost Kylie. He is running as fast as he dares in the dark basement, calling out to both Andrew and Kylie.

"Andrew, where are you? Kylie, wait for me!"

"I'm here," Andrew cries back, his voice a cracked shell of panic. "Hurry, I can't hold them! Ahhhhh…"

Dylan does not hear a sound from Kylie.

Kylie runs in the direction she is sure Andrew cried out from. She feels reckless racing so fast through the dark in unknown territory.

She can hear Dylan calling her. She fights the urge to answer.

"I'm not going to let that smelly vagrant catch me again," she thinks, the vivid memory of his grabbing her still making her stomach sick with fear. "We can't leave Andrew down here alone in trouble either."

She turns down another hallway, following Andrew's cries for help. She can hear footsteps behind her. "Only one set. That's good. It's probably Dylan then. Maybe that creep gave up and left."

She stumbles in the dark, catching herself before she falls.

"That guy is crazy, all his talk about monsters and beasts. There is probably nothing more scary down here than rats and a scraggly stray cat."

No matter which way she goes Kylie seems to go the wrong way. She hears Andrew cry out again, answering Dylan's call. The sound seems to always come from the wrong direction. She stops and looks around.

"I'm completely lost down here."

She spots a crack of light coming in between two boards blocking off a window. "An outside wall!" she gasps. "If I follow the wall I'll have to find something!"

It proves to be easier said than done. Kylie gets as close to the wall as the jumble of discarded furniture and other stuff will let her and tries following the wall, keeping it in sight when she can and trying to keep her bearings in relation to that wall when she has to go down a hallway and can't see it anymore.

Kylie stops. She hears something moving in the shadows but can't see what it is. It's staying out of her sight behind the piles of junk.

"Dylan?" she whispers, her voice shaky. She hears Dylan call out from somewhere in the basement and Andrew call back. "Whatever it is, it's not Dylan."

"Uh, Mr. Um Mr.-?" She doesn't know what to call the vagrant. It has to be him.

It moves again and her heart lurches in fear. "Why doesn't he just come out?" she thinks. "Why is he hiding and sneaking up on me? I have a really bad feeling about this."

Madison and Anna hear Dylan call out for Andrew and the answering call.

"Andrew, where are you? Kylie, wait for me!"

"I'm here," Andrew cries back, his voice a cracked shell of panic. "Hurry, I can't hold them! Ahhhhh..."

"Dylan is here too," Anna says in relief. She feels a little better knowing someone else is here too, a boy who is stronger and braver than she is.

"This way." She leads the way.

"Which voice do we follow?" Madison's voice is a high shaky tremor. "Dylan and Andrew's voices are coming from different directions."

"Dylan. Andrew sounds like he is in trouble, but if we find Dylan he can help us help Andrew."

"But Andrew sounds like he is really desperate. Dylan is already looking for him. If we look for him too we will probably run into Dylan there."

"That makes sense. Okay, let's go this way then." Anna changes course, Madison on her heels. They race off following the sounds of Andrew's frantic cries for help.

They charge around a corner and they both cry out in surprised fright, trying to skid to a stop, finding something suddenly looming tall before them.

At first, they thought it is a monster. It smells like a monster and is dirty and ragged. "A monster in ragged clothes?"

The monster grunts, stopping its forward motion. It reaches for them, lunging at them as the girls turn and flee. It catches Anna and she screams and fights against it. "How many more are down here?" it growls.

Madison falters, keeps going, and then stops. With a regretful frown, she comes back, crying at the monster. "Let her go!"

"Stop it," the monster growls, firmly holding on to Anna despite her frantic squirming to break free. He swats at Madison, trying to catch her too.

Madison dodges back, his fingers just missing her.

"Wait, you are not a monster!" Madison demands.

"No I am not!" he growls gruffly. "What are all you kids doing down here? How many of you are there?" It is the vagrant who had tried to get Kylie and Dylan out of the basement.

"Uh, I don't know," Madison says.

Anna is still fighting his grip. "Let me go!"

"If I let you go, do not run," he warns. He lowers his voice to a whisper. "There's something down here. You have to get out of here before it gets you."

"You are just trying to scare us," Anna accuses.

He turns one red-rimmed eye on her. "You should be afraid," he says in a low voice.

The girls are not sure if it is a threat or a warning. Either way they want nothing to do with this homeless man.

"Promise you won't run."

"I won't run." Anna's voice is petulant. She has no intention of keeping this promise.

He releases his grip on her.

"Come," he urges, "this way to get out. We have to get your friends too before the beast gets them."

"Not a good idea," Anna mouths to Madison.

Madison shrugs as if to say, "what else can we do?"

They follow the vagrant.

Kylie stands uncertainly, trying to see who or what is hiding behind the looming piles of clutter in front of her. She hears it shift its weight. It seems big, really big for a rat or stray cat. If it is not the same man who caught her earlier, she is sure it has to be one of the other homeless people she is now sure are living down here.

"Who-who's there?" she asks nervously.

Kylie hears the clicking of nails on the floor and heavy breathing like panting. It is coming from behind her.

Her throat constricts with fear and she is suddenly chilled. Kylie turns around slowly.

"Caesar!"

The large dog is standing there staring at her. He lowers his head and his hackles rise, making the hair on his shoulders across his back stand up, making him look even bigger. A line of hair down his back towards his tail is also standing up. It makes the dog look more dangerous.

A low rumble comes from deep in the dog's chest.

Kylie swallows.

"Ok, maybe Caesar is scarier than Old Man Hooper," she whispers.

She raises her voice a little. "Uh, Caesar, good boy. Nice doggie." Kylie tries to talk to the dog, hoping he will not attack her but is sure he will.

Caesar's lips curl up, wrinkling his nose and showing his wicked teeth. He growls louder and takes a stiff step in her direction.

Kylie's stomach swims with dread, making her feel nauseous. "I am about to be torn to pieces."

She pauses.

"But, if Caesar is there, then what's behind me?"

19   The Kids Have Gone Missing

Keys jingle just before turning the lock on the front door. It is Kylie's mother's signal that it's her at the door. She opens the door, stepping inside and pausing for Becca to follow her in. She is exhausted from work and wants only to fall into bed and sleep. But that is not to be.

Becca sister flounces down on the floor to take her shoes off.

Kylie's mother looks around. The house is silent and has an empty feel.

"Kylie, we're home," she calls out.

When there is no answer, she decides Kylie just did not hear her. The empty silence nags at her subconscious.

Becca runs off, leaving her shoes in an untidy pair in the middle of the floor.

Julie puts down Becca's backpack, tidying the shoes. Leaving her purse on the living room chair, she goes to the kitchen to make the girls' supper. She does not feel like eating herself. She has not felt much like eating in days and today the exhaustion hangs off her like a lead-weighted coat.

She is stirring a pot of macaroni when Becca comes running into the kitchen.

"Mommy, Kylie is not here!" the little girl says.

Julie looks down at her, not understanding. "She must be in her bedroom."

Becca shakes her head. "Nu-uh, she is not there. Not in the bathroom or living room either. Kylie is not here."

Alarm flashes in Julie's head. She turns off the stove and moves the pot to a cool element.

A search of the house quickly becomes frantic. Kylie is not there.

Julie finally stops searching places she already searched repeatedly. She wavers on her feet, looking faint.

"Where is she?"

"I don't know," Becca shrugs, looking as worried for her mother as she is for her missing sister.

Julie grabs the phone and starts calling around Kylie's friends, neighbors, and anyone else she can think of. None of them have heard from Kylie or know where she is. The only one she does not get an answer at is Anna's house. She leaves a message. Feeling lost, she puts the phone down and looks at Becca, who is staring up at her with a worried frown.

It is the worst feeling a mother can have. Her daughter is not here and she does not know where she is. Fear fills her with dread of the worst.

She looks around uncertainly, feeling lost. "What do I do?"

Sickness washes over her with her next thought.

"Her father. What if he has her?"

She moves to dial her ex-husband's number. Her finger twitches and she stops. She puts the phone down.

"If he has her, he will either deny it or yell and swear at me." She's afraid of the confrontation and what might happen to Kylie if she makes him angry. "If he doesn't have her, he'll use this against me in court. Either way, if I call him I lose and so do Kylie and Becca."

She keeps these thoughts to herself. She looks at Becca, who is still looking at her with a frown and waiting for her to do something more to find Kylie.

Finally, she picks up the phone again to call the police.

One thought keeps playing through her mind. Her ex-husband, Kylie's dad, has taken her.

"Please don't hurt her," she whispers as she waits for someone to answer the phone.

Dylan's parents are beside themselves with worry. He should have been home hours ago.

His dad is driving around in the car searching the neighborhood, checking at the parks and anywhere else he can think of. His mom is calling all Dylan's friends.

She calls Andrew's house. Andrew's mother answers.

"Hi, this is Dylan's mom, Shannon. Is Dylan there?"

Surprised because the boys haven't talked to each other in months, Andrew's mom has to think for a second. "No, we haven't seen him."

"Could you ask Andrew if he's seen him? He hasn't come home." The worry in her voice is clear on the phone.

Andrew's mother shakes her head at the voice on the line. "Andrew is sleeping. It's late and he's been sleeping for hours. He couldn't have seen him."

"Okay, thanks." Shannon hangs up the phone with a frown.

She turns at the sound of the door opening, looking at it hopefully. She deflates when she sees it's only her husband coming in alone.

"You didn't find him?"

"No." He shakes his head. "Any luck with his friends?"

"None of them have seen him." She keeps to herself the comments she received from some of the parents, how their sons don't hang around with Dylan anymore and how he has been bullying everyone at school. It pains her. No parent wants to be the parent of that boy, the bully.

Dylan's father's shoulders sag. "I'm calling the police. See if you can find anything in his room that would give us any idea where he went."

Dylan's mother nods unhappily, her face etched with worry. She goes to his room and stops inside the doorway, looking around. She does not know where to start or what to look for.

She starts with his desk, turning on his computer and rifling through the contents on the desktop and in the drawers. When the computer finishes booting up, she takes a quick look at the items on the screen desktop. She flips quickly through his email and his chats and scans his browsing history. There is nothing there.

She moves on to looking through the stuff on top of his dresser, and in his dresser drawers. She finds a notebook and skims the pages. There are a few notes jotted, test study notes, websites to check out, and random drawings and other notes. She pauses over one page.

Her husband appears in the doorway, leaning against the doorframe with a defeated look.

"Anything?" he asks.

"Apparently he has a crush on some girl called Kylie." She shakes her head. "Nothing."

He sighs heavily.

"What is it?" She looks at him with concern.

"The police sounded like they think Dylan probably ran away or is just staying out after curfew. They didn't seem too concerned. They said he would probably come home when he gets hungry."

Dylan's mother shakes her head in stunned shock. "No, he didn't run away. He wouldn't."

Her husband looks around the room. "Is any of his stuff missing? Kids that run away usually pack a bag."

"No, I don't think anything is missing. There is no way Dylan ran away. I know in my heart he would not run away." Tears sting her eyes and she sniffles back a worried sob.

"I don't think he ran away either. Get on the phone again. Call his friends, neighbors, anyone you can think of. Ask about this Kylie girl too. Someone knows where he is. I'm going back out searching the neighborhood again."

Andrew's mom has a bad feeling. The fear in Dylan's mother's voice on the phone unnerved her.

When they got home the house was silent. The lights were on, but that was no surprise. It was late and they assumed Andrew was in bed sleeping. His bedroom door was closed and only darkness showed beneath the door. They did not actually check.

Drawn by an uneasy feeling she cannot explain, Andrew's mom slips down the hall and quietly opens his bedroom door a crack, peeking into his room. She stiffens and opens the door wide, letting the hallway light splash across the floor and the empty bed. She scans the room automatically.

She turns and runs down the hall calling out to her husband, "He isn't here! Andrew isn't here!"

"What?" her husband asks, coming from the bathroom.

"Andrew is not here!"

"He has to be."

They search the house, starting upstairs and moving down. His father walks into the basement storage area and stops, staring at the mess of stacked boxes that were knocked down and scattered.

"What happened here?" he mutters, shaking his head.

Andrew's mother steps in behind him, seeing the fallen boxes. "Andrew!" She darts forward, frantically moving boxes. "Help me! He could be under there!"

They work together pulling the boxes away, afraid their son is under the pile of fallen boxes. He could have been hurt by the falling boxes. Some of them are somewhat heavy.

They've moved enough boxes to know there is no body beneath them.

"He isn't here," Andrew's mother sniffles. "Where is he?"

"How did these get knocked down?" her husband complains.

He steps over a box and is reaching for another when he stops and just stares. He has discovered the large hole in the wall.

"How did that get there?"

Dylan's mom comes to see and suddenly has a really bad feeling, worse than the one before.

"Do you think something got in and got him?" She has visions of stories, old urban legends that could not possibly be true, of alligators flushed down toilets that grow and come up from the sewer to eat pets and children.

"That's impossible," her husband says. But what he is thinking is what if Andrew crawled into the hole for some reason. He is a boy, after all.

He jumps over the boxes still scattered on the floor and races up the stairs, rummaging in the kitchen junk drawer for a flashlight. He turns it on to test it and it flickers off. A quick battery change and he is racing back downstairs.

Shining the light in first, he pokes his head into the hole.

"There's a tunnel in here," he exclaims in shock. The tunnel goes impossibly beyond their basement. He can't fit his whole body but he is suddenly sure Andrew did go in there. He would fit.

"Do you think he went in there?" His wife's face is a mask of worry now.

"Yes. We have to call the police." He meets his wife's worried look.

Madison's parents are sick with worry. She was not home when they got home and they have not heard from her. She should have been home hours ago.

"We never should have let her be a latchkey kid," Madison's mother moans. She blames herself for Madison being missing.

"Let's start phoning her friends," her husband says.

They get on the phone and call around, phoning all her friends. She runs down the list, none of them know anything. Finally, with the list of people to call down to the last two numbers, one of them has some information.

"I don't know where she is, but she's been hanging out with Andrew," the girl's voice on the phone says.

"Thank you." Madison's mother hangs up the phone and turns to her husband.

"She's been hanging around with a boy."

"Who?" Madison's father's voice is tight.

"If she's late because she's hanging around with some boy, she's in trouble," he thinks.

"Andrew? I don't know who that is."

"I think I know."

He takes the phone and looks up a number, dialing and waiting through the rings.

"Hello," he says when a voice answers on the other end.

"This is Madison's father. I'm looking for her. One of her friends told me she has been hanging around with Andrew a lot. Can you ask him if he has seen her or knows where she is?"

There is a pause on the line. "Andrew is missing." The worried voice becomes more hopeful, "Could they be together?"

Anna's parents rush home from the hospital. They have wonderful news. Her brother has improved and he might just beat this disease. They had a pretty bad scare earlier in the year and his chance of surviving the cancer is very small. Now the doctor thinks he has a good chance of beating it.

They rush into the house excitedly, her mother calling out her name. She is a little deflated when Anna does not answer or come to hear the news.

"She's probably in her room with the headphones on," Anna's father says. He lets his wife take the lead to Anna's bedroom. She is bursting to tell the news.

They knock, barely wait a heartbeat, and open the door eagerly. They stop in the doorway. Anna is not there.

"Where is she?" Anna's mother asks, turning to her husband.

He frowns. "It's too late for her to be out. Let's check the house."

They call out to her, searching the house. Anna is not home.

"Where could she be?" Anna's mother asks, worried.

"We'll call her friends," her husband says.

"Friends?" She blinks, her expression turning to guilt then sadness. "She doesn't have any friends." She pauses. "Does she?"

"She must have some." He sounds uncertain.

"I don't know of any."

"None?"

She shakes her head. Another thought comes to her.

"She ran away!" she wails, feeling like a bad mom and suddenly realizing just how much they've neglected Anna since their son became sick. She cannot remember when the last time she saw her daughter was.

"No, she wouldn't do something like that," her husband says. But he can't ignore the nagging doubt. Did she?

"I'll search the parks and neighborhood and you call whoever you can think of, neighbors, other kids in her class," he says, grabbing his keys and heading for the door.

With a worried look, Anna's mom picks up the phone, grabs the phone book, and starts dialing.

Anna's dad is driving around and calling her out the open car window when another car approaching from the other way slows and honks. The driver waves at him urgently.

"Are you looking for someone?" Dylan's dad asks when he pulls alongside his car.

"My daughter, Anna. She's out somewhere and we don't know where."

"Well, if you see a boy, Dylan, tell him to get his butt home. We're looking for him too," Dylan's dad says.

The dads give each other an understanding nod and head in opposite directions, looking for their kids.

It does not occur to them the boy and girl might be together.

After a long search, Anna's dad gives up and finally returns home. He goes into the house, hopeful she came home.

"Any news?" he asks, entering the kitchen.

His wife looks up from where she is sitting at the table looking wrung out and exhausted. She shakes her head and looks at him, her face filled with worry.

"I ran out of people to call." There is a long moment of silence between them.

Anna's dad's shoulders sag and he suddenly looks like he aged fifteen years. "We might have to face the possibility Anna ran away."

His wife brings a hand to her throat as if to ward off the possibility, looking stricken.

"I'll call the police."

His wife chokes off a sob while he calls the police. Neither knows when she might have run off, or the last time they knew she was home. It is embarrassing that they cannot answer these questions. But more than that, they feel like they completely failed their daughter. She had to run away just to get their attention, to remind them that she is still there.

After hanging up, he notices the message light blinking on the answering machine.

"You didn't notice this?" He points at the light blinking its accusation of their bad parenting at them.

"No," his wife sniffles, staring at the blinking light. She feels both shame for not seeing it and hope it is news about Anna.

"It had to be Anna calling us. She is probably someplace safe, maybe waiting for us to pick her up."

He presses the button and the answering machine beeps then plays out the message to the accompanied hissing of static.

"Hello," the woman's voice crackles, sounding shaky and full of hesitations. "This is Kylie's mom. I, um, Kylie has been hanging around with Anna. Kylie didn't come home and I am, I was, hoping that, um, you can ask Anna if she knows where she is? Maybe she knows where Kylie might have gone? Please call me as soon as you get this." She rattles off her phone number almost too fast to catch, her voice cracking with strain. The machine bleeps and goes silent.

The message chills them. Another girl is missing too.

Anna's father looks at his wife gravely. She meets his look, her eyes hollow with worry and her mouth drawn. Worry lines crease her brow.

"I ran into another dad out there looking for his kid, a boy," he says.

His wife puts her hand to her throat again, her eyes full of fear.

He plays the message again, skipping ahead to get the phone number.

Picking up the phone, he dials Kylie's house.

As word of each child's disappearance spreads through the community, the news collides and people quickly realize each one is no isolated disappearance. There is more than one child missing.

The count starts to go up. Two kids are missing. No, three. Four. A total of five kids have mysteriously gone missing over the course of two days. Given Anna's parents uncertainty when they saw her last, she might have vanished the same day as the others or a day earlier. All in the same neighborhood.

This is unheard of.

A massive search is coordinated out of the local community center as the night grows later. It is all over the news and people come from other neighborhoods to help search for the missing children. Flashlights bob all over the neighborhood as searchers look.

The search lasts through the night and into the next day.

Police question anyone who could possibly have been involved with kidnapping them, know where a group of kids might have snuck off to, or seen anything.

The first suspect in Kylie's disappearance is her dad. The police show up on his doorstep. He opens the door and a look of surprise flashes across his face. It is quickly replaced by anger.

"Whatever she's saying about me this time, she's lying," he growls defensively, gripping the door tight as if he might slam it closed at any moment.

"Mr. Martin, do you know the whereabouts of your daughter, Kylie?"

"Her mother has her. Maybe you should check there."

"Are you sure you don't know where she is? Can we take a look inside?"

"Do you have a warrant? No, you can't look inside. What did their mother say? I haven't even seen my kids in days, not since my last court ordered visit. This is probably some trick their mother is playing. She's always lying and turning the kids against me. Trying to get me in trouble for stuff I didn't do with her lies. Why don't you go check that out? I bet she knows where Kylie is. She's probably hiding her and then lying and saying I took her. You go talk to her. She knows where Kylie is."

The officer levels an unimpressed look at him.

"Sir, are you aware that your daughter has been missing since yesterday? Are you sure you have not seen or heard from her? We are concerned for her welfare."

Kylie's dad sneers at them and chuckles. "Her mother can't keep track of her? Sweet. This is going to kill her in court."

"Mr. Martin, your daughter may be with four other kids who are missing. Anything you can tell us will help, even if it seems unimportant."

"So what, do you think I took my own kid? I can't kidnap my own kid, she's mine." His voice is defensive, angry. "Do you think I kidnapped that kid and her friends? I don't even know who her friends are."

One of the officers holds out his card to Kylie's dad.

"If your daughter contacts you or you think of anything that might help, please contact us."

He looks at the proffered card, almost refuses to take it, and grudgingly changes his mind, taking the card.

The officers turn and leave and he closes the door on them.

"Do you think he's good for Kylie Martin's disappearance?" one of them asks the other.

His partner shrugs. "It's an ugly divorce and custody dispute. He's one slimy character. He might have kidnapped his own daughter, but not all five kids."

"I just hope she's with the other kids, not with him. You read the file on him?"

"Yes. I think we need to keep an eye on him. If he did anything to that kid we will find out and hopefully he will go to jail for a very long time."

His partner nods agreement. "If he did hurt that kid, we'll be coming back for him."

On the other side of the closed door, Kylie's dad is breathing fast ragged breaths. He looks like a trapped animal.

"I didn't have anything to do with Kylie's disappearance, or any of those other kids. They probably all went off somewhere together."

He's pacing the floor, looking around as if for an escape route, working himself up to greater agitation.

"They're going to pin this on me. I know it. She told them all kinds of lies about me."

He refuses to consider his attempt to take Kylie as an attempted abduction. Refuses to accept he could hold any blame or that he did anything wrong. He refuses to acknowledge even to himself that the event happened at all. As if accepting that fact for himself will somehow make it true.

"They're going to lock me up if they don't find that kid. All of those kids. Kylie, I can't believe you and your mother are doing this to me." He lets out an animal-like growl of anger and fear.

Pale and shaking now, Kylie's father hastily packs his bags and rushes out to his car, speeding off.

He wants to hurt his ex wife, but not at the expense of himself. He doesn't even know why he wants to hurt her. He is just angry and feels the need to. But he is a coward and takes the coward's path. He runs.

Half the neighborhood is at the community center while the other half are out searching for the missing children. The place is filled with strangers too, all the people who came in to help search. Police, fire fighters, and even the army came. They are all busy coordinating the search, sending groups out to search different areas and other groups to search the same places again after.

The police Sergeant leading the search is addressing the crowd before another group of searchers are sent out into the growing darkness.

"No stone will be left unturned and no place searched less than three times. We will find those missing children!" He does not add the last thought in his mind, "Whether they are dead or alive." He needs to give the families and searchers hope.

He pushes that gruesome thought away. "Don't even think it, man. It's not true. We will find those kids and it will turn out they were just up to mischief somewhere."

There is almost a carnival like feeling to the whole thing. A terrible carnival of dread and high anxiety where you are sure anyone might vanish at any moment to suffer a terrible fate and never be found.

Parents keep their kids close, afraid they would be taken or lost too. Fear clings to the hearts of everyone.

Almost everyone.

Amber, Jessica, and Brooke are lounging together.

"This is so boring," Amber complains with a pout. "I can't believe our parents made us come."

"I know, right?" Jessica agrees. "It's not like we are actually going to go look for them or anything."

"I wish we were somewhere else," Brooke complains.

Small kids, too young to understand the gravity of what is happening, race around squealing and playing. It is a sick contrast to the heaviness pulling at everyone else's hearts.

Amber makes an annoyed face at them and turns her attention back to her friends.

"Why do we even have to be here?" she complains.

"Our parents are paranoid," Jessica mutters unhappily. She would rather be online playing games or in the chat rooms.

"So what if a couple kids are off goofing around somewhere?" Amber whines. "Nothing ever happens to anyone here. They are probably just hiding because they are in trouble."

Brooke looks at her uncertainly. "I don't know. Everyone seems pretty freaked out about it. They were not even all friends either. There is no way they all went somewhere together."

Amber snickers with a nasty sneer. "That dumb Kylie is one of them. Whatever happened to her, she deserves it."

The other two just look at her. They can't believe she said that.

A few heads turn in their direction, people who overheard what she said.

"I mean who even wants that witch around anyway," Amber continues. "I hope something happened to her, something really bad. I bet she went off and killed herself. Well I say good! She is so stupid and ugly."

Jessica is looking around nervously as more people turn their attention to the three girls.

"I wish Amber would just shut up," Brooke thinks. Listening to her is putting a sick knot in her stomach. "We have done some pretty mean things to Kylie, all because Amber pushed us to. If Kylie did kill herself, it is on Amber's hands." She looks down at her own hands. "On mine too," she thinks miserably.

"I don't know about you, but I hate Kylie and I hope she killed herself." Amber continues her rant. "I hope she suffered for hours before she died too and that they never find her ugly body." It came out a lot louder in the sudden silence than Amber intended.

She looks around, startled, and realizes everyone stopped talking and is staring at her. Her face flushes in embarrassment. She looks around sheepishly at all the people staring at her with shocked expressions and turns to her friends, her allies.

Brooke turns away from her in disgust. Jessica is staring at her with a shocked look, afraid and embarrassed by everyone staring at them.

"What?" Amber demands smugly.

Brooke turns on her. "You are a horrible person and uglier on the inside than anybody is inside or out," Brooke growls. "I hate you and always have. I only pretend to be your friend because you are so mean and it is the only way to not be a victim of your nastiness."

Brooke glares at Amber, who is trying to recover her cool after flinching at her hurtful words. Brooke's heart is pounding wildly in her chest with her fear over confronting Amber.

"I am so dead," Brooke thinks, feeling sick with it. "She is going to be after me every day now too, just like with Kylie."

Brooke is spurred on, though, from being in the center of the spotlight on Amber. Everyone is staring at them in silent shock. Shame flushes through her and anger takes over her fear again.

"You have no friends," Brooke says. "Nobody likes you. You are too mean. You are the one who should go kill yourself. Do the world a favor."

Brooke stalks off into the crowd without looking back.

Amber is hurt and shocked. She turns to Jessica for support.

"Dylan doesn't like you either," Jessica says coldly. "You look pretty enough in the mirror, but you are just plain ugly. You are mean and ugly inside and I don't like you either."

She turns and walks away, following Brooke and leaving Amber standing alone.

Tears well up in Amber's eyes and she tries to fight them back. Everyone is standing around staring at her with looks of shock, disgust, and anger.

Her mother pushes through the crowd angrily, stepping forward and staring at Amber in dismay.

"How could you say such a thing?" she demands with a hurt look. She turns away sadly from Amber and goes to Kylie's mother, Julie.

Julie is staring at Amber with tears in her eyes, her expression devastated.

"Let's find your daughter," Amber's mother says.

Julie looks at her, blinking and nodding tearfully.

Everyone seems to turn away from Amber as if she suddenly is not there anymore. Or maybe they just can't stand to look at her anymore.

Amber looks around at them feeling more alone than she has ever felt in her life. Her eyes are pleading for someone to side with her, anyone. She feels like the whole world has just broken and turned against her.

A man walks through the crowd, stopping and looking around in the empty space where Amber is left alone. She looks at him unhappily.

"Maybe he's coming to stand up for me," she thinks miserably. "He isn't giving me the same angry hateful looks everyone else is." Hope stirs in Amber.

"He is a nice looking man, probably around my dad's age. But it's like his eyes have a terrible sadness that can never be fixed. He looks like he might be kind, if he didn't look so sad."

His eyes stop on Amber. He pauses, then walks up to her.

She looks up at him, wondering why he looks so sad.

"Amber? You are the girl who goes by the screen name MG1?" he asks.

"Yes," she says. Amber feels on edge. She has the uneasy sense that something is up and she does not know what. She does not like not feeling in control.

"Why is he asking me that?" she wonders. "Maybe I shouldn't have answered."

A good-looking boy comes through the crowd and stands next to the man with a pretty little girl with braces on her legs to help her stand.

Amber's heart flutters. "They feel sorry for me and came to give me sympathy," she thinks. "Finally, someone who cares about how I feel."

She can't stop looking at the boy. "He is so hot," she thinks. "And he is about my age too."

The boy and little girl both have a deep sadness in their eyes too. A sadness that Amber somehow knows will never leave their eyes.

"He keeps looking at me. Oh my gawd, he likes me. I would totally date him," Amber thinks. "That sad thing makes him even hotter, I think. He is even better looking than Dylan." She feels a little thrill. He is staring at her and she is sure he is thinking the same thing.

"I've been looking for you," the man says. "You know my daughter."

Amber's gaze shifts to the little girl in leg braces. She has never seen any of these three people before. "Who are they talking about?" she thinks. "The other missing girls' parents are over there." She tries a brave smile, although the hot boy's stare is making her nervous and giddy.

"Who is your daughter?"

"You would know her by her online user name," the man says. "I am Chattymay1's dad. This is her brother and her sister."

Amber is confused. The user name is familiar, but she has no idea who he is talking about.

"Her real name was Kerry," the boy says. "She was getting bullied at school by girls like you."

Amber looks at him in surprise. "I didn't bully her," she stammers, "I-I don't even know a Kerry."

Her mind races. "Does he think I bullied his sister? They don't even live around here or go to my school. If they did, I would have noticed him for sure."

"No, you didn't" the boy says coldly. "You didn't know her."

Amber stares back at them in confusion.

"You said some pretty mean things to her online," Kerry's father says. "She left her screen open to the chat."

Suddenly Amber remembers the faceless person she attacked in the chat room. She had been extra nasty to this Chattymay1. It had been a fun game.

"Yeah, whatever," Amber mutters and starts turning away, disappointed this might ruin her chances with that hot guy.

The little girl's words stop her.

"You killed my sister," she says loud enough for everyone to hear. Her eyes are bright with the tears that are about to fall. She bravely holds them back.

People drop what they are doing and turn to stare.

Amber's mother looks confused and shocked. She starts hurrying over to her daughter's defense, mouth open to tell these people to leave her daughter alone.

"I did not!" Amber cries, turning back to face them, shocked at the accusation.

Chattymay1, Kerry's, father looks at her with his pained eyes.

"We came to see the face of the person who killed Kerry. She killed herself because of you. I just wanted you to know that." He turns, walking away carrying the world of weight of pain and loss on his shoulders. The boy and girl follow.

The boy pauses, turning back to give her one last look, shaking his head as if she had done something to disappoint him deeply. He turns away, following his father through the crowd.

Amber is stunned. She never imagined anyone would actually kill their self because of her. She feels numb inside, like this is not real. She is already putting up an emotional wall between herself and all these people staring at her in shock.

The little girl looks back and sees Amber's shocked and hurt look and runs back awkwardly, her leg braces clacking. She hugs Amber.

"It's okay, I forgive you," she whispers to Amber. "Kerry would have wanted me to." She runs back to catch up with her father and brother who stopped to wait for her.

"I don't," the boy says to Amber. "I never will."

They keep going, people turning to stare at them in shock then back to Amber.

Amber is suddenly the center of everyone's world and it is not a place she wants to be. She feels awful. She just wants to be invisible, to be anywhere but here, to just be dead and never even be born maybe.

The hurt look on her mother's face is more than she can bear. She has never seen her in so much pain. "She'll never forgive me," she thinks miserably.

A voice behind her startles Amber. "Amber Shaw, you are under arrest for the death of Kerry Hamilton. You are being charged with felony aggravated stalking, criminal harassment, intimidation, mischief in relation to data, unauthorized use of a computer, false messages, indecent or harassing communications, counselling suicide, incitement of hatred, and defamatory libel."

Amber whirls around to see two police officers standing behind her looking huge and stern. She is filled with fear.

"Mom! Dad!" she cries as they put handcuffs on her.

Her parents stand together and just shake their heads sadly at her. The pain in their eyes is like a knife to her heart. They turn away from her as the police officers lead Amber through the crowd.

"Mom! Dad!" Amber cries again, sobbing. "Help me! Why won't you even look at me? Look at me!"

"Do you think she made Kylie kill herself too?" someone asks.

Amber's dad nods sadly and Kylie's mother breaks into desolate tears.

"Mom, Dad, help me!" Amber cries back to them as the officers take her away to their car. "I didn't do anything, I was just messing around!"

Her mom looks utterly devastated. She stares back after her daughter, feeling sick at heart. She knows all too well her daughter is more than capable of doing what she is accused of. She is sure she is guilty, maybe even guilty of doing harm to Kylie or any of the other missing kids.

She knows her daughter is a mean twisted creature behind that pretty face. She has always turned away from it, refusing to acknowledge the truth while she defended her daughter from being punished again and again for bullying over the years.

"She will be safe there," Amber's dad says, comforting his wife. "Maybe letting her sit and stew for a while will teach her a lesson."

As much as he loves his daughter too, he does not like her as a person. "She really is a nasty thing and I have seen it too many times," he thinks sadly. He feels like he failed her somehow.

"Her mother might turn a blind eye and not want to see it," he thinks, "but I can't deny that Amber is not a nice person."

"Now we need to find those missing kids," he says.

Mr. Hooper comes shuffling into the community center. He looks around, hollow eyed and looking worse than ever.

"My dog," he says quietly. "Has anyone seen my dog Caesar?"

A woman turns on him furiously. "We are here searching for missing children and you are asking about a dog?"

Hooper blinks in confusion. He does not quite seem to know where he is. "Caesar-," he begins to say and stops.

He looks around at all the commotion with a confused look, at the woman who is still glaring at him angrily. He has not slept or eaten since Caesar went missing. He is absolutely exhausted and has spent the whole time desperately looking for his dog. He needs that dog.

He starts trembling and the little color left in his face drains, leaving his pallor pasty and grey.

He turns around and hobbles back out, muttering. "Kids, I know where they are. The old abandoned plant. The basement, the beast in the basement."

If anyone had paid attention to hear, they might have stopped the old man.

Mr. Hooper leaves and hobbles down the road towards the old abandoned brick building.

20   Escape from the Darkness

Searching the dark maze, Anna and Madison turn a corner, running down another hallway. They reach a doorway, skidding as they slow to look in the room.

They stop in stunned surprise, staring at Andrew, coming on him by accident. He is pale and shaking and pushing a legless dresser against the wall with everything he has. His eyes are wild with terror.

"Help me!" Andrew cries hoarsely the moment he sees them. The desperation cracking his voice fills them with dread. The dresser is rocking and shaking and pushing back.

"They are getting in!" Andrew cries. "Help me! Block the hole!"

Madison breaks her trance and rushes forward, throwing her weight against the dresser although she has no idea why.

Anna rushes forward a few heartbeats later, adding her weight to the dresser, pushing back at it with them.

"I can't believe the strength behind this dresser," Madison cries. The dresser is bucking and fighting back. "How were you able to hold it for so long?"

"What's behind this thing?" Anna says, trying to put more weight and muscle against it.

The vagrant followed the girls. He steps into the open doorway and just stops and stands there looking at the dresser for a moment, the three kids fighting to hold it against the wall.

He turns around slowly, scanning the dark shadows. "They could be hiding anywhere," he thinks.

The dresser bucks hard and almost flies away from the wall despite their frantic efforts to hold it in place.

"What's behind there?" Madison cries.

"Monsters!" Andrew sobs.

"Help us mister!" Andrew begs, noticing the dirty homeless man, but the vagrant does not come to help.

"It is useless," the vagrant mutters. "We should have run when we could. It is too late." He sounds defeated, like he has given up.

Dylan hears the voices ahead and speeds up, racing mostly blindly through the basement. He arrives out of breath and looks at them, wondering what is going on.

The dresser bucks hard again, pushing back against Andrew and the girls, and they almost lose it. Dylan rushes in and squeezes in between Andrew and the girls. He puts his shoulder into it, pushing against the dresser.

"Why are we holding the dresser?" he asks, looking at them.

Suddenly the dresser stops bucking and pushing. It goes still like any old ordinary scratched up dresser with the legs broken off.

They all look at each other uncertainly.

"What just happened?" Anna asks.

"They gave up?" Andrew suggests. His teeth are chattering with shock and he can't stop shaking.

"Who gave up?" Dylan asks.

Kylie is frozen in fear, staring back at Caesar. He just stares back at her, motionless. They both seem to be stuck, waiting for something to happen.

With a vicious snarl, the dog lunges forward.

Kylie screams.

They hear Kylie's scream echo through the basement. Without a thought or pause, Dylan bolts into the darkness, tearing off after the sound.

"Stop!" Madison cries. "Come back!"

"Let him go," the vagrant mutters in defeat. "We're lost."

Anna glares at him angrily. "No we're not!" She stalks off. "Let's go, our friend needs our help."

With a fearful look at each other and back at the motionless dresser, Madison and Andrew follow.

The vagrant shakes his head and mutters. "It is no good, no good. We're dead, all dead."

Kylie flinches, unprepared for Caesar's attack.

He brushes against her as he lunges past her and goes after whatever is hiding in the dark.

Kylie yelps in shock and fear.

The dog disappears behind the wall of piled high furniture.

Kylie steps back woodenly, staring fearfully at the mountain of junk. She can hear the dog snarling, his nails clattering on the floor. He barks. He yelps. She is not sure what she hears from whatever the dog went after. It is not a growl; it's more like a groan. It does not sound human. There is a slithering sound that sends chills down her spine.

Caesar comes barreling from behind the junk, limping and bloodied. He stops and stares at Kylie.

She backs away, staring at him in fear. "I don't know what I should be more scared of, whatever Caesar just fought or Caesar. Why won't he stop staring at me?"

Caesar shifts, taking a step closer to her, ears alert and a low rumbling growl in his chest.

"This time he's going to attack me and rip me apart. He is one mean dog."

Caesar's ears go down, laying back. He lowers his head and snarls, teeth bared as he turns around, positioning himself between Kylie and whatever he attacked. It is still unseen on the other side of the piled high junk furniture.

Caesar steps back against her, pushing against Kylie like he is trying to push her back.

Kylie takes a step back and another. The dog moves with her, keeping himself pressed against her legs, staring at whatever is beyond the furniture.

"Caesar!"

Kylie and the dog's heads snap around in surprise.

"It is old Mr. Hooper!" Kylie thinks, almost voicing it in alarm.

The old man hobbles forward. He looks at the dog and puts one hand on Caesar's head, his hand smearing the blood wetting the dog's fur. He looks at the girl, saying nothing.

The dog's stance does not soften. He continues staring fixatedly at something in the dark, a low rumble vibrating up his chest, his lips wrinkled back and teeth bared.

Kylie can only stand in stunned shock staring at the old man.

Mr. Hooper raises his other hand and Kylie sees for the first time that he is holding a gun.

Her blood freezes. "He is going to kill me!"

Mr. Hooper raises the gun higher, turning to the mountain of rubble, his back to Kylie.

"Get out of here girl, while you can," he says. The handgun is shaking in his trembling hand.

Caesar looks back at her, up at his master, then turns his attention back to the hidden beast, growling low and menacing.

Dylan comes running around the corner and skids to a halt, shocked to see the old man and the dog. It takes a pattering of heartbeats for the gun to register.

"Don't shoot!" he cries.

Anna comes around the corner just as Dylan yells and almost runs into him in her shock.

"Shoot? Who's going to shoot?" It does not make any sense to Anna. Then she sees the old man. She does not see the gun.

"What is he talking about, don't shoot?" she thinks. Everything seems to be whirling at breakneck speed.

Dylan edges closer to Kylie.

Andrew and Madison come around the corner slowly, pale and shaking. They are looking around them at the dark shadows, not at the others.

"We have to get out of here," Andrew whispers hoarsely. "Th-they are everywhere."

"What is?" Anna asks, not taking her eyes off the mountain of junk. She heard the slithering sound behind it.

Dylan and Anna are focused on Mr. Hooper and Caesar.

"Them," Madison gasps, pointing.

The others turn to look and a hairy creature the size of a large cat waddles from the darkness beneath a chair. Its beady eyes reflect the light, making them shine.

Another follows the first, slightly smaller. They are not cats or rats or anything else recognizable.

They are ugly and terrifying.

Eyes shine from the darkness, pair after pair as they come out of hiding, the eyes announcing the creatures right before each creature crawls out of the black shadows.

They are surrounded.

"Those are the little ones," the vagrant says behind them.

"The beast is behind there," Mr. Hooper says, keeping his gun and his eyes trained on the mountain of rubble.

"Wh-what's going on here?" Dylan asks shakily.

"We've been hunting the beast," Mr. Hooper says, "me and Caesar. I caught one of the small ones in the basement years ago. I searched the basement and found a hole in the wall with a tunnel behind it."

He turns and looks at them, his eyes haunted.

"I could hear them in there. Then they were gone. There was something wrong about the one I caught. It was bad. Like it just wanted to kill me. I could not seal the hole. I had to find out where they went because I knew they would come back.

I could just squeeze through and I crawled through the tunnel to see where it went. Whatever that thing was, it came from the tunnel.

I ended up here in this basement. I found myself trapped. I could not get out of the building and I could not let the monsters get out either.

The only way out was the tunnel back to my own basement. But it was not my basement I ended up in."

They are all stunned except Andrew. He already learned about the tunnel to his basement. A cold chill fills him.

Mr. Hooper continues.

"After that I explored the tunnels, for years, ending up in many different basements. Whenever I found one of these creatures, I killed it. These things have access to the basements of many homes, and to the people in them. "

He looks frailer suddenly. "Sometimes I found people in the basement too. What was left of them after those things got them. Other times I could hear them moving around upstairs, unaware of what is happening beneath their feet and thinking they are safe in their own homes."

Mr. Hooper turns to Kylie.

"Nobody is safe in their home. Last winter I had just chased some out of your basement when you came crawling in the window. They looked hungry too, as hungry as you looked cold."

Kylie pales, remembering the day those bully girls attacked her in the park and left her to walk home with no coat or boots or anything. It was so cold that day that she was sure she would die before she made it home.

Then the realization hits her. The old man had been in her house. Her knees go weak and the room starts to spin.

"Then one day I came across the beast," Hooper says. "Thought I was dead for sure. And I almost was. I barely escaped alive."

He points to the vagrant.

"I met Harry then. He is the only reason I got out. He carried me out from this here basement."

They turn to look at the vagrant in surprise and he looks embarrassed.

"That is when I got Caesar," Mr. Hooper says. "I trained him to warn me when the creatures are near. I trained him to find them and kill them too. They are not just in the basement anymore. They are getting braver. They are coming out above ground now."

Mr. Hooper looks at them all meaningfully, trying to drill the significance into them with his eyes.

"They are here to kill me," he says, "and everyone else in this neighborhood. I am sure of it."

Mr. Hooper spins, surprisingly agile on his age-ruined legs, at a slithering sound behind the mound of garbage furniture, levelling his gun with a shaking hand towards it.

The vagrant, Harry, steps forward, watching the small creatures surrounding them with a terrified expression.

"No sudden moves," he warns, keeping his voice almost a whisper.

"We watched the abandoned plant together after that, taking turns," Harry says. "Before it was just me alone, guarding it against the beast escaping. The little ones come and go through the broken windows, but the beast was somehow trapped inside.

The little ones would swarm over you, devouring you alive, leaving nothing behind. But the beast is the bad one."

Harry shivers as if Death had just traced his fingers down his spine.

"We have both seen it happen. Mr. Hooper saw them go after a curious cat that got too close to one of the windows. The cat screeched and howled and fought for its life. It was no match for them. They pulled it in through the window where they had reached out to surprise and grab the cat that had been sniffing around it.

I saw them take down a man when I was working in this basement of the plant, right before it was closed. I saw the big beast too. We both have."

"We have to get out of here," Mr. Hooper says. "Harry, we have to get these kids out of here."

"It's too late," Harry says. "I've done it."

Mr. Hooper turns to look at him.

The whole world seems to explode at once. Flames erupt ahead of them down a hallway beyond the area are in.

Hooper's gun goes off with a flash in the dark and a roar that echoes deafeningly in the basement.

The wall of rotting furniture blows out with a guttural sound that is neither snarl, or growl, or shriek.

Anna dodges sideways; a reflexive move without thought, barely avoiding being hit with a flying chair. The chair hits something behind her with a loud thud.

Dylan dives into Kylie, tackling her and taking her down; trying to shield her from the falling furniture.

Mr. Hooper screams.

Andrew falls with a cry, knocked down by a small table that hits him in the head. He sprawls on the floor, dazed, blood oozing from a gash his head.

Harry lunges and grabs Madison. She shrieks and tries to fend him off; not knowing what is attacking her in that sudden lunge. He shoves her back, pushing her out of the way of being crushed by falling debris.

Caesar bolts forward with a snarl, attacking something, yelping in pain almost immediately.

The not rat creatures seem to explode into the room everywhere, filling the area with their ugly hairy bodies. They shriek and squeal a very un rat-like sound, leaping and darting frantically.

Another fire erupts in another direction and they shriek and squealed louder, swarming in a frenzy to get away from the terrifying flames, ignoring the humans trespassing in their lair.

The beast from behind the wall of furniture stands hunched over its fallen hiding place. The falling furniture does not seem to affect it even as heavy objects tumble against it.

The beast grows. It rises slowly up from its crouched position, bigger and bigger, towering over them. It seems to be filling the whole room.

Harry shoves Madison harder, pushing her away behind him.

"RUN!" he screams. "FOLLOW THE FIRE IF YOU WANT TO LIVE!"

Madison stumbles and stares at him in uncertain shock. "I would burn alive in the fire," she thinks desperately.

Another fire erupts nearby and half the kids scream.

"Where are all these fires coming from?" Dylan cries. The kids are all in stunned shock at the sudden pops and roars of the little explosions and the leaping flames they are creating.

"I set them to kill the monsters," Harry shouts. "I thought that if I could get them all out of the basements and trap them here, I could kill them all! Now RUN! RUN!"

The small creatures are attacking anything in their way in their frenzy to escape, furniture, walls, and each other. They are blindly tearing and biting, even at their own bodies.

Anna yanks at the still dazed Andrew's arm, half dragging him as he stumbles to his feet. She kicks desperately at one of the creatures as it latches onto his leg with its nasty teeth. It spins to attack her only to be attacked by one of its brothers.

Anna pulls Andrew. "Come on," she screams.

"Go, go, go!" Harry is yelling, grabbing the kids and shoving them towards the path through the flames behind him.

The beast is still growing, filling the room with its terrifying ugliness. It is hairy but half-bald in patches, as if the hair does not want to grow on its mottled leathery skin. The skin itself looks like it falls somewhere between flesh and scales. Its mouth is a huge slash across its wide face and is filled with wickedly sharp teeth. Slimy drool drips and rolls down its huge body. Its eyes gleam evilly in the flickering light of the roaring flames.

Another fire erupts.

"Go! Hurry!" Harry screams. He grabs Kylie, pulling her and pushing her towards the exit, dragging Dylan along because he refuses to give up his grip on her. "Before the path is closed! Go! Follow the fire!"

The kids are screaming and crying, stumbling in the basement. It is getting harder to see despite the light thrown off by the fires boiling and growing all around them. Their eyes burn and their lungs ache from the air that is quickly growing un-breathable. The place is filling with thick smoke.

"Caesar!" Mr. Hooper cries out.

Harry grabs the old man, dragging him out even as Hooper fights to break free and grab the dog.

Everything is a blur of running blindly through smoke and fire after that.

Fires are still erupting everywhere, filling the basement with boiling leaping flames that roar loudly and hungrily. Where the fire still fights to take over, the smoke boils and thickens.

By the time they reach the stairs they are fumbling blindly. They climb by touch, crying and choking, thick smoke scorching their lungs.

"Keep going, keep going," Harry keeps screaming hoarsely at them.

The stairs vanish and they stumble onto the flat surface of the floor above. They are still blinded, their eyes watering from the burning pain of heat and smoke. The flames are quickly devouring the entire building. Windows explode from the pressure of the immense heat forcing its way up and out through the main floor.

Most of the first floor is being devoured by flames now. The floor blackening then turning yellow orange as the fire takes its place. Sections of burning floor crumble and fall into the basement. The old building is burning hot and fast, its timber dried decades ago and left to rot and neglect.

A group of searchers are on the way to search the old abandoned plant when someone spots smoke rising from it. It is one of the few places left they have not searched yet.

"Look, smoke!"

They hear the muffled boom of one of the explosions in the basement.

"Call the fire department!"

"Call the search command center. If the kids are in there, we need to get them out fast!"

People in the neighborhood start emerging from their homes in confusion after feeling their homes shake with the dull reverberating thuds of the shock waves of the explosions reaching their basements through the underground tunnels. They look around, wondering what is happening.

The search group leader phones the command center while someone else dials 911 and word is spread through text messages going out to all the search groups.

Word spreads quickly that the old abandoned building is on fire and fear courses through the searchers. What if the kids are in there?

More people rush into the area and are drawn by the muffled sounds of the small explosions going off in the building, the black smoke wafting up into the sky, and the growing roar of the fire that is growing and engulfing the building.

The crowd grows with the thickening smoke filling the sky. Smoke is pouring from the windows now and flames can be seen leaping in the blackness within the building.

"We have to go in to look for the kids," one of the men yells. Others agree and they start heading for the burning building, but others in the crowd hold them back, wrestling with them.

"You can't go in there! Wait for the fire department." The wail of approaching sirens can be heard in the distance.

Anguished cries from some of the parents of the missing kids chill the crowds' hearts with each muffled explosion from inside.

A louder explosion makes the ground tremble and a new wave of smoke boil from the windows, forced out by the shockwave of displaced air from the blast.

A collective moan moves through the crowd. If the children are in there they are lost now. There is no hope of rescuing them.

Too late, sirens scream up the street accompanied by a cacophony of flashing lights as fire trucks and police cars arrive on the scene. The distant wail of more rescue vehicles is almost drowned out. Ambulances race against time, hoping to get there in time to save any survivors.

A blackened shape stumbles out the back door of the old brick building.

The first police and fire trucks screech to a stop in the front street. The firemen are running before their feet hit the ground, rushing to pull out and hook up the hoses.

The wail of more sirens crying out in the distance grows steadily louder, multiple sirens clashing in a frantic song.

Someone in the crowd filling the yard behind the abandoned factory cries out, spotting the child stumbling blindly behind the building.

People rush forward, yelling, "It's one of the kids! It's one of the missing kids!"

They surround Andrew, wrapping a coat around him and leading him away from the burning building.

A scream fills the air.

"Where's the others? Are they inside?" The words are said with a mix of hope and dread and they are repeated through the crowd.

Another figure stumbles from the smoke now billowing out the back door and a police officer is on the child instantly, throwing his arms around the child in a bear hug, scooping them up and carrying the child away from the building. He throws the child to the ground, throwing himself on top, using his own hands to put out the fire that has just started licking at Anna's clothes as she stumbled out.

Anxious faces stare at the burning building.

Is that all? Only two? Where were the other three?

A thundering boom rocks the neighborhood as something inside the building explodes. The force flattens people to the ground, knocking them off their feet. The remaining windows are blown out of the brick building and wood boarding up the windows is blown off and sent flying.

Mr. Hooper comes stumbling from the boiling smoke carrying something.

It is Madison. He staggers under the weight. It is too much for him.

The crowd gapes in shock.

More fire trucks are skidding to a halt, firemen leaping off before they come to a complete stop. Two firemen race in with blankets, covering Mr. Hooper and Madison to smother any flames that might be burning on the old man and child, taking the child from him.

The old man staggers and falls, moaning something unintelligible.

A fireman helps him up, trying to make out what he is moaning about. "Caesar? Over there? What are you saying? Are there more inside?"

Another figure stumbles out, pushed from behind, and firefighters are on him immediately, wrapping a blanket around him.

Dylan fights against them, trying to go back into the building. "Kylie is still in there!" His voice is a hoarse whisper from the smoke and heat searing his throat and lungs.

A dark shape moves unnoticed in the commotion, on the side of the building where there is a tangle of overgrown bushes, tall grass, and weeds next to the building near the back corner. Smoke boils up from an open door laying on the ground where the weeds were pushed away to reveal two doors on the ground.

It is the kind of basement entrance that is reminiscent of an old bomb shelter or basement dug out later beneath a house, access granted through two doors that lay on the ground as if discarded. An orange glow flickers in the blackness below. Dark shapes move below, a sea of motion surging up to the opening above.

In ones and twos, they emerge, keeping stealthily to the shadows, darting off into the night.

The crowd is focused on the back door, waiting in desperate hope for more kids to come stumbling out of the burning building.

A large hulking figure stumbles out, dragging something. He coughs and doubles over with the force of the harsh coughs wracking his whole body.

Firemen rush at him and he pushes them off, shoving what he dragged out at them. Ambulances are beginning to arrive. The paramedics race against time, their first aid packs and oxygen tanks bouncing on the gurneys as they push and pull them over the rough broken pavement to the back of the building.

"Caesar!" Mr. Hooper wails piteously, reaching one arm out as if he can somehow reach into the ruined building and pluck the dog to safety.

"Here," a weak girl's voice calls, breaking into horrid gut-tearing hacking coughs.

The firefighters step back from the large figure, wrapping blankets around the girl the vagrant dragged out and thrust at them.

Kylie's hands still grip Caesar's collar, dragging him as she was being dragged all the way up and out of the basement and through the burning main floor of the building.

The dog lies limp and lifeless on the ground.

A fireman is trying to put an oxygen mask over Kylie's face and she looks up at him, her eyes full of sorrow and loss. She looks down at the motionless dog. Another fireman runs forward, putting an oxygen mask on the dog, cupping his hands around it to try to direct the oxygen into the dog's nose instead of it escaping around the face it is not meant to cover.

Kylie looks around for the others, finding them one by one, wrapped in blankets with oxygen masks on their faces and being fussed over by paramedics and their parents.

Mr. Hooper pushes his way through the people blocking him, the paramedic trying to triage him trying to dissuade him from going anywhere.

He pushes the paramedic off, stumbling to the dog and falling to his knees on the ground before him, sobbing his name over and over. "Caesar. Caesar. Caesar."

Caesar wags his tail weakly.

"Him!" a woman screams. "He did it! He took the kids!" She is pointing at Harry.

Police are on him in seconds. They swarm him, wrestling the large man to the ground and handcuffing him. Harry struggles, lost in a haze of shock and too weak to put up a fight. He stops fighting when he realizes it is the police and not hideous hairy monsters that are attacking him.

Word spreads through the crowd like a virus. Some homeless man kidnapped the kids! He will go to jail for the rest of his life.

"No," Madison cries weakly, breaking into a coughing fit that shakes her whole body violently. "He saved us, he saved us all."

Nobody hears her soft cry and she lapses into unconsciousness. They put her in an ambulance and its sirens scream as it races down the street.

Mr. Hooper wails when someone tries to take Caesar away from him. They are talking at him, but he does not hear their words.

Blankets wrapped around them and looking alien with their oxygen masks and covered head to toe in black soot, Kylie and Dylan come to stand on either side of Mr. Hooper. They each put a hand on a shoulder.

"It's okay Mr. Hooper," Kylie kneels down to talk to him.

He finally looks at her and she points.

Dylan kneels too. "Mr. Hooper, my dad is taking Caesar to the vet." He looks up at his dad standing over them with a hurt look. "You won't let them just put him down, will you?"

Mr. Hooper looks at Dylan's dad, his eyes hopeful through the pain of loss.

"I'll do everything I can to make them save him," Dylan's dad says.

Mr. Hooper watches miserably as Dylan's dad gently picks up the dog, soot from the fire smearing his clothes as he lifts Caesar and carries him away.

"It's going to be okay Mr. Hooper," Kylie says.

A pair of paramedics come and gently help Mr. Hooper to his feet, laying him down on a gurney to take him to the waiting ambulance.

Kylie and Dylan stand up. Anna comes to stand with them, all three watching Mr. Hooper be wheeled away.

Harry is being placed in the back of a police car. He looks at them, meeting their eyes. His eyes are haunted. The car pulls away, taking Harry with it.

"We have to do something to help him," Kylie says.

"We will," Dylan says. "Later, when we have a chance to tell them what happened."

"They'll never believe us," Kylie says.

"Probably not," Dylan says.

"So, what do you want to do this summer?" Anna asks.

Dylan grins. "I'm planning to have a quiet summer."

Kylie turns to look at the burning warehouse. The fire is roaring and the firefighters are spraying water on it, smoke and steam billowing out the windows with a hissing popping of the building being consumed by flames.

"What if he didn't get them all?" she asks quietly.

Outside of town, a boy moves in the darkness, a darker silhouette against the side of his grandparents' old farmhouse.

He moves warily, hesitantly.

He pauses next to a pair of old worn heavy wooden doors lying on the ground. They are not randomly abandoned there, left to rot on the grass. The old farmhouse has one of those basements that were dug out from outside the house decades after it was built, with the double doors that lay on the ground against the back wall of the house.

The basement was built in 1962, after the bomb shelter craze hit the nation, originally intended as a fallout shelter and later converted to a cold storage. Later still, it was converted again to a place to store old items that served past their usefulness and were not discarded.

It is the creepy kind of basement that fills a child's active imagination with night terrors.

He stares down at the doors, pulled by the urge to open them and investigate, but held back by an icy chill of fear.

He imagines himself struggling to open one of those heavy wooden doors, pulling it up and over on its hinges. The door bangs down on the ground when he drops it, leaving the dark rectangle of open blackness below. He moves around and struggles to open the other door, widening the hole in the ground.

Steep stairs that are more ladder than stairs vanish down into the blackness below.

The boy looks down into the darkness, trying to dare himself to go down. He hears a noise. Something is down there. He jumps to the other side of one of the doors, lifting it up to push the door over its apex and letting it fall closed with a loud bang. He hurries to close the other door too, but something reaches up and grabs him from below.

He pushes the thought away, staring down at the still closed doors.

"I know I heard it."

He hears the sound again, the same sound he is sure he heard coming from beneath the floor of the kitchen inside the house; the sound that drew him outside to investigate.

There is a rustling and a wet slithering sound coming from the other side of the doors.

END

Other books by Vivian Munnoch:

<u>Latchkey Kids Series:</u>

The Latchkey Kids

What would you do if you came home from school alone and heard noises in the basement?

Five kids, twelve and thirteen years old and on their own before and after school, each faces their own struggle. A broken home, illness, crushes, bullying, depression, absent parents, suicidal thoughts, broken friendships, and fears of being only a kid and home alone.

Madison, Andrew, Kylie, Anna, and Dylan are brought together by circumstances that feel overwhelmingly out of their control. The temptation of exploring an old abandoned brick building, loneliness, and fleeing an attempted abduction, each is drawn to the old abandoned building for different reasons.

There, they will fight for their lives, where the monsters in the basement nest.

The Latchkey Kids: The Disappearance of Willie Gordon

Spring break is over and, still in shock from the events of the night of the fire; the kids are forced back into everyday life as if nothing happened. But it did happen. And it is happening again.

While the kids try to come to terms with what happened the night of the fire at the abandoned factory, nothing in their lives seems to have changed when everything feels like it did.

A broken home, illness, crushes, bullying, depression, absent parents, suicidal thoughts, they all continue as before.

Amber Shaw returns to school and the Mean Team is broken up, but will it last?

Everything is back to normal. Right?

And then Willie Gordon vanishes.

While new jealousies burn, problems kept secret are revealed and Joshua joins the group after his sister committed suicide, the group feels they are the only ones who can find Willie. Nobody believes them the monsters are real.

The kids have to face the monsters again, in the basements where they nest.

<u>Wishing Stone Series:</u>

Madelaine & Mocha

It started with a walk in the woods.

Madelaine and her family are on a boring, no electronics and thank you very much for ruining my life, camping trip that changes Madelaine and her life forever.

First, her little dog Mocha is lost in the forest. Then Madelaine vanishes from their tent without a trace in the night. Everyone assumes she snuck out to look for Mocha.

Madelaine wakes in the dark, dressed only in her nightgown, with no idea how she got where she is, locked in a small room.

While searchers comb the forest looking for her, Madelaine is trying to figure out how to escape and return to her family. But they will never look in the right place.

Only her little dog Mocha knows what really happened to Madelaine.

About the Author

Vivian Munnoch is a Canadian author, a member of the Manitoba Writers' Guild, the Horror Writers Association, and Authors of Manitoba.

Vivian grew up with a love of the darker side; sneaking down to the basement at night to watch the old horror B movies, devouring books by horror authors, and has always had a passion for books and the idea of creating stories and worlds a person can get lost in since reading that first novel.

This love of storytelling has this author working writing and editing into a busy life that includes a full time job, family, and doing the little things to help the writing community including offering encouragement to others in the online writing community and volunteering time helping with the Manitoba Writers' Guild Facebook presence, proofreading for the HWA newsletter, and visiting schools for I Love to Read month.

Vivian Munnoch currently lives in Winnipeg with two rescue dogs, spouse, and kids.

Follow Vivian Munnoch:

Facebook:
        https://www.facebook.com/VivianMunnoch.author/
Twitter: @VivianMunnoch
Wordpress: https://vivianmunnoch.wordpress.com/

The Latchkey Kids

The Latchkey Kids Series Book 1

There is something about basements that always seems just a little creepy, that cave-like place where sunlight doesn't quite reach.

Andrew feels it, although he would never admit to anyone he is scared of the basement.

Madison, new to being a latchkey kid, even admits she is scared of the dark . . . to herself. Her biggest fear is losing her key.

Kylie is too busy being afraid to think about being scared of the basement. She has bigger problems in her life; the Mean Team tormenting her and making her life miserable, and her dad.

Dylan is afraid of being home alone; ever since his house was broken into, almost burned, and dog beaten. He won't even admit to himself the basement makes him nervous.

Anna, tough and impervious to rules Anna, would tell you nothing scares her. Spiders do. There are spiders in the basement.

There are other things in the basement too.

While the five kids struggle through their own problems, trying to survive their final years before high school, they become unlikely friends.

They are each drawn to the abandoned factory by their own circumstances, pulled together into something bigger than themselves. There they will discover the noises in the basement are real. They will discover the monsters where they nest.